THE HIGH COUNTRY

Molly Barclay opened her mouth and shut it again; her cheeks were pink.

'So,' Kurt continued, 'I trekked over that never-to-be-forgotten route again, Adrian, old friend. With a properly equipped expedition, this time. And I chose my spot, and I built myself a house, and I began to ranch.'

'God, but I envy you,' Adrian said. 'And to be able to leave your stock, and come away like this...you must have them eating out of your hand.'

'Well,' Kurt said, 'I have some help. But not enough.'

Adrian looked at him, aware that the three women were looking at *him*.

'It is not the same, without experience,' Kurt explained. 'And the Masai, well, they are suspicious and changeable people. But do you know, they still ask after you, Adrian, old friend? They still dream that one day you will return to see them. Be with them. Well, I know that is your dream too. Unless it has changed.'

'No,' Adrian said slowly. 'No, it hasn't changed.' He refused to look at any of the women.

'Well, then, old friend, will you not come and be my...head overseer? And my friend, and mentor, again, in dealing with the Masai?'

THE
HIGH
COUNTRY

Christopher Nicole

THE SHERIDAN
BOOK COMPANY

This edition published in 1994 by
The Sheridan Book Company

First published in Great Britain by Century 1987
Random House, 20 Vauxhall Bridge Road, London SW1V 2SA
Arrow edition 1988

Printed and bound in Great Britain by
Cox & Wyman Ltd, Reading, Berkshire

ISBN 1-85501-648-6

CONTENTS

'In the highlands [of Kenya] you woke up in the morning and thought, here I am, where I ought to be.'
Karen Blixen, *Out of Africa*

PROLOGUE

Prologue

'One day, maybe two,' Safah said. 'We will see the grass-land.' He was a Somali, tall, thin, gravely decorous at all times. Now he bowed to each of the three white men in turn as he handed them their tea.

It was dawn, and chill; a mist clung to the giant trees which surrounded the encampment, making them loom out of the green gloom like relics of the original, pre-historic, earthswamp . . . as perhaps they were, Adrian Barclay thought; it would not have seemed amiss to hear the pounding tread of a dinosaur just beyond the mist wall.

But to his companions, the forest was an obstacle, not a thing of beauty or romance.

'There'd better be more than just grass, you long streak of misery,' growled Kurt von Schlieben. 'How far do you reckon we've come, Captain John?'

John Barclay shrugged as he lit his morning pipe. 'Maybe four hundred miles from Mombasa.' He was nearly twice the age of the German, and had the ruddy complexion of a seafaring man; indeed, even in the East African jungle he still wore a battered old peaked cap and dungarees. Both men were tall and powerfully built, but the German had the edge: six foot one, he had heavy shoulders and massive arms and legs. Bluntly handsome where the Englishman's features were surprisingly small and delicate, with a mass of black hair where Barclay's was pale and thinning, he knew nothing of the sea. Neither man knew much of the forest, either. Schlieben was more at home in it, simply because, being a landsman, he regarded all life as a challenge to be met and overcome; again unlike Barclay, who had seen sufficient of nature at her most awe-inspiring to know how puny his own efforts were likely to be when set against such primeval power.

Yet John Barclay had inspired this expedition. An act of madness, most of the Europeans in Mombasa had said. They were sufficiently few in number to force them to band together, regardless of nationality, whether one was Portuguese and might perhaps claim descent from one of the original white settlers who had arrived hot on the heels of Vasco da Gama at the turn of the sixteenth century, or French and hotly antagonistic, or British or German and well on the way to becoming rivals for this rich coast, but aware of having been allies in almost everything for almost two centuries and certainly not about to change that fortunate state of affairs. If the new German Empire was, in this early spring of 1875, flexing its muscles, if only four years before it had decisively defeated France to claim at least the military hegemony of continental Europe, it was still grateful for Great Britain's neutrality – some would call it isolationism – during the Franco-Prussian War. And in Africa there was surely room for joint exploitation, for working together against the natives in a search for wealth, rather than against each other, as the French seemed so determined to do. Any eyebrows raised when Kurt von Schlieben volunteered to accompany John Barclay on his absurd safari into the interior had been because few other Mombasa residents could conceive of using one's precious 'long leave' – when one should be hurrying home to visit family and heritage – to walk several hundred dangerous miles into the bush.

The middle-aged Englishman, romantic but patient, and the young German, aggressive but determined, made a splendid team, Adrian thought, complementing each other in almost every way. A team of which he was well aware he was not yet a part. He was too young, too clearly inexperienced and naïve, to share the mental intimacy of the men. He had had to bully, cajole and beg to be here at all. As John Barclay's only son he had been able to bring family ties to bear; as Molly Barclay's only son he knew his father had been reluctant to risk both the male members of the family on such an adventure. As a giant of a youth – at eighteen he was six feet four inches of glittering blond manhood, towering even above Schlieben – he was obviously, whatever his inexperience, a useful accumulation of muscles to have around; as an apprentice on board his father's ship, he was expected to show more devotion to duty than most.

But the ship was why they were here. The ship and that unforeseen storm, as they had left Durban to work their way north, which had dismasted them and forced them to crawl into Mombasa under a jury rig. Their cargo was for the East African port, and they had delivered it; but their journey home, around the Cape of Good Hope and out into the Atlantic – for the owners were not yet convinced of the viability of the newfangled Suez Canal – would have to wait for the ship to be repaired. It meant several months in Mombasa. Months in which John Barclay's time would be wasted. He was not the man to accept that.

He had always dreamed. John Barclay had first come to East Africa thirty years before, and talked, and listened, as was his nature – preferably to the natives rather than the rumour-beguiled white men. From the Kikuyu, who often visited the coastland to market their goods, and from the Somali, who, always eager to seek their fortunes in the less arid south, were already almost indigenous on the coast, he had heard about the great lands beyond the forest. The high country, the natives called it, and the Arab merchants of Mombasa had traded with the people who lived in that fabulous place, for ivory and other valuables, for several hundred years. If it was inconceivable to a European to imagine a grassland set several thousand feet above sea level, for so the Somali described it, it was none the less an entrancing idea. It had taken hold of John Barclay and gripped his mind with the fervour of a crusade. One day, before he died, he would look upon this fabulous second, superior world. The dismasting of his ship had seemed a message from the gods. A message and an opportunity, he had at last been persuaded, to be shared with his son.

'Four hundred miles,' Schlieben remarked. 'To look at a little grass.'

But he smiled as he spoke, to take any sting out of his comment. Kurt von Schlieben smiled easily, and attractively. He was an attractive man. But Adrian had early recognised that it was a mistake to suppose the geniality of the smile hid any softness of character. As this was his first trip to Africa, it was the first time he had met the German. His father had known the vice-consul for several years, and Adrian knew he had the utmost respect for him. Certainly that respect contained a recognition of background. Schlieben had not, like too many of his countrymen encountered in faraway places, accumulated a 'von' to sound better than he was. He was a genuine Prussian junker. That his family had decided he was best remotely hidden away in an East African seaport for a few years while the consequences of an unfortunate duel – fatal to his opponent although he also carried a scar – were perhaps forgotten, merely added to the excitement of the man.

Yet Adrian doubted that even Father had considered the matter fully. He had sought a companion, just as he had sought a guide and an overseer for his bearers. He had welcomed the uncompromising Somali, Safah, for his knowledge of the Kikuyu people and the Swaheli language, and also for his knowledge of the interior; he had welcomed the tough, good-humoured, capable Schlieben as the ideal man to have at his side in chancing the unknown, assuming

14

that the younger man was also concerned merely with seeing something out of the ordinary, doing something unusual, adventuring, which was *his* only purpose. Adrian had immediately understood that Schlieben had more than adventuring in mind. What, he did not yet know, nor could he, until they reached their destination, but he was pretty sure it had, as an end result, a return to Germany in triumph. To do that, he would need to discover either wealth or fame.

Whatever the treasures which might or might not lie ahead of them, the route was certainly guarded by almost every danger nature could imagine. Snakes, spiders, scorpions and incessant rain were accepted as part of the natural order of things in Mombasa. Stout boots, thick breeches, broad-brimmed hats, had been regarded as essential – and wearing those, the journey should have been merely exhausting. They had not expected that within a week of leaving the coast the daily rain would stop, and with it the trees, and they would find themselves in a red earth desert. The desert did not mean any diminution in the snakes, spiders and scorpions – rather they increased. And the dry heat was far less pleasant than the rain, because the red dust got everywhere, into the tea and coffee, the whisky sundowners, the meat, and into the eyes, the ears, the mouth, the nose and every other conceivable crevice in the human body.

By then they were grateful for the cool certainty of Safah. He was a Muslim, and therefore, by European standards, a difficult companion at times. Not only did he find it necessary to order the expedition to a halt at regular hours throughout the day while he knelt and prayed towards Mecca, but he naturally pursued a Muslim's attitude towards game. Schlieben was an excellent shot, and they never went short of fresh meat – but Safah occasionally did, whenever Schlieben killed the kongoni outright, or the unhappy animal managed in some other way to die before

Safah could reach it and slit its pulsing throat. But he knew the country; he told them the desert was nothing and would soon be behind them – and it was. Then they pressed on, always climbing, but now into a pleasant grassland. Foolishly they supposed they had already reached their destination, and were disappointed – this was no second world. Safah merely smiled. 'There is much journeying to be done yet, to reach the high country, bwanas,' he pointed out. 'This is but Tsavo. It is best we pass here with all haste.'

They did not immediately understand why. Never had they seen such an abundance of game – giraffe, wildebeest, gazelle, and also elephant – it was a hunter's paradise, and it was even cool. Schlieben immediately brought down their dinner, and again they were unable to understand when Safah made the Kikuyu bearers light an additional four fires round the camp perimeter. But by dusk they had begun to realise on whose domain they were now treading, as they heard the guttural roaring on every side. By dawn they had fought a regular battle with at least a dozen huge, fearless, thick-maned lions, had lost the remains of their kill and two bearers besides, and had as a reward three of the magnificent beasts stretched dead on the ground.

'They will attack, again and again,' Safah warned. Then they followed his advice and hurried, but the crossing of the plain of Tsavo, accompanied by several other concerted attacks, was not something Adrian would ever forget. Nor was it possible to forget that the plain had to be crossed again on the way home.

From Tsavo they climbed again, until their shortage of breath told them they were perhaps three thousand feet above sea level. And then, walking the floor of a canyon, they looked to their left and saw the twin peaks in the far distance. 'Kibo,' Safah said reverently. 'Mawenzi. The roof of the world.' They were glad he was not proposing to lead them up there.

Now they encountered the forest, but a special kind of

forest, this, far removed from the steamy jungles of the coast, or of West Africa, where John Barclay had also traded. This forest was dry and cool, even cold at night. The undergrowth was not so thick a man might hack at it all day and still be uncertain if he had made any progress, as in the Congo. The trees clustered, and in their search for light, reaching ever upwards, excluded the heavens from those on the ground. But they were splendid trees, dominated by the remarkable boabab, which suggested a wooden fortress rising out of the soil, grey and gnarled as if from withstanding a thousand sieges. The forest abounded in game, too, and above the travellers' heads the monkeys swung to and fro, and chattered in unison with the birds. There were leopards prowling, and hyenas scavenging, and bush pigs hurrying, in sufficient abundance to be exciting, but lacking the menace of the massed lions of Tsavo. It was an enjoyable place, but still not the ultimate they sought.

It was also the frontier of the land of the Kikuyu, in their natural state a far more noble people than might be supposed from those of their compatriots who sought instant wealth on the coast. Safah was well known to them, and the white men were received in their kraals with friendship and entertainment. That too had been an unforgettable experience, for a great *ngoma*, or dance was held in their honour, in which several hundred young people of both sexes took part, mostly naked, but covered in a kind of red paint which Safah explained was actually mud. The dancing was purposeful, consisting in the main of stamping the feet and slow gyrations, and was accompanied by chants and even individual songs recalling the past glories of the tribe; some of it was also suggestive in the extreme, as the maidens would place their bodies against those of their male partners as if seeking succour from the perils of the forest. If Adrian was aware of being surrounded by a large number of well-armed Africans – however apparently friendly, and childishly interested in the white man's dress and weapons – Schlieben

17

was clearly more interested in the girls, with their high, small breasts and their curiously shaven heads, which actually enhanced their attractiveness.

John Barclay sought only information, through Safah, from the older men. But the Kikuyu chieftains were just as amazed, and disturbed, at their intention as the settlers on the coast. They spoke of the Masai Morani, shaking their heads. 'The Masai are the people of the high lands,' Safah explained. 'They are an extremely fierce people, especially the Morani, the young men, eager of reputation. The Kikuyu have had many wars with them, because the Masai sometimes raid down into the forest to steal cattle. The chiefs think they will kill you.'

'Then will they not also kill you?' John Barclay asked.

Safah allowed one of his very rare smiles, and looked at the three rifles carried by the white men. 'I do not think they will kill us,' he said. 'They have seen but few white men.'

He had meant, of course, that they would be overawed by the power of the guns. But, in fact, Adrian knew he was speaking nothing less than the truth. If the Europeans, led as always by the Portuguese, had been probing at Africa for some four hundred years, the probes had seldom penetrated more than a few miles inland from the coast, whether the quest had been for gold or for slaves or for trading concessions. Because his father traded with the huge dark continent, Adrian had read everything he could find on the subject, even before he had been old enough to join John Barclay's ship. He knew that the Portuguese had first visited the Canary Islands as far back as the fourteenth century, and, under the impetus of Prince Henry the Navigator, the Azores and Madeira a hundred years later. He knew that voyage after voyage, year after year, the intrepid sailors from Lisbon and Oporto and Sagres had pushed south, rounding Cape Verde itself in 1445, to discover that wonderland of slaves and gold that was the Bight of Benin, and thus encouraging still further explorations, until in the winter of 1487, Bartholemew Dias had doubled the Cape of Good Hope, entirely by accident, to be sure – he had been driven by a storm far to the south while coasting down the west side of Africa, and when he had regained sight of land, it had been to the west of him – but leading directly, a dozen years later, to the exploit of da Gama in not only rounding the Cape and reaching the already thriving Muslim seaport of Mombasa, but in opening up the sea route to India.

The Portuguese had been followed by others, but always seeking profit. The search for sheer knowledge of the continent had been tardy. Portuguese missionaries and Portuguese soldiers reaching Ethiopia had led the way, but they too had been seeking profit of a sort, the conversion of the natives and the securing of political influence. It had not been until 1616 that Gaspar Boccaro, another Portuguese, had journeyed from the Upper Zambesi to Kilwa on the coast, the first known white man to have plunged into the heart of the continent.

For another hundred and fifty years exploration had concentrated on the more accessible west. The east had remained a land of mystery until in 1768 James Bruce had explored Ethiopia and the Blue Nile. Just over a century ago, Adrian thought. And still no one had penetrated the high country until Richard Burton and John Speke, a scant seventeen years before, in 1858, had followed the river south from Ethiopia, and returned to talk of a huge body of water which they had patriotically named after the Queen . . . and of which, strangely, Safah knew nothing. Since then Speke had returned, with James Grant, while the famous David Livingstone had penetrated the land to the south, and died there only two years before. And so far as Adrian was aware, Livingstone's equally famous discoverer, Henry Morton Stanley, was at this moment somewhere to the west of them, having set out the previous year to circumnavigate Lake Victoria Nyanza, amidst a blaze of publicity. But all of those added up to no more than half a dozen white men to have ever trodden this virgin earth, and there was no record of any of them having come directly inland from the coast. There had been no publicity attached to John Barclay's expedition, save locally. Yet they were exploring, and learning . . . was that fame the goal Schlieben sought?

'Besides,' Safah added more seriously, 'it is a vast country. If we are wise and careful, the Masai will not even know we are there. It will only be the four of us.'

The bearers from the coast had only been contracted as far as the Kikuyu kraals. Safah was not concerned at this, and said they would procure fresh bearers here, and was right. But these also would contract only as far as the land of the Masai; they would not venture to trespass on it. Two days later, therefore, Safah told them they must make a base camp where they were, leaving all their heavy equipment, as the bearers would go no further. Schlieben was doubtful about this, but Safah assured him of the honesty of the forest men, and that the baggage would be awaiting them on their return. With that, John Barclay, who had developed the highest regard for the Somali, was content. So each of the four of them humped a knapsack containing the essentials: a change of clothing, tea, sugar, quinine and, of course, a bandolier with an ample supply of cartridges. Safah knew nothing of firearms, and carried the spear with which he had left Mombasa. Then they set off again, four men, Adrian thought, seeking the roof of the world.

Once more they climbed, through a belt of unexpected moisture, which was not actually rain but rather like a Scottish mist, and was, Adrian realised, in fact cloud. Then they emerged into brilliantly hot sunshine. Now the trees began to thin, and their heartbeats to quicken. Next morning they awoke to an even thicker white mist, and a cold which hurt their nostrils as they breathed, and made their teeth chatter. Safah was as cold as they, but he smiled. 'Soon it will be very hot,' he warned. 'We have arrived at the high land.'

They remained in camp until the mist cleared, which was about nine in the morning. Then as the sun soared into an intensely blue sky and it did indeed become very hot, they walked out with Safah to gaze at the most amazing vista. They stood on the edge of a vast plain which stretched as far as the eye could see. The plain clearly undulated to a considerable extent, but nonetheless gave an impression of flatness, while it gradually faded into a blue haze. In the haze, a great distance off, could be made out the shadowy shapes of mountain ranges, so immense and so final, observed in such a situation, that they suggested that there the world might end.

As it was near the end of the dry season, much of the plain was brown and sun-scorched, but it was studded with flame-trees and acacia, and there were patches of green, grass and bushes, and even little copses, clustered where there was obviously water close to the surface.

Above all, the clarity of the air almost seared the lungs, and gave an overwhelming feeling of having left the humdrum requirements of man's daily life, the problems and even the dangers of having to exist in a hostile environment, far behind. Adrian had a strong impression of having climbed a staircase to the heavens, and arrived at eternity while still alive. The blood coursed through his artteries, filled his brain with a sensation of power, even of immortality, which he had never known before.

John Barclay had a more prosaic cast of mind. 'What a place for cattle,' he remarked. 'If there is sufficient water.'

'There is sufficient water,' Safah told him. 'The Masai have cattle.'

'And no lions?' Schlieben asked.

'There are lion. There is everything, here on the high grass,' Safah said. 'But the Masai are mighty hunters.'

'How high are we, do you think?' Adrian mused.

'The roof of the world,' Safah said proudly.

'Well, a good six thousand feet above sea-level, anyway,' John Barclay suggested.

But Safah had not yet shown them the true wonder of this world. They walked all day, and then the next, while the mountains seemed to come no closer, and the blue horizon merely receded. They threaded their way through little dry river beds, where multicoloured flowers still peeped through the dry earth; they found themselves surrounded by gleaming white butterflies, with red or orange wing-tips; they disturbed yellow-necked spurfowls, scratching amongst the dirt, and they watched the hideous hooded vultures circling overhead; and they saw vast herds of game, which Safah identified as impala, a species of antelope, or kongoni, or hartebeests, and the sight of which had Schlieben stroking his rifle thoughtfully.

Then, on the second evening, after they had pitched their camp close to a stream, almost dry but containing sufficient water for their purposes, and even more important, providing a stand of trees for shade, he took them for another, shorter walk, which ended in a sudden escarpment they had not expected to exist. Then they caught their breaths yet again, for the plain, so unending to the north, here to the west suddenly dropped right away, for several hundred feet, and they looked down on a vast valley, a wonderworld of woods and open country, containing a string of lakes, and suggesting a greenness, even in the dry season. Adrian realised that his earlier estimate had been wrong. If the high country had indeed been heaven, he had yet had to make his way across it to look down on paradise itself.

Safah might have felt the same way. 'The other world,' he said proudly.

Barclay and Schlieben were for a moment speechless, because even they could not help but agree with him. 'This must be the finest country in existence,' Schlieben said at last, his normally harsh tones hushed.

22

'It beckons,' John Barclay said, thoughtfully. 'Do you realise that if we are indeed six thousand feet up, here, then the floor of that valley has to be at least three? Think of the climate down there.'

'It is good enough up here,' Schlieben pointed out.

'Nevertheless . . . is it possible to get down there, Safah?'

'Of course, Bwana Barclay. It is not difficult. But there is the land of the Masai.'

'You mean up here isn't?' Schlieben asked.

'Up here also, Bwana Schlieben. The Masai are the masters of all the high country. But they are wanderers. They follow the seasons. Sometimes they are here, then another time they are there.'

'There is a fire,' Adrian said, pointing to the north. 'A big one. What would be the cause of that?'

Safah shaded his eyes as he looked at the rolling clouds of white smoke, a long way away, but still on the grassland. 'The Masai,' he said. 'That is not good. They are closer than I had expected, for the time of year.'

'Are they fighting a battle?' Schlieben asked.

'No, no,' Safah said. 'It is the Masai way. Just before the Long Rains come, they set fire to their crop lands, that the rains may the more easily fertilise them. That is another reason for us to return without delay. The Masai know the weather, therefore it is possible that the Long Rains may be coming earlier than usual, this year. We must be back at Tsavo before they begin or we shall be forced to remain here for several months.'

John Barclay nodded, and they returned to their encampment.

'You cannot mean that we have come this far to take one look, and then go home again?' Schlieben asked.

Adrian had to sympathise with him.

'That is what I said I would do,' John Barclay reminded him. 'None of us can afford to become trapped up here for several months, nor did I come here to confront the Masai.

23

We've seen the most fabulous place on earth. I want to go away and think about it, because I've a notion to come back, before I'm too old to make this journey any more. With maybe a well-equipped expedition, so that we needn't fear the Masai. Maybe even with the idea of settling here . . .' He glanced at Adrian.

'Oh, yes, sir,' Adrian cried, eyes glowing. 'That would be magnificent.'

'Do you think your mother and Mandy might like it?'

Mandy was Adrian's younger sister.

'I think they would love it. If we could get them through that bush.'

'Aye,' Barclay said. 'It's no country for white women, that's certain. But . . . it is a paradise, eh, Kurt?'

Schlieben made no reply, but he leaned back to gaze at the grassland, and his eyes were also glowing.

'We will spend one more day here,' John Barclay decided the next morning, and when Safah looked doubtful, he said, 'Come now, old friend. No one knows we are here. You must allow us time to drink in these surroundings. Besides, we could do with a rest. One more day will not hurt.'

He needed the rest more than any of them, Adrian knew. He had indeed been increasingly worried about his father, who, at fifty-two, and having spent most of his life on the poopdeck of a ship, had probably in the past month taken more exercise than in his entire previous life, with an equal journey to come. Of course, going back they would be descending rather than climbing, but it was still a long way. A leisurely day would do them all good.

They pursued their own pleasures. Schlieben went hunting, accompanied by Safah. John Barclay went walking, intimating that he wished to be by himself, dreaming no doubt, visualising perhaps a future when he could live here, were that ever possible. Adrian returned to the escarpment with a pair of binoculars and stared down at the valley floor, so far beneath him. He could see movement down there, herds of giraffe or zebra, at that distance he couldn't be sure even with the glasses. But no people, and no sign of any human habitation. If they were in the land of the Masai, it was, as Safah had said, a vast country, and they need not necessarily be discovered.

Not even when announcing themselves? He cocked his head as he heard the report of the rifle, oddly dull because of the huge open plain, but still clearly audible more than a mile away. Then there was another. But Schlieben had Safah with him, and the Somali must feel sure the noise would not carry far enough to be overheard by a hostile ear.

He walked back to the stream. None of the others had yet returned, and he sat down beneath the trees, and then lay, his hands beneath his head, gazing up through the some-what thin foliage at the enormous blue vault of the sky above him. He had never been this high in his life before — none of them had, except perhaps Safah — and he was aware of a kind of light-headedness, perhaps partly because of the rarity of the air, but equally, he was sure, because of the feeling of being at one with the entire universe, and even the Creator. The sea often induced similar feelings, when he was far away from land, in good weather, with blue below and blue above, and the knowledge that there was no other man for hundreds of miles. But the sea always contained an element of lurking danger, a knowledge that, were its mood to change, it could become the most implacably deadly force on earth. He could not envisage this pleasant land ever becoming hostile, whatever creatures might roam it.

He sat up to watch Schlieben and Safah returning. Lack-ing bearers, they were carrying the eland themselves, sus-pended from a pole slung between their shoulders. Adrian thought it was a fortunate thing that they were both big, strong men, for the buck had to weigh something like two hundred pounds. It made rather a sad sight, its huge horns scraping the dust, its expression surprised that death should

25

have overtaken it from a distance, and without warning. But perhaps that was the best way to die.

'I'm going to mount those horns,' Schlieben said. 'I have never seen a pair as splendid.' He knelt beside the carcass as it was laid in the dust, and got to work with his knife.

'Where is Bwana Barclay?' Safah asked.

Adrian shrugged. 'He went walking.'

'And it is now halfway through the day,' Safah said severely. 'He should have returned. I will find him.'

Adrian got up. Safah regarded all three of them as children, to be cared for and scolded when they did something foolish, which in the forest had been often enough. But now there was something in his tone which was alarming. 'You don't think something may have happened to him?'

'He should have returned by now,' Safah repeated, more severely yet, and set off, following John Barclay's boot tracks, which were distinct enough.

Adrian hesitated, then picked up his rifle and went behind him.

'Mind you're back for lunch,' Schlieben called. 'That will be in half an hour.' He was already slicing off some magnificent steaks to be barbecued on the fire.

Safah and Adrian followed the tracks for over a mile, then they came to a rocky outcrop, perhaps twelve feet high, and there the bootprints ceased. Safah climbed up on the rocks, and Adrian joined him; from here they could once more look down into the valley – it was, in fact, not very far from where he himself had been earlier that morning.

'Your father was here. He has fallen in love with this place,' Safah commented.

'That wouldn't be difficult to do,' Adrian said.

'But he should have come back.' Safah climbed down the other side, and stood stiffly, arms suddenly hanging straight at his sides, the spear point touching the dust. John Barclay lay at the foot of the mound, on his face. His captain's cap had come off and rolled about a foot away, leaving his head exposed to the sun. Blood trailed away from the balding scalp.

Adrian jumped down beside the Somali, knelt and turned his father over. 'He's alive, thank God,' he muttered, watching the front of his father's shirt rise and fall, and the dust fluttering away from his nostrils. 'But what can have happened?'

Safah squatted beside him, raised the stricken man's hands and arms, looked at them, inspected his trousers and boots, looked around, and saw the rifle, which had been thrown several feet when Barclay had fallen. 'He must have slipped and struck his head,' he suggested. 'Perhaps he was overcome by the heat. I have often said he should wear a white man's hat.'

Adrian had already examined his father's scalp; it was cut, but not deeply – the worst bruise was on the side of his face, which must have made the first impact with the ground. And he was certainly very hot. 'We must get him back to camp, to shade and water,' he said.

Safah nodded, and between them they lifted the inert body. Safah carried him over his shoulder, while Adrian retrieved the cap and the rifle. They changed burdens quickly enough, as Adrian was so much the stronger. But both were exhausted when they inhaled the delicious aroma of cooking meat, and regained the camp. 'We don't know what happened to him,' Adrian confessed, as he tenderly laid his father down in the shade of the trees. 'Save that he fell off some rocks.' He hurried to the stream to fetch water.

Schlieben frowned at his friend, then knelt and tested Barclay's pulse. He raised the unconscious man's arm, attempted to fold the fingers and laid the arm down again. 'I have seen illnesses like this before. He has had a seizure.'

'A seizure? Father?' Adrian stooped and bathed John Barclay's face, praying for his eyes to open. 'I don't know what that is.'

27

'It is to do with the blood. See the mottled colour in his cheeks? Hear the stertorous breathing? It may have been caused by the altitude and the exertion. But look here . . .' he tried to bend the fingers again. 'Paralysis has already set in.'

'Paralysis?' Adrian shouted.

'It is often a result,' Schlieben told him. 'Even when the patient makes a recovery, partial paralysis may ensue.'

'My God! What must we do?' Adrian asked, aghast. His father had never been ill in his life. His brain found it difficult to accept the catastrope.

'Do?' Schlieben asked. 'What can we do? We are not doctors. Although not even doctors would be much help here. We must wait, and hope, and see what happens.'

Adrian's shoulders slumped as he looked at the face he loved, respected, honoured, admired. It was impossible to imagine Father paralysed. Even partially. And how would he walk back to the coast?

'If the paralysis reaches his heart or his lungs, he will die,' Safah said.

'Now there is an obvious statement,' Schlieben agreed. 'But it need not necessarily do so.'

'Perhaps in another week, the Long Rains will come,' Safah went on.

'I hope you are not suggesting what I think you are suggesting,' Schlieben said.

'I would not abandon my friend, Bwana Barclay,' Safah said with dignity. 'But I do not think we can risk spending several months here, either. The Masai would certainly find us, in time. In any event, we have not sufficient provisions; white men cannot live off game alone. One of us must return to the base camp and secure sufficient help to carry Bwana Barclay out, at least as far as the Kikuyu kraals.'

'Then it'll have to be you,' Schlieben decided. 'Only you know the way.'

Safah inclined his head in recognition of that fact. 'I will try to persuade bearers to come up here with a litter,' he said. 'I will be back in four days.'

'Mind you are,' Schlieben agreed. And grinned. 'Bwana Adrian and I would not like to have to find our way back to the coast alone.'

'Four days,' Safah said. He regarded the stricken sea captain for a moment, his face solemn. Then he picked up his spear and a haunch of the raw eland, and walked away from the camp, stiffly and confidently. He didn't look back.

'Will he return?' Adrian asked.

'He'll return,' Schlieben said. 'His reputation would be lost forever if he abandoned two white men in the bush.' He handed Adrian a steak. 'Eat. You have to keep up your strength. Eat, and watch, and maybe pray.'

On the high grass the dawn was even colder than in the forest. Adrian had awoken during the night to an immense rustling sound, and sat up, supposing the Long Rains had indeed arrived early, but then realised it was the wind, sweeping across the plain, and already chill. There were certainly clouds gathering in the sky, but the rain was not yet ready to fall. He checked his father's covering, re-wrapped himself in his blanket and lay down again, but stayed awake, watching his father by the flickering light of the fire; they had seen leopards on their first day, and there was still a great deal of the eland waiting to be eaten. But the night was quiet.

He gazed at his father's face. John Barclay breathed slowly and heavily, and occasionally he made a sound, although his lips hardly seemed to move. Once or twice his eyes opened, but it was clear he saw nothing. Adrian did not know what to hope for. Father, paralysed? Even a partial paralysis would be unbearable for so active a mind, but supposing it was total . . . of course, even that would be preferable to death, but it seemed tragically ironic that he should have been struck down just as he had seen the sight

29

he had dreamed of for years, and had been in the midst of plans for making his future here.

Unless it had been the realisation of that dream which had induced the seizure.

Towards dawn Adrian dozed, but awoke with a start, discovering it was daybreak. He sat up again and looked at his father, who also slept, it seemed, then at Schlieben, snoring contentedly, then at the eland, and the camp, and the now only glowing fire, and then beyond – and felt his blood slowly freeze.

A man stood, looming out of the morning mist as if he had dropped from the heavens – or risen from beneath the earth. At least, Adrian had to presume it was a man, for the apparition was so perfectly still it could have been an ebony statue. But it was a sufficiently awe-inspiring sight, tall, straight, very stiff, quite naked save for a leather belt over one shoulder, like a bandolier, long legs thin and hips narrow, but chest and shoulders wide and powerful. It was the head which was terrifying. The black features were cold and intensely arrogant, the jaw thrust forward, the lips wide and flat, the expression disdainful. The eyes, too, still as only an African's can be, appearing almost blind in the way they stared straight ahead, were cold. The hair, unlike that of the forest Africans, was long, worn in a heavy pigtail down the back, while round the forehead there was another leather band. The man carried a spear in his right hand, the haft resting on the ground, and the bandolier contained a hunting knife in a rough sheath. But even more disturbing than the weapons or the expression was the complexion of the skin, blue–black in colour, drawn tight and full in the most perfect smooth darkness; there was not a line, not a dimple – it might have been the face of a plump new-born babe.

But Adrian knew it was the face of a Masai Morani. Very slowly and carefully he began to move both his arms at once, the right to reach for his rifle, the left to touch

Schlieben's shoulder. Schlieben was awake in a moment, not immediately moving as he saw Adrian's expression and understood there was danger about, then turning on his stomach and seizing his rifle with the same movement, cradling it in his shoulder and levelling it; just in time Adrian slapped it down. 'You cannot shoot him in cold blood,' he protested.

Schlieben rose to his knees, the blanket falling about his waist. 'I would say his blood is quite hot enough. Christ, if his friends also find us . . .'

Adrian turned his head, the hairs on the back of his neck prickling. On the far side of the stream, also shrouded in mist, stood another six warriors. 'Had you fired, we'd be dead men by now,' he said.

Schlieben also turned. 'Don't you think we are dead men anyway, unless we fire? There are seven of them. We can drop them all before they can get at us.'

'And what if there are others close by? And anyway, Father swore he had not come here to start a war with the Masai.'

'So we wait for them to start a war with us,' Schlieben observed. 'There is no other way, boy. If we do not strike first, our heads are going to be stuck on some totem pole.'

'There has to be another way,' Adrian insisted, trying to think if it was possible to impress these young men with their strength and their desire to be friends.

Slowly he rose to his feet – and watched the Masai move. It was not a positive gesture, rather a kind of contraction of the entire body – and he realised that tall as the warriors were, for Africans, none of them had ever encountered a man as large as himself. Nor perhaps a man so fair. But it was the size, added to the fairness, that would matter. Immediately he knew he had found the answer to their dilemma. He stooped and laid his rifle on the ground. Schlieben watched him, frowning. Adrian walked away

31

from the weapon to where the carcass of the eland lay by the fire. Only a few steaks had been cut from the body, and it must still weigh more than any single average man could possibly lift. Adrian stooped again, lodged his hands in the bloodied meat, straightened, and with an enormous effort lifted the carcass above his head.

Once again a ripple of movement came from the Masai. 'Cover me,' Adrian said softly, and walked towards them, carrying the dead beast. Already his muscles were straining and sweat was running down his face, but he did not change the slow rhythm of his step as he waded the stream and went right up to the waiting men, who continued to stare at him, their expressions slowly changing from arrogance to alarm mingled with curiosity. Now he knew he was at most risk. A panic reaction, a single thrust from one of those spears- . . . but the men did not move until he stood immediately before them. Then he slowly lowered his arm, teeth gritting against the burning temptation to drop the enormous burden, and held it out, arms extended. The Masai gazed at him, understanding his invitation, but knowing that not one of them was strong enough to take the gift in the manner in which it was being offered. Adrian made himself stand there for ten seconds, then he slowly placed the carcass on the ground at their feet, stood back, gazed at them a moment longer, turned his back on them and walked back to the camp.

'Jesus Christ,' Schlieben remarked. 'You have got good nerves, boy.'

Adrian knelt beside him, and at last turned to look at the men again. They hesitated for a moment longer, then turned and left, disappearing almost instantly into the mist; the solitary man followed their example. The eland was left lying where Adrian had placed it.

'Well, I have to hand it to you,' Schlieben observed. 'That was damned impressive. But . . . we'd better get out of here. They'll be back, you know.'

'That's what I'm counting on,' Adrian said. 'We'll wait for them.'

They waited, for what was undoubtedly the longest day of Adrian's life, while the sun rose and the mist cleared to reveal an empty landscape. They looked at each other without speaking – they had expected to see the warriors still there, or the entire Masai nation assembled, waiting to assault them, and now did not know whether to be glad or sorry.

For them, there was nothing to do but wait. Even Schlieben, ever anxious to be up and doing, understood that as the Masai could easily track them now they knew they were there; their only hope was to face it out and attempt to cash in on Adrian's feat of the morning. He also understood that they must stick together, and instead of hunting contented himself with angling in the stream, actually catching some small fish which he added to their lunch.

Adrian could do nothing but sit beside his father, washing his face every time it grew hot and flushed, and occasionally attempting to dribble some water down the tightly clenched mouth. By now he realised that the chances of John Barclay making any sort of a recovery were slim, yet, unsure as to whether or not he would himself be alive by nightfall, it was difficult to feel any true grief or even concern. There was in fact no part of the future he dared think about, as it was at least possible that the Masai had found them in the first place through coming across Safah, in which case there was not even any prospect of native bearers coming to their assistance. Only the Masai mattered, now.

It was late afternoon when Schlieben, who had appeared to be dozing, said quietly, 'They are here.'

Adrian stood up and gazed at a large number of men, not less than fifty, he estimated, approaching across the plain. They shimmered in the afternoon heat, their numbers seeming to swell and then diminish with every blink of the eyelids. As they drew closer, he saw that most of them were young, and presumably included their acquaintances of that morning, but there were also several older warriors, perhaps even more statuesque and arrogant in bearing than the Morani. They gathered before the encampment, while one of the young men, definitely a morning visitor, whispered in the ear of the most senior of the elders. He did not point, save with his eyes, but that he was identifying each of them was obvious.

'God, to have Safah here,' Schlieben muttered. 'To tell us what they intend.'

'Well, we must make do with signs,' Adrian said. Strangely, he was not afraid. Indeed, he did not think he had been afraid that morning. He was concerned about the coming moments, as he had been concerned all day, but the matter still appeared simply as a problem, to be solved if he could – even if failure to do so might mean death. Now he took off his hat to expose his yellow hair, and stepped forward, holding out both hands, palms uppermost and fingers spread. The Masai watched him approach, insensibly moving closer together, and one or two of the young men let the hafts of their spears strike the earth with dull thuds, but no one made an aggressive move.

The elder gestured his young companion to step back, and waited alone for Adrian to come up to him. He gazed at the huge body in front of him, then up at the yellow hair, then pointedly at the dead eland. The carcass was now becoming somewhat high, but Adrian understood that a demonstration was required, and returned to heft it once more and offer it to the group. Still they stared at him in consternation, and began to mutter amongst themselves. Adrian laid the carcass on the ground at the chief's feet and then extended his hands again. After a moment, the chief took the fingers in his own. His flesh was dry and coarse, but Adrian wanted to shout with joy.

'By God,' Schlieben said behind him. 'You've done it.'

The chieftain released Adrian, stepped past him and entered the camp to stand above John Barclay. Then he uttered a single word, and three more of the older men came forward, one stooping beside the sea captain, looking from John Barclay's face to the small, delicate features Adrian had inherited, and understanding. The chief pointed at the sick man and shook his head, then grasped Adrian's hand again in a gesture of sympathy. Then he pointed across the plain towards the valley. Adrian nodded, but in turn pointed at his father; the African might consider the case hopeless, but he was not going to abandon him here. The chieftain almost seemed to shrug, then gave orders to his young men, who immediately made a kind of stretcher by criss-crossing several spears. On this John Barclay was laid, and six men lifted him from the ground. The chief then pointed towards the valley again.

'Seems like a fair offer to me,' Schlieben said, and also squeezed Adrian's hand. 'You've saved our lives, boy. I won't forget that. Now let's go and see how these Masai live.'

As the chief had indicated, the Masai encampment was situated down in the Rift Valley itself, and was a good distance away; indeed, it was dark by the time they reached the floor of the valley, but by then the landscape was bathed in the purest of moonlight, which, while hiding many of the features they longed to see, bathed the overall scene in a glowing white light that made it the more dramatic.

The camp itself was actually a village of small huts surrounded by a rough stone wall and close to a fast running stream, which apparently emptied into a large lake only a short distance away. It appeared to be surprisingly permanent for a nomadic people, as Safah had described the Masai, but Adrian and Schlieben were later to learn that although the tribe, or clan – for each group was composed entirely of relatives in some degree or another – did move their herds of cattle and sheep and goats north in the dry months to seek new pastures, they always returned to this same spot. The lake, called Naivasha, they discovered the next day, was a place of the utmost quiet beauty and the home of magnificent pink flamingoes, which seemed totally unconcerned at the near presence of human beings and remained standing on one leg, only occasionally flapping their great wings and moving to some better fishing ground. It was easy to see they had never been hunted.

The kraal was also close to the area which had recently been burned, and it showed in the moonlight as a vast expanse of white ash. Occasional flames still darted, giving the whole area a vaguely sweetish, nostril-tingling smell. Adrian and Schlieben were struck by the difference between these people and any previous Africans they had encountered. To their surprise, the houses were downwind of the scorched area, and when the night wind sprang up, the entire kraal and its occupants were covered in the ash, but this did not seem to concern anyone. Unlike other Africans, especially the scrupulously clean Somalis, the Masai were a dirty people, caring little for the state their bodies were in. They lived close to their cattle, for their cattle were their wealth, and also to their sheep and goats, which provided them with meat and milk. The animals were guarded day and night by the young warriors, ready to repel any onslaught by lion or leopard.

At the same time, being plainsmen instead of forest dwellers, they were intensely attractive physically, with their long, slender and yet powerful legs trained to carry them for miles on foot, for they had no horses, in pursuit of the lion – the killing of which was the achievement of manhood – or of human adversaries, and their powerful shoulders, their proud faces, and above all, their marvellous complexions, which were to be found only in the young men, although it was easy to discern that the elders had also once possessed such perfection, however gnarled they might now be. Not that the women were unattractive. Far from it. Tall and straight like their brothers, and similarly naked unless married, some of them were quite beautiful. In another vital difference to the Kikuyu maidens, who had displayed a total shyness towards the white men, and of course the Somali girls, none of whom Adrian had ever even seen, because, as Muslims, they were kept in strict purdáh and were veiled when on the street, these girls were immediate coquettes. They cast sidelong glances at both the white men and assumed suggestive expressions with their mouths and eyes.

'By God, a man must be careful here,' Schlieben muttered, clearly thinking entirely of his own problems.

For Adrian there were other, more immediate situations to be resolved. He was surrounded by children of the tribe. Both sexes were naked and inquisitive, and, having clearly heard all about him from the warriors of the morning, anxious to have him lift several of them from the ground at once. He accommodated one or two groups, but was grateful when the chieftain waved them away with a few peremptory words and then ushered him into a low hut, gained by a circular entrance through which he had to bend double, to enter a small, utterly dark interior, on the beaten earth floor of which his father was being reverently laid. He did not like to leave him there, exposed to every crawling creature which might take it into its head to assault him. But as the chieftain was clearly waiting for him, he went outside and was shown to a place round the fire. Schlieben was already there. The German was eating meat, as were the elders, but the young men only drank from a kind of gourd, and one of these was passed to Adrian. He sipped without thinking, presuming it was some sort of alcohol, and was nearly sick on the spot; it took all his sang-froid not to drop the contents on the ground. 'My God,' he gasped to Schlieben. 'What is it?'

Schlieben took the gourd, and cautiously sniffed. 'I have

heard of this,' he said. 'The Morani are fed only upon blood and milk until they reach manhood, which of course is young in an African. And even then it remains their favourite food until their fighting days are done. That is the reason for their remarkable complexions, and the thinness of their bodies.'

'Blood and milk?' Adrian gazed into the gourd, his flesh seeming to crawl as he now inhaled the stench of the liquid. 'Whose blood?'

'Oh, that of a lion, perhaps. Who knows? I doubt it will be human, if that is what is bothering you.' Schlieben grinned. 'They regard you as being worthy of treatment as a Morani, Adrian. You cannot let them, and us, down now. Besides' – his grin widened – 'I suspect it is all you are going to get.'

They slept in the same hut as John Barclay. It was actually quite free of bugs except for some harmless ants, and Adrian slept very heavily, despite his unsatisfactory meal, which he had only kept down with an effort. He awoke at dawn, as the entire village stirred, sat up, and stared at Schlieben in amazement and embarrassment – and concern – for in his friend's arms there lay one of the native girls: both were naked. 'Oh, hell,' Adrian said. 'Really, Kurt . . . this will mean trouble.'

'I didn't go looking for her, if that's what you think,' Schlieben said. 'She came crawling in here. And she knows how to make a man happy. I don't suppose you understand anything about that; you're too young. Off with you, Fräulein,' he said, slapping the naked bottom. The girl giggled and left the hut. Adrian tensed himself for an explosion from outside, because there had to be a great many people about, and no one would have any doubt where she had been or how she had spent her night. But although there was certainly some excited chatter, there was no indication of anger.

'I have heard too,' Schlieben said, sitting up in turn, 'that

38

the Masai are a most immoral people. Well, as they say, one man's meat is another man's poison. I feel a new man, this morning. Perhaps it is something you should study. How is Captain John?'

Adrian knelt beside his father, whose eyes were shut. His body was strangely inert, with no movement to the chest, and no sound of breathing, either. He touched his father's cheek, and shuddered. 'Oh, God,' he said. 'While you . . . God!'

'How was I to know?' Schlieben asked, reasonably enough, and knelt beside the boy. 'He was breathing when last I listened.'

'Father,' Adrian said. There were no tears. He had known this was inevitable. But for him never to have regained consciousness . . .

Schlieben rested his hand on his shoulder. 'I am truly sorry, boy. He was a splendid companion. The best I have known. And I think, after having had a seizure, this is the most merciful way for him to have gone, without even knowing what had happened to him. Believe me.'

Adrian sighed, knowing he was right, and raised his head to gaze at three of the elders, who crouched in the low, round doorway of the hut. His shoulders slumped, and the Masai understood what had happened. One of them came forward, touched the dead body and shook his head. Then he placed his hand on Adrian's shoulders, the fingers tight on the flesh.

'They are a decent people,' Schlieben said.

He took charge of the burial, as the Masai did not really understand what he wanted. But they were willing to carry out his wishes with that silent curiosity which was their principal characteristic. John Barclay was carried by the warriors back to the very spot where he had fallen, over-looking the Rift Valley. At the foot of the stony outcrop the warriors dug a grave with their spears, and in it the sea captain was laid to rest, while Schlieben said a half-forgotten German prayer over him. Then he had the natives erect a cairn of stones over the grave, so that no hyena could come and dig it up. Then he stood next to Adrian, who had been a silent spectator of the scene. 'We can do no more.'

'You have done enough,' Adrian said. 'I am very grateful.'

'He was my friend,' Schlieben said, and was silent for some seconds. Then he said, 'Well, now we had better go and find Safah, or he will fear the worst.' He went up to the chief, who had supervised the burial from the Masai point of view, touched him on the arm and pointed to Adrian and himself. 'We must leave,' he said.

The chieftain certainly understood what he meant, if not the words. But he shook his head, his face grave.

Schlieben frowned. 'Now you listen to me, old man,' he said, still speaking quietly, but his face beginning to glow as it did when he was angry. 'Don't try any funny stuff with us. We are grateful for your assistance, but we will not be your prisoners.'

The chieftain never changed expression, merely pointed at the sky. Schlieben and Adrian both turned to look, and saw the great black clouds banking up below the mountains.

'He could be right,' Adrian said.

'The Long Rains,' Schlieben muttered. 'Well, they do say that man proposes and God disposes, and allowing that, everything must be for the best.' He turned back to the chieftain. 'All right, old man, you have made your point. How long do the rains last?' He pointed at the clouds, then at the sun, pressed his hands together and placed them on his cheek, closing his eyes, and then repeated the pantomime several times.

The chief looked even more sombre, and in reply opened and closed his hands several times rapidly.

'I'd say he means for some time,' Adrian said.

'Hell and damnation. But let us use our time well, and choose our allotments.'

They walked back to the encampment with the Masai, who were now in a state of unusual excitement as they saw the approach of the most vital weather of the year.

'Do you seriously intend to come back?' Adrian asked.

'Indeed I do, boy. This place is a paradise. You will not find a better no matter how hard you look. Think of the climate. No beastly malaria up here to give a man the shakes, I'll wager. A man might live forever. Forgive me, but your father certainly carried the seeds of his collapse in him before he ever set foot on this plain. And all of this land . . . why, we each could farm a million acres and no one would be any the wiser.'

'Save the Masai,' Adrian suggested.

Schlieben grinned. 'But the Masai are our friends. I'll bet you something else: they'd be more than happy to have us settle up here with them, especially if we brought in a few more rifles; then they could relax a bit about their herds.'

Adrian thought he was perhaps being sanguine, if not about the Masai, then about the possibilities of the place. It was certainly far more beautiful than anything he had ever known, and he would agree that it was probably far more healthy. But . . . 'Supposing we did farm here,' he ventured. 'How would we export our surplus?'

'Export our surplus?' Schlieben laughed. 'You think too far ahead too fast, boy.'

'We would have to do that, in order to purchase the necessities of life,' Adrian argued.

'Necessities of life? Up here we would be self-supporting.'

'Even for bullets? We would have to earn some money, somehow.'

Schlieben gave him a curious glance; clearly the necessity of earning money had never been a problem to the son of a Prussian landowner, even if temporarily disgraced. 'Why,' he said, 'if we had a surplus to export, why . . . we would build a railroad, from here to the coast. Oh, aye, that's what we'd do, build a railroad.'

Clearly he was as much a dreamer as his father had been, Adrian thought. But dreams were forgotten when they regained the village and he was beckoned by the chieftain to go into the large hut which was the centre of the kraal. Here he found several of the elders assembled, together with one of the tallest and fiercest-looking of the Morani, who he had gathered already was the chieftain's son and his appointed successor. Adrian found himself standing in the middle of these men while they quite openly inspected him, discussing him amongst themselves, and occasionally addressing him, although he could not understand a word that was said. Finally, the chieftain tapped him on the chest, touched the cloth of his shirt, and then his own naked flesh.

'He wants you to strip off,' Schlieben said.

'Like hell he does,' Adrian growled.

'Well,' Schlieben said. 'I have a notion we'd better humour him. What the hell? They're all men.'

Adrian hesitated for a moment, but reflected that Schlieben was undoubtedly right. He took off his shirt and handed it to his friend. The Masai crowded round, certainly impressed with his physique, the breadth and depth of his chest, the broadness of his shoulders, and chattered amongst themselves. Their only concern was a thorn scratch on his shoulder, and to his amazement one of them tore away the scab to inspect the clean blood welling up from underneath – this seemed to reassure them.

Then the chief pointed at his pants.

'I'm afraid it's the lot,' Schlieben said, clearly amused; no one had suggested *he* undress.

'If there is any funny business . . .' Adrian warned.

'I don't think these fellows know the meaning of the word,' Schlieben said.

Adrian took off his trousers, and once again the Masai were impressed by the long, muscular legs. But they pointed at his drawers in a mixture of consternation and amusement, making unmistakeable gestures.

'They want to know if you have anything under there,' Schlieben suggested.

Adrian drew a long breath, but there seemed no help for it, so he removed the last of his clothing. The men once again crowded closer to stare at him, and then seemed transported with delight, clapping their hands. The chieftain was the most pleased of all. He waved them away and stood before Adrian, making a most solemn speech, with much waving of his hands and arms and touching of his own genitals. As he spoke, the gathered men stamped their feet with a thunderous sound, and outside they could hear the Morani thumping their spear hafts on the earth.

'I don't like the look of this,' Adrian said. 'I have a distinct feeling that they want me for the pot. Can you reach our rifles?'

'No,' Schlieben said. 'Anyway, the Masai are not cannibals. And in fact, I don't think they mean you any harm at all. I think they are inviting you to become a Morani.'

'Are they?' Adrian was amazed, but also both relieved and complimented. 'You mean we're accepted?'

'If you accept their offer, yes. However . . .'

'Then I do,' Adrian interrupted. He stretched out his hand, and the chieftain, after a brief hesitation, grasped it, while the watching men murmured their appreciation.

'Ah . . .' Schlieben chewed his lip. 'You may have been a trifle hasty.'

'We have to be friends with them.'

'Oh, I agree. But . . . there will be a certain degree of initiation necessary.'

'I think I can do anything a Masai can,' Adrian pointed out. 'What is it, killing a lion or something?'

'That will come later,' Schlieben agreed. 'But . . . have you not noticed anything about these men?'

It was difficult to notice anything at all at the moment, as the warriors were forming a sort of guard of honour to escort Adrian to the door. 'Hey,' he said. 'They're not taking me outside like this?'

'Yes,' Schlieben said, hurrying behind him.

'But . . .' Then he was outside, in the bright sunlight, surrounded by all the men of the tribe, and all the women, too. Then he did notice what was basically different between the Masai men and himself; the Masai were all circumcised.

It was clearly too late to turn back, without causing mortal offence and endangering their lives. And apparently the induction of a new warrior was a very special event, of which circumcision was only the climax. The Masai had no doubt that he was already a proven warrior; his size and strength showed them that. They were only concerned to make sure he had not yet been taken into any other tribe, and that his skin was free of any blemishes – either would have barred him from acceptance. That being established, the lengthy ceremony could proceed.

The whole business was conducted by the senior Morani, who happened to be the chief's son. First came a period of private contemplation, when he was presumably intended to reflect upon the responsibilities and pleasures which were rushing at him, but he could only wonder how painful the coming ordeal was going to be. Then he was made to stand in the centre of the assembled tribe while the Morani solemnly slaughtered a bullock – a rare and costly event – whereupon he was led forward to be the first to drink the blood spurting from the dying animal's neck. This was nauseating enough, but then he was led into a specially prepared hut and made to lie on a goatskin mat. He was given something to chew, which had the effect of sending his brain spinning away into the wildest of fantasies, and only dimly became aware of men holding his legs and arms, and of a sudden searing pain. He reacted immediately and violently, flexing his muscles and having to be held down by what seemed the entire clan. Then he was given something to drink which again had his head spinning, and this was kept up for some twenty-four hours. The following twenty-four hours were even worse, as the drugs were withdrawn, the pain persisted, and in addition his bladder was full; he was so uncomfortable and weak and generally unlike himself he began to wonder if he had actually been castrated.

But on the third morning he was able to pass water without screaming in agony, and the pain began to recede. He had spent the entire time in the hut attended only by men, and had no idea what had happened to Schlieben. Nor was he yet allowed out, but was instructed by his mentor, whose name he gathered was Kainairju, to sit on the same bloodstained mat on which he had been circumcised, to have his head shaved and then painted with a mixture of pig's fat and red ochre. This ceremony was carried out by an old woman, who he understood to be Kainairju's mother, the chieftain's head wife.

Now at last he was invited to go outside. Somewhat apprehensively he obeyed, to find the chieftain, Schlieben and the entire clan assembled to meet him, with much stamping of feet and spears. Standing beside the chieftain was a Masai girl, hardly fifteen years of age, he estimated, but as tall and straight and attractive as any of her compatriots. Her head was shaven, her handsome features carved from ebony, her breasts small and high, her limbs slender and strong. The chieftain placed his hand on the girl's head, then on his own heart, then he took her hand and placed it in Adrian's.

'By God,' Schlieben said. 'He's marrying you.'

Adrian had no idea what to say, or do. Of course he could not be being married . . . but he was most certainly being presented with the girl.

'Lulu,' the chieftain said. 'Lulu.'

'Lulu?' Adrian looked at Schlieben.

45

'I would say that's her name.'

'Lulu?' He found it difficult not to smile.

As Schlieben saw. 'No joke, boy. I think, unless my memory plays me false, that Lulu is the Masai name for dawn. Now there is a beautiful name, for a beautiful girl. Do you know, I am almost tempted to remain here, and make a home, and live out our days in peace, as your father wanted to do.'

'No,' Adrian said. 'Not now. I cannot disappear without trace. I have a mother and sister to care for. The moment the rains cease we must leave.' He looked down at the black fingers still resting in his, and knew an irresistible stirring within him; he had not been as unaffected by the sight of Schlieben and the other girl, or by his own recent experience, as he pretended. 'But I shall come back. That I swear.'

PART I

The Quest

1

Adrian Barclay reached the head of the little Southampton side street, turned into it and stopped to straighten his jacket. It was new, as were most of his clothes; partly because Schlieben had advanced him the money to make some purchases in Mombasa, and partly because he had earned sufficient on the voyage home to outfit himself with at least one decent suit of clothes, bought within the last hour, following his discharge. But having been bought hurriedly, and from what was available, neither jacket nor trousers fitted very well, and he had tied a handkerchief round his neck to keep out the winter air, for he had no cravat.

But he was home at last, that was the important thing. Or was it? Sometimes he could not be sure.

He walked down the street slowly, came to the gate, and there hesitated. The little house looked much the same as when he had last seen it, and that had been more than a year ago — save that it sadly lacked a fresh coat of paint; the windowsills were cracked and peeling. Yet the little garden was as neatly tended as ever he remembered it. The garden was his mother's pride and joy, and in that, as in all things when she was free from school, Mandy was her loyal assistant. That the garden was as it should be was reassuring.

He pushed open the gate, went up the path between the

rose beds, banged the brass knocker, and a moment later faced his sister.

'Adrian,' she whispered. She was very clearly his sister, even at fifteen tall for a girl, and with splendid blonde hair. On her the delicate Barclay features were even more exquisite. 'Oh, Adrian.'

He swept her into his arms, held her close and looked past her at the woman who came out of the kitchen. Once she too had been blonde and with some pretensions to beauty; now she looked tired, and her hair was more grey than he remembered. But her eyes could still light up as she saw her son.

'Adrian!' she said, and he extended his hug to include both of them. 'I had almost given you up.'

'Did you not get a telegram? From Kurt von Schlieben?'

'From a German man. Yes. But that was months ago. He said you would soon be home.'

'Well . . . I had to find a ship, and then work my passage . . .'

Molly Barclay gazed into his eyes. 'And now you are home,' she said. 'Oh, thank God for that. Now you are home.'

They sat in the little parlour, where once again there were evidences of a certain stringency. But there was a bottle of cordial to be opened, to celebrate his return. The women wanted him to talk. How they wanted him to talk, to tell them everything that had happened.

But where was he to begin? Simply with the death of Father, the starkly beautiful funeral? His mother wanted to hear about that in considerable detail, when it was a memory he wished to forget because of the guilt involved. He had not felt sufficient grief. Everything during those couple of days had happened too fast, with crisis piling upon crisis, and too unexpectedly. Emotions had been driven across his mind with kaleidoscopic rapidity. And that same evening, before he had even properly accepted the fact of his father's death, had come the start of his induction into the tribe. That was not something he could ever talk about, to anyone, much less his mother; for the rest of his life he must change his clothes in private.

It was easier to talk of the Masai themselves. He had lived with them for five months, learned their language, hunted with them, come to be accepted by them as indeed a Morani, a young warrior. These things he could talk about freely, and they were fascinated. He could excite them with tales of stalking lion, horrify them with his description of drinking blood and milk. But they naturally also wanted to know about the women. On that subject he pretended ignorance. He could describe them, and their scanty clothing, and their habits, and the food they cooked, and their ways of having babies and bringing up children . . . and still claim to know little of *them*, which did not appear unreasonable in a nineteen-year-old boy.

To his relief, they were at least as interested in his tale of how he and Schlieben had escaped, when the Long Rains finally ceased. For they had had to escape. The Masai chieftain, Uthuli, who had given his own daughter to the huge young white man, wished to keep them there permanently; he could see that the possession of someone like Adrian Barclay would be a great advantage to his tribe. He hoped, and had been led to believe by Adrian and Schlieben's dissembling, that the months of the Long Rains, and the attentions of Lulu, would make them content. Fortunately, he also never truly understood the power of the rifle, and thus never sought to confiscate theirs.

When the rains finally ceased in the summer, and the tribe prepared for its migration towards the north, having planted its crop, which would be waiting to be reaped when it returned in the autumn, Adrian and Schlieben found it a simple matter to slip away. They were missed and pursued, of course, but by then they were as fit and capable of long hours of loping under the African sun as any of the Morani, and although the Africans slowly gained on them, they lacked any effective missile weapons, their bows only being capable of execution at relatively short ranges. The power of the white men's rifles kept them safe. Adrian did not permit Schlieben actually to kill any of their erstwhile comrades, but a rifle carefully aimed at a piece of rock or a tree and shivering it into splinters was sufficiently discouraging. Thus they gained the forest and the Kikuyu kraals, where they were welcomed as souls returning from the dead. Indeed they had been supposed dead; Safah, on regaining the encampment, had found only the evidences of its being overrun by many feet – and even the Somali had not been prepared to enter the Masai village in search of them.

Then the coast, to find that John Barclay's ship, having been remasted, had sailed away under the command of First Officer Garroway; Safah had also convinced him that they had been murdered by the Masai. People in Mombasa were sympathetic, but there was a strong suggestion of 'I-told-you-so' when they spoke either of John Barclay's death or their own captivity. Only Safah understood. He was in any event guilty over what had happened, feeling that it somehow had been his fault; but he lacked the means to help Adrian, penniless and with only rags on his back.

Adrian did not know what to make of Schlieben. No two men could have spent six months together, in the most trying of circumstances, relying entirely upon each other for survival most of the time, without becoming the best of friends. No one could have been more sympathetic than Schlieben over John Barclay's death, or expressed more feelings of friendship and admiration for the sea captain. Yet Adrian always felt there was no real warmth behind the words. They were what Schlieben felt needed to be said.

Thus Adrian did not feel he knew the German at all. He understood that he was a lusty character, with a gigantic

52

appetite for life; where Adrian had contented himself with Lulu – indeed both his youth and his Puritan upbringing would have made any polygamous relationship utterly distasteful – Schlieben had found his pleasures where he could, and amongst the Masai the opportunities were plentiful. His courage could not be doubted, but he had never sought to display it unnecessarily, any more than he had ever shown the slightest pique at being relegated to a role of second player, as it were; the Masai were clearly interested in him only as Adrian's companion, and never thought to discover if he too might be capable of the feats of strength which they found so fascinating in the younger man – and on which they called at every opportunity. Even Schlieben's marksmanship was not as admired as Adrian's muscles – the Masai regarded firearms as a sort of magic, which could be appreciated and even used, but never understood.

Additionally, while they had both taken their places in the male life of the village, hunted lion – and entranced the Morani with that magical ability to kill from a distance and in comparative safety – and herded cattle, and stood guard like any other warrior, Schlieben had always worn on these occasions a thoughtful and almost distracted expression, as if his mind was far away upon other matters. Of course Adrian understood that no doubt he too was concerned to think his family must suppose him dead, that his position might well have been filled – as indeed it had. Yet on their arrival back in Mombasa he did not seem particularly bothered by that, and far from immediately informing his family of his safe return, merely used his father's name to negotiate a loan from the main German trading house in the port – and left them to relay the happy news back to Berlin.

From the loan he was able to stake Adrian in a modest fashion. But by then a curtain had fallen between the two men – or perhaps it had always been there, and Adrian had not noticed it.

53

'What will you do now?' Schlieben asked as they sipped coffee together, for all the world like two casual acquaintances rather than men who had shared everything for the past six months.

'Find a passage back to England as quickly as possible. Would it be possible to get a message to my mother.'

'Of course. I will attend to it.'

'It should say . . .' Adrian checked. He had no idea what it should say.

'Leave it with me,' Schlieben said. 'And then?'

'Well, I imagine there will be my father's affairs to sort out . . . oh, I will repay you your loan, of course.'

'Do not think of it,' Schlieben said. 'It is a gift. You saved my life. A loan would be a scant repayment of that.'

'I appreciate your generosity,' Adrian said. 'But I will repay you, whenever I can. Will you remain here?'

Schlieben shook his head. 'I think I too should go home.'

'Then will you give me your address in Germany?'

Schlieben grinned. 'I will write you.'

Almost as if he wishes to be rid of me, Adrian thought. But then Schlieben asked, 'Will you ever return to the high land, as you said you would?'

Will I ever go back? Adrian wondered then, as he was wondering now. Back to the highlands, the pure air, the magnificent scenery, the feeling of being one with God?

Back to the lions of Tsavo, and the desert, and the forest? Back to his father's grave?

And back to the Masai, and Lulu. There was the most taxing question of all. Because there too, he could feel no certainty in his mind that he understood his own feelings, or hers. She had been presented to him within a week of his father's death. Having spent his brief career at sea under his father's eye, he was a virgin, uncertain of his physical desires; even if he had been aroused by Schlieben's antics. But at that moment, he was so confused and upset by the events of the week that he truly wanted to hold someone tight in his arms, just to feel the reality of being alive, and perhaps to assuage some of that grief he could not reveal.

Lulu was also a virgin, but she had been given to a man, and she understood, like any young African girl, what was required of her. Her satin-like flesh was impossible to resist, and being totally inexperienced, he did not attempt to make love with any preconceived ideas, but allowed himself to follow her lead, guided by her actions and positions. And knocked on the door of paradise. To be entrapped between Lulu's tight buttocks was the most glorious sensation in the world, as was the caressing of her equally tight breasts with their cone-like nipples. They never kissed. She knew nothing of kissing, and neither did he, and where she did not lead, he did not press the matter. She did like to nuzzle him, and that too was an unforgettable experience.

But had they loved? He did not believe so, which was why he resisted any temptation to take her with him when he left. Besides, he had learned that the Masai could not exist outside their own lands and their own way of life; to imprison a Masai, they said in Mombasa, was to pronounce a rapid sentence of death, hardly more than three months. He could not help but feel that Lulu would regard removal from her tribe as an imprisonment, certainly in European society, with its strict rules of dress and conduct. She was a creature of the high land, and could only be happy there.

But there were of course other reasons. If he could not imagine Lulu in England, he could even less imagine himself in England, and certainly here in this parlour, with a black girl on his arm. Mother's reaction just could not be contemplated. So, had he deserted her? The matter had worried him, in the beginning, and still did, on occasion. But it was gradually being resolved in his conscience. It *could* well have caused her death, and there had been no true love between them. They had been placed together, because a warrior must have a woman, and because Uthuli had wished to make his blond protégé a gift of the best woman

55

he could think of. Lulu was probably very happy to have seen the last of him, and would now be able to settle down with one of her own people, to a life she understood.

But would he go back?

'Yes,' he had told Schlieben. 'I wish to go back. I would like to make my father's dream come true.' He had waited, and when Schlieben made no comment, asked, 'And you?'

Schlieben's eyes had worn that faraway look. 'Oh, I will go back as well,' he had said. 'When I am ready.'

'It sounds a frightful experience,' Molly Barclay said when he was finished, while Mandy still clung to his arm, gazing open-mouthed at his face. 'Poor John . . . but to have done such a thing in the first place, and taking you with him . . . you could both have been killed.'

It occurred to Adrian that his mother, used in any event to seeing her husband for only a couple of months in every year, had perhaps not properly realised that from this voyage he never was going to return. It seemed to be John Barclay's fate not to be mourned.

'It was dangerous, perhaps,' he admitted. 'But exciting. And it was not the country or anything in it that killed Father. He could have had his seizure on the deck of the ship. The country is the most splendid, the most healthy, anywhere in the world. I wish I could paint, that I could perhaps recreate some idea of it for you. But not even a painting could capture the quality of the air, the feeling of being on top of the universe . . . our guide called it the roof of the world, and he was just about right. Mother' – he leaned forward and took her hands – 'Father fell in love with it. He had dreamed of it for so long, and it was even better than he had dreamed. Almost his last words were a wish to give up the sea and take us all up there, to live.'

His mother frowned at him, uncomprehending. 'He wanted to go and live in Africa? In the jungle?'

'This isn't jungle. Oh, there is jungle around it. But the

high land is . . . like Scotland, only on an incomparably larger and grander scale, and with an incomparably better climate.'

'But what would we do there?' Mandy asked.

'Well, we could certainly ranch cattle. But I am sure there are a great many other things we could do as well. There is so much land it is unbelievable.'

'My God,' Molly Barclay said. 'I do believe you are serious. You must be mad, Adrian. Are there white women there?'

'Well, none in the interior, of course. There are no white men, either. But there are a few white women on the coast. Portuguese, mainly, but very nice.' He had not actually met any of them. 'Oh, it would be a difficult journey for you, I'll not deny that. But it would also be a unique adventure, and I would be there to show you the way, and make sure nothing happened to you.'

'I do believe you *are* serious,' Molly Barclay remarked again.

'You mean . . . leave England?' Mandy asked in wonderment.

'For somewhere far better,' Adrian repeated. 'Where there is no winter, just a perpetual cool summer; where there is no illness . . .' He paused, gazing at his mother's expression, because of course Father *had* died there. But as Schlieben said, Father had surely already been carrying the seeds of death within him.

'I think your adventure has gone to your head,' Molly Barclay said. 'And it does seem to have been the most remarkable adventure. But it is over now, Adrian, and must be put out of your mind. You have a great number of things to do.'

'Mother . . .'

She continued as if he hadn't spoken. 'There is very little money. In fact, there is almost none. Which is why we have prayed for your return. Mr Dringle has been very kind, but he is not a charitable institution, nor would we accept his charity if he were. I have had to take Amanda out of school.' She glanced at the girl, who gave an uncertain smile and squeezed Adrian's arm as if to reassure him that it had not been his fault. 'However,' her mother went on. 'Immediately on hearing that you were actually alive, Mr Dringle told me that you were of course still employed by his company, and he then gave me an advance on your wages. There is a berth waiting for you on one of his ships. I am sorry to have to ask you to go back to sea again so soon, but there it is. There is the advance to be repaid, and your wage is all we shall have to live on.'

'Mother . . .'

'There is no money,' she shouted with sudden vehemence. 'You can dream, Adrian, like your father. He always dreamed, and left me poorly provided for. And where did it get him? A grave not even in consecrated soil, hundreds of miles from a church. But even if this place were the paradise you have suggested, and I would say that by your own account it is not, how would we get there and begin a new life? There is no *money*.'

Adrian gazed at her for several seconds, while Amanda looked from one to the other anxiously. If she had always worshipped her big brother, her life had been built around her mother – her father she had hardly known. Then Adrian nodded. 'I understand the situation, Mother. I shall see Mr Dringle in the morning, and take his offered berth.'

'Oh, thank God, Adrian. Thank God.' She held him close. 'I knew you would. You have always been a good and faithful boy, thank God.' Her tone suggested she could not say as much for his father. She kissed his cheek. 'You have had a great adventure, if also a tragic one. Something to look back upon. But now you must think of the future.'

The only future worth considering is the high country, Adrian thought. But he did not tell her that.

*

58

'Your father was a fine seaman,' Alexander Dringle said. 'Oh, yes, a fine seaman. But a dreamer, too. Dreams lead to irresponsibility. Leaving his ship and wandering off into the jungle . . . that was an irresponsible act. So was taking his only son. Would you not agree, Adrian?'

Adrian supposed the shipowner was right, at least about leaving the ship. It was easy to see that Alexander Dringle had never dreamed in his life. He had inherited his cargo line from his father, and to do him justice, far from letting it decline as so many born-rich men would have done, had built it up even more. But he remained a small, pinch-faced fellow, who preferred to sit in his gloomy office looking at manifests and schedules than inhaling the open air.

'I asked him to take me, sir,' he said. 'And it was a worthwhile dream, because it is there. The land he had always dreamed of. There, and waiting to be used. To be enjoyed.'

'So is heaven, no doubt,' Mr Dringle remarked piously. 'And heaven is the reward for hard work and good deeds. The firm will expect hard work from you, Adrian.' Clearly he was not so optimistic as to expect good deeds as well.

'The firm will have it, sir.'

'I expected nothing less. You have another couple of weeks on shore, then you will ship as fourth mate on the *Sara Dringle*.'

'You are generous, sir.'

'I know you have neither the experience nor the qualifications for such a position, yet. But I expect you to study.'

'I will do that, sir.'

'Good. Good. Pass your examinations, and you will climb the ladder of success. I see you a master in ten years' time.'

'Thank you, sir.'

'As long as you do not waste your time in dreaming, eh?'

'I shall hope never to waste my time, sir.' Adrian chose his words carefully. 'But the *Sara Dringle* . . . she is a new ship, sir?'

'Launched seven months ago. Named after my youngest daughter. This will be her maiden voyage. She is a fine ship. You will do well in her. And you will not be away from your poor widowed mother all that much; she will sail between Southampton and New York, scarcely two months around, if the wind is fair.'

'New York?' Adrian cried in dismay. He had anticipated being on the East Africa run, and thus at least able to keep an eye on his dream, and renew it, year after year, by talk and hearsay.

'New York,' Mr Dringle repeated firmly. 'We agreed that you were going to work, not dream.'

It occurred to Adrian that his mother and Mr Dringle were working in close accord. But there was nothing for it. Jobs were not so plentiful in the shipping industry since the Argentinian financial collapse had induced a worldwide recession in trade and banking three years before. Staying with Dringle and Company, where his father was remembered with affection, promised him a smooth ride upwards, and in any event, as his mother kept reminding him, there was no money for gambling, especially with one's life and career. John Barclay had done that, without making adequate provision for his family, which was why they were in this unhappy strait.

And the North Atlantic was the most exacting of all proving grounds for sailors. There were worse places in the world, and he had sailed some of them. Particularly he remembered the passage round the Cape of Good Hope – called the Cape of Storms by some early seamen – and up the south east coast of Africa, where the Agulhas Current ran strongly; in any sort of weather the seas could be frightening, and even in a calm the swell was immense. But there was no sea passage in which, taking the year as a whole, the weather was so unfailingly bad as on the North Atlantic run. Each voyage might see the ship experience as many as seven gales, some of them major storms, and he saw seas off Newfoundland quite as large as any in the Indian Ocean. A seaman, and especially an officer, had here to put theory into practice every day of the week, learn, during the several days at a time when the sky was completely overcast, and thus no sun or star sights were possible, to work out an accurate dead reckoning of the ship's position, or become as much as a hundred miles off course. Perhaps more important yet, he needed to learn how to drive men to change sail every few hours, in appalling conditions, and when they were already wet and exhausted . . . and yet not become hated by them. That could only be accomplished by leadership rather than bullying, an art which perhaps had to be born into a man rather than attained by study. Not every officer possessed it, and some had even achieved master's rank without it, and were loathed and feared by their crews. Adrian was proud enough to feel that he did possess it, inherited perhaps from his father, and Alexander Dringle thought so too, it seemed, as promotion came steadily, with the passing of each examination.

Making four Atlantic crossings a year, each way, and having a great deal of studying to do in between times, left little leisure for dreaming. Which no doubt was what his mother and Mr Dringle had intended. Not that he ever mentioned Africa to them again. Indeed, as year succeeded year, even his sharp memory of the high grassland began to fade, and he wondered which *was* memory and which imagination. Soon the whole episode became dreamlike, and even his recollection of Lulu's brother, Uthuli's son Kainairju, who had been the nearest thing to a friend Adrian had had amongst the Morani, grew indistinct. Nights standing guard over the herd, shivering in the intense cold; days stalking lion or leopard, perspiring in the intense heat;

61

sitting round the fire for his daily imbibition of blood and milk; accepting the annoying practical jokes the Masai had delighted in playing on each other, and on him; the occasional surprising unbending of the proud warriors – all seemed part of some previous existence. It was amazing to him how he could have lived so intimately with a people for five months, and accumulated nothing of permanent value – probably because from the start his mind had been set on eventual escape.

And then, without warning, he would remember how the fields of white carnations had sprouted on the plains after the rain, and the plovers wheeling and crying above them like seabirds, and he would know that it had been no dream.

Not altogether to his surprise, he never did receive a letter from Schlieben. If he found it regrettable that, after all they had experienced together, the German should wish to forget *him* so completely – and even wondered if perhaps Schlieben was embarrassed at the adventure, and the outcome of it, and his loan, of course – he could also recognise that Schlieben too must have found nothing worth retaining from his adventure, not even their friendship. There was little he could do about that. And at last even Lulu, whom he had supposed would remain sharply etched in his mind for all time, became an odd sort of half-dream, an erotic thought of which he was ashamed. She coloured his relations with women of his own race, almost as much as his fear of amusement or contempt should they ever discover his un-English physical characteristics. He made no attempt to seek women out, save for the occasional prostitute, with whom it was necessary to share nothing but money.

Yet he still had every intention of one day returning. Dringle could not keep him on the North Atlantic run forever. One day he would sail back into the harbour formed by Mombasa Island, and look across the sound at the mainland, and know what lay behind the trees. He continued to read everything he could discover on Africa, and especially East Africa, and to look out in the newspapers for word of developments there, of any other white men who might have trodden that sacred ground. Thus he devoured the reports of Stanley's great expedition, which, after duly circumnavigating Lake Victoria Nyanza and then visiting Lake Tanganyika in the south, actually crossed the entire continent, reaching the Congo and thence following that great river down to its west coast exit. He read with concern of the foundation of the International Association for the Exploration and Civilisation of Africa, under the auspices of King Leopold II of Belgium, his mind filling with horror as he imagined the highlands invaded by European soldiers and settlers – and had to smile at his own dog-in-the-manger attitude; if he could not enjoy them, he did not wish anyone else to. Then he was reassured to read that the Sultan of Zanzibar, Barghash Sayyid, who had for years been under considerable British influence – mainly because both the islands which were his principal cities, Zanzibar and Mombasa, were vulnerable to bombardment by the Royal Navy – and who, only a few years before, had agreed to put an end to the slavery which was endemic in those waters – had offered his entire continental possessions, and he claimed some thousand miles of coastline, to Sir William Mackinnon. He was the chairman of the British India Steam Navigation Company, which, like Dringle and Son, traded with both Mombasa and Zanzibar, although on a far grander scale. Mackinnon, apparently feeling that this was too large a gift for a private individual or even a private company to accept, put the matter to Her Majesty's Government, asking for support, and was politely told to forget it. Mr Disraeli had, while Adrian and Schlieben were with the Masai, purchased on his own initiative a controlling interest in the Suez Canal at the other end of the coast; he could see little of value in taking over the problems of the Sultan of Zanzibar. The hinterland, for the time being, was again safe.

Actually, Adrian did not know if the Sultan of Zanzibar claimed suzerainty over the high country, however many years the Arabs of the coast had traded with the Masai. He was more concerned with the activities of British missionaries, who, following Stanley's discoveries, were beginning to penetrate to Lake Victoria and beyond. But so far as he could gather, they were interested only in reaching the African kingdom of Uganda, which lay on the western side of the lake, and where King Mtesa was one of the few native sovereigns to welcome the white man. There was no word that any European other than his father, Schlieben and himself had ever looked upon the high country. Or even knew of its existence, outside legend. His private paradise would remain a paradise for a while longer.

In the spring of 1880, Adrian received his first mate's ticket. It was an occasion for great celebration, for he was still only twenty-three years old, and Alexander Dringle was delighted. 'When I prophesied that you would be a master in ten years, I was underestimating your ability,' he declared. 'It is only four since your return from Africa, from the dead, and you have made great strides. Oh, indeed, Adrian, we are all proud of you.'

Mother was proudest of all, and Amanda, now a perfectly beautiful twenty-year-old, had eyes which shone like stars. Neither Mother nor Dringle, however, were so well pleased when Adrian hinted that he would like to broaden his experience, and perhaps transfer from the North Atlantic to the Eastern routes for a few years.

'You'll not find promotion easy to come by on the Eastern route,' Dringle told him. 'The North Atlantic is where there is most profit, and most notice taken of those who earn it. You stay with that, for a few years more.'

A few more years, Adrian thought bitterly. While Europe was slowly becoming aware of Africa, while his dream might at any moment be realised by someone else. And while he was helpless to do anything about it; he was still his mother's sole support, and Mandy's as well – although that might not continue for very long, as she did not lack admirers. But that again was a reason for him to be at least in the background, at regular intervals: he was also playing the father she no longer had, and could not pretend that every young man who came knocking on their door exactly filled his ideal for her.

So once again he sadly relegated his dream to the back of his mind, and set to work to gain that master's ticket which would perhaps give him more freedom, little suspecting that Fate, having chosen to show him the high country, was not prepared to let him slip from her clutches.

In the August of that year the *Sara Dringle* encountered very heavy weather on the New York crossing. Incorporating as she did the latest in marine design and technology, she was powered by an engine as well as by sail. Soon the engineer was panting white-faced up to the bridge to inform the captain that several of the bolts bedding the engine had sheered, and that he feared the whole massive piece of machinery might break loose. All the hands that could be spared were sent below with warps and hawsers to prevent that catastrophe, but it was obvious the engine could not again be used until it had been rebedded. The storm blew itself out, and they limped on under canvas, finally arriving in New York nine days late. They had been posted as missing, presumed lost; everyone knew that a hurricane had crossed their track.

Alexander Dringle was telegraphed, and after congratulating them on their good fortune and seamanship in bringing the ship through the storm, made the obvious decision: that no attempt was to be made to recross the Atlantic until the engine had been fully repaired. The ship was therefore towed up the Hudson River to the yard of Meachem and Company, who were specialists in marine engineering. John

Meacham, who owned the yard, was also a shipowner, a big, bluff, confident man with a red face and an inevitable cigar. He had a reputation for being a hard-driving man and rough on his crews, but he also knew both sides of his business, and personally inspected the damage – Alexander Dringle was an old friend as well as a long-standing rival for the Atlantic trade.

'That'll take not less than two weeks to put right, Captain Lewis,' he declared.

'I was wondering what the lads and I should do in the meantime,' Lewis said.

'You can't go home and back. Take a holiday. What else can you do? I tell you what, Captain, bring your officers up to the house for lunch tomorrow. No point in getting all fretted up about a thing like this. They happen, and there's an end to it.'

'Well, sir, of course we accept your kind invitation with pleasure,' Lewis said, but that evening he brooded over his glass of whisky with his first officer. 'Every day we sit here is costing the company money,' he grumbled.

'I've known it happen before,' Adrian agreed. 'It really can try a man's patience.'

'And that last time cost your father his life,' Lewis pointed out.

'Well,' Adrian said, 'there's not much exploring left to be done in the United States. Our only danger lies in being bored to death.'

Although he was struck by the similarity of the situation, as the United States, full of bustling and spreading civilisation, was *not* Africa – even the wild Indians of the Midwest had recently been pacified following their spectacular victory over General Custer at the Little Big Horn – Adrian did expect to be bored. And to allow himself to feel resentful of the Meachem fortune, as lack of wealth was preventing him from achieving his ambition.

The Meachem estate was a little farther up the Hudson

than the shipyard, set in magnificent grounds sloping down to the river itself, and containing a four-square mansion with colonial pillars, bow windows, several clusters of chimney pots and a terrace, surrounded by a park of copper beeches and elms. It was undoubtedly a lovely place, but money aside, it was too much the epitome of civilised success to attract Adrian.

The entertainment was on a scale to match the surroundings. The Meachems had invited several friends, but the five officers from the British ship – dressed in their best shore-going outfits of blue serge jackets with brass buttons, and smart caps – were treated as guests of honour at a huge banquet, taken outdoors under the trees and served by a score of obsequious black servants. Remembering the innate pride of all the Africans he had encountered, be they Kikuyu, Masai, or above all, Somali, Adrian found this rather offensive, but he smiled and determined at least to enjoy the food.

Yet the company was pleasant enough, as well. The Meachems had four daughters, and each, with her silky dark hair and slender body and somewhat bold features, was as pretty as any picture. But obviously they were slumming, and knew it. Adrian was thus the more completely taken aback when, after the meal, when the entire party was strolling the grounds, he suddenly found himself beside the eldest of the girls – although she could hardly be more than twenty, he was certain – who announced, 'I'm Joanna, but you may call me Jo.' While he was still digesting so frontal an assault, she went on, 'And you're Mr Barclay. Papa has told us how you once spent a whole year as a prisoner of the Hottentots.'

She was the handsomest of the sisters, Adrian had already decided, with hair not quite dark enough to be black, hazel eyes, a pronounced but most attractive nose, and a firm mouth and chin. And a definite awareness of who and what she was, as he discovered when he burst out laughing.

'Was it so amusing?' she snapped, the eyes suddenly brittle.

'Well, it is, Miss Meachem,' he said. 'Because it's not quite true. But I am flattered that your father should have mentioned me to you at all.' And who had mentioned him to Meachem? he wondered. Probably Dringle.

'Are you suggesting that my father has lied about you?' she asked coldly.

'By no means. But the information he was given was not quite accurate. The Hottentots live in South West Africa. I have never been there. I lived with a people known as the Masai, for five months. That was in East Africa. As to whether I was a prisoner, they and I had differing opinions about that. I managed to prove my point.'

She had stopped walking, so he naturally had to do the same; the rest of the party drifted away from them. 'I stand corrected,' she said, but some of the annoyance had left her voice. 'Still, five months is a long time. Wasn't it a terrifying experience?'

'Not really. They treated me very well. They thought I was an exceptional being, you see.'

'Of course,' she agreed. 'As no doubt, you do yourself.' With which she turned and began to walk very rapidly after her family. He caught up with her in two strides.

'I learned to speak their language,' he said lamely.

'How very nice for you,' Joanna Meachem replied. 'We really must see if we can find a . . . Masai, was it? A Masai-speaking American for you to chat with.'

After that he gave up, and was therefore the more astonished when, three days later, he heard a voice say, 'Why, good day, Mr Barclay.'

He was on the foredeck at the time, for Captain Lewis had not been able to bring himself to declare a holiday after all, and had decided that as the ship was perforce lying idle she should be given a complete painting and re-caulking. Adrian was in his shirt sleeves, and surrounded by seamen

68

stripped to the waist, forcing the thick caulking material down between the deck seams, while others stood waiting with the heated tar. And Joanna Meachem was standing above them on the bridge deck. She had apparently come on board unnoticed, which would not have been difficult, as it was her father's yard and there was no one on the gangway. Hastily Adrian raised his cap. 'Miss Meachem. Apologies for the state of my men. And myself.'

'I have been on board ships in dock before, Mr Barclay,' she said, and turned away, twirling her parasol, to look towards the stern of the ship. Her message was clear, or she would not have addressed him in the first place. In her yellow dress with its black trim, the skirt fluttering in the breeze to give glimpses of her high-sided elastic boots, and her parasol and matching yellow and black bonnet, she was even prettier today than she had been at the luncheon.

'You'll carry on, lads,' he said, and picked up his jacket before hurrying for the ladder and joining her on the bridge.

'She's not a very big ship, is she,' she remarked as he reached her.

'Big enough. Dringle and Company is not a passenger line.'

'Do you never take passengers?' she asked. 'Under any circumstances?'

'Oh, well, there are two cabins aft which are available for friends of Mr Dringle who want to make a cheap crossing.'

'I was reading a book on Africa the other day,' she said, changing the subject without warning. 'And I wondered if you might care to look at it and tell me if it is at all accurate.'

'I doubt I am qualified to do that, Miss Meachem,' he said.

'I am sure you are. And I seem to remember asking you to call me Jo,' she said. 'When next do you have some time off?'

'Well . . .' he ventured cautiously.

'I shall expect you tomorrow afternoon at three,' she said.

'And now I really must be getting back.' She smiled at him, and then descended the ladder and made her way ashore, where her pony and trap were waiting.

Adrian discussed the matter with Lewis that evening, having in any event to ask for shore leave, were he going to accept her invitation – or command, as seemed more accurate a description. But what he actually wanted was some advice. He had never encountered anyone quite so forward, and was keenly aware of the difference in their stations. As the Captain understood. 'Of course you cannot refuse her,' he said. 'We are very much in Mr Meachen.'s debt. But I do suggest you behave with the utmost propriety. Endeavour to make sure you are never left alone with her.' Then he gave Adrian a hard look. 'I presume you do find her attractive?'

'I find her most attractive,' Adrian confessed. 'But you cannot really suppose she has any . . . well, ulterior motive in inviting me to call?'

'If you do not suppose so, why have you come to me for advice?' the Welshman asked bluntly.

'It just seems incredible. I mean, a girl like Joanna Meachem must have the pick of every beau in New York.'

'Of a certain class, no doubt. Perhaps for that very reason she wants some decent manhood,' Lewis said wisely. 'Don't sell yourself short, Adrian. You're a very handsome young fellow. And when you've a body as big as yours, well, the ladies get to wondering what else about it might be outsize.'

Adrian found himself flushing. 'Now you are being extraordinarily vulgar.'

He was entirely relieved the following afternoon, when, again wearing his best blue jacket and his shore-going cap, he was shown by the black butler from the house and through the trees to a little arbor where there was a summer house, in which all four of the sisters were gathered. As Lewis had suggested, he only had to make sure they always had company, and how could they not, with so many siblings about?

Each of the girls made quite a fuss of welcoming him, and he was given a glass of lemonade to drink, and then sat down on one of the bench seats that circled the walls, with the offending book, which was shared between Joanna and himself. This necessitated their shoulders touching quite regularly. She was wearing pink today, and grew prettier every time he saw her. The book was actually about South Africa, and he had only touched at Cape Town on the way to Mombasa five years before, but he did his best to comment on the various descriptive passages, becoming quite interested, until he realised that the girl sitting on his other side was no longer there. He sat straight in alarm, and discovered that all three of the younger sisters had disappeared. That could hardly be a coincidence.

'I expect they found it boring,' Joanna explained unconvincingly.

'Ah. Well, I suppose I should be going.'

'Of course you should not. You've only just got here. Have another glass of lemonade.' She went to the table and poured two, and brought them back to where he sat. 'I adore Africa. Everything about it. I mean to go there one day.'

'Do you?' His surprise was genuine.

'Of course. Don't you want to go back?'

'Oh . . .' Then his enthusiasm ran away with him. 'How I want to go back. To the high country. It is the most fabulous place. I would give anything to be able to return this minute.'

She sat on the floor at his feet. 'Tell me about it.'

He hesitated. She was actually leaning her shoulder against his knee, and now she looked back up at him, her head bent right back so that he could see her neck, her hair cascading on to the ground. She was a most attractive girl. Perhaps she would never be beautiful, as Mandy was, but

71

she had a far more compelling face, vibrant and alive, and above all, eager. And to feel they might actually share a common dream . . . Before he could stop himself he was telling her everything he could remember, and once he had started speaking it was remarkable how memory came flooding back. He omitted Lulu, of course, but he was now used to doing that, even in his dreams.

She sighed, when at last he paused for breath. 'It does sound, as you say, fabulous. Will you take me there?'

'Eh?'

'Well, I could hardly go alone, don't you see? And Papa and Mama are the most hidebound of old stick-in-the-muds. A trip to Boston is as much trouble to them as if they were going to the moon. Besides, you know the way. And you would protect me. After what you've told me, I certainly mean to visit there.'

He knew she meant it. And he also knew that Joanna Meachem was a girl who made her dreams come true.

'Yes,' he said. 'Well, of course I would protect you. And it sounds a most delightful prospect. But I'm afraid, Miss Meachem . . . Jo,' he hastily corrected himself as he saw sparks gathering in her eyes again, 'that young ladies do not go gallivanting off into the jungle with men who are not related to them, not if they are ladies. And in any event, ladies do not go into the jungle at all. It is no place for gentlewomen, believe me.' He was quite forgetting that he had once proposed taking his mother and sister into it.

'Oh, stuff and nonsense,' she declared, scrambling to her feet and standing in front of him. 'I am quite capable of going into any jungle in the world. I can shoot a rifle. I'll show you. I have one of my own, and sometimes Papa and I go up into the mountains shooting together. I have shot a bear,' she said proudly. 'As for propriety, why, obviously you would have to marry me.'

'Do what?' He was aghast.

She frowned at him. 'Don't you find me attractive?'

72

'Why, of course I do. I think you are quite lovely. But really, Miss Meachem, we hardly know each other.'

'I thought you were very handsome when I first saw you,' she pointed out.

'I'm enormously flattered. But looks are not everything.'

'They're a start. I mean, I would never dream of marrying you if I didn't know what you looked like, now would I? Now tell me, where do you live?'

'In a place called Southampton,' he replied without thinking.

'Should I know where that is?'

'It's a seaport, in southern England,' he explained.

'Of course it would be. Do you have rooms, or a house?'

'I have a house.'

'Oh, I'm so glad. All by yourself?'

'Well, no. I have my mother and sister living with me.'

'Gee, I'll adore meeting them. When can we go?'

Adrian scratched his head, and decided to fall back on first principles. 'Jo, please . . . come here and sit down.'

She obeyed, sitting beside him on the bench.

'We cannot possibly marry,' Adrian said carefully, and raised his forefinger as she would have spoken. 'Just listen. We do *not* know each other at all. The thought of marriage has never entered my mind. But there are even more important factors than that. It would mean your leaving New York for a totally strange land . . .'

'We speak the same language.'

'We don't, really. And we have utterly different customs and ideas on things. That would only be the beginning. I am a ship's officer. I am away from home for something like ten months in every year . . .'

'You wouldn't be, because we'd be going to Africa together.'

That stopped him for a moment, because the idea was quite entrancing. But he recovered himself. 'No we wouldn't. Not right away. I do not have a penny in the world. You are the daughter of a millionaire. Now, what do you suppose your father would say to such a match?'

This time she answered without thinking. 'He'd throw you out.'

'Exactly. And so, you see . . .'

'So we will have to elope,' Joanna Meachem said happily.

'To . . . my God!'

'I think it would be rather fun.'

'Miss Meachem . . . Jo . . .' He paused in desperate anxiety. It was not that he could not fall in love with her very rapidly, he knew; indeed, he was doing so more and more with every moment he spent in her company. She looked delicious, she smelt delicious, her total confidence in the future was delicious, and he had no doubt at all that she would feel even more delicious than all the others put together. And in addition, she was the first person he had met since leaving Schlieben who had shown any enthusiasm for Africa at all.

Neither was it the fact that she was totally unlike any other woman he had ever met, and in her utter commitment to the mood of the moment appeared as almost irrational, to someone with his sober upbringing, anyway.

It was not even that he considered himself as married to Lulu. He had never thought of the Masai girl as more than a mistress. But, apart from the very real financial and social objections he had put forward, he possessed a private but growing fear that apart from his mutilated penis – of which perhaps a well-brought-up young lady would know nothing – he did not know how to behave himself sexually with any lady. None of the waterfront girls he had been to bed with had actually said so, but they had passed remarks such as, 'So you like to doggy paddle, do you?' which had suggested he was not being absolutely orthodox; one wise old bird had actually discussed it with him, and pointed out the error of his ways. He had not told her where he had got his notions, but had agreed to do it in what she had called the

74

'proper' way, and had found it not half as enjoyable, principally because he had been afraid all the time of crushing her – she had been about the same size as Jo.

These were utterly indecent thoughts to be having while in the company of a young lady, and he guessed his face must be as red as a beetroot. 'We simply cannot marry,' he said lamely.

She had been gazing at him very intently while he was choosing his words, and now she took his face between her hands and kissed him on the lips. His mouth was open, as was hers. Her tongue was the sweetest thing he had ever tasted. He could not stop his arms from closing on her back and shoulders, and if slender, they felt every bit as delicious as he had anticipated. Then he raised his eyes and watched John Meachem coming down the path towards them.

2

'You, sir, are a rogue and a rascal,' Mr Meachem declared.

'Don't you dare be rude to Adrian, Papa,' Joanna said, disentangling herself.

'Adrian, is it? You go to your room, miss. I'll deal with you later.'

Joanna glanced at him scornfully, and then turned back to Adrian. 'Remember our plans,' she said, and darted past her father and up the path to the house.

'Plans, are there?' Meachem inquired.

'I assure you, sir, it was . . . well . . . rather sudden,' Adrian said, wishing there could be an earthquake, or another hurricane, or that one of the trees would fall.

'I can believe that,' Meachem said surprisingly. He did not look as angry as Adrian had expected. 'That daughter of mine is going to get herself into real trouble one of these days.'

Adrian frowned at him.

'Oh, sure, you didn't realise, eh?' He sat down on the bench. 'I am not going to pull rank on you, boy. I'm just going to tell you some of the facts of life. Sit down.'

Cautiously Adrian lowered himself to the seat.

'Joanna . . . what shall I say? I guess she was spoiled from a child. First-born and all that. I have only daughters. You know that. Maybe if I'd have had a son things would be different. But girls . . . you can't put them out to work, teach them the business. You can only let them be, and if you love them, spoil them rotten. So Jo . . . she takes a fancy to something, she has to have it. Always has. Never considers that it might not be the right thing for her. Maybe I should've taken my belt to her long ago, knocked some common sense into her. Maybe . . .' His expression brightened. 'Maybe I'll do it today. And then I'm going to marry her off, no matter what she says.'

Adrian was not at all sure what he had just been told, but it seemed to him that he had been presented with an opening, one honour dictated that he take, if only to save the silly girl from a whipping. 'I . . .' He licked his lips. 'I would very much like to marry Miss Joanna, sir,' he ventured. 'If . . . if it would be appropriate.' So there it was. He was being as much a fool as she. But he had no choice.

Meachem raised his eyebrows. 'You?'

'I think Joanna would accept me, sir.'

'Holy Christ! Joanna would accept the garbage collector, if she was in that kind of mood. You? What do you earn, boy?'

'Ah . . .' Adrian hesitated.

'Forget it. I could pay your wage out of the small change in my pocket.'

'I have every prospect of being a master within the next few years, sir,' Adrian said, beginning to bridle.

76

'I'm sure you do. Is that supposed to interest me? I'm talking about money, boy. About this . . .' He gestured at the estate. 'Joanna has known nothing else. Nor will she ever know anything less, if I have anything to do with it.'

'Perhaps she *wants* something else,' Adrian argued.

'Now you listen to me, son, if you want to get that master's ticket. You clear off my property and skedaddle back to that ship of yours, and you stay there until she's ready to put to sea. If I ever find you on my land again, or if I ever hear of you speaking to my daughter again, I am going to have the law on you, and I am going to have your scalp. You won't ever work on any ship again, except maybe before the mast. I never threaten. I state facts. You want to be certain about that. Now git. And if you behave yourself, I'll say no more about this afternoon.'

Adrian hesitated, and glanced along the path where Joanna had gone. However shocked he had been by her behaviour, he still wanted her to be there, perhaps looking at him a last time, so that he could wave goodbye. But she wasn't, so maybe her father was right about her. That didn't make him feel any less embarrassed or angry; it made the temptation to tell Meachem to go to hell and do his damndest even stronger. But he'd be ruining himself to no purpose – he knew Meachem was a big enough man in the shipping world to implement his threat. And besides, had the roles been reversed and he been dealing with Mandy and an obviously unsuitable match, he would have acted no differently.

'Thank you, Mr Meachem,' he said, and walked the other way.

He remained heartily ashamed of himself. Had he not had the responsibility of Mother and Mandy . . . but that was futile reasoning. There was no way he could have stood up to Meachem no matter what the circumstances, except in a

77

purely physical sense, and that would probably have landed him in gaol for assault.

To Lewis' inquiry, he replied that he and Miss Meachem had merely read the book, in the company of her sisters. He knew he had to forget her, but during the remainder of their stay in Meachem's yard he could not help hoping she might one day appear on the bridge deck again. She never did.

And then they were at sea again, homeward bound. Now he could stop trying to forget her, and instead savour her memory. A brief memory. But he did not suppose he would ever forget the scent of her, or the feel of her, or the peculiar little smile she had . . . he realised that for all the absurdity and impossibility of the situation, which he had recognised from the start, he had just about fallen in love with her. He didn't think he had ever been in love before. What a way to start! But more than anything else, she had actually wanted to go to Africa, with him. That was the most encouraging thing he had heard for years. Joanna Meachem might be as far beyond his reach as the stars, but if there was one woman in the world capable of sharing his dream, surely there would be another, somewhere.

The *Sara Dringle* went into dry dock for a complete refit on her return to Southampton, and Adrian was given extended leave for the first time since his return from Africa, now nearly five years ago. It was a time to fix up the house, work in the garden – it was not really cold in southern England in the autumn – and enjoy the company of Mother and Mandy. His sister had a new admirer, an assistant in a local grocer's, actually the son of the grocer himself, with whom she seemed, if not exactly smitten, more than pleased. Adrian supposed that, being his sister and John Barclay's daughter, Mandy also dreamed, from time to time. But she had enough of her mother in her to have the sense to keep her dreams under careful control, to recognise what was practical and what was not. And if she was pleased, he could see no reason to stand in her way. To him, to be the wife of a grocer's assistant, even if he one day became a grocer, and never again leave the confines of Southampton, would be a dreadful prospect. But there again, no doubt, Mandy had her head set very straight on her shoulders.

More surprisingly was a letter he received towards the end of November from Kurt von Schlieben. After five years! His hand almost trembled as he slit the envelope, but it turned out to be a very ordinary and unexciting letter. Kurt merely apologised for not having written before, explained that he had been very busy, and said that as he would be in England in December, he would like to call. Adrian was delighted with the prospect of seeing his old friend again, although he saw no means of replying to say so; the letter had taken six weeks to reach him, which was not really surprising, he supposed, as it was post-marked Mombasa. So Kurt's family had packed him off back to his old position as vice-consul. Adrian grinned. It was nice to think that someone was even more restricted than himself. In any event, December was only two weeks off, so Kurt would just have to assume that he would be welcome.

The thought of his old friend coming to visit put him in the best of humours, even if he had no idea how Kurt would take to the rather humble surroundings in which he would find himself, and both his excitement and his apprehension communicated itself to Molly and Amanda. There was a great cleaning and scrubbing, and he had to spend most evenings telling them again about the adventures he had shared with the German. Actually putting Kurt up would be no problem, as he could share Adrian's room, but extra food and some German wine was laid in, and Adrian gave the little dining table a fresh coat of French polish. He also worked harder than ever in the garden, and was thus occupied on the first of December, which happened to be just a week before his birthday, when he heard the sound of wheels and looked up to see Joanna Meachem descending from a pony and trap at his gate. Adrian dropped his trowel and stood up. Joanna was waiting while the driver got down the suitcase which had been beside her on the seat. Now she turned to Adrian. 'I suppose we had better give him something,' she said. 'I have quite run out of money.'

Adrian put his hand into his pocket, only then remembering it was covered in soil, and found a shilling. He opened the gate, gave the coin to the driver and looked at the girl. He honestly had no idea whether he was standing on his head or his heels. She looked utterly entrancing, in a cape trimmed with fur over a heavy blue travelling gown, and with the winter breeze filling her cheeks with rosebuds. But . . . here?

'How on earth did you find my house?' he asked, curiosity getting the better of his manners.

'You told me you lived in Southampton, England,' she reminded him. 'I knew your name, and that you were a sailor, so I simply asked at the dock. You might look pleased to see me,' she said severely. 'I'm sorry I took so long getting here. But it wasn't quite as easy as I thought it was going to be. And I've been travelling second class. It was quite terrible. I suppose men think a woman alone is fair game for anything. It's a good thing I had this.' She reached into her handbag and produced a little pearl-handled revolver.

'For heaven's sake put that thing away,' Adrian begged, resisting the temptation to point out that this was England and not America. 'You'd better come in. But Joanna . . .'

'Jo.'

'Jo . . . I mean, what are you *doing* here?'

'I've come to be with you, silly.' She restored the pistol to its hiding place and stood before him. 'Aren't you going to kiss me? No, perhaps not,' she added, as she saw his hands. 'I shall kiss you.' She put her arms round his neck and virtually crawled up his body to reach him, but by then he was assisting her anyway, even if he did leave earth stains on her cape. She tasted just as good as the last time, and smelt just as good; he seemed to be holding all of heaven in his arms.

Incredibly, she seemed to feel the same way. 'Oh, Adrian,' she said. 'I have missed you so. And I've had the most terrible time. Would you believe that Father beat me, that afternoon? With his belt. Me! I think it was that more than anything which decided me I wasn't going to put up with any more of his bullying. I was sore for days. I had to sleep on my tummy. And then, announcing my engagement to that crazy Jerry Bailey . . . ugh!'

'Oh, my God!' Adrian said, an enormous and dreadful suspicion starting to fill his mind. He turned, still holding her, towards the house – the garden was overlooked by their neighbours – and discovered his mother standing in the doorway watching them. 'Oh, my God,' he said again. 'Jo . . . I'd like you to meet my mother.'

Joanna slid back down his shirt front and ran to the door. 'Mrs Barclay! You must think it simply terrible of me just to appear like this. But I didn't have the time to write. When the opportunity came, I just had to grab it, and I knew I'd get here in person quicker than any letter.'

She was holding out her hands, and even Molly Barclay could not resist such an appealing picture. She squeezed the hands while looking totally mystified.

'Ah . . . Joanna Meachem,' Adrian explained. 'We met in New York.'

'I see,' Molly said, getting a great deal of comment into the last word.

'Oh, it's not what you think,' Joanna cried. 'We're engaged to be married.'

'*What* did you say?' Molly inquired.

Joanna looked at Adrian. 'You mean you haven't told her?'

'Inside,' Adrian decided. The neighbours couldn't help but be interested in this.

'Now, Jo,' he said. 'Perhaps you'll explain what this is all about.' Sense and practicality were what was needed here, obviously; to give way to his bouncing elation could well be disastrous.

She gazed at him, her pointed chin slowly slackening. 'I told you. Didn't you know I was going to come?'

'Of course I didn't,' Adrian said. 'When you didn't come to the ship . . .'

'I was too sore. Anway, Papa had me under lock and key until after you'd left.'

'Good Lord! But . . . are you trying to say that you've run away from home?'

'Of course I've run away from home. Didn't you expect me to?' She was keeping her temper with an effort, and he also suspected that tears weren't too far away.

'Well,' he said. 'Actually, no, I didn't. I thought . . . well . . . I explained that we couldn't . . . I mean, that I couldn't . . .'

'Man talk,' she said. 'Man talk. Always about support and money. Oh, Adrian – you mean you don't want me?'

'I . . .' He knew he was flushing, and gazed at his mother in dismay. How I want you, he thought. I just can't afford you.

'We were going to go to Africa together,' Joanna explained. 'Oh, I was so looking forward to that. Now . . .' she sighed. She stood up, picked up her discarded cape and with an effort hefted her suitcase. 'I won't stay where I'm not wanted.'

'Adrian,' Molly protested, 'Miss Meachem must at least spend the night, until we decide what's best to do.'

'That's too kind of you, Mrs Barclay,' Joanna said. 'But . . .' She looked at Adrian. She wanted the invitation to come from him.

'Adrian can sleep on the settee in here,' Molly decided, misunderstanding.

Joanna continued to gaze at Adrian. 'You mean you don't like me at all?' she asked.

82

'Oh, Jo, you know how much I like you.'

'I meant, love me.'

Love you, he thought. Love you. Did he? Of course he did. If he could only believe *her* apparent emotions were genuine. How he yearned to take her in his arms and say, You're all mine, all I've ever wanted. But her father's words haunted him. In any event, he had to make her realise just what she was doing, and risking. 'Jo, how old are you?'

'Twenty.'

'That's what I thought. Don't you realise that your father can, and most certainly will, haul you back to America?'

'He won't do that.'

'You're an eternal optimist, I know. But even if we got married . . .'

'That's what I'm here for,' she interrupted.

He sighed. 'He could have the marriage annulled, Jo. Because you're under age.'

'He won't do that either,' Joanna continued patiently. 'Simply because he doesn't know where I've gone. I didn't tell *anybody*,' she finished proudly.

'He'll very soon work it out.'

'Maybe he will, but not very soon. I deliberately allowed myself to be courted by Jerry after you left. I could've gone anywhere in the world. Anyway, all we need is one month.'

'A month?'

'Because then I'll be twenty-one,' she said triumphantly.

Adrian looked at his mother, who looked back at him, her face still stony. 'I think it would be best if Joanna and I had a private chat,' he said.

'It would be highly improper.'

'Well, what's proper about this entire business?'

Molly Barclay hesitated, sighed, shrugged and withdrew to the kitchen, closing the door behind her.

'You're going to throw me out,' Joanna said, sitting down so as perhaps to make that more difficult.

'I'm going to try to talk some sense into you.' He sat

beside her, held her hands, looked into that gorgeously mobile face, which was attempting to look attentive and miserable at the same time, inhaled that irresistible scent, gazed into those huge hazel eyes . . . and had to exert an enormous effort of will to stop himself kissing her, which would make any reasonable discussion of the situation impossible. 'Jo,' he said. 'When you're twenty-one your father isn't going to have any legal hold on you. But that's only the start of the matter. If we marry without his consent, he'll be very angry. I'm sure you know how angry he can be. You'll never see your family again, any of them.'

She shook her head. 'I'll see Prissy and Hetty and Pru,' she said. 'Whenever they can manage it. I know I will. They'll never let me down.'

'All right, you'll see your sisters. But not your father or your mother. And he'll almost certainly cut you out of his will and stop your allowance, or whatever it is that you have.'

'So what? I'll have you to look after me.'

'Yes, but . . .' Her fingers were tightening and his responded. But she had to be made to understand. 'I have nothing except my wage as a ship's officer. That has to support my mother and sister as well as me, and you, if we married. We're pretty poor, and low down the social scale as well. If I get my master's ticket, things will improve, but we'll still always be poor, at least in comparison with what you've known all your life.'

'You're not going to get your master's ticket,' she said. 'We're going to Africa.'

'I can't. Not until I've provided for my family.'

'Okay. So we'll wait a while. Do you really think I mind being poor?'

'Have you ever tried it?'

'Oh . . . I love you, Adrian. That's all that matters.'

'How can you be sure. This is only the fourth time we've met.'

84

'I was sure the first time we met.'

'You didn't show it.'

'So was I to throw myself at you?'

He decided not to remind her she had done just that, from their second meeting. 'You really don't know anything about me.'

'You don't know a lot about *me*, either. But we know the important things. The rest, we'll have fun finding out.'

'Jo . . .' In desperation he charged straight through the final limits of good manners. 'We might not see eye to eye . . . in bed.'

'Well,' she said, 'there's only one way to find that out.'

Her fingers were tighter than ever. 'Do you . . .' he bit his lip. He simply had no idea how to continue.

'I'm a virgin, if that's what's bothering you,' she said.

'Oh, my God!'

'You're a strange guy. Most men I know would be pleased about that.'

'I am pleased. It's just that . . .'

'You mean you are too?' she cried. 'Oh, boy. We're going to have such *fun*.' She kissed him.

'It is quite out of the question without your parents' permission,' Molly Barclay declared, for about the tenth time in three days. But now her tone was desperate; they had an appointment with the vicar.

She looked at Amanda for support, but got none. Amanda, having met Jo, had fallen in love with her at first sight – she had always regretted not having a sister – and having been apprised of the situation, had fallen in love with that too. She had all her father's romanticism, Molly thought sadly.

'But *why*?' Joanna asked for the tenth time also, maintaining her devastatingly simplistic approach to the problem. 'The old guy's agreed to meet with us. We just go along

85

to the church tomorrow and tell him we want to get married.'

'You are not over twenty-one.' Molly's tone was tired.

'We tell him that I am. It won't be much of a lie. By the time we actually get married, I'll be within a couple of days of it.'

'It is still dishonest,' Molly Barclay said. 'And I cannot permit that. Besides, it will bring untold trouble in its wake. Adrian.' She appealed to her son, knowing it was probably for the last time.

Adrian gave her a hasty smile, and then bestowed one on Joanna as well. She responded by kissing him on the cheek. The three days which had so irritated his mother and delighted Amanda had been sheer heaven for him. Even his suspicions, which he knew arose mainly from his innate caution, had been virtually allayed. She was even more attractive than he remembered. And she shared his dream of Africa!

'But we love each other,' Adrian said, unequivocally declaring his feelings for the first time.

'Oh, *sweetheart*,' Jo cried, throwing her arms round his neck. 'If you knew how much I've wanted to hear you say those words.'

'How can you possibly know you love each other on so brief an acquaintance?' Molly objected.

'I'm sure they can, Mother,' Amanda protested.

'Of course we can,' Joanna agreed. 'We do. We . . .' she paused, her mouth forming an entrancing O, as there was a heavy rap on the front door.

The same thought was obviously in each of their minds. Molly Barclay turned red, and Amanda turned white. Adrian grabbed Jo's arm and bundled her into his bedroom, closing the door on her. Then he returned to the parlour, glanced at his mother and sister, who were speechless, drew a long breath, and opened the front door, trying to remember all he knew about demanding to see search warrants and the like. But his jaw dropped in amazement as he gazed at the man standing in the doorway. Far from being either John Meachem or a policeman, the visitor was Kurt von Schlieben.

'I got here earlier than I had hoped,' Kurt explained, and looked from face to face. Joanna had been retrieved from the bedroom, and he had been introduced; now his smile embraced all of them, however shocked their expressions remained.

'Well, it is grand to see you, Kurt,' Adrian said. 'So very good.' He had in fact forgotten his friend was coming at all in the distraction of Joanna's visit. And now obviously some sort of explanation was required. 'I'm afraid you have arrived in the midst of a family crisis.'

'Ah. Perhaps I should leave.'

'Not on your life.'

'Oh, please stay,' Joanna said. 'Perhaps you could give us the benefit of your advice.'

Kurt sat down and was given a glass of beer. Molly frowned. She couldn't feel happy about confiding such a situation to a total stranger . . . but both the girls were obviously bubbling with anxiety to tell someone, and Kurt was of course Adrian's best friend, of whom he had told glowing tales. Besides, he did look a very sensible young man. He might be just the person to talk some sense into Adrian.

Kurt listened, his face slowly relaxing into a smile. 'But that is magnificent. I never knew the English had so much romance in them,' he said. 'Oh, Mrs Barclay, you cannot stand in their way. Is it not love that makes the world go round? Did not one of your great poets say that? Shakespeare?'

'I think it was somebody else,' Joanna ventured.

'Still the sentiment is both admirable and accurate.'

Molly sighed, and took a drink herself.

'And I will stand as your groomsman,' Kurt announced.

'Oh, would you?' Adrian cried. 'Why, that would be splendid.' Because it was splendid, to have Kurt here, in his own house, and such a changed Kurt. This man was relaxed and happy and confident . . . well, Kurt had never lacked confidence, he supposed. But Adrian remembered it as a defiant confidence, which was not quite the same thing.

'Providing you are going to be married within a month,' Kurt said. 'I can stay no longer.'

'Four weeks from Sunday,' Joanna promised him.

'And then you're off back to Mombasa,' Adrian said enviously. 'Tell us what it's like nowadays. Jo is terribly keen on Africa.'

'Is she?' Kurt asked, eyes playing over her lazily.

'Oh, yes,' she declared. 'Adrian and I are going to go there to live, just as soon as we can afford it.'

'Oh, my God,' Molly muttered.

'Are you, now?' Kurt asked. 'That is a strange coincidence.'

'Not really,' Adrian smiled. 'We don't have any intention of settling in Mombasa, I'm afraid.'

'I did not think you would have. But I no longer live in Mombasa either, you know.'

'Don't you? Your letter was postmarked from there.'

'Yes, I suppose it would have been. But I have given up the diplomatic corps. I have taken up farming. Ranching, to be more exact.'

'On the mainland? That sounds tremendous. Where about?'

Kurt slowly drank the remainder of his beer, leaned back, stretched out his legs and smiled at Amanda. 'In the high country.'

'The high country?' Adrian shouted. 'You're not serious?'

Molly and Amanda exchanged glances, while Joanna looked from one to the other, uncertain exactly what they were talking about.

'The same.'

'But . . . how? When? Where?'

Kurt grinned, and held up his empty tankard. Amanda hastily refilled it. 'It is a long story. Well, not so long, perhaps. You know I always wanted to return there. As did you.'

'Of course.'

'It was difficult, naturally, without sufficient funds. I supposed I would have to bury the idea for a while. So I settled down once again to being the dutiful son in Koenigsburg, and then, what do you think happened two years ago? My father died.'

'Oh, I am sorry,' Molly said.

Kurt smiled at her. 'I am not, Mrs Barclay. He was a dreadful bully. And I was his only son.'

'Gee,' Jo commented. She understood about inheritances.

'So there it was. I suddenly found myself a very wealthy man. And I knew what I wanted to do with my wealth, even if my mother and sisters' — once again he smiled at Amanda — 'did not approve. But I would not be deterred. I sold up such of the estate as I needed to raise sufficient capital for my project, put the rest in the hands of an attorney so that my family would never want, and returned to Mombasa.'

'Good Lord,' Adrian commented, dazed by such decisiveness.

'You abandoned your family?' Molly asked, losing some of her sympathy.

'A man must make his own way, Mrs Barclay. I am sure you would not stand in the way of Adrian, now would you? Indeed I know you have not, as he is still a sailor, gone for most of each year.'

Molly Barclay opened her mouth and shut it again; her cheeks were pink.

'So,' Kurt continued, 'I trekked over that never-to-be-forgotten route again, Adrian, old friend. With a properly equipped expedition, this time. And I chose my spot, and I built myself a house, and I began to ranch.'

"But what about the Masai?"

'Oh, they visited me. And remembered me. Indeed, I think they were glad to see me back. They were more than pleased to sell me some head of cattle to start my herd with.'

'Sell you?'

'Well, as you know, they have no use for money. I gave them a rifle.'

'You gave the Masai a rifle?'

Kurt winked. 'With a defective sight. And only fifty cartridges. They were perfectly happy. But I can promise you they will never hit anything with that rifle at more than fifty yards' range. That is good, eh? It will make them understand that rifles are strictly white man's magic. But for the time being they are happy. So am I. I am living in paradise.'

'God, but I envy you,' Adrian said. 'And to be able to leave your stock, and come away like this . . . you must have them eating out of your hand.'

'Well,' Kurt said, 'I have some help. But not enough.'

Adrian looked at him, aware that the three women were looking at *him*.

'It is not the same, without experience,' Kurt explained. 'And the Masai, well, they are suspicious and changeable people. But do you know, they still ask after you, Adrian, old friend? They still dream that one day you will return to see them. Be with them. Well, I know that is your dream too. Unless it has changed.'

'No,' Adrian said slowly. 'No, it hasn't changed.' He refused to look at any of the women.

'Well, then, old friend, will you not come and be my . . . head overseer? And my friend, and mentor, again, in dealing with the Masai?'

3

Adrian sat down with a thump.

'Gee,' Jo commented. 'Oh, gee!'

Amanda gazed at Kurt, open-mouthed.

While Molly Barclay's mouth closed like a steel trap. 'Adrian, you cannot.'

'I know how you must feel, Mrs Barclay,' Kurt said sympathetically. 'But just stop and think a bit. Suppose Adrian were transferred to the Australian route? He'd be going just in the direction I am proposing, only a good deal further. He'd be away for perhaps nine months. What's different about his coming to Africa to ranch cattle? Nine months at a time, and he'll be home on furlough. I'll tell you what the difference is. Working with me, he'll be bringing home a lot more than he ever will as a sailor.'

'But he won't be a sailor,' Molly pointed out. 'What do we live on until he does come back?'

'She's right, Kurt,' Adrian said with a sigh. 'Can't be done.'

'Of course it can be done,' Kurt insisted. 'Anything can be done if you put your mind to it. Listen, agree to come with me, and I'll pay you your first nine months' wage in advance, here and now. Your living is all found anyway, so you can leave everything with your mother.' He smiled at Amanda as he spoke.

'Hell,' Adrian said, forgetting his manners. 'That's a very generous offer.'

'I need you, boy,' Kurt said simply.

Adrian looked at Jo. Her eyes were as big as saucers.

'Of course it's generous, Mr Schlieben,' Molly agreed. 'But there is more to it than just money. Adrian, as you know, is about to get married. How can you possibly expect him to leave his bride like that?' She seemed to have entirely forgotten that only an hour before she had been strenuously objecting to the marriage.

'Wouldn't he have to leave her if he went back to sea?' Adrian scratched his head.

'Now wait just one moment,' Jo interrupted. 'Let's not get carried away. I'm going with Adrian. And Kurt,' she added.

'That would be quite impossible,' Molly declared, as usual.

'Well,' Adrian said.

'I think your mother is right, Adrian,' Kurt said. 'You know it is quite a trip. Not at all suitable for a white woman.'

'Stuff and nonsense,' Jo declared. 'I am quite capable of walking through any bush there is. I'm a crack shot, too. I couldn't bring my own rifle with me, but just let me have one and I'll split the hair on your head at a quarter-of-a-mile range. Just so long as the sight hasn't been tampered with.' She glanced at Kurt. 'There's no way you are leaving me behind. It's what I've always wanted to do. Adrian,' she appealed. 'You said we'd do it together, whenever we got the chance. Now we've got the chance. You *can't* leave me behind.'

There was a brief silence.

'I'm sure you'll manage very well,' Amanda said at last, her eyes glowing. She was obviously wishing she could go too.

'Well,' Adrian said again.

'Quite impossible,' Molly repeated.

'I'm going,' Joanna said, with stubborn determination,

92

her eyes taking on that brittle look Adrian was coming to know so well.

'I wonder if I could have a word with you in private, Adrian?' Kurt asked.

'I'm going,' Joanna repeated. 'You're going out there to live, aren't you, Adrian? To make a home. How can you make a home without your wife?'

Adrian scratched his head.

'Just a brief word,' Kurt begged.

Adrian nodded, and the two men went out into the garden. It was a crisp, clear night, cold enough for their breaths to mist in front of their faces.

'You must talk her out of it,' Kurt said.

'I don't altogether see why,' Adrian said. 'I believe she is quite capable of making the journey. She's a lot tougher than she looks. I mean, she crossed the Atlantic all on her lonesome, with a pistol tucked away in her handbag. She's totally unafraid of anything. Even . . . well, the discomforts of a safari. And frankly, Kurt, I don't want to let her out of my sight. She's the most wonderful thing that has ever happened to me. And besides, we haven't even come up to the crunch yet, which will be when John Meachem discovers where she's gone, and decides to come looking for her. I couldn't let her face that on her own.'

'And what about the Masai? They remember you, boy. They remember you as if it was yesterday. The giant with the golden hair.'

'So? Why shouldn't they adore the giant's wife? Even if she hasn't got golden hair?'

'Will Lulu feel like that?'

Adrian frowned at him. 'Lulu? You've seen her?'

'Ah . . . no,' Kurt said. 'But I'm sure she's still there.'

'And still carrying a torch for me? After five years. That's nonsense. She'll have married, and be a mother at least four times over.'

'Yes,' Kurt said thoughtfully. 'It's possible. You feel no kind of . . . well, affection for her?'

'Of course I do. I remember her with great affection. But I was never in love with her. Are you trying to tell me you were in love with any of those girls you took to bed?'

'Well, no,' Kurt agreed. 'However, I didn't really shack up with just one of them in particular.'

'I was a boy, then,' Adrian reminded him.

'Yes.' Kurt continued to speak thoughtfully. His face was lost in the gloom.

'To tell you the truth, Kurt, much as I want to do it, I really don't think I can, without Jo. It was a mutual dream of Africa that brought us together. I couldn't realise my dream without letting her realise hers as well.'

'Of course,' Kurt said. 'I have been stupid and thought-less. It will work out.' He slapped Adrian on the shoulder. 'By all means bring your lovely and charming wife along. We must think of ways and means of providing some company for her. But now, if you are really serious, then let us make plans. You realise that we must be in Mombasa not later than the end of January, if we are to be sure of reaching the ranch before the beginning of the Long Rains.'

Adrian hadn't thought about it; he had forgotten the Long Rains, which controlled all life in East Africa. But of course he knew Kurt was right. He nodded.

'Well,' Kurt went on, 'if you are not getting married until the end of this month, we are going to run short of time.'

Adrian's frown was back. 'I'm afraid I cannot possibly ask Jo to come away with me until we *are* married. She'd probably say yes, but it would put her in a hopelessly compromising position.'

'And I would not wish you to think of it, old friend. I am only suggesting that we expedite matters.'

'How?'

'There are two possibilities. A special licence, or a visit to Gretna Green. The latter is best, I think, as a special licence

94

involves various questions, and there is still the business of residence. In Gretna, as I understand it, legal residence is a matter of staying there overnight.'

'By God,' Adrian said. 'I never thought of that.'

'It will still be necessary to lie about the lady's age.' Kurt grinned. 'But everyone who goes to Gretna has to do that, or they would not make the journey in the first place.' He gave Adrian another slap on the shoulder. 'Leave the details to me.'

'Oh, my darling,' Joanna said, resting her head on Adrian's shoulder. 'I am so very, very happy.'

As they had now, at least in Molly Barclay's opinion, firmly put themselves beyond the limits of conventional morals by agreeing to the Gretna plan, she had been persuaded to allow Kurt to take Amanda and herself out to dinner, and leave them alone in the cottage. Kurt had invited them to come along, but Joanna had declined. They had actually had no time alone together since her arrival.

Now they sat together on the settee, which was still to be Adrian's bed for another week; Kurt of course was putting up at an hotel – he had realised at a glance there was no room for him in the little cottage.

'I'm so excited I could die. Except . . .' She sat up and held his hands. 'Adrian, is Kurt really a friend?'

'Well, he's always proved so in the past. He was a friend of my father's, first, and after Father died, why, I suppose he felt responsible for me. No man could have been more faithful. As he's proved so again now.'

'Um.' She got up and walked about the room with the vigorous animal energy she always exuded. 'I don't like him.'

'Jo!'

'Sorry. I always say what I think. It gets me into some terrible trouble, nearly always. Have I offended you?'

She stood in front of him, looking anxious. He caught her

round the waist and swept her on to his lap. The concept of being able to do that to a girl like Joanna Meachem left him breathless.

She laughed happily and nuzzled his neck. 'Have I?'

'Of course you haven't. It's just that . . . you're going to see an awful lot of him. There'll be nobody else up there, save him, you and me.'

'And a whole nation of Africans,' she reminded him, and kissed his cheek. 'That'll be okay. I'm not going to tell him I don't like him. I just wanted you to know. I guess . . . I don't *trust* him, would be a more accurate way of putting it.'

Adrian frowned. 'What have you to trust him with?'

'Our lives?'

'Oh, nonsense. Anyway, I know as much about the bush as he does.'

'If you knew how reassuring I find that thought,' she confided.

'And anyway, would he come all this way to hire me if he meant me any harm?'

'He is hiring you, I guess,' she said thoughtfully. 'But that's still not right, is it? Coming all this way to hire *you*.'

'I know the country.'

'Others could learn.'

'I don't quite follow what you're driving at.'

'Well, you and he both had a dream. He's managed to realise his. Yet he's come back to get you up there as well.'

'Wouldn't you describe that as true friendship?'

'Maybe. But then, maybe not. He must know that, having had your dream, you'll one day try to make it come true. One day soon. Your own spread, your own herd . . . if you got on better with the Masai than he did there's every prospect of your becoming a bigger wheel up there than he could ever be. I would have thought you were the very last person he would want up there.'

Adrian frowned. He had never known her so serious, had not really considered that she *could* be this serious.

96

'And all this talk about the Masai wanting to see you again . . . that doesn't ring true to me,' Joanna persisted.

'So what do you think is the truth?'

'I have no idea. I'm just sure there's something he hasn't told us.'

'Well, you could be right. But on the other hand, my sweet, there is no other way for us to get up to the high country in the near future.'

'I know. I'm not trying to stop you going. I'm as anxious to get up there as you are. I'm just trying to get you to maybe sprinkle a little salt on everything that's handed to you.'

Suddenly she was sounding almost as cautious as he. But of course he knew she was right; he was inclined to accept people and things at their face value. And it was odd, Kurt showing up like this, with, as she put it, such generosity in mind, when he had made no attempt to contact him for five years. He nodded. 'I promise. We'll let him use me, us, even, to get there, and see what's going on. Then we'll start thinking about our own place, and if necessary kick him in the teeth.' He grinned. 'Does that sound cynical and tough enough to match your papa?'

'Every time, if I had the smallest belief you would ever actually do something like that. I do love you so.' She kissed him on the mouth, deep and slow, and he felt her bottom wriggle on his lap. He realised this evening was the first time they had really got close to each other, in every sense. And her remarks about Kurt made him feel intensely guilty, so much so that he was almost tempted to tell her about Lulu. He didn't want her ever to feel *he* was not being completely honest with her. But it would have no point, and might upset her. She wouldn't really understand, with her sheltered background and upbringing. When she had seen the country and the Masai, things would be different. Besides, they would also have been married for some time.

Perhaps similar thoughts were passing through her own

97

mind, because without warning she asked, 'Adrian, are you really a virgin?'

He kissed her on the nose. 'Not really. I'm sorry.'

'Oh, don't be. You have no idea how relieved that makes me. Because I . . . we . . . well . . .'

'You're not either?'

'Oh, you rotter! What I meant was, well, Prissy and Hetty and Pru and I talked about it, of course, but Mama never would. And they were so young, they didn't know anything.'

'Did you?'

She shook her head, gazing at him intently. 'Adrian . . .'

He shook his head in turn.

She pouted. 'It'd just be a sort of lesson. You needn't . . .'

'Needn't what?'

Pink flared in her cheeks. 'Well, whatever it is you do.'

'Didn't they teach you at school?'

'I never went to school. None of us did. What, John Meachem's girls rubbing shoulders with the *hoi poloi*? We had a governess. Hetty and Pru still do. So you see, I do need a lesson.'

'When we're married.'

'But don't you think you should sort of, prepare me? I think that would be a great idea, as we're alone. Heaven knows when we'll get the chance again.'

'On our wedding night. If I started taking your clothes off now, my darling girl, I wouldn't be able to stop. I'd really like to leave that until we're married.'

The pout slowly faded as she realised he was not going to be tempted. 'Just tell me . . . it won't hurt, will it?' she asked anxiously.

He wondered if any man had ever been vouchsafed such innocence and trust into his keeping, and kissed her again. 'I'm told it might, the first time,' he said. 'But I'll be so very careful.'

'I knew you would,' she said, with her usual confidence.

*

'That was a delicious meal,' Molly Barclay said. She had never enjoyed herself more. This was a restaurant she had always dreamed of visiting, in the past – but John had never been a man for eating in expensive places. And since he died she had been forced to abandon all her dreams. She had hoped to be able to live them vicariously through her children, but there too she knew she was doomed to disappointment. Amanda's young man had very limited views and a permanent sniff, and now that Adrian was going to disappear into the African jungle with this runaway American heiress, a character so positively unusual, in Molly's view, that she had to be regarded as at least eccentric . . .

But Mr Schlieben was a charmer. And that he was very wealthy no one could doubt. His clothes showed that, even if he had not ordered oysters and champagne; she wished her gown, and Amanda's, had been a little more up to it. Nor could she really condemn him for wishing Adrian to work with him in the bush. That was a compliment to Adrian, really. As for taking that Yankee hussy along . . . the sooner and the farther she was removed from England the better. Out there in the wilds Adrian might even be able to look at her with less starry eyes. In fact he almost certainly would, the moment she began to moan and complain.

If only Mr Schlieben were a proper businessman in England or Germany, then the whole world might have been perfect. Still, she smiled at him, and he smiled back.

'I'm glad you enjoyed it, Mrs Barclay. I'm told it's about the only decent place in Southampton. I have it in mind, with your permission, of course, for a small reception for your friends, after we return from Scotland.'

'Oh!' she exclaimed. 'I don't think we can rise to a place like this, Mr Schlieben. As you know, Miss Meachem doesn't really have any parental support for her wedding, and so . . .'

'I think, in such circumstances, that I should take over the responsibilities of the father of the bride,' he said easily.

'You? But we couldn't permit that, really.'

'It's the least I can do,' he said, smiling at Amanda, as he was wont to do whenever he made a significant statement.

'Oh, well, you'll have to discuss that with Adrian, I'm sure,' Molly said. 'But to have a reception here . . . that would be very nice, wouldn't it.' She looked around her at the drapes and the silver and the white-jacketed waiters and the dinner-jacketed orchestra and the ladies in expensive gowns . . . she would have to get one of those for the occasion. As would Amanda, of course.

'As I say, I don't think there is anywhere else,' Kurt said. 'I will have a word with the management.'

'You said, "when *we* return from Scotland",' Amanda said. 'Are you going too?'

'But of course. And you.'

'Me?'

'And your mother as well,' Kurt added hastily.

'Me?' Molly squeaked.

'Well, don't you want to see your son married?'

'But I thought Gretna Green was strictly for people who were eloping.'

'It is for people who are in a hurry to get married,' Kurt pointed out. 'Of course, every eloping couple is in a hurry to get married, but not every couple which is in a hurry to get married is necessarily eloping.'

'Ah,' Molly said, confused. 'Won't Adrian mind?'

'Adrian will be delighted. I don't think it has crossed his mind that we would not be there.'

'On their wedding night?' Amanda murmured.

Kurt patted her hand. 'I am sure we will occupy ourselves usefully, Fräulein. Now, ladies, a liqueur with our coffees?'

'Oh, that would be very nice,' Molly said. It must have been fifteen years since she had had a liqueur. But she had a problem, compounded by her excitement. 'Would you mind if we left you to order for us?'

Kurt was on his feet in an instant. 'Of course not. If you will trust my taste.'

'Willingly, Mr Schlieben. Amanda?'

'I'll stay here, Mother,' Amanda decided.

Molly raised her eyebrows, and considered the situation. But in the middle of a crowded and expensive restaurant, and with the band playing . . . 'Suit yourself,' she agreed, and left the room.

Kurt signalled the waiter, ordered brandy, *crème de menthe* and coffee, and smiled at Amanda. 'Your mother is a most charming woman.'

'I'm so glad you like her. She is having the time of her life.'

'That pleases me. And how could I not like her, when her son is my best friend, and her daughter is one of the most beautiful women I have ever met?'

'Oh, Mr Schlieben,' she flushed.

'Kurt,' he suggested.

'Well . . . Kurt. Adrian has told me so much about you.'

'Has he, indeed. All good, I hope?'

'Oh, yes. I think he admires you enormously.'

'Well, that is nice to know,' Kurt said thoughtfully. 'And equally, he told me a great deal about you, when we were in the land of the Masai together. But he was describing an adorable fifteen-year-old. I imagine it never crossed his mind that you would one day be an absolute princess.'

Amanda didn't know what to say; Wally Brown had never flattered her in such terms – he would have been too embarrassed.

'Do you approve of Adrian's marriage to Miss Meachem?' Kurt went on.

'Oh, I do,' Amanda said, happy to change the subject. 'She is such a lovely girl. And madly in love with Adrian.'

'So it appears. How do you think she will fare in the wilds of Africa?'

101

'Well . . . I don't know anything about the wilds of Africa, except what Adrian has told me. I wish I did. But I am sure Jo will never let Adrian down. Or you.'

'And I am sure you are right. But would you really like to know about the wilds of Africa? You?'

'Oh, yes,' Amanda breathed. 'It sounds so . . . so tremendous. I do envy the three of you, setting off on that sort of adventure. And Adrian has told me about the highlands. He says it is the most beautiful place on earth.'

'It is that,' Kurt agreed. His hand drifted across the table to touch hers. 'I am a great believer in making ambitions, dreams, come true. So is Adrian, I know. Are you?'

She gazed at him, open-mouthed, and he gave her fingers a squeeze, and then released them, as the waiter with the coffee and liqueurs, and Molly Barclay, arrived back at the table together.

'Adrian,' Alexander Dringle said, clearing papers on his desk. 'I am pleased to see you. I was just going to send round to ask you to stop by. All well at home?'

'Yes, sir,' Adrian said, and took the offered seat. The office was situated on Southampton Docks, and looked out at several ships of the Dringle line moored alongside, either loading, or discharging cargo. For a moment he felt a pang of nostalgic regret; he had never known any other life than the sea, had been destined for it ever since he could remember – John Barclay's son. Now he was turning his back on it. But for something far better, he reminded himself.

'And are you ready for sea in January?' Dringle asked.

'Ah,' Adrian said, reaching inside his jacket pocket for the envelope. 'Well, sir . . .'

'Good, good. You'll be happy to get back to work, I have no doubt,' Dringle went on. 'Being ashore never does any seaman any good. Now, the matter in hand. I have received this telegraphic message . . .' It was lying on his desk, and he regarded it with some suspicion; the cable between England and America had been laid less than twenty years previously, and the idea of virtually instant communication between the two countries was still rather daunting.

'Indeed, sir?' Adrian asked. He had come here in the highest of spirits, certain of success with Kurt's backing, but as he could guess what was in the wire he had a sudden start of apprehension.

'Yes, it's from John Meachem. You met him, didn't you, when the *Sara Dringle* was undergoing repairs in his yard in August.'

'Yes, sir.' Slowly Adrian released the letter of resignation. First things first.

'Well, I have known him for years, of course. He's a very decent fellow, although like all Americans a bit apt to fly off the handle at times. Now he has sent me this telegraphic message . . .' Once again he peered at the paper, as if wondering how it had possibly got on his desk in the first place. 'It makes very little sense to me, but it does seem to involve you . . .' He glanced up.

'If I could see it, sir . . .'

'I think I had better read it to you,' Dringle decided. 'It says: "DAUGHTER JOANNA LEFT UNDERSTOOD TO HAVE TAKEN ATLANTIC PASSAGE STOP." The stop isn't actually part of the message, if you follow me. It appears to be some sort of punctuation.'

Adrian nodded, glad of the opportunity to consider his reply.

'It goes on,' Dringle read, ' "CONSIDER IT PROBABLE HAS GONE TO YOUR EMPLOYEE ADRIAN BARCLAY STOP MUST BE APPREHENDED AT ALL COSTS AND PLACED UNDER DURESS PENDING MY ARRIVAL STOP IF ANY CRIMINAL LIAISON EXISTS BETWEEN BARCLAY AND HERSELF INSIST ON BARCLAY'S ARREST AND CHARGE WITH SEDUCTION AND RAPE STOP WILL ARRIVE ENGLAND

TWELVE DECEMBER STOP RELY ON YOU TO PRE-VENT DASTARDLY OUTRAGE STOP REGARDS MEACHEM".' Mr Dringle laid down the paper and peered at Adrian over the top of his glasses. 'Can you make any sense out of that?'

Adrian did some quick calculating, with a sinking feeling in his stomach. Today was the sixth of December; Meachem was arriving in six days' time.

'Well?' Dringle inquired.

'I can make no sense of it at all, sir,' Adrian said. 'I did meet a Miss Joanna Meachem on a couple of occasions, when Mr Meachem was kind enough to invite us to his house. I thought she was a pretty and high-spirited girl.'

'But why should Meachem suppose she's run off to see you?'

'You will have to ask Mr Meachem that, sir.'

'Yes, I suppose I shall have to await his arrival before I get an explanation,' Dringle said. 'These Americans. So boister-ous in all they do. Still, you had better see him yourself to refute all his allegations.'

'I doubt that will be possible, sir,' Adrian said.

Dringle raised his eyebrows. 'Why not?'

'Because, sir, my purpose in coming in this morning was to tender my resignation.' Adrian at last placed the envelope on his employer's desk.

'Your resignation?' Dringle looked flabbergasted. 'But . . . you are joining another shipping company?'

'No, sir,' Adrian said. 'I am taking a shore job.'

'You? A shore job?' Dringle was amazed.

'In Africa,' Adrian explained. 'And I am leaving almost immediately.'

'God bless my soul,' Mr Dringle remarked.

Some of the spirit of the adventure even communicated itself to Molly. Adrian did not, of course, tell her, or the two girls, about Meachem's telegram or his imminent arrival.

104

He did tell Kurt, who pulled his nose and grinned. 'That creates an interesting situation.'

'I'm glad you think so. It could be disastrous. I suppose he would be within his rights to have me arrested, at least until Jo comes of age.'

'Well, I certainly will not allow that to happen,' Kurt said. 'Just leave it with me. I will simply alter one or two of our arrangements. But I agree, there is no need to upset the ladies.'

Adrian was happy to do that. The umbrella of Kurt's money and determination was the most reassuring feeling he had ever had. And this was the man who was using him? Jo must be wrong about that, just as Kurt must be the truest friend he had ever had.

He was in a state of considerable excitement, as were they all, Molly most of all; it was some years since she had left Southampton, except to visit her sister in Ramsgate. They travelled in a first-class railway carriage, of course, as Kurt was paying, and were waited on hand and foot. This was clearly nothing less than Joanna was accustomed to, or Kurt, but Amanda and her mother were in a whirl of exhilaration.

Amanda had suddenly blossomed over the past couple of days. Undoubtedly it was because of Kurt's presence, his constant attention. Before, she had seemed consciously to subdue her beauty by wearing the dowdiest of fashions, more often than not concealing her magnificent yellow hair in a tight bun, just as she had equally subdued her natural vivacity, allowing herself only quiet smiles, never a laugh. Presumably this had all been for the benefit of Wally Brown. Now she was almost the match of Joanna in her sparkling gaiety. The pair could almost have been sisters, as they were going to be. It was only a pity they would have to be separated immediately after they got to know each other.

They reached Gretna that evening, and found that even if *they* were not actually expected, people like them were expected on every train. They were shown to a comfortable little inn and informed that the blacksmith opened for business at eleven o'clock the following morning.

'What do we have to do before then?' Adrian asked.

The landlord shrugged. 'Be patient, laddie. And good,' he warned. 'I'll have no sneaking up and down the passages, that I won't. I've put the ladies in one room – ye'll no mind sharing a bed, two of ye, I'm sure – and you gentlemen in the other.'

'But . . . is there no one we have to report to?' Adrian asked. 'No forms to be filled out?'

'Hamish will gi'e you a licence when he's done wi' you,' the landlord told him. 'What else were you wanting? Enjoy your tea.'

'I didn't know there was such a civilised place in the whole world,' Joanna said, trying to decide whether to start on the muffins or the salmon; tea in a Scottish inn took on an entirely different connotation to anywhere else on earth.

'Aye,' the landlord said. 'Well, lass, let's hope you feel like that in twenty years' time, when maybe it's your own daughter away up here, and you in London fretting your heart away.'

'Are we to understand that you don't approve of Gretna marriages?' Kurt asked.

'Approve? Who'm I to approve, mister? It's a business, see. I'm not in this business for ma health. Without yon couple, and others, I'd be working a plough.' He bustled off to his bar.

'Well,' Molly commented, clearly wishing she had sampled this demi-monde existence a good deal earlier in her life. 'That is the most amazing thing I've ever heard.'

'Is it, Mother?' Amanda asked, and Adrian discovered to his consternation that she and Kurt were holding hands.

'It is a most convenient place, for those with things to do,' Kurt agreed. 'There is no necessity for the locals to approve, and we are not interested in their disapproval, I am sure.

106

Mrs Barclay, Adrian . . . Amanda and I would like to make it a double wedding.'

Molly Barclay's jaw dropped. So did Adrian's. Joanna clapped her hands in delight.

'You and Amanda?' Adrian asked stupidly.

'Of course.'

'But . . .' You've only known her a few days, he wanted to say. And you're really a stranger, from another country. You've swept an innocent girl off her feet with your good looks and your confidence and your sophistication, and your promise of high adventure . . . and your money. She knows nothing of your habits, of your vices, of your beliefs.

But wasn't that exactly how John Meachem must be feeling? Except that Meachem knew there was not even ample wealth involved.

And at least they'd be together, so that he and Jo could look after her if Kurt let her down.

The same thought was occurring to Molly. 'You mean to take her to Africa?'

'Oh, Mother,' Amanda said. 'Isn't it marvellous?'

Molly gazed at her, open-mouthed. 'You're leaving me all alone,' she said.

'Oh, Mother . . . but if I were marrying Wally I'd be moving out.'

'Not to Africa,' Molly said, starting to cry.

'Oh, Mother.' It was Adrian's turn, and he put his arm round her shoulders, his own brain still in a turmoil.

'What about Wally, anyway?' Molly sobbed, concentrating on detail.

'Well . . . we were never officially engaged, you know,' Amanda pointed out.

'As you are now,' Kurt said. 'The ring, Amanda.'

Amanda obediently took it from her handbag and slipped it on her finger. It was a large diamond solitaire.

'Oh, my, how gorgeous!' Joanna cried. 'So that's what the pair of you sneaked off to do yesterday.' She glanced at

Adrian and flushed at his expression. They had mutually decided against an engagement ring, to save money. It had anyway seemed pointless, with the wedding only a few days away. But she knew how he must be feeling.

'Wally probably thinks you are engaged,' Molly said, drying her tears with Adrian's handkerchief.

'Then I'll have to explain it to him when we get back,' Amanda said.

'When you'll already be Mrs von Schlieben,' Adrian pointed out.

'Mrs von Schlieben,' Amanda breathed.

'Have you any objection to our marriage, old friend?' Kurt asked gently.

'Of course I haven't,' Adrian lied, unable to think of anything else to say. 'Your announcement was a little sudden, that's all. I mean . . .' He looked at his mother, who was still stifling tears.

'That is a matter which has greatly worried me,' Kurt confessed. 'Of course we cannot think of leaving you on your own, Mrs Barclay. You are so welcome to accompany us to my ranch . . .'

'Africa? Me?' Molly gave an almost hysterical laugh. 'I'm too old for that kind of thing.'

As Kurt had obviously guessed she was going to reply. He did not attempt to persuade her. 'Well, in that case,' he said, 'you must let me get you really settled in, wherever you wish to be.'

'I am quite happy in Southampton, thank you, Mr Schlieben. I suppose I will see my children again occasionally?'

'More often than that, Mother,' Kurt promised. 'You do not mind if I call you Mother, I hope?'

Molly Barclay simpered through her sniffs.

'Because now that you are my mother, virtually, I must take care of you. You do not mind if I accept this responsibility, Adrian?'

Adrian didn't know what to say. He was sure his friend had no intention of humiliating him yet again – and he also knew that only someone with Kurt's wealth could possibly take care of the situation.

'So what I would like to do is this,' Kurt smiled. 'I would like to give you, as a present, a sum of money sufficient to enable you to live as I would wish you to live, for the rest of your days.'

'Oh, my,' Molly said.

'Shall we say . . . five thousand pounds? Together with an income of fifty pounds a month for the rest of your life.'

'That is incredibly generous of you,' Adrian protested.

'She's my mother now too,' Kurt reminded him.

'Oh, I couldn't accept that,' Molly protested, with no suggestion of firmness.

'You can and you must and you will,' Kurt said, and kissed her on the cheek. 'But first, there is something you must do for me. I wish you to take a holiday. When we get back to London, I wish you to go on holiday. Where would you like to go?'

'I don't know of anywhere to go,' Molly protested. 'I could go and stay with my sister, I suppose; she's moved out to Ramsgate.'

'Then why not do that. Go and stay with her for several months. It will be company for you, almost until Amanda and Adrian are due to return to visit you. We will see to the Southampton house. Will you promise me to do that?'

'Well,' Molly said. But it was clear she would at that moment promise Kurt anything.

Adrian had at last grasped what he was driving at. As usual, Kurt had confided none of his plans, and Adrian was rather surprised that they had not merely packed up the Southampton house and taken all their clothes with them when they left for London the previous day. But Kurt had merely winked, and said he had it all worked out. Now he obviously wanted Molly to dissociate herself from whatever might happen.

Amanda hugged Joanna. 'I'm coming with you,' she whispered. 'Oh, I'm so excited. I'm actually coming with you.'

Joanna hugged her back, but the expression on her face as she looked past Amanda's shoulder at Adrian was a compound of a variety of emotions, not all of them revealing as much happiness as her first enthusiastic reception of the news.

Adrian could guess what she was probably thinking. That Kurt von Schlieben had, very simply, just bought them all, with his smile and his money and his promises. But he wondered if she was also trying to decide whether Amanda had been swept off her feet by the man, or by the thought of the adventure that was Africa.

And then he wondered if that might not be *her* real motivation as well – she had certainly suggested that in their early acquaintance. He hated himself for thinking it. He blamed her for filling his mind with suspicions, and Kurt for making those suspicions so plausible. Because surely the really important question was, *why* was Kurt going to all this trouble and expense to buy the Barclay family?

'There it is,' said the blacksmith. 'You may kiss the bride.'

Adrian looked down into Joanna's face, and they smiled at each other. If they had both had so many doubts about the way things were working out, there was no room for them now.

He lifted her into his arms and kissed her, a slow, lingering kiss, while the others waited patiently, as they had waited for two other couples before them; Gretna was doing a roaring trade. Now they stepped back, to allow Amanda and Kurt to have their turn.

His sister, and his best friend, Adrian thought, as he gazed at their backs and listened to the words. Could any man ask

110

for anything more? Was it simply that he could not bring himself to believe that a man of the world like Kurt could possibly have fallen so rapidly and apparently completely for a total innocent, who certainly did not have the background of family or position which should be required for the wife of a von Schlieben? Mandy was certainly a most beautiful girl. Why should it not all be genuine? After all, Kurt, buried away in darkest Africa, couldn't have encountered that many beautiful blondes during the past few years. Why should they not, after such an uncertain life as during the past six years, all now be embarking on a prolonged period of total happiness? It was certainly far more pleasant to believe that than to keep worrying about what Kurt might be going to do next.

'Happy, my dearest girl?' he whispered to Joanna, over the glasses of champagne they were sharing with their landlord and his wife, following a Scottish high tea which had contained everything from steaks to scones, and had lasted for several hours – he gathered the feast and the champagne would simply be added to Kurt's bill.

'Oh, happy,' she whispered back, even her doubts temporarily forgotten.

Amanda and Kurt were similarly billing and cooing.

'Well,' Molly decided, 'I think I will take a walk and look at the scenery. I have never been to Scotland before. I am told it is very beautiful.' She smiled at each of her children in turn. Her spirits had quite revived – following an obligatory cry at the actual ceremonies – with the realisation that she was now, by any standard she had ever known, a wealthy woman. 'I suggest you have an early night,' she added archly.

Joanna and Amanda gazed at each other, their thoughts mingling although they did not exchange a word. They did not need to; each was about to leave girlhood behind and embark upon the real business of life – with the promise of a fabulous adventure lying beyond. Now was no time for

111

doubts or fears. 'I think Mother is right,' Joanna said.

They now had a room each, and the landlord and his wife were waiting to beam at them as they mounted the stairs. 'I've filled your hotties,' Mrs McGregor said.

'Hoots, woman, d'ye think they'll need hotties the night?' her husband demanded.

Joanna darted into her room and leaned against the door when Adrian shut it behind him. 'You'd think they'd be blasé,' she said. 'Having this happening all the time.'

'I think it's a difficult thing to be blasé about,' Adrian said.

'And there speaks the voice of experience.' She lay on his chest across the bed. 'How many mistresses have you had?'

They were married. Perhaps there would never be a better time than now to make a full confession. 'Just one,' he said. 'Do you want to know about her?'

'Never,' she declared. 'She was before you met me, I hope.'

'Long, long before.'

'Do you still ever see her?'

'I haven't seen her for five years,' he answered truthfully.

'Then never,' she said again. 'Life began for both of us the day you came to lunch. Promise?'

'Oh, promise,' he said, greatly relieved. 'I'm sorry about not being able to give you a ring like Mandy's.'

She stroked the plain gold wedding band he had placed on her finger. 'This is all I want, Adrian. This, and you.'

He smiled at her. 'I thought maybe . . . forget it.'

'Tell me,' she insisted. 'No secrets.'

'Well, I thought maybe the necessity of escaping Jerry Bailey, and the idea of maybe going to Africa . . . might have influenced your decisions. Just a little.'

'Maybe they did,' she said seriously. 'Without knowing you were so interested in Africa, I wouldn't have been so interested in you. Without Papa's threat of marrying me off to Jerry, I mightn't have summoned up the guts to run away.

112

But I always intended to marry you, almost from the day I saw you. And I did run away to be with you, Adrian. I'd have gone anywhere in the world for that.'

'I know you did, my darling girl,' he said.

'Well, then . . .' She raised herself on her elbow and stared into his eyes. 'You are going to have to show me everything. And tell me everything, too. Lesson number one starts here.'

How lovely she was. And they would share everything, every secret, from this moment, without ever a glance over their shoulders. Then why was he not truly the happiest man in the world? Could it possibly be the thought that Amanda, no less innocent, might be saying those same words to Kurt at this very moment?

'And you'll try not to hurt me,' Joanna reminded him.

He kissed her, held her close and rolled on his side with her, heart pounding, feeling the urge he had kept so carefully repressed for so long becoming irresistible.

She cradled her head on her arm, still staring at him. 'Do you want me to undress?'

He nodded.

'Everything?' Her eyes were large as saucers, and colour flared into her cheeks.

'Everything.'

She sat up with great determination. 'I'll have to hurry, or I'll freeze.' She tore at her clothes, throwing them on to a chair. Clearly cold was less important than embarrassment. Adrian followed her example, but she did not look at him; indeed, she turned her back on him, then dived beneath the covers, a sliver of pink and white.

He finished more slowly; her eyes were tight shut. 'Lesson number one,' he said. 'All the senses need to be used.'

Cautiously she opened her eyes, gazing resolutely at the ceiling.

'All,' he said again.

Slowly she turned her head, rosebuds again blazing in her

113

cheeks. 'Oh,' she said. 'Oh, God! Adrian . . .' She sat up, the coverlet held to her throat, then lay down again, her hair scattered around her on the pillow.

He sat beside her and gently pulled the sheet from her fingers. She gasped, because she had been holding her breath, and the chill of the room seemed to inflate her breasts as well as her nipples. She was a small woman, the smallest he had ever been with, but also perhaps the most exquisite. As he slowly pulled back the sheet he revealed a tight rib-cage, flat belly, fluttering as she breathed, silk-covered groin, and straight, slender legs. Her arms lay at her side, and she might have been on parade, lying down. The whole was encased in marvellously white velvet skin.

Her lips were slightly parted, but she didn't speak, just gazed at him, waiting. He lay on his elbow to kiss her mouth, caress her body. Now her arms did move, to go round his neck and hold him tightly. Her kissing paused for only an instant when he sought to discover if she was ready for him, and then she parted her legs willingly enough; if she shivered when he touched her, it might have been the cold.

And then he hesitated. He knew how he wanted her, but was afraid of her reactions. But where he was the teacher and she the pupil, what did he have to fear? He raised his head to look at her, and she held her breath again, aware that the moment had come. 'Now turn over,' he said quietly. 'And kneel, with your head on the pillow.'

The train rumbled across the snow-covered countryside, bathed in the dim rays of the setting sun. Each clackety-clack of the wheels seemed to shout, We love, we have loved, we will love. For all of them? Adrian sat with Joanna huddled against him, his mother on his other side. Certainly Joanna loved, and he loved. Soon the steward would be in to make up their beds, and they would be alone again.

Opposite them, Amanda was similarly leaning against

Kurt. Kurt looked supremely happy. Amanda merely looked drowsy. She had indeed looked drowsy all day, as if she had not slept at all. And happy? She did not look *un*happy, Adrian thought. But there was no such glow as emanated from Jo. Just exhaustion. And a certain amount of apprehension coupled with a total subservience to her husband. Well, Kurt was the sort of man who would demand that from his wife, but Adrian wondered how *he* had made love. Amanda was his sister; but she was also another man's wife, now, and that man was the core around whom he was building his life.

It occurred to him, perversely, that he was starting to dislike Kurt. He was objective enough in his consideration of himself to know that it was partly jealousy, and was therefore a quite unworthy emotion. And also partly it stemmed from the seeds of mistrust planted by Joanna. But was it also a result of sheer masculine rivalry? When last they had been in Africa together, he had been the more important; the friendship of the Masai had been based upon his strength, his complexion, his *difference*. Now the situation was entirely reversed. For the foreseeable future it would be Kurt who was top dog. It was equally unworthy to resent that, he supposed; Kurt had done, while he had only dreamed – and Kurt was financing the realisation of his own dream. But it was still a situation he longed to change.

They reached London at dawn, and there said farewell to Molly, seeing her on to a train to Ramsgate. As Kurt had so obviously calculated, her grief was well tempered by her desire to show off her new-found wealth and independence – Kurt had, it now appeared, made all the necessary financial arrangements with his bankers before even broaching the subject. The farewells *were* tearful, but Adrian and Amanda were equally distracted, apprehensive and excited about the coming hours – and at the thought that at the end of it they would be on a ship bound for Africa. Then they took the train, in the afternoon, to Southampton. They hired a cab from the station to the cottage.

'It seems an age since we left,' Amanda said, hurrying into the kitchen. 'I'll put a kettle on, shall I?'

'I'll help you,' Joanna decided, joining her.

'Well, don't be long,' Kurt called. 'I want to be out of here in half an hour. Let's get these suitcases ready, Adrian.'

Adrian had been about to follow the girls, but checked himself. This would be the first time the two wives had been alone together since their weddings. Would they compare notes? Undoubtedly, but hardly as to detail. And was his conscience to haunt him throughout his life? When they had sex the second time, Joanna assumed the required position without hesitation or prompting, and when, if only for variety, he suggested the missionary position, and then with her on top, she confessed that she liked the first one best, even if it had been, that time, the most painful. The second time was not painful at all. She could hardly condemn him for behaving like a heathen now, even if she ever discovered that his love-making was not that approved by polite society.

'You are pensive,' Kurt observed, pouring them each a glass of beer as Adrian placed the three suitcases by the door. Another cause for dislike, perhaps; he had this habit of behaving as if he owned the world. But no doubt he considered that he did own this cottage, now. He had virtually bought it twenty times over.

'Being married makes a man think,' Adrian replied.

'It does. Or it should,' Kurt agreed easily. 'Well, now we must start thinking about the next few months. There has been no time properly to outfit either you or the girls, but I think we will be able to do that either in Alexandria, or certainly in Cairo. We will break the journey in Egypt.'

'That sounds fabulous.' There had been no time for him to be told their exact itinerary, either. 'And there *is* a ship leaving Southampton tonight?'

116

'Tonight,' Kurt agreed. 'Our passages are booked. But first, it seems, you will after all have to fight for your right to happiness.'

He was looking out of the window, and something in his tone made Adrian hurry to his side. Getting out of a cab at the gate was John Meachem, accompanied by another man in civilian dress, and two uniformed policemen.

'Holy smoke!' Adrian gasped, letting the blind fall back into place.

'I suspected this might happen,' Kurt agreed. 'I noticed someone who could only have been a spy standing on the street corner when we arrived. Clearly he had been keeping the house under surveillance.'

'And you never warned me,' Adrian said bitterly, once again aware that his friend seemed merely to be enjoying the situation. 'What can we do?' Where he had felt quite at home when faced with the possibility of having to take on the Masai, or at sea when encountering a storm, like so many Englishmen he was totally aghast at the thought of opposing the law – and he still had a guilty conscience as regards Meachem.

'Tell the girls to stay in the kitchen, for a start. And then . . .' Kurt pulled out his fob watch and flipped open the lid. 'Yes, we shall have to hurry. Are you prepared to commit a criminal act?'

Adrian hesitated only a moment. Whatever his suspicions of Kurt's motives, here was the pair of them standing shoulder to shoulder as they had against the Masai, and as they might have to do again. Besides, the alternative meant giving up Joanna. 'I'm your man.'

There was a bang on the street door, and Kurt opened it. 'Good afternoon, gentlemen. Can I be of service?'

'Is your name Adrian Barclay?' someone asked. It was not Meachem, and was presumably the other plainclothes man.

'No, sir, it is not,' Kurt said. 'My name is Kurt von Schlieben.'

117

'Of course he's not Barclay,' Meachem snapped. 'I know what Barclay looks like. Big, fair-haired scoundrel.'

Adrian had closed the kitchen door, and now came into the room.

'That's him!' Meachem shouted. 'Seize the rascal.'

'Adrian Barclay?' inquired the plainclothes man.

'That's me.'

'We have a warrant here, signed by a justice of the peace, empowering us to search your premises, Mr Barclay,' the man said. 'I am Detective Sergeant Crawford, by the way. I believe you know Mr Meachem.'

'A warrant, eh?' Kurt asked. 'Then you had all better come in,' he invited, to Adrian's consternation.

'I've come for my daughter,' Meachem declared, shouldering his way through the policemen to face Adrian. 'I know she's here. My man saw you arriving not an hour ago.'

Adrian looked at Kurt, who was carefully closing the door to enclose the six of them inside the cottage. 'Indeed you saw them arriving, sir,' Kurt said. 'They were with me and my wife. In fact, the four of us were returning from our weddings. Our honeymoons, you might say.'

'Your *what*?' Meachem shouted. 'By God . . .'

'If you'll pardon me, sir,' the detective sergeant said. Meachem glared at him, but Crawford had already stepped in front of the shipowner. 'Are you married to the young lady in question, Mr Barclay?'

'I am.'

Crawford glanced at Meachem. 'Does this make any difference, sir?'

'Difference?'

'Well, we are faced with a *fait accompli*, as it were. And the young lady, well . . .'

'Has been raped,' Meachem bawled. 'I want this rat strung up, sergeant. That's what I want.'

'Yes,' Crawford agreed doubtfully. 'Mr Barclay, when

you eloped with Miss Meachem, were you aware that the lady was under the legal age of consent, and that she did not possess her father's permission for this marriage to take place?'

Once again Adrian looked at Kurt.

'He did,' Kurt agreed.

'Then, sir, you understand that Mr Meachem has every right to regain possession of his daughter and have the marriage annulled. He also has every right to charge you with abduction, and, in the circumstances, with rape, as he has intimated. There might also be a matter of perjury, if you have told lies to any court or religious minister in order to accomplish your purpose.'

'Attaboy,' Meachem declared. 'He is going to get the whole book thrown at him. I want him locked away for so long no one will even remember him.'

Crawford waited for him to finish, with a somewhat tired expression. Then he said, 'So now, sir, I must ask you to produce the young lady, otherwise I shall exercise this warrant and find her. I must also ask you to accompany me to the police station, where charges may be laid against you.'

Adrian looked at Kurt. If he did not understand why Kurt had allowed this to happen, he still had no doubt that his friend had worked out a solution to the problem.

But he was totally unprepared for that solution. 'I think not,' Kurt said, and stood against the wall, a large revolver in his hand; it had apparently been concealed under his jacket, suggesting he had had this in mind from the beginning.

'Oh, hell,' Adrian remarked.

'For Jesus' sake!' Meacham exclaimed. 'He's got a gun.'

The policemen exchanged glances, and Crawford turned to face Kurt. 'I would put that down, sir, if I were you,' he said. 'A foreign gentleman, are you?'

'I am not English,' Kurt agreed.

'Well, sir, we don't hold with that sort of thing in this country. Come along, sir, hand over that weapon, and you may avoid very serious trouble.'

He took a step forward, and the gun came up. 'If you come any closer, sergeant,' Kurt said in a quiet voice, 'I am going to blow you into two pieces.'

Crawford hesitated; it was difficult to doubt that Kurt meant what he said.

'Kurt!' Adrian begged.

'No half-measures now, boy,' Kurt said. 'Mr Barclay will tell you, sergeant, that I am a very good shot,' he went on. 'And I am not the least afraid of using this weapon. I do so all the time in my native surroundings. Now, gentlemen, I wish you to enter that bedroom over there.'

'For Jesus' sake,' Meachem complained. 'Why don't you guys shoot the bastard?'

'We are not armed, sir,' Crawford informed him.

'For Jesus' sake . . .'

'Let's go,' Kurt suggested.

'I'm afraid we have no choice but to obey him, at this moment, sir,' Crawford explained to Meachem.

'Christ in heaven, what are you guys *for*?' Meachem demanded.

'As soon as it is possible, we shall obtain a warrant for the arrest of this gentleman. Both of these gentlemen, sir. Never fear,' Crawford reassured him.

Adrian very much feared the sergeant would be proved right, but Kurt showed no hesitation at all. 'Now, gentlemen,' he said. 'If, one at a time, you will lie on those beds – there is room for two on each – Mr Barclay will tie you up. I suggest you tear the sheets into strips, Adrian, and the blankets, and you can also use your spare belts and neckties,' he added. 'Anything to keep them quiet for a couple of hours.'

'By Christ,' Meachem snarled.

'And if anyone attempts to move, I will shoot him,' Kurt

said, levelling the pistol. He made the three policemen stand against the wall while Adrian secured Meachem.

'You are going to suffer for this, boy,' Meachem promised. 'When I get through with you, you not only won't ever sail again. You're not even going to *walk* any more.'

Adrian made no reply. He dealt with each of the policemen in turn, and then with Sergeant Crawford.

'I'm afraid Mr Meachem is right, Mr Barclay,' the sergeant said. 'You are going to go to prison for a very long time. Assaulting a police officer in the execution of his duty is a very serious offence.'

Adrian secured him as well, and when he had finished, Kurt added his own expertise. He made sure the knots were in as inaccessible places as possible, and then, using spare blankets again torn into strips, secured the men to the beds. 'Now let's leave,' he said. 'We have that steamer to catch.'

They closed and locked the door, and found the two girls already in the living room, looking desperately excited and anxious.

'We listened,' Amanda confessed.

'Papa will be *so* angry,' Joanna said, but she giggled as she spoke.

'He is already pretty angry,' Adrian told her. 'And I would say we are in deep trouble.'

Kurt winked at him and picked up one of the suitcases. Adrian took the other two, one in each hand, and the girls lifted the lighter bags. 'They have to catch us first,' Kurt said.

'Do you suppose they'll find that difficult? This steamer we're booked on, don't you suppose they'll find out soon enough which one it is?' Adrian demanded. 'Especially since you were careless enough to tell them that's what we were doing. Where is our first port of call?'

'Gibraltar,' Kurt said, leading them down the garden path.

'Well, they can telegraph Gibraltar, and it's British

territory. There'll be armed policemen waiting for us when we arrive there.'

'I am sure you are right,' Kurt agreed. 'Their problem will be that we will not be on the steamer.'

'But you said . . .'

'Oh, we are booked on it, and as it will have sailed before our friends back at the cottage can get there, they will certainly assume we went on it, and will do exactly as you say. But instead of that, we are going to the ferry dock to catch the night boat to Le Havre. That is why we are walking instead of taking a cab – they will find our actual movements that much more difficult to trace. We have just sufficient time; the ferry leaves in three quarters of an hour. From Le Havre we will take a train to Marseilles, and there pick up a ship for Alexandria. Do not worry. I have worked it all out.'

'And when we get to Mombasa?'

'Supposing they ever find out that is where we are going,' Kurt agreed. 'But there is no telegraph to Mombasa and, in any event, no English law to be enforced there.'

'You do seem to have worked it out,' Joanna said in grudging admiration, hurrying at their sides.

'Save that it all seems so unnecessary,' Amanda commented. 'If we had just taken another ship from, say, London . . .'

'Ah, but it was most amusing, wasn't it?' Kurt asked, blowing her a kiss.

'Amusing,' Adrian growled. 'You do realise this means I can never return to England?'

'Ah,' Kurt said. 'Well, perhaps it may be inadvisable for you to do so for a while. Do not worry, I have promised to arrange for you to be able to visit your mother, perhaps in France. And you would not have been able to return anyway, after having absconded with John Meachem's daughter. No, no, old friend, I see this as the hand of Fate, guiding you to the highlands, for better or for worse. There

122

is where your future lies. Nowhere else.'

Adrian glanced at him, a whole succession of fresh suspicions suddenly racing through his mind. Kurt was right: whatever he found when he reached the land of the Masai, he could not now turn back. He had burned his boats.

Or Kurt had burned them for him.

4

'Mombasa,' Kurt said, pointing.

The girls held hands as they stood at the rail of the ship and gazed at the palm trees, the brilliant pinks and whites and pale blues of the houses, the minarets – at this distance they all seemed to be rising out of the sea.

But beyond was Africa, and a blue haze of distant mountains. This was a sight they had seen before, almost every day for the past week, yet it had never been as dramatic as now.

The voyage had been one long exhaustion of the senses. Under Kurt's expert direction they had had the journey of a lifetime, snuggled in their berths as the mail packet rolled its way across the Channel in a December gale; arriving in Le Havre in a cold, grey dawn, wildly apprehensive that somehow their prisoners would have got free and worked out their true route in time to wire the gendarmerie; boarding an overnight train for Marseilles and once again enjoying first-class luxury as snow gave place to green; honeymooning dreamily the length of the Mediterranean, undisturbed even when a winter mistral had the winds howling and the seas crashing against the ship; and then gasping at their first sight of Egypt.

At Alexandria they had left the vessel – to confuse any pursuers who might somehow have followed their trail, and also to complete the equipage of the women and Adrian. Here they purchased sun helmets and thick boots; almost equally thick stockings and heavy drill skirts; spine pads, which were considered essential to withstand the heat; and, for the girls, yards of red flannel to be made up into long johns for wearing next to the skin.

'That just doesn't sound right,' Joanna objected, regarding the unfeminine material with total distaste. 'Inside that lot, we'll sweat like pigs, if you'll pardon the expression. Shouldn't we really wear as little as possible?'

'Good heavens no,' Kurt said. 'You will still sweat, and the sweat will dry, and before you know it you will have caught a chill, and then malaria. You have heard of malaria?'

'Sure I have.'

'Well, then, you will know that while nobody is absolutely sure what causes it, informed opinion is convinced that it is a matter of catching cold from excessive sweating and cooling. They even call it the sweating sickness. You must be careful.'

Joanna had accepted his ruling, because Amanda so clearly wanted to, but she remained doubtful. She was totally restored to humour, however, when Kurt made her a present of a light sporting rifle, a beautiful little weapon over which she went into raptures and very rapidly demonstrated her skill. He bought one for Amanda as well, but she had very obviously never even touched such an object before and was terrified of it.

Yet again their personal apprehensions were swept away as they visited Cairo and saw the pyramids, before moving back to Suez to pick up another ship, their present one, bound from Port Said to Mombasa.

They had been a total of five weeks on the journey from England, and every moment of it had been utterly enjoyable, with Kurt, the omnipresent host, smilingly guiding them through every pitfall. What then of suspicions and apprehensions? It seemed churlish even to consider them. If Adrian and Joanna had gazed at each other that first night, in the privacy of their small cabin on board the Channel packet, their expressions reflecting the enormity of what they had done, regretting it seemed a waste of time. She had turned her back on her family, irrevocably, and he had turned his back on his country, irrevocably. Yet they were both young enough and optimistic enough and confident enough to suppose that irrevocably might not mean forever. And always the pull of the adventure that was Africa loomed ahead.

Now they hugged each other, she with sheer delight, he as he began to remember all of those things he had almost been trying to forget, in despair that he would ever know them again.

Amanda hardly seemed less happy, although her total subservience to her husband continued to bother and disturb Adrian. One morning during their passage through the Mediterranean he was sure she had been crying in the night; her eyes were puffy. Yet as she revealed every indication of adoring Kurt as much as ever, he said nothing. Nor did Joanna make any comment.

They could hardly wait to disembark, now properly clad in all the protective clothing deemed necessary for Europeans in the extreme tropics, and Mombasa was just four degrees south of the Equator. 'I feel as if I'm wearing armour, and I'm sopping wet already,' Joanna complained as they climbed down the ladder and boarded the waiting rowing boat.

Amanda, taller and stronger, was less handicapped but was having trouble with her veil, which was suspended from the inside brim of her topee, as was Joanna's, to save her face from the sun.

'You'll be much wetter before you're any drier,' Kurt teased, and Adrian gave Joanna's fingers a quick squeeze. Then they were ashore, the ladies having to be carried by their husbands to save them from splashing through the shallows, watched by a crowd of people, mostly young Arab men, who were predictably fascinated by Amanda's hair; Adrian's was hidden by his slouch hat. Immediately the heat seemed to redouble itself, bouncing off the houses; even the sea breeze coming in off the Indian Ocean was suddenly hot, where before it had only been warm. It was salty too, and they immediately became aware of a consuming thirst.

Kurt guided them to the shade of an enormous mango tree, where several people had already gathered, chattering at each other in Arabic or Swaheli, while they waited for the arrival of the second boat with their gear. He busily engaged young men to carry it for them, speaking Swaheli with perfect fluency – something he had not done six years ago, Adrian realised.

'It's not as hot as this at night?' Joanna asked hopefully, fanning herself with her hat.

'Down here, yes, I'm afraid it is,' Adrian confessed. 'But not in the high country. Up there you need a blanket.'

'Oh, goodie,' she said. 'I never thought I'd ever wish to see a New England winter again, but right now I could do with a good roll in the snow.'

'All arranged,' Kurt said, rejoining them, 'and I have arranged the hotel as well. Tomorrow we cross to the mainland.'

It was clearly visible across the water, coconut trees waving in the breeze, with the forest waiting behind.

'I am so excited I could scream,' Joanna said.

There was no actual bath in the hotel, merely a room where by pulling a chain one released a few drops of tepid water from a pipe in the roof, but it did cool them off somewhat, and was accompanied by a wonderfully wicked sense of intimacy. The walls did not reach the ceiling, either in the bathroom or in their bedrooms, so they could all chat to

126

each other while they bathed and dressed. 'Real togetherness,' Joanna commented. 'I'm going to *love* Africa.'

Waiting for them downstairs was a delicious if unusual meal, in which strange fish and equally unknown vegetables, which went by exotic names such as okra and sweet potato, comprised the main course. There were sliced mangoes to follow; after a slightly apprehensive approach, the girls found these most enjoyable, even if the trickling juice made a sad mess of their toilettes. 'Time for another bath,' Joanna giggled as she tried to clean herself up.

Wearing light silk gowns, with their hair pinned up and thus their shoulders bared to enjoy the warmth of the verandah – although immediately a target for a myriad of insects, dominated by mosquitoes – they were clearly the best thing that had happened either to the hotel or to Mombasa for a very long time. They were the only ladies present; the other diners, mostly wealthy Arabs with only a smattering of European officials and businessmen, gazed at them in consternation and admiration.

Nor was Kurt the least bit averse to telling everyone who would listen of the adventure on which they were about to embark, which caused even more consternation and a good deal of shaking of heads and pessimistic comment. But Kurt rejected all attempted criticism with his boisterous laugh; there was of course no alcohol to be had on the premises, as it was a strictly Muslim establishment, but Kurt had brought ashore several bottles of gin from the ship, and the landlord had no objection to their consuming them at his table. The party got quite merry, in celebration, Kurt said, as he looked down Joanna's *décolletage*, of the fact that their wives would never look quite like this again.

'Oh the contrary,' Joanna retorted. 'I intend to dress for dinner every night when we get to your ranch. Don't you, Mandy?'

'If you will,' Amanda agreed.

'Bravo!' Adrian cried, having also been at the gin.

'Oh, indeed, bravo,' Kurt agreed. 'Do you mind if I hold you to that promise?'

'You won't have to,' Joanna declared.

'I am beginning to wonder how I survived all this time without your company. And yours, my sweet,' he smiled at Amanda. Then the smile faded and he muttered, 'Oh, God in heaven; here comes Mr Misery himself.'

The man approaching them was tall and thin, clearly European because of his brick-red complexion, and even more clearly English, with his white suit and his narrow tie, and his thin, somewhat ascetic features. 'Herr von Schlieben,' he said, and gave a brief bow.

'My pleasure, Mr Moore,' Kurt said, without rising. 'May I introduce my friend and colleague, Adrian Barclay.'

'Barclay?' The Englishman frowned. 'Not the Adrian Barclay who accompanied you into the interior six years ago?'

'Indeed.'

'Well, sir, the pleasure is mine.' Moore shook hands enthusiastically. 'William Moore, Her Majesty's vice-consul in Mombasa. I was not here in 1875, as you will appreciate, but I have heard people speak of your safari. A famous exploit, sir.'

'Won't you sit down, Mr Moore?' Adrian invited, 'and meet Frau von Schlieben, my sister Amanda, and my wife, Joanna.'

'Ladies!' Moore bent over their hands, while obviously drinking in their beauty and European-style clothes. 'This is a great pleasure. Now you must reassure me as to the absurdity of a rumour I have just heard, that you intend to accompany your husbands into the interior.'

'Well, we sure don't mean to let them out of our sights,' Joanna told him.

Moore did not appear to appreciate her humour. 'My dear lady,' he said, 'I do most sincerely beg you to reconsider. I do not think you can have any idea of what lies ahead of you.'

'But we do. Both our husbands know the country pretty well,' Joanna explained. 'I think we'll be able to cope.'

'With the desert? And Tsavo? And then the real jungle?'

'Sounds fun,' Joanna riposted, while Kurt and Adrian watched her with admiring amusement. 'Have you ever been up-country yourself?'

'Good heavens no, dear lady. My job is representing Her Majesty's Government in Mombasa, not traipsing about the interior.'

'Then I reckon you should leave criticism to those who have done so,' Kurt suggested.

Moore flushed. 'I do know, Herr von Schlieben, that where you propose to go is the home of the Masai. Do you think it is right to expose these two lovely ladies to that risk?'

'We're looking forward to meeting them,' Joanna told him.

Moore looked at Adrian in desperation. 'I would say it is some years since you have been here, sir.'

'Some,' Adrian agreed.

'And are you as friendly with the Masai as Herr von Schlieben?'

'I think I can say that,' Adrian agreed.

'I think you are mad, all of you. Mad to suppose you can live alongside such vicious savages, and absolutely irresponsible to suppose you can risk taking white women into such country.' Moore stood up. 'I must advise against it in the strongest terms, gentlemen. You'll excuse me. Frau von Schlieben; Mrs Barclay.' He bowed and walked away.

'Wow,' Joanna remarked. 'He certainly had a bee in his bonnet.'

'Oh, Moore takes his job very seriously,' Kurt said. 'And he is right, the Masai are a warlike people. But are not the Germans also warlike people? Yet we are perfectly capable of getting on with those who would do business with us. Here on the coast the Masai Morani are legends, and are

129

used by mothers, I am sure, to frighten their babies to sleep.'

'He's right, you know,' Adrian agreed.

'Frau von Schlieben,' Amanda said, half to herself. 'I've never been called that before. It sounds just superb.'

'Frau von Schlieben,' Kurt smiled, squeezing her hand.

'What's that noise?' Joanna asked.

They listened, to a snapping of whips and a melancholy shuffling of feet. 'Ah,' Kurt said, turning his chair to look out at the street. 'I'm afraid there is far more misery here on the coast than ever in the land of the Masai. There are no slaves in the high country.'

'Slaves?' Joanna got up and went to the verandah rail. It was quite dark by now, but there was a moon and she could make out the column of young black men, most of them only boys, winding its way down to the waterfront; the boys were yoked together in rows of four, and were controlled by several Arabs, very well armed and wielding the bullwhips. 'Oh, the poor creatures,' she said. 'Where are they being taken?'

'I imagine down to Zanzibar. That's where the principal slave market is. They'll be castrated down there.'

'Castrated?' She stared at him with her mouth open.

'Castrated?' Amanda also echoed, clearly not knowing what he was talking about.

'It means they will have their genitals removed, my dear,' Kurt explained, 'with a sharp-bladed knife. If they survive the operation, and quite a few do not, then they are ideal for domestic work.'

'Oh, my Lord!' Amanda turned quite pale. 'What sort of domestic work?'

'Well, you see, they can be used as harem attendants and guards. Obviously, without their penises, and thus largely without sexual desire, they can be allowed to work in the seraglio without risking any of the women.' He grinned. 'Although one does hear tales of apparent eunuchs who have been allowed to retain the shaft if not the testicles, and

130

are therefore quite capable of whiling away the boring hours when the lady of the house is separated from her lord and master — without any risk of conception, of course.'

'Ugh,' Amanda commented.

'And then some of them, the more attractive boys, will not be castrated at all,' Kurt went on, 'but will be kept as male prostitutes.'

'*Male* prostitutes?' Joanna asked.

'Indeed. Most wealthy men in the Orient or Africa are, shall we say, ambivalent in their sexual desires. There is no stigma against homosexuality here as there is in Europe. A pretty boy is just as sought-after as a pretty girl.'

'I feel quite sick,' Joanna said, returning to the table and sitting down with a bump.

Adrian thought the conversation had got quite indecent enough. 'I'm sure I remember reading somewhere that slavery had been abolished by the Sultan of Zanzibar,' he said.

Kurt guffawed. 'It was, while there was a British cruiser actually anchored in his harbour. But as soon as the Union Jack departed, he was back to his old tricks. If anything is to be made of this country, we Germans will have to do it.'

'Or we British,' Adrian suggested.

This time Kurt smiled. 'You British are not interested, old friend. That is official — I believe from Mr Gladstone himself.'

Joanna lay awake half the night, staring at the ceiling through the cloudy white mosquito netting which was supposed to protect them from the bugs. In fact it had so many holes it kept no insect out, but the gauze was thick enough to repel what little breeze there was, while with the window wide open they listened to the constant rumble of surf on the reef. Thus they lay and sweltered, so much so that daringly she took off her nightgown to be as naked as

131

Adrian. But she had more on her mind than just heat and noise. When he would have reassured her with more than words, she couldn't respond. 'It just can't be real,' she said. 'All those young men . . .' She touched him for the first time, but protectively rather than passionately.

'As Kurt said,' he whispered, 'there are many terrifying things happening down here on the coast. Far more than in the high country.'

'Where there are only the Masai.' She shivered.

'Who will not trouble us, as long as we do not offend them. I told you, they regard me as a superior being.'

'Yes, you did,' she said thoughtfully. 'I'd forgotten that.' She kissed him. 'I'm sorry I'm being such a goose. It was just the *idea* . . . ugh! I'll be okay tomorrow.'

Next morning she was quite her old self again, and Adrian's day was made when just as they prepared to leave the hotel, he was informed that a certain Safah-ben-Ali was waiting to see him. 'Safah, old friend,' he shouted, squeezing the Somali's hand. 'How very good to see you. I wish you to meet my wife, Mrs Barclay, and my sister, Frau von Schlieben. Herr von Schlieben you surely remember.'

Safah straightened from a deep bow to the girls. 'Everyone in Mombasa knows Herr von Schlieben,' he said. 'He has gone amongst the Masai, and returned.'

'Well, we are going up there again now, with him,' Adrian told him.

Safah looked as surprised as any Somali ever would. 'With the ladies, bwana? On safari?'

'Indeed. But this is no safari, Safah. We intend to make our home up there.'

Safah digested this for several seconds. Then he announced, 'I will come with you.'

'You?'

'You already have a guide?'

'Yes,' Kurt said. 'I have two Kikuyu arranged on the mainland.'

132

'But they will leave you at the land of the Masai,' Safah reminded him. 'I will remain with you.'

'Well, I would very much like to have you along,' Adrian said, and looked at Kurt. 'We know he can be relied upon.'

Kurt shrugged. 'You are entitled to a personal servant, by all means. But we are leaving in fifteen minutes.'

'I have my requirements, Bwana Schlieben,' Safah said, without taking offence.

'Then let's go,' Adrian shouted, suddenly happier than he had been for some time.

Joanna saw, and understood.

'Now there are four of us,' she said enigmatically, and then added, as she saw Amanda watching Kurt with adoring eyes, 'Well, maybe just three.'

They crossed on the ferry – a raft dragged on rope cables – to the mainland, where indeed Kurt had, as usual, arranged everything. It took some time to round everybody up, but the message that he had arrived had been sent over the previous afternoon, and by evening the entire expedition was assembled, the various boxes allotted to their respective bearers, and, to Adrian's surprise and somewhat to his dismay, they had made the acquaintance of Hans Pitzer, who it seemed was also in Kurt's employ, and would be accompanying them. Pitzer was a Bavarian, small and dark, unshaven and distinctly unclean, who leered at Joanna and Amanda, and shook Adrian's hand effusively.

'We're not going to wind up looking like that, are we?' Joanna whispered. Both she and Amanda had been in rhapsodies at actually standing on the mainland of Africa at last, but Pitzer's appearance was most off-putting.

'No chance,' Adrian reassured her. 'But I suppose it's quite easy to do, when living with people who wear nothing most of the time and have little idea of hygiene.'

She gave another of her little shivers.

That night they sat around a campfire and exchanged

reminiscences, while the girls listened, savouring the excitement of actually being on safari, for even if the lights of Mombasa continued to gleam across the water, they were constantly starting at odd rustles or birdcries from the forest which was now only a few yards away, listening to the slither of the cicadas, and gripping their husbands' arms at the distant roaring of a baboon.

They were also obtaining their first intimation of the discomforts which lay ahead, as the mosquitoes whirred around them – no evening gowns tonight, but thick blouses buttoned at wrist and neck; the myriad fireflies were more attractive.

Pitzer, it appeared, had also made the journey into the interior, with Kurt, and Adrian now found himself once again very much the junior partner, although Pitzer continued to treat him with great respect.

Pitzer made no better an impression on Safah than on Joanna. 'These people are so loud,' the Somali commented, as he prepared Adrian and Jo's folding cots. 'I wonder the Masai put up with them.'

'I'm inclined to agree with him,' Joanna said, lying on her side and gazing at Adrian. 'Are you?'

She was trying to arouse his suspicions again, he knew, simply because of Pitzer's unexpected appearance; Kurt had never mentioned him before. Certainly the Bavarian's presence added to the mystery of why Kurt had gone to so much trouble to secure Adrian as an aide if he already had another experienced white man available. But it was easy to see that Kurt would hardly find anything very congenial in the company of someone like Pitzer.

However, they were actually embarked on their safari, and thus far everything Kurt had promised them had come true, usually manifold. He pulled Joanna on to his cot. 'We're here,' he said.

She giggled. 'It'll give way.'

'I'll be careful,' he promised.

134

At dawn the next morning they plunged into the forest, a column nearly a mile long, with the two Kikuyu guides out in front, then the white people and Safah, followed by the bearers in a long file. Pitzer brought up the rear with Kurt's Somali servant, Omar, in order to prevent any desertions. The beginning was like a vast picnic, as the bearers chanted and the girls exclaimed over the butterflies and small birds which fluttered from tree to tree, and went into rhapsodies over their first monkey, which swung above their heads as he removed himself from the vicinity of the intruders as rapidly as possible.

By mid-morning the sun was high, and the trees not yet thick enough to offer much protection. Sweat rolled down their faces and Joanna looked enviously at the half-naked bearers, as well as the open-throated shirts of the white men. Now they were beginning to tire as well, and when Kurt at last called a halt the two girls just collapsed where they stood. 'We may have to take it a bit easier than on our last safari together,' Adrian suggested.

Kurt shook his head. 'We must hurry,' he said. 'The rains are not that far away. They will toughen up.'

'I'm not going to drop by the wayside,' Joanna promised, as he sat beside her for lunch. 'I just wish I could get out of this Turkish bath I'm wearing.'

That afternoon they forded a stream, having to wade up to their thighs, which again the girls found an ordeal, as for an hour afterwards their heavy skirts, now wet, clung to their legs and constantly threatened to trip them up. Now, in any event, the walking grew more difficult, as the bush thickened and the way began to ascend. By evening they were absolutely exhausted, and Jo was thankfully stripping off in the shelter of their tent when they were alarmed by a piercing scream. 'Mandy!' Jo gasped, wrapping herself in a towel as she followed Adrian outside in a rush.

Amanda and Kurt were in their tent, and now Mandy was sobbing. 'Are you okay?' Jo called.

135

'Oh, Jo, my God . . . . come in.'

Jo went inside. Adrian started to follow her, and then checked; his sister had rolled down her longjohns and was virtually naked. 'Whatever is the matter?' he asked, dropping the tent flap back into place.

'She has accumulated a bush tick,' Kurt explained through the canvas. 'There is absolutely nothing to be alarmed about, my dear girl. I will have it off in a moment.'

'Ugh,' Joanna commented. 'What a horrible-looking thing. And in such a place! I've never seen a tick that huge,' she confessed.

'Well, they are larger than normal,' Kurt agreed. 'But this one is of course swollen with Mandy's blood. Now, bend over, my dear, and please try not to scream so loudly.'

A match scraped, and Amanda did have to stifle another scream. Adrian knew that Kurt was touching the tick's head – which also meant touching Amanda's flesh, as the head would be half-buried in it – with the hot match in order to make the creature relax its grip; merely to pull it off and leave either the head or legs buried could result in infestation and tick fever, which could be fatal.

'There we are,' Kurt said. 'Now, my dear, there was really nothing to worry about, was there?'

'It was just awful,' Joanna told Adrian. 'Right up where her thigh joins her bottom, and at the back. Ugh. If I ever get one of those . . .'

She did, the next day, behind her knee, and submitted to the ordeal by match with good spirits. Within a couple of days ticks were accepted as part of a day's routine, as were the sudden, heavy rain showers, the unexpected ants' nests, the vicious-looking spiders, the occasional snake, and worst of all, the drooping branches which threatened to flick off their hats and tugged at their clothing. Even the variety of flora and fauna, which included huge-eared bush dogs, scavenging hyenas and hurrying warthogs – which Kurt would not let anyone shoot, as they always travelled in

136

packs and could be remarkably vicious when aroused – as well, of course, as hundreds of monkeys, failed to offset the discomforts. 'How much longer does this go on?' Jo asked on the fifth night.

'Not much longer,' Adrian promised her. 'But this is the easiest part of the journey.'

She stuck out her tongue at him.

She discovered he was right when they reached the desert, where the daily rain showers ceased and their parched throats were soon intensified by the red dust which smothered them whenever there was the slightest breeze; they made their way looking like Western desperadoes, bandannas tied across mouths and noses. Now they lost their first bearer, who trod on a scorpion and as a result developed an acute fever. Two other bearers were deputed to take him back to the coast, their loads being redistributed.

'This will slow us up,' Kurt grumbled. 'And it is a waste of time and manpower. He will be dead long before they can get him to a doctor. It would have been better to shoot him now and put him out of his misery – and lose only one man instead of three.'

'Kurt,' Amanda protested.

'Well, my dear,' he said. 'We are living in a different world now. You must remember that.'

'Why don't they wear boots, like us?' Joanna asked Adrian that night, as they undressed in their tent. 'The idea of walking barefoot over this ground gives me the heebie-jeebies.'

'I suppose they've never tried them,' Adrian said, and frowned. 'What's that noise?'

They listened to a sort of half-yelp, half-moan. Joanna flushed. 'That's Mandy,' she said softly.

He stared at her with his mouth open.

'It appears Kurt is a violent lover. But she adores it,' she

137

added hastily. 'I don't think he's actually hurting her.' Then she saw the expression in his eyes. 'Do you think *we* could leave it until I can have a bath? This God-awful dust has got *everywhere* – I honestly don't think there's any room for you in there.'

Again Adrian had to remind himself that how Kurt and Mandy made love was no concern of his, especially if it was what Mandy wanted. But he felt very inclined, the following night, to have Safah pitch his tent a good deal further away, and would have done so but for the reflection that the Africans and Pitzer must also have heard Mandy's moans, and for him to show any reaction might cause comment.

They plodded onwards beneath a burning sun, hating even the breeze which would from time to time spring up, because far from cooling it was hotter than ever, and merely hurled the dust into their faces. The girls' veils were already torn in places, and there was no doubt their complexions were going to suffer dreadfully. But all the while they were climbing, and now they saw for the first time the twin peaks away to their left, clearly covered in snow. 'Kilimanjaro,' Safah said reverently. 'The roof of the world.'

'Those must be twenty thousand feet high,' Joanna remarked in wonderment.

'Not quite,' Kurt said. 'But high enough. There is another mountain to the north of the high lands, equally high and snow covered. The Masai call it the Ol-Doinyo Keri, the striped mountain, because of the snow and the various strata. This is a land of mountains. Once upon a time, it must have been a mass of volcanoes. Can you imagine them, erupting day and night for perhaps thousands of years on end?'

'Oh, boy,' she agreed, her enthusiasm quite restored, especially as the dust was giving way to scrub, and soon to trees.

'Tsavo,' Safah said, fearfully.

Immediately the column was closed up, the bearers now marching three abreast across the grassland, while Kurt and Pitzer walked to either side, commanding Adrian to remain in the centre of the column with the women; the two Somalis brought up the rear. Joanna and Amanda had of course been told about the packs of lion which roamed this plain, and to begin with stared about themselves apprehensively, but for Joanna at least that prospect soon paled as she saw the tremendous herds of game. 'Surely we can have a shot?' she begged.

'You will,' Kurt promised, and they pitched camp early, in a delightful vale shaded by trees. Here Pitzer and Omar set the Africans to work felling some of the smaller trunks to erect a barricade around the camp, while the other two white men, with Joanna and Safah, went hunting, taking two of the bearers to transport their anticipated kill. Amanda went too, although she did not bother to carry her rifle.

'What is it you would like to shoot?' Kurt asked Joanna. 'As you see there is every possible variety.'

'Something exciting.'

He scanned the plain with his field glasses. 'Like that?'

She took the binoculars. 'Oh, boy. Are those really elephants.'

'Indeed they are.'

'Let me see.' Amanda took the glasses.

'Can we shoot one?'

'Well, they are a long way away. Oh, shooting elephants is great sport and rewarding as well. I regard those fellows — or their tusks, I should say — as money in the bank, should I ever need it. But I think you should begin with something of more value as food; we are short of meat. What about those?'

They had just topped a shallow rise, and Joanna caught her breath as they looked down into the next valley and saw the herd of buffalo, huge horns standing away from their heads like the branches of trees, grazing close to a waterhole not half a mile away. 'Oh, boy,' she whispered again.

The breeze was in their faces, and Kurt was able to take them much closer, bending double to conceal themselves behind the grass and the occasional thorn tree. 'Now,' he said, when they were within a quarter of a mile. 'Choose your target.'

Joanna lay on the warm grass, topee pushed back on her head, legs spread as wide as her skirt would permit, rifle nestled in her shoulder, and sighted. Adrian knelt behind her to watch. The rifle barrel moved once or twice, then settled, and she squeezed the trigger. The sound of the shot alarmed the herd, which promptly galloped off into the distance, but one of the huge creatures lay inert on the ground. 'Got him!' She scrambled to her feet.

'Good shooting, bwana,' Safah commented.

'Come on.' She ran down the slope, Adrian at her heels.

'No, no, bwanas,' Safah called, but they ignored him.

Amanda would have followed, but Kurt checked her with a word.

The rest of the herd were now almost out of sight, and Joanna and Adrian were running across the grass towards her victim, panting with excitement, when without warning the apparently dead animal rose to its feet, with a couple of mighty heaves, gave a few more snorts, lowered its head, pawed the ground and charged at them.

'Oh, my God!' Joanna stopped so suddenly she lost her footing and sat down with a thump; winded, she dropped her rifle.

Adrian gazed at the red eyes and steaming nostrils of the enraged animal, now only fifty feet away, raised his own rifle and fired, but without taking adequate aim; the bullet screamed over the buffalo's back. Desperately he reached for another bullet, knowing he did not have the time, knowing they were lost, listening to Joanna screaming as she got her breath back . . . and another shot rang out. The buffalo collapsed again, only ten feet away from them.

Slowly Adrian lowered his rifle, listening to Kurt laughing as he now followed them down the slope with Amanda and Safah and the bearers. 'Never a single bullet for a buffalo,' Kurt roared. 'Those fellows will charge you when they're dead.'

Adrian helped Joanna to her feet. 'You didn't try to stop us,' he said. 'Jo could have been killed.'

'Not with me around,' Kurt said. 'Besides, one example is worth a thousand lectures. You'll think twice about approaching a wounded buffalo again, eh?'

'I hate him,' Joanna growled in their tent that night. 'Oh, how I hate him. And I thought you knew about things like that.'

'We never shot a buffalo on my last safari,' he admitted. 'I really thought it was dead.'

'So did I,' she said. 'Oh, I feel such a fool.'

'Why?' he asked. 'We all have to learn. And it was a damned good shot.'

'Um,' she remarked, and rolled on her side, away from him. He hesitated above her; this night was considerably cooler than any they had known since leaving the ship, and she had not bothered to take off her long-johns – the garment was stiff with dried sweat. But she still looked magnificently attractive, and he was hardly any cleaner himself – and they had not had sex since their first night on African soil. But she was clearly not in the mood. He sighed and lay down himself, immediately falling into a deep slumber, out of which he was awakened by a tremendous uproar.

He knew at once that a lion was attacking the camp. He seized his rifle, pulled on his trousers and rushed outside. Kurt was already there, with Pitzer, firing into the darkness, while the bearers set up a tremendous hubbub, and in the flickering firelight several of the huge creatures could clearly be seen scampering to and fro as they sought both the

141

buffalo meat and any human flesh that might be available. Adrian joined the other white men in advancing on them, firing as they did so and bringing down two of the beasts, before he was alerted by a terrified scream from behind him, followed instantly by the crack of a revolver, repeated several times. He turned round to see a lion actually tearing at the tent he had just left.

He raced back, yelling and whooping to attract the creature's attention while he hurriedly reloaded. With a sweep of its paw the lion had torn the canvas down one side, and now, attempting to enter the hole it had made, it collapsed the centre pole, to the accompaniment of another shriek from Joanna, who had stopped shooting, probably because she had emptied the chambers of her revolver. But the lion's attention had been attracted by Adrian's shouts, and with another sweep of its paw it emerged to find him.

Adrian halted and dropped to one knee. If not a natural marksman like Kurt, or Joanna for that matter, he had a steady hand and eye when he remembered to use them. Now he desperately tried to control his breathing while he sighted the rifle; the lion tossed its mane and ran towards him, only thirty feet away, gathering itself for a spring. As it left the ground, Adrian squeezed the trigger, then hurled himself to the right. But the beast was already dead as it hit the earth.

He picked himself up again, ran to the tent and pulled at the torn canvas. Jo lay beneath it, still in her collapsed cot, and still clutching her revolver. 'I hit him,' she gasped. 'I know I hit him. But it didn't seem to matter.'

'It's all right, my darling.' He helped her to her feet and out of the destroyed tent, to where Kurt and Pitzer and Amanda were gazing at the dead lion.

'Nice shooting, Adrian,' Kurt said. 'He was coming straight at you, and that can be unnerving. Oh, yes, nice shooting.'

'*You* shot him?' Joanna whispered.

'Well . . . there didn't seem anything else to do,' Adrian pointed out.

'You saved my life,' she said, and hugged him. He gathered he was forgiven.

But the attack had been severe enough. If four lions were dead, so were three of the bearers, and the camp was a mess. As soon as they had buried the dead, they hurried to leave Tsavo behind them and climb into the forest. Here the going was harder than ever, but the girls did not complain, and to their great joy when they came across a fast-running stream Kurt allowed them to bathe while the men set up camp some distance away. They were able to rinse out their clothes and even wash their hair, and returned refreshed in every way. That night Joanna was again the girl with whom Adrian had fallen in love, her confidence in him totally restored. And now, surely, the end was in sight.

They were, as before, welcomed by the Kikuyu, because Kurt had taken the trouble to load one of the bales with everything a forest African might wish, from a bolt of bright cloth to several strings of beads, and not forgetting a couple of rifles which had seen better days. 'It is best to stay on their right side,' he confided to Adrian. 'There are tales on the coast of their attacking Arab caravans with poison-tipped arrows.'

Adrian entirely agreed with him. 'But,' he asked, 'do we have to do this every time we travel up or down from the high country?'

'Ah . . . I imagine we will, until we muster sufficient force to overawe them,' Kurt said.

Strange, Adrian thought; he doesn't seem sure. But his reflections were interrupted by the interest the girls were both attracting and expressing in their surroundings, a mutual mixture of embarrassment and delight. The Africans as before put on a dance for them, leaving Amanda and Joanna starry-eyed at the sight of so much uninhibited nudity. 'Oh, my,' Joanna commented. 'If Papa could only see this.' It was the first time she had mentioned him since leaving England.

That night she was more passionate than ever he had known her, but it turned out it was for an even more exciting reason than being surrounded by a horde of naked warriors. 'I've missed two periods,' she whispered as she lay on his chest. 'I've never done that before. I reckon you must have got to me that very first night.'

He hugged her against him. 'Then we must take it easy from here on.'

'No, no,' she said. 'I want to get to the ranch just as quickly as possible. I'll be all right, believe me. The little fellow is no kind of a problem at the moment.'

They decided not to tell their companions for the time being, and the safari pressed on, climbing ever upwards, shivering at night before warming to the heat of the sun at noon. Kurt kept casting anxious glances at the sky, where the clouds were beginning to gather, suggesting that the Long Rains might be early this year. A week later they crossed the great swamp which lay just below the highlands themselves, and knew they were about to debouch on to the plains. Here, as usual, the bearers departed, leaving the stores in a great mound in a carefully selected place.

'How do we get them to the ranch?' Amanda asked.

'We will have to transport them ourselves, piecemeal,' Kurt explained. 'But these cowardly fellows will not risk an encounter with the Masai and, in fact, I would not wish to tempt the Masai into attacking us by appearing with an army of forest Africans.'

Each of the five remaining men – Kurt, Pitzer, Adrian, Safah and Omar – hefted a well-laden pack. Amanda insisted on bearing at least a haversack, as did Joanna, to Adrian's concern. But she seemed perfectly well and happy, happier indeed than he had ever known her when they at last gazed across the plain.

'My,' she said. 'Oh, my.'

'It is dry, and brown, and parched, at this time of year,' Kurt explained. 'But when the Long Rains come, then it will spring into every variety of flower and shrub.'

'Those mountains,' she said, peering into the distance.

'Oh, indeed, but they are not the greatest wonders of this land.'

'Where's the ranch?' Amanda asked, looking from left to right; there was no habitation of any sort in sight.

'Oh, we are still two days away from it,' Kurt told her. 'But there is so much to see first.'

The next day he took them to the precipice from which Safah had first shown them the Rift Valley, eliciting even more exclamations of wonder. 'It's like a lost world down there,' Joanna said. 'Can we go down?'

Adrian hugged her. 'My first question on seeing it too. We will go together, when we've made our number with the Masai.'

From there they went to John Barclay's grave, and the others stood back to allow Adrian and his sister to approach it by themselves. The cairn of stones was untouched by the passage of nearly six years. 'What a magnificent place to lie forever,' Amanda said, and a tear trickled down her cheek. 'I wish we could persuade Mother to come up here one day, just to know that Father wasn't just a foolish dreamer. That he did find his paradise, even if he died doing it.'

'We'll get her here,' Adrian promised.

They walked all the next day, heading north-west towards the mountains, which never seemed to come any closer. The ground undulated, sudden escarpments hiding unsuspected valleys. There was almost no shade, except beneath the gnarled and twisted branches of the thorn trees, and where, from time to time, there was water and a clump of acacias or a huge euphorbia. But there was as ever an enormous variety of game, and in the afternoon Joanna shot her first

145

kongoni for their dinner. Soon after the kill they saw men in the distance, but they were not approaching. 'Are they Masai?' she asked anxiously.

Kurt nodded. 'They have been stalking us ever since we left the forest. But they know it is I. They will not harm us. Now, let me see – over there, I think.'

Once again he seemed oddly unsure, Adrian thought, as if this was only the second or third time he had made this journey. Although he understood it was quite easy to lose one's bearings in this unchanging landscape, he had supposed there would be some kind of trail, beaten down by the passage of previous caravans such as this, or by the cattle; but the grass was largely unmarked.

Kurt seemed to have remembered where he was, however, and pointed again. 'Nearly there.'

They turned to the right, topped another small rise and looked down on another well-wooded, shallow valley – and a lean-to hut, close by a little stream which bubbled out of the earth before disappearing into the trees. 'Home!'

Adrian and Joanna and Amanda stared at it.

Pitzer joined them. 'I hardly expected it still to be there.'

'Ah, the Masai are patient people,' Kurt said.

'But . . . where's the ranch?' Amanda asked.

'There, my dear. Here. We are standing on it. For as far as the eye can see, and beyond, is our property, if we wish.'

'I mean . . . where's the house?'

'Well, I haven't actually had the time to build a house yet. That is what we are going to do now, together.'

Amanda's legs gave way, and she sat on the grass without warning, as if all the exhaustion of the safari had suddenly gathered on her shoulders.

Joanna said nothing; her expression revealed her feelings.

'Where are your cattle?' Adrian asked.

'Ah,' Kurt said. 'They will be well scattered in search of fodder. We will have to see about rounding them up, when we have got the rest of the gear here and built a house.'

'*Are* there any cattle?' Joanna asked.

Kurt grinned at her. 'There are a great deal of cattle up here, my dear. Of course, the Masai believe they all belong to them. Still . . . there are enough to go round.' He began to stride down the slope.

Adrian hurried behind him. 'You mean there *aren't* any cattle actually belonging to us?'

'As yet, none with our brand on them, if that is what you mean. But there will be. You and I are going to build a great empire up here, Adrian. That is my ambition. Is it not yours?'

'Ambition,' Adrian said bitterly. 'All this is still just a dream. I suppose you never did even treat with the Masai? They could come storming over that hill at any moment.'

'Oh, no,' Kurt said. 'I did treat with the Masai. Indeed I did.' They reached the hut. 'We will sleep in the open, at least until the Long Rains come. But by then I would hope to have built something more substantial. Is it not a delightful spot? We have everything, because I chose it with great care. Here there is the stream, the trees, sanitation and shade, as well as good drinking water. You will be very happy here, my darling girl,' he told Amanda, who had followed them down the hill with the others. She continued to gaze around with horrified eyes.

'Well, there sure is a lot of country,' Joanna remarked, determined to be cheerful. 'I've always wanted to do a Thoreau and start from scratch.'

Adrian scratched his head. Safah got to work immediately, pitching their tent.

'That was quick,' Pitzer muttered, peering into the distance.

They turned, reaching for their rifles, and watched the woman approaching across the plain. She was tall, and straight, and handsome, naked except for an apron, and alone . . . save for a little boy, about five years old, who trotted at her side. A strange little boy, for although he

147

looked like an African, his hair was a fuzzy yellow.

Adrian's heart seemed to constrict as he looked at them. 'Oh, Christ,' he muttered. 'Lulu?'

'As I said, the Masai have been watching us for some time,' Kurt agreed. 'But I did not expect her so soon.'

'But . . .'

'Oh, yes, the boy is your son. She is very anxious for him to have a father. In fact,' Kurt said, 'that is part of the deal I made with the Masai.'

PART II

The Rivals

5

'The deal?' Adrian asked in bewilderment.

'I will explain about it later,' Kurt said. 'Do you not want to greet your son?'

Adrian glanced at Joanna. She could have been turned to stone as she watched the approaching pair. No one could have any doubt that the child was his son. Amanda put her arm round the American girl's shoulders. Safah and Omar had stopped working at the sight of Lulu, but now they resumed; the coming crisis was a white man's affair. Pitzer stood by himself, watching.

Lulu stopped several feet away. She was far more handsome than he remembered. He realised she must be about twenty, and she possessed a quite superb mature figure. Now she lifted the little boy in front of her.

'Your son,' Kurt said again softly

Adrian glanced at him. He was beginning to realise that he had been tricked, outwitted and led a dance like a bull with a ring in its nose. He also understood that he did not as yet even know how *much* he had been tricked. He knew how angry he was, knew that there was going to have to be a settlement between Kurt and himself. But he also knew he was face to face with the greatest crisis of his life. As Kurt had reminded him, this was his son.

He took a step forward, and Lulu set the little boy on the ground. He had clearly been well rehearsed, and ran forward immediately. Adrian stooped, and the boy was in his arms. He straightened again, holding him close.

'I have called him Bar,' Lulu said, in Masai, as if Adrian had only been away for the term of her pregnancy.

The words sounded strange, after so long. Bar – he thought – all she could remember, or pronounce, of his name. Bar Barclay. 'It is a good name,' he said.

Now she came forward herself and knelt, and then prostrated herself at his feet. He didn't know what to do or say. The silence was broken only by a sound from Joanna which might have been a sob.

Safah and Omar finished pitching the tents and got to work on a fire, then prepared the antelope Joanna had shot earlier. Pitzer made a great show of supervising. Lulu sat and watched them, and Bar played in the dust beside her. She also watched Adrian, but she did not seem put out that he had not been more demonstrative in his greeting. He was a warrior, and she was his woman; she was simply content that he was back. Nor did she appear at this moment to connect him with Joanna. He wondered if it would matter to her when she did.

Kurt unpacked his knapsack. 'I think a celebratory drink is in order,' he said, producing a bottle of whisky.

'I ought to break your neck,' Adrian said.

'Would you have come, if I had told you the truth?'

'You still have not told me the truth.'

'I will do so, when we have had a drink, eh?' He poured two cups.

Adrian turned to look at the women. Amanda also clearly did not know what to say or do, and was playing at unpacking her haversack. Joanna sat with her back to everyone, gazing out at the high country. She had dreamed of coming here for years, and now she had arrived. And how she must hate the reality, Adrian thought.

'To our future success,' Kurt said, raising his cup.

Adrian considered. But more than ever, now, he had to make this into a success. He sipped, then walked to where Joanna sat, gazing out at the sunset. It was at once beautiful and idyllic, on the gentle slope down into the next valley, with the brilliant red sky as a backdrop. There was little noise from behind them, now, and the tap-tap of a woodpecker from the little copse sounded clearly in the still air.

He knelt beside her. 'A drink?'

She turned her head to look at him, then turned away again. Her face was frozen.

He looked with her down the slope, at the huge ten-foot-high tower which rose about two hundred yards away. 'That's a termite hill,' he said. 'I'll show you it, tomorrow, if you like. They really are works of enormous complexity. They have watchtowers and air-passages . . . regular communities.'

She gave no sign of even having heard him. He sighed. 'I would have told you of her,' he said. 'I tried to do so. But you did not wish me to.'

'You said she was in the past.' Her voice was low, and angry. 'I did not know she would be waiting for you. With your son. You spoke of a mistress, not a wife.'

'She is not my wife. And I did not know she was waiting, either. She was an incident, six years ago. I did not know I had a son.'

Joanna said nothing.

'I . . . I cannot send her away,' he explained. 'She is the chief's daughter. There would be immediate trouble. And . . . I have a son.'

Still Joanna did not speak.

Adrian got up and walked back to the now blazing fire. 'She is very upset.'

Kurt refilled his glass. 'Of course she is. She is a woman. But, being a woman, she will get over it.'

'Will she?'

'Of course. Mandy, my love, come and have a drink of

153

whisky. And then go and talk some sense into Joanna.'

Amanda came to the fire and stood for a moment looking at her nephew. Then she looked at her brother, as if trying to envisage the circumstances in which Bar had been conceived. Perhaps, Adrian thought, she succeeded in doing so – she gave a shudder and sat down. She accepted a mug of whisky, sipped and shuddered again. 'Is there any sense to talk?'

'Of course. So Adrian is fortunate enough to have two women. What is wrong in that? I have told you this is a different world to any you have ever known. Most men in this country have several women, if they can afford them. Would you object if I had a native mistress?'

'I . . .' She flushed. 'I have never thought of it. But do you?'

'As it happens, no. But I easily could have.'

'I don't think Joanna will accept that reasoning,' Adrian said.

'Well, she will have to, won't she?'

'Will she? I think you had better do some explaining, Kurt.'

Kurt looked at him, as if debating whether or not to tell him to go to hell, then grinned, shrugged and sat down. He drank some more whisky.

Adrian squatted beside him, and Amanda sat on his other side. As Joanna had predicted in Mombasa, Amanda was staying loyal to her husband, whatever her real feelings.

'Well,' Kurt said. 'I had a dream. A dream you shared, because it was your father's dream. I had the money to make that dream come true, when my own father died. All I needed was to be able to treat with the Masai. I could have recruited an army, of course, but I knew that would be a mistake, unless I was prepared to build and garrison a fortress for the rest of my life. So I came up here with Hans Pitzer and Omar. Just the three of us. Of course the Masai found us, very quickly, and we were in some danger. But

154

they remembered me – as your friend.' He gave one of his grins. 'They had always known their yellow-haired demigod would come back to them.'

'Go on,' Adrian said.

'Well, they supposed I was bringing them news of your return. They entertained me. And I told them I had actually come to live in the high country, to farm cattle. They did not seem very happy about that, but intimated they would not oppose me, on condition I brought you back to them. When I said I would, they could not have been more friendly. They offered me cattle, told me where was the best place to make my camp. There was only one thing; I had to promise to bring you back by the next Long Rains. This was last September, so you will see that I had to hurry. And we have only just made it.' He pointed to where the heavy dark clouds were massing above the mountains to the north.

'You promised them Adrian?' Even Amanda was aghast.

'I promised he would come to live in the high country. Nothing more. I was not going to deliver him to them bound hand and foot, if that is what you think. But you see, he is of great importance to them. Six years ago Uthuli, their chieftain, virtually adopted Adrian as his son, gave him his daughter as a woman, and now in addition, he is the grandfather of Adrian's son. He wants his son-in-law back again. After knowing such a man, and fathering such a child, Lulu could go to no one else. But there was far more. The whole tribe wants Adrian back. During the months we lived with them, purely by chance they prospered. Their cattle got no disease, and the rains were good and plentiful. After we left, there was an outbreak of rinderpest, which killed half their herd, and they nearly starved. Nor have they done well since. They are certain that with Adrian's return, they will again prosper. We may smile at such a childish superstition, but to people who live this close to nature, everything is related to specific events, specific signs. Adrian is a sign.'

'And if they do not prosper?' Amanda asked.

Kurt grinned. 'I think that is a bridge we must cross when we come to it. But the fact is that I am sure, I *know*, that we can now do good business with them and raise cattle and crops, and make a fine home for ourselves and our children. You have seen how Lulu arrived here within an hour of ourselves. She can hardly have been more than a mile away at any time. The Masai have been watching us since we left the swamp. They know Adrian is here. Uthuli himself will probably be here tomorrow. It is going to work out very well.'

'But you did not feel able to tell me all this in England,' Adrian said.

'As I said just now, would you then have come?'

'Probably, yes.'

Kurt raised his glass. 'Then I misjudged your steadfastness of purpose, and apologise unreservedly.'

'You could at least have told me that Lulu was also waiting.'

'I did try,' Kurt reminded him.

'Not very convincingly. Nor did you mention my son.'

'Well, the mood you were in, I did not think it would be tactful to do so. You were about to get married.'

Adrian stared at him. Kurt smiled back. Because he was pleased, Adrian knew. Kurt had done what he had promised the Masai he would do. So what was *he* to do? Get up and march back to the coast, with only Safah as bearer? And with Joanna pregnant? And the rains about to start and make the swamp and the forest impassable? And then the law waiting for him if he ever set foot on English-controlled soil again? Oh, Kurt had worked it all out to perfection.

And how could he ever abandon Amanda to such a monster? Or to the risk of murder by the Masai; if he left Kurt could not fulfil his promise. That was another rope securely tied round his neck, again as Kurt had foreseen. Indeed, was that not the reason Kurt had married Amanda?

156

He was Kurt's passport to prosperity, here in the high country, and Kurt clearly intended to make sure that he could never leave. For a pragmatic scoundrel like Kurt, to give his name to a woman he probably did not love would be of little importance; his wife was certainly beautiful and compliant, which was all he required of her.

Lastly, could he ever contemplate abandoning his son? Or of taking the boy away from his mother?

'You realise you are several kinds of a swine,' he remarked.

Kurt shrugged. 'Of course you feel that now. When you have had the time to think about it, my friend, you will realise that I have planned your life most carefully to be nothing but success. Is not this where you have always wished to be, more than anywhere else in the world?'

Safah bowed to them. 'The meal is ready, bwanas.'

'And I am starving.' Kurt got up and looked at Amanda. 'You had better go and fetch Joanna.'

Amanda hesitated, then went to where Joanna still sat staring at the dusk. 'She will be hungry, too,' Kurt said reassuringly. 'I see a house here,' he went on expansively, as the two men sat by the fire. 'And another over there, for you and' – he grinned – 'your women. And one for Pitzer. Oh, indeed, we will make this into a paradise. And we will farm cattle, and grow crops, and raise our families, and be happy. And do you know what else we will do?' He lowered his voice. 'Once a year we, you and I and some picked men, will go down to the Tsavo grassland and shoot elephant and market their tusks. We will become enormously rich. Then we may be able to devise a way of getting our cattle and produce to the coast for marketing. A railway is the answer, of course. But I suspect that would be an impossible task. Those escarpments, that desert . . . the expense would be unimaginable. No, we shall have to consider the matter. But it will not be that important, because we are living in paradise.'

Adrian said nothing. He did not wish to think about paradise just at that minute.

'Ah, Joanna,' Kurt said, as the women returned. 'Do sit down. Have some meat.' He speared a steak with his knife and presented it to her. 'I seem to remember your promising to dress for dinner once we reached the ranch. But tonight, I will let you off. First night at sea, eh? Nobody dresses for dinner on the first night out.'

Joanna sat down, but she ignored the steak. 'I would like to leave tomorrow,' she said, preferring to gaze into the fire rather than look at either of them.

'Leave?' Kurt asked. 'To go where?'

'Back to the coast, and then home. Perhaps' – at last she glanced at Adrian – 'you would be good enough to let Safah accompany me.'

'That is absurd,' Adrian said.

'I am not staying here,' she said in a low, determined voice.

'Dear lady,' Kurt said, 'you have no choice. You and Safah alone would never make the coast. You might as well just cut your throat. You would not make it in the best of conditions, but in about three days' time the Long Rains will start. The forests will become impassable.'

She gazed at him. 'How long do they last?'

He shrugged. 'Three, four months.'

'Four *months*?'

'At the end of which time you'll be six months pregnant,' Adrian reminded her.

'Pregnant?' Amanda shouted. 'Oh, my dear, are you pregnant?'

'God, I am,' Joanna said. 'I had almost forgotten.'

'But that is marvellous,' Amanda cried. 'I . . . well . . .' She glanced at Kurt.

He smiled expansively. 'You may tell them now, my dear. In all the circumstances.'

'Well,' Amanda said, blushing, 'I think I'm pregnant too.'

158

'That's tremendous,' Adrian said. 'Isn't it, Jo?'

'Congratulations,' Joanna said. 'So I am to be kept a prisoner here for the next seven months, is that it? Until my baby is born.'

'By which time you will think of it as your home, as it will be,' Kurt said.

'Never,' she said. She got up. 'This is paradise? This . . . this watering hole? You lied to us and tricked us to get us up here.' She turned to Adrian. 'Just as you tricked me over that woman. Well, I will stay because I have to. But I want nothing to do with any of you. If you attempt to lay a finger on me, Adrian Barclay, I'll kill you, so help me God.' She went into the tent Safah had erected for them.

'Just like a woman,' Kurt laughed. 'Laying down the law, and calmly appropriating what is yours as hers. I am glad you are not like her, my sweet. Not that I would allow you to behave that way, of course.'

'Do you think I should go to her?' Adrian asked his sister.

Kurt gave a bellow of laughter. 'Of course. When you are ready. When you have finished your meal and had another drink. Go to her, and beat some sense into her. That is the only language she is going to understand now. Whip her to make her submit to you, and then mount her and fuck her into exhaustion. Better yet, take your other woman with you, and make her share you.'

Adrian ignored him; he remained looking at Amanda, whose cheeks were pink with embarrassment at her husband's vulgarity. 'Should I?'

Amanda hesitated, then sighed and shook her head. 'I think maybe she may feel different in the morning. Right now I think she hates you.'

He finished his meal, got up and walked away from the campfire to stare out at the darkness. His paradise. His dream. Turned into a green and brown hell. But he realised he would have come back anyway, given the opportunity, even if he had known exactly what he was coming to —

especially a son he had never seen, had not even known existed. And he would still have brought Joanna, had she wanted to come. But would he have told her? Would he not still have decided to chance it, rather than risk losing her; and put his faith in their growing love, and in her great desire to realise her dream, and in the beauties of the high country and everything it had to offer, to offset any sense of betrayal?

He heard a soft footfall behind him and turned, his brain dancing at the thought it might be her. But it was Lulu. She had put Bar to bed, and she carried a blanket for them to share. Now she took off her apron.

'We have at the most a week before the rains start,' Kurt announced next morning. 'We must use that time well. I would have preferred to commence by bringing up as much of the rest of our gear as possible, but that will have to wait until Uthuli has given us the go-ahead. So let's get to work on the house, eh?'

Pitzer, Safah and Omar immediately went off into the wood to select the appropriate timber; amongst the gear they *had* brought with them were axes, adzes, saws, planes and chisels.

'I'll go and give them a hand,' Adrian said, finishing his coffee.

'Did you sleep well?' Kurt asked, grinning. Everyone knew with whom he had spent the night.

'Yes, thank you.' Because he had, despite all. Or perhaps because of all. He had forgotten the uninhibited splendour of Lulu's lovemaking. But now he suffered from conscience and felt at odds with the world.

'That is the great thing about having two women,' Kurt agreed. 'When one is not available, the other always is. I am fortunate, in that my wife is always available. Is that not so, my sweet?'

Amanda was returning from the stream, where she had

160

been washing her face and cleaning her teeth; she wore a nightdress and dressing gown, and looked, as always first thing in the morning, utterly exhausted. 'I am sure you are right, Kurt,' she said, and went into their tent.

So, what sort of a night did *you* spend? Adrian wondered. But Kurt at least still had a wife. He looked at the other tent, where there was no movement.

Adrian went to join the other men, followed immediately by Lulu and Bar. Not long afterwards Amanda also made her way through the trees to where they worked, stripped to the waist, stacking the timber they were sawing.

'Look out, there!' Pitzer shouted, as one of the trees Safah had been cutting started to scythe through its neighbours. 'Timber!'

Amanda side-stepped without difficulty, but both Pitzer and Adrian ran towards her. 'You should have told us you were coming.'

'I wanted to talk to you,' she said.

Adrian glanced at Pitzer, and Pitzer grinned. 'I'll get back to work.'

'About what?' Adrian asked, when they were alone.

'Well, about Kurt.' She kicked the dust with the toe of her boot; she was now fully dressed in blouse and skirt and topee, her hair gathered up beneath the hat to cool her neck. 'I would hate you and him to quarrel.'

'After the way he tricked us? I don't see how we can avoid it.'

'He had very good reasons,' she said, gazing at him.

'And you love him.'

Her chin came up. 'Yes. Yes, I do.'

'I don't see how you can. I feel an utter louse for having introduced you. As for agreeing to your marriage . . .'

'I love him,' she said again. 'And if he tricked us, as you say, he did it with our good at heart.'

'Oh, come now . . .'

'Of course he did. Is it not possible that he sees life,

161

objectives, just a little bit more clearly than you? Or I?'

Adrian scratched his head.

'You know I'm right,' she said. 'Promise me you won't quarrel, Adrian. Promise. For all of our sakes.'

He sighed, then shrugged. 'Not unless he does something else to upset Jo. Or harms you.'

She smiled and kissed his cheek. 'I'll see that he doesn't. He'll be so glad to have you his friend again.'

She hurried off, leaving Adrian gazing after her, wondering if she had been sent. But there was no reason for her to lie to her own brother, when they were alone. She actually *loved* Kurt. Presumably that was all that mattered.

He rejoined the men and they worked until noon. By the time they regained the camp, dragging the lengths of timber they had cut and shaped, Joanna was up, also fully dressed, sitting with her back to the tents, staring out over the plain.

'She had a cup of coffee and something to eat,' Amanda told him. 'I would say she is feeling a lot better this morning.'

'Think I could speak with her, then?'

'Ah . . . give it a little while longer,' she decided.

He nodded and got up, then he noticed Safah was pointing. The tall Somali was exhibiting as much agitation as it was possible for him to do, in that he was holding his beard with his left hand and tugging it. 'The Masai come,' he said.

6

'No weapons,' Kurt snapped, as they all stood up and instinctively reached for their rifles. 'We could not take on so many, anyway.'

Adrian realised he was right; there were perhaps a hundred men approaching them, and as he watched them approach he was aware of a quickening of his heartbeat, a sudden rush of sweat between his shoulder-blades – he had forgotten what a majestic and indeed awe-inspiring sight the Masai warrior was, when dressed for war. The Morani had daubed their naked bodies with red clay, and their elders wore ostrich feathers or lion-mane headdresses – Uthuli's was the finest of all. More important than their accoutrements, however, or even their weapons, was the rigid poise of each man, standing absolutely straight and still as they came to a halt, and the utter arrogance of their gazes as they surveyed the intruders.

But they could not have come for war, he reminded himself. They had come to seek Bar-clay.

He stood next to Kurt. Pitzer backed off to stand near the rifles, obviously determined not to be taken alive if anything were to go wrong with the coming negotiations. The two Somalis stood together, some distance away, nervous, but anxious not to show it. Amanda stood by herself, behind her husband; Joanna had also risen and turned, but remained some thirty yards away – Adrian could not imagine what thoughts must be going through the minds of the two girls.

Lulu went forward, walking in her usual stately fashion, Bar running at her side, to greet her father. And her brother, Adrian realised, for Kainairju was there as well, also resplendent in a lion's mane headdress, as befitted the son of a chief.

Lulu spoke to Uthuli, who listened and then stepped away from his people and gazed at Adrian.

'Up to you, boy,' Kurt muttered.

Adrian went up to the chief. As usual at moments like this, he was unaware of being afraid, although his throat was dry and his stomach muscles were tight enough.

'My son.' Uthuli placed his hand on Adrian's shoulder. 'You have been a long time in returning to your people.'

'I have had many things to do,' Adrian replied.

Uthuli gazed into his eyes for several moments, and then nodded. 'A man must perform his duty,' he agreed. 'But now you have returned.' He looked to left and right, but did not find what he sought. Then he gestured Lulu to his side, again gazing at Adrian.

Adrian understood what the chief had been looking for, and what he wanted. As did Lulu. But she was proud to be part of the coming demonstration. She tensed her muscles, and Adrian seized her by one thigh and one shoulder, and while she held herself rigid, swung her above his head, holding her there for several seconds. He knew his fingers, biting into her flesh, must be very painful, but she uttered no sound.

The warriors, reassured that he had not lost his strength, drummed their spear hafts on the ground. Uthuli was delighted. 'Now indeed you have returned to us,' he said, as Adrian set Lulu on the ground again. 'Are you pleased with your wife and son?'

'Well pleased,' Adrian said.

'Then I am also pleased. Your friend would stay here. And you will stay here too.'

'With my friend,' Adrian said carefully.

Once again a long look into his eyes. 'That you are in the land of the Masai is sufficient,' Uthuli said at last. 'You will not leave this land again.'

'No,' Adrian agreed, prepared to face that problem when the time came.

'Then we are pleased.' He turned to face his warriors. 'Bar-clay is home,' he said.

The warriors again drummed their spear hafts on the ground, causing little eddies of dust.

'You will live here?' Uthuli asked, looking at the copse and the stream with faint disapproval.

'Yes,' Adrian said. 'We will plant crops and farm cattle.'

'It is too late to plant crops for this year,' Uthuli said. 'We will share ours with you. Cattle . . . there are cattle.

You are pleased with your wife and son?'

This obviously worried him more than anything else. 'Yes,' Adrian said again. 'Well pleased.'

Uthuli stepped past him and went up to Kurt, followed by Kainairju and Lulu, who was now carrying Bar. Adrian accompanied them. 'You are a man of your word, Von,' the chieftain said, 'in that you have brought Bar-clay to us before the coming of the Long Rains. I am pleased. Now we will prosper. We will all prosper. My men will cut wood for you.'

'There are goods in the forest, by the swamp,' Kurt said. 'We need those here before the water rises.'

'My men are not carriers of goods,' Uthuli said. 'Like the Kikuyu.' His tone was contemptuous. 'I will send women to help you.' He looked at the two Somalis.

'They are our friends,' Adrian said.

'They are from the far land,' Uthuli said. 'I have seen their kind before. They are our enemies. They have come here in great numbers and sought to carry off our young men and women. They are our enemies.'

'These two are *our* friends,' Adrian repeated. 'And therefore yours.'

Uthuli considered, then nodded. He glanced at Pitzer without interest, and then looked at Amanda, who had just taken off her sun topee to fan herself; her yellow hair was fluttering in the breeze.

Behind them, spear hafts drummed on the ground, and Amanda suddenly realised everyone was looking at her. She flushed and held the topee in front of her protectively; it was in any event too late to repair the damage by attempting to conceal the hair.

'My sister,' Adrian explained.

'That I see,' Uthuli agreed. 'Can she not come closer?'

'Come over here, Mandy,' Kurt commanded.

Amanda gave a quick glance from left to right, as if seeking support, then came forward.

165

'Bar-clay's sister,' Uthuli said thoughtfully, no doubt wondering what superhuman gifts she possessed. 'Why does she conceal herself?' He looked pointedly at Lulu, who was as usual wearing only her apron.

Kurt looked at Adrian.

'You can't,' Adrian said in English.

'I think we must,' Kurt said. 'Mandy, take off your blouse.'

Her jaw dropped.

'Do it,' he snapped.

'No,' Adrian said. 'You cannot permit this.'

'She is my wife,' Kurt reminded him. 'And will do as I say. Like you, she is our passport to a fortune if we manage to remain friends with these people. Mandy!'

'No,' she whispered. 'Please, Kurt . . . not in front of all of these people. I couldn't.'

'A different world, remember,' he said. 'These men are used to nudity. It is the clothes you are wearing that offends them. Now do it.' He was speaking in a low voice, but with an intonation she had obviously heard before. Adrian again wanted to interfere, but again knew that Kurt was right; they would exist here, and prosper, by humouring the Masai. His sister was being asked only to act like a Masai woman, as he had been forced to become a Masai man.

Mandy hesitated for a last moment, then slowly unbuttoned her blouse and shrugged it from her shoulders; in the cool of the highlands she had at last discarded at least the upper half of her longjohns.

Uthuli stared at her appreciatively, as did everyone else; with the larger breasts of the Caucasian, the pink nipples studded against the marvellously white skin, she was a more superb figure than even Lulu – as Lulu knew, from the expression on her face.

'I am pleased,' Uthuli said. 'She is truly Bar-clay's sister. But has she no legs?'

'Drop the skirt,' Kurt commanded.

'Kurt . . .'

'Now,' he insisted.

Her shoulders seemed to square with resolution, then she unfastened her skirt and allowed it to fall to the ground. Adrian discovered that she had indeed utterly discarded her longjohns, and wore only drawers. Her legs were as magnificent as the rest of her.

He held his breath as he waited for Uthuli to require more, but the chieftain understood that she was Kurt's woman, and that her genitals were not to be displayed save to her husband. Kainairju, however, stepped past his father and went up to her, staring at her. Amanda was also holding her breath. When Kainairju's hand moved, Adrian also moved, but Kurt gripped his arm. Kainairju stroked Amanda's breast, and she breathed at last, in a great gasp. Kainairju stepped back. 'I will give you three cows,' he said.

Kurt grinned. 'She is not for sale.'

'Ten cows,' Kainairju said, and his father gave a little snort of disgust; not even a demigoddess could be worth ten cows.

'That is a splendid offer, my friend,' Kurt said. 'But she bears my child.'

Kainairju stared at him for several seconds, then shrugged. 'Perhaps afterward.'

'Perhaps,' Kurt agreed with his easy good humour.

Uthuli could sense the tension between the two men. He stepped forward to touch Kurt's arm. 'She is a lily,' he said. 'Your woman. And the other?'

'Barclay's second woman,' Kurt replied without hesitation.

'Can she not also be seen?'

Kurt glanced at Adrian.

'She won't do it,' Adrian said in English.

'I think she will have to,' Kurt said.

Adrian hesitated, then walked to where Joanna waited. She had been watching the scene; Amanda, not having been

167

commanded to dress, still stood all but naked in the sudden gloom, the sun having disappeared behind the clouds – she made an incongruous figure, not only because of her whiteness, but because she had replaced her topee on her head.

'I would rather kill myself,' Joanna said in a low voice, anticipating his request.

'You would rather kill all of us as well? And your unborn babe?'

'My unborn babe,' she said in tones of the most utter contempt. 'That lump in my belly, you mean. Yes, let them kill us all.'

He chewed his lip, knowing he would have to use force . . . and was struck a stinging blow on the shoulder. He turned, and was hit again on the face. He gazed at Uthuli, who had raised his arms to the skies, Joanna forgotten for the moment at least. 'The Long Rains,' the chieftain said happily.

'The Long Rains,' his warriors chanted.

'They have come early,' Uthuli said. 'Because Bar-clay has returned to us.' He dug his fingers into Adrian's arm. 'Now it is well,' he said. 'The heavens are pleased.'

The rains fell, sometimes heavily, sometimes lightly. Often there would be entirely dry days, but the threat of the rain was always present, and it could be counted upon to rain at least once in every forty-eight hours. The nights were chill. It was enormously exciting and pleasurable to watch the plain sprout into green, the stream bubble and overflow its banks, the flowers break out in wild, brilliant profusion – pinks and blues and yellows against the encompassing green and brown – the birds cluster, the storks wade, the plovers wheel overhead, the mountains emerge and then disappear behind the swirling dark clouds.

'It is the best time of the year,' Kurt declared. 'It is like the beginning of life, every year. It is magnificent.'

He was on top of the world in every sense because he had

168

achieved his dream. Now it was simply a matter of implementing it. The rain did not prevent the work from going ahead. True to his word, Uthuli sent a regiment of young girls, who were marshalled by Lulu, and accompanied Pitzer and Omar to the edge of the swamp to bring up the rest of the gear before the forest became impassable. The warriors were prepared to test their skill and their muscles with the axes, which they clearly fancied as possible weapons of war. As a result the building of the first house went on apace.

The rains meant there was a great deal of discomfort, as the white people were still living under canvas, and the ground was invariably soggy and there was mud everywhere, as well as every possible variety of crawling thing from ants, spiders, beetles and scorpions to lizards seeking shelter from the wet – but they knew this was a temporary state.

Even Amanda seemed perfectly happy, as she could watch her house slowly rising from the plain and begin to picture the garden she would have and the lawn, and as she planned her nursery. For a few days after the first visit of the Masai she had been in a state of total embarrassment with everyone, and more especially the warriors, who gazed at her, even when she was fully dressed, obviously remembering. That soon faded. And always there was Kainairju, for Uthuli's son always led the warriors who came to the ranch, for whatever reason, and then he would stare at Amanda — insolently, as the Masai did everything.

Amanda knew nothing, of course, of the final interchange between Kainairju and Kurt, as that had been in Masai, but she could remember the touch of Kainairju's hand, and knew that he was remembering it too.

Kurt was aware of Kainairju's continuing interest in his wife; it was impossible to overlook. Wisely, he never showed offence or even concern. But after everything that had happened, Adrian was determined to make sure where his brother-in-law stood.

'I would hope you would never let expediency or greed ever get the better of you regarding Amanda,' he told him.

Kurt grinned. 'It always amazes me how a white man will quite happily couple with a black woman, but the thought of the reverse taking place makes him reach for his rifle.'

'She is my sister,' Adrian reminded him. 'You have humiliated her sufficiently.'

'She enjoyed it. Every woman enjoys being admired. She will enjoy it even more as time goes by and she has only the memory of it.'

'None the less, Kurt,' Adrian said, 'if I thought you were ever even to consider trading Amanda to Kainairju, or any Masai, I swear on my father's grave that I will kill you.'

Kurt's grin faded; he had never heard Adrian speak quite so solemnly. In the superiority of his increased experience and his inherited wealth, and in view of Adrian's own naïvity with Joanna and his new circumstances, he had forgotten that beneath the youthful uncertainties was the boy who had first faced the Masai on his own terms, and gained the day.

'Mandy played her part in securing our acceptance by Uthuli with her beauty, just as you did with your strength. You should be proud of that,' Kurt said quietly. 'But I will never forget that she is my wife and the mother of my child. As she will be the mother of many more children for me. Do you take me for an animal?'

It was a question, Adrian supposed, that was better left unanswered.

Adrian's own hopes that Amanda might be right, and Joanna would soon come to terms with her situation, began to fade as the rains came to an end. His wife remained as coldly angry, at least externally, as ever. She maintained her own tent, and while she was careful to eat and drink all that she considered necessary for the health of herself and her

170

child, she preferred to do that alone as well. The child remained his best hope – but he had no means of knowing if she would have carried out her threat to destroy them all rather than undress before the Masai; if that were true, then not even the child could save his marriage.

Sometimes he would become impatient and angry with her, and would wonder if he cared *what* she did. And then, when he looked at her sitting silently staring out over the plain, he knew how much he loved her and how much he longed to take her in his arms. Meanwhile, he made do with Lulu, which undoubtedly exacerbated the situation, as Joanna was aware that Lulu went to his tent every night. But Lulu sought her rights as well as being a great comfort to him. In any event she could not be repudiated without causing offence to Uthuli.

Besides, there was the boy. He was bright, intelligent and tireless, and he knew who his father was. He accompanied Adrian everywhere, galloping along on his strong little legs, and when he was exhausted, he was delighted to be swept from the ground and placed on his father's shoulder, to survey the world from nine feet and more above ground level. Adrian adored him, which was another reason he could never repudiate Lulu. He had some hopes that the charm of the little boy might do something towards warming Joanna's heart, but she continued to regard him with distaste, and to stay wrapped up in her own anger, an anger which seemed to grow as her belly began to swell. Only to Amanda, who was in approximately the same condition, did she ever even deign to speak.

'What does she *want*?' Adrian would ask his sister in despair.

'She wants to go home and forget that she ever met you,' Amanda told him bluntly.

'But . . .'

'Of course, she cannot do that, because of the child. She does not want the child, because it is yours, but yet she

171

cannot bear to think of losing it, ever. She is afraid that you could not let her take it with her, should she decide to leave. Would you?'

Adrian had no reply to that, because he knew he would not – if it meant losing Joanna.

'She is very miserable,' Amanda said. 'And very lonely.'

'No more than I,' he replied.

Kurt, of course, maintained his different point of view. 'You are making a mistake,' he warned repeatedly. 'You are allowing her to establish a situation. There is nothing a woman likes more. She will have you surrendering to her.'

'I would willingly do that,' Adrian said, 'if she would accept it.' There was absolutely no point in remaining angry with Kurt. He had been engineered into this position, but he knew it was what he had always longed for – apart from Joanna's hostility. Could she but be brought around, he could be the happiest man in the world.

'Then you are a fool,' Kurt told him. 'Never surrender to a woman. They know nothing of victory. They cannot treat, they can only demand.'

'Is Amanda, then, so demanding?' Adrian asked.

Kurt gave one of his slow grins. 'She is my wife, and knows it. But I will tell you something else, women do not *want* victory. It makes them unhappy. They want to be dominated, and led, throughout life.'

At times like this he was at his most hateful. But no one could fault his energy, or the breadth of his ideas, or his determination.

By the time the rains began to dwindle and the skies to clear, the house was all but complete; in early August the room was on, and they moved in. There were only two bedrooms, and Joanna intimated she would rather remain in her tent than share. Amanda managed to persuade her to change her mind, as they were both now clearly close to delivery, and it was Adrian and Lulu who remained in the tent, with Bar.

172

Kurt shook his head at this fresh evidence of masculine weakness on the part of Adrian, but was already busily designing furniture, all of which would be homemade and hand carved by himself and Omar, who had some skill as a carpenter. 'Then we will commence your house, Adrian,' he said. 'And then Pitzer's. Oh, yes, it is all falling into place.'

Adrian was more concerned about the thought of the coming deliveries. It was something he had never thought of, in England or at sea, and he found the concept frightening, entirely removed as they were from any medical assistance. That Joanna was also afraid was obvious, although she would not share her feelings with anyone; it was indeed difficult to decide what she thought about, wrapped up in her lonely anger and misery. He was sure Amanda was right, and she *was* utterly miserable; she could not be anything else, especially with the beauty and interest of the land, which she had so long anticipated, clouded by her sense of outrage. He knew he still loved her. Almost he made a resolution that when the baby was born, and she had recovered her strength, he would even take Kurt's advice and force her to his arms and his bed, overwhelm her with love – and pray that she would respond.

Amanda, on the other hand, was utterly confident, simply because Kurt himself was confident. 'Childbirth,' he said with one of his enormous bursts of laughter, 'is a natural function. Animals do it all the time, without the assistance of doctors or midwives. And what is a woman but an animal?' He chucked Amanda under the chin. 'A very beautiful animal, to be sure.'

'What a pity you are not able to show us how it is done,' Joanna remarked, one of the very few times she entered any of their conversations.

A week later she was glad of his confidence, as her labour pains commenced. Kurt certainly seemed to know what to do, and although she was horrified at the thought of his manhandling her naked body she quickly became grateful for his reassuring touch. Soon she was past caring, and even accepted Lulu. When she first saw the black girl at her side she shouted at her to go away, that she did not want to be touched by those filthy fingers, but Lulu knew even more than Kurt about childbirth, and Joanna surrendered to their care, with some assistance from an increasingly distraught Amanda. Adrian knew he had nothing to offer, he was too distraught himself, and Pitzer kept him by the fire while he fed him copious draughts of whisky.

Joanna was in labour for several hours, and then gave birth to a baby girl, somewhat small and querulous, but alive, and with no obvious defects. 'There,' Kurt said, as proudly as if he himself had been the father. 'What were you afraid of?'

Joanna made no reply, she was too exhausted. And when the baby was placed in her arms by Lulu, she wept. It was the first sign of a break in her ice-cold demeanour for several months. Adrian stood by the bed, looking down on her, and she raised her head to return his gaze. 'Are you satisfied?' she asked, her voice low.

'I am overwhelmed,' he said. 'And I love you so very much.'

'I hate you,' she said. 'So very much.' She closed her eyes.

Amanda followed her sister-in-law after three days, and gave birth to a boy. Her delivery was easier, as perhaps she trusted her midwives more.

The children were christened together. As Joanna refused to express a choice, however lovingly she hugged the baby to her breast, Adrian decided on Catherine, the name of Joanna's mother – but even that did not appear to please her. Kurt named his son Heinrich, after his own father. 'He was a fearful fellow,' he said. 'But after all, without him we would not be here. And now I have a son,' he said proudly. 'Now indeed we have two ready-made families. We are the founders of a new nation, a new civilisation here in the high country. And these two little babes will be our inheritors.' He glanced at Bar, who was as usual watching with intelligent eyes – and Adrian had made some progress in teaching him English. 'A new nation,' he said again, thoughtfully.

It was difficult to argue with his enthusiasm. Once the rains were over, the Masai reaped their crop of grain, which they shared with the white people as they had promised, and then abandoned their village to move their cattle herds to the north in search of fresh pasturage before the weather could grow too hot. Here again Uthuli was as good as ever in keeping his word, and the ranch was stocked with a dozen sheep and goats to keep them in meat; the Masai only killed their cattle – their estimate of a man's wealth – on special occasions, and for meat relied mainly on their sheep and goats. For religious reasons they were forbidden to eat the meat of any wild animals save buffalo and eland.

Uthuli had understood, from the moment he had seen the size and solidity of the house Kurt was building, that his white friends were not nomadic. Remembering how they had broken away seven years before, he made no attempt to force them to accompany his people north. But he rested his hand on Adrian's shoulder in saying goodbye, and looked into his eyes, and said, 'You will be here when we return, my son.'

'I will be here, my father,' Adrian promised willingly; he now had even less encouragement to leave, if it would cost him Joanna.

With the tribe's departure, the Europeans, and even more the two Somalis, felt less on edge all the time. True, they had lost their labour force, but now it was simply a matter of extending the ranch by building a house for Adrian and his women, as Kurt would always put it. This the five men were quite capable of doing, with considerable help from Lulu. The small flock they now possessed had to be kept close at hand to discourage prowling leopards, but only one of the

175

men was needed as herdsman at a time, and the two Somalis took turns. They also built a pen into which the livestock could be enclosed at night – this would not keep out a leopard, but made the animals easier to watch and protect. Kurt decided against slaughtering any of them, except in extreme necessity; there was so much game available that, suffering from no religious scruples, they could go hunting twice a week and secure all the meat they wished, while the goats provided fresh milk.

Thus, if at the moment it was difficult to see any financial prosperity coming their way in the immediate future, with the Masai grain to supplement their meat diet, and fish in the stream, and the days a succession of perpetually blue skies and warm sunshine, and the nights cool enough to enjoy one's bed; with the great plain a mass of waving grass and brightly coloured flowers, only beginning to fade as the rains became a memory; with the constant parade of game – zebra and wildebeest, buffalo and hartebeest, gazelle and giraffe, and even, on occasion, a short-sighted, suspicious rhinoceros – to watch gathering at the stream in the evenings, carelessly unafraid of the white people seated on the house verandah not fifty yards away; with the variety of birds – egrets and herons seeking the water, black crakes and kingfishers overhead, plovers further out on the plains, and above them all, stately and menacing hooded vultures wheeling out of the sky – to be admired; with the huge mountains ringing them on three sides, with the world apparently their very own, no one could dispute that they were living in a paradise.

Only their own tensions were disruptive. But the tensions were entirely between Joanna and Adrian. Once the second house was completed and he moved into it, with Lulu and Bar of course, he invited her to do the same, but she refused. 'I will stay with Amanda,' she said.

'Fifty yards?' he asked. 'You can talk to her from my front verandah.'

'I prefer to stay here,' she repeated. Both she and Amanda were feeding, so it made some sense for them to remain together, he tried to reason, with his usual inclination to see both sides of a question. And indeed the obvious delight with which she viewed her baby, the obvious pleasure she found in playing with her and bathing her – there was little dressing or undressing to be done as neither child had any clothes – was the most reassuring thing he had seen for a long time. To his relief, she did not raise the matter of a return to the coast again. Presumably even she could understand that was not practical as long as the baby was at her breast. Once again he determined to practise patience, for all Kurt's coarse attempts to egg him into action.

'They are at their bests when feeding,' he said. 'Their breasts are bigger, their bodies more receptive. They are never sweeter.'

Presumably he was speaking from experience; certainly Amanda had never looked happier. Adrian contented himself with saying, 'I will not force her,' and Kurt shrugged and walked away.

They celebrated Christmas in style, for although their stock of whisky was all but exhausted, Kurt had some bottles of claret, somewhat sour after their long journey in the tropical sun, but still alcoholic enough to induce laughter and even bring half a smile to Joanna's face, while the teetotal Somalis watched them with polite indulgence. Kurt began to hint that one of them should make a trek back to the coast to replenish their European supplies, but he knew this was a subject not to be mentioned in front of Joanna, nor could the journey be made until Adrian had resolved his relations with her.

In any event, they had first to await the return of the Masai. This they were sure they could now do without apprehension. Until one day in late January 1882, when the Africans could be expected back at any moment to clear the ground for sowing their crops, Safah, who had been out hunting, came back in a state of some agitation. 'There are many men over there.' He pointed to the south-east.

'Masai?' Kurt demanded.

'They would not come from that direction,' Adrian pointed out. 'They aren't Kikuyu, I hope?' He knew from his time with the Masai seven years before that the Morani often raided Kikuyu territory in search of women and cattle, and had always been worried that one day the forest dwellers might seek their revenge.

'These are white men,' Safah said.

Adrian and Kurt looked at each other in consternation, unsure whether to be pleased or aghast at the thought of their paradise being invaded. Next day they were definitely aghast, as a very large safari approached the ranch. It was German – led by a Dr Gustav Fischer, who was small and moustached and bustling – and was certainly enormous, being composed of some forty very well armed white men, with more than a hundred bearers (not Kikuyu, but from further to the south). They had apparently made their way up from the coast opposite Zanzibar.

For their part, the newcomers gazed in wonderment at the cluster of houses, at the white men who greeted them, and most of all at the two white women. 'I had heard a legend that there was a white family living in the interior,' Dr Fischer confessed. 'But I did not believe it. How long have you been here?'

'A year, all but,' Kurt told him. 'You will have to provide your own whisky; we have exhausted our supply.'

Fischer laughed. 'You will have all the whisky you can desire, my friend. I brought a great deal of it, to feed to the natives. But I think it would be better fed to you. You are German. I am pleased about that.'

They feasted around the fire by the stream. The visitors had shot sufficient game for the meal, but Kurt told Omar and Safah to kill two of the sheep in any event, to show their

178

hospitality. Joanna and Amanda preferred to remain with the children on the verandah as they spoke no German, but this night, for the first time since leaving the coast, they each put on an evening gown, and attracted repeated glances from the men.

Adrian had picked up enough German from Kurt to carry on a conversation. 'What is the purpose of your safari?' he asked Fischer.

'Why, to see, and map, and perhaps . . . there is no doubt that this could be a wealthy country.'

'It belongs to the Masai,' Adrian said.

'This we have heard,' Fischer agreed. 'A fearsome people, we have been told, hence our determination to defend ourselves. But they are surely indigenous savages. They cannot stand in the way of progress.'

Adrian and Kurt exchanged glances. 'Progress being what, in your estimation, Herr Doctor?' Adrian asked.

'Well, in the first instance certainly, trade with us on the coast. Later, perhaps, we may consider colonisation. Do you find the climate healthy for Europeans?'

'It is the best climate in the world,' Kurt declared.

'An opinion we have formed for ourselves these past few days. Well, then . . .'

'The country belongs to the Masai,' Adrian repeated. 'By what authority do you come here supposing you can simply appropriate it?'

Fischer frowned at him. 'By what authority do *you* live here?'

'By the authority of the chief of the Masai in this area.'

Kurt guffawed. 'Adrian is a member of the tribe.'

Fischer raised his eyebrows. 'Is that so? Well, we are very pleased to meet you, Herr Barclay. We are quite prepared to treat with the Masai and bargain with them fairly for our requirements. Perhaps you would care to assist us.'

'Me?' Adrian demanded.

'It is my intention to push down into that great valley we

179

have seen. I am told it is the heartland of the Masai.'

'It is.'

'Then we should encounter them, which is what I wish to do. If you were with us to act as interpreter, to talk to their chiefs on our behalf and make them understand that we intend them no harm, so long as they are not obstructive and attempt no harm to us . . .'

Once again Kurt and Adrian exchanged glances. 'It might be a good idea for you to do that,' Kurt suggested. 'Otherwise there may be trouble. We do not want that.'

Adrian reflected for some minutes. 'I will accompany you,' he decided at last. 'And I will interpret for you to the Masai chieftains. But I will not forward your plans in any way. It is for the Masai to say.'

Fischer gave a twisted smile. 'You would preserve this little paradise all for yourself,' he remarked. 'Well, no man could blame you for wishing to do that. But you will not succeed.'

'That is for the Masai to say,' Adrian repeated.

The news of his intended departure with the German party caused consternation in the ranch. Amanda clearly did not want him to go; he could not determine whether she was afraid for his life or did not want to be left alone with Kurt. Equally, Joanna, although she did not say so, looked very unhappy at the prospect – which pleased him greatly. Lulu wanted to accompany him, but as wherever she went Bar also went, and he was in a hurry, he told her to stay – besides, he did not want to expose the Germans, not all of whom were as refined as Fischer, to temptation; he was already disturbed by the way the men looked at all of the women. Thus he took only Safah. His principal intention was to prevent any trouble between Fischer's men and the Masai. Quite apart from any land-grabbing ideas they might have, he had no doubt that the sight of the naked and handsome Masai maidens might well provoke a crisis.

In fact he found the Germans very good company. If more than half the party were coastal roughnecks, there were also several scientists accompanying Fischer, and these were enthusiastic, learned, charming and enormously interested in himself and Kurt and their success in settling here, and in treating with the Masai. But they were also very determined men who saw the highlands and the valley as at once a paradise in which white men could prosper, a vast research laboratory in which to investigate the habits and life cycles of a hundred varieties of animal – including indigenous man – an inexhaustible sporting playground, a very profitable trading reservoir . . . and the ideal place for planting a German colony.

The apprehensions he had felt on first meeting them settled into a great lump in his stomach. He tried to tell himself that it was absurd to feel that way. Of course these highlands would eventually be discovered by other white people. Indeed, that was *their* best hope of future prosperity. Certainly his. Yet in his bones he also knew it would have to bring strife and sadness, and the eventual ruin of this heaven on earth. And here he was being instrumental in bringing that about, because he had no choice.

He led them down on to the floor of the Rift Valley, where he had so longed to bring Joanna, and on towards Lake Naivasha, whence he knew the Masai would be returning to their village. They had been gone from the ranch for three days when Fischer hurried up to him to tell him that their scouts had seen three tall black men armed with spears looking down on them from a bluff.

'They didn't shoot, I hope,' Adrian said.

'They reported back to me,' Fischer told him. 'But I have ordered the camp to be pitched and put into a proper state to repel any attack.'

'Isn't that why you have me along?' Adrian asked. He picked up his rifle and, accompanied by Safah, left the camp – where the white men had already formed a perimeter, lying amidst the grass and stones, rifles and bandoliers at the ready – and approached the lake itself. The Germans watched him go with pessimistic concern; clearly they did not expect to see him again, alive.

The lake, although the waters had receded in this dry spell before the rains, was as lovely as ever, and the pink flamingoes as incuriously solemn. This was the first time Safah had seen these stately birds, in many ways so reminiscent of the Somalis themselves, and for all his apprehension of their mission, he was entranced.

They were of course under constant surveillance, and when they awoke next morning at dawn, they found themselves in the midst of several warriors. No words of greeting were spoken; the Masai merely headed in a certain direction, and Adrian and Safah accompanied them. They reached a war party of some three hundred men, daubed with red mud and wearing lion manes or feathered headdresses, carrying spears and clubs and bows; there was undoubtedly more than one clan gathered here in alliance.

Uthuli was waiting to greet them, looking more grim than Adrian had ever seen him. 'Your visit surprises me, my son,' he remarked. 'You have too many friends. And too many long spears.' He touched Adrian's rifle.

'They are no friends of mine, my father,' Adrian said. 'They are white men who have heard of the wondrous beauty of the high country and come to seek concessions of you.'

'Concessions?' Uthuli asked.

'They wish to trade, and perhaps farm, in time. And they wish to explore the wonders of your world.'

'And will they not be followed by others? Tell me, how many white men are there in this world?'

Adrian sighed. 'They are like the grains of earth upon the plain, my father. But not all of them will come here.'

'None of them will come here,' Uthuli stated. 'I have given a home to you and your friend. This is enough. We

182

have not sufficient grain, sufficient flocks, for so many. And they have brought with them many black men who are our enemies. They must leave this place.'

Adrian nodded. 'I will say that to them.' He glanced around him, noticing that Kainairju and a large contingent of the Morani whom he knew personally were absent. 'You will start no war until I have spoken to these men?'

Uthuli inclined his head. 'But my men will prepare for war, should they not heed your words, and wish to fight us.'

Adrian scratched his head. Spears and short-ranged bows against modern rifles – and Kainairju already on the loose. 'Where is my brother?' he asked.

'He is out watching the white men, to discover their purpose,' Uthuli said.

'If he attacks them, they will fight,' Adrian warned.

'If they fight with us, they will all be killed,' Uthuli said uncompromisingly. 'Tell them this.'

Adrian and Safah hurried, but it was the next day before they regained the German encampment, to find it still in a state of readiness. 'We have seen some of the savages,' Fischer told him. 'But a few shots scared them off. And we are very pleased to see you back again. We supposed we had sent you to your deaths.'

'You risk your own,' Adrian replied, and told him of Uthuli's ultimatum.

'Well,' Fischer remarked, 'this old savage has a high opinion of himself. You expect him to attack us at any moment, then?'

'He will not attack you at all if you immediately break this camp and begin to withdraw,' Adrian said.

'He must take me for a fool. Then he would be able to ambush us on the march.'

'He will not do that,' Adrian promised. 'He is a man of his word.'

'I will take leave to doubt that,' Fischer commented. 'In any event, I have never turned my back on any savage yet.

183

Any civilised man, either. Nor do I intend to do so now. You are convinced he *will* attack if we remain here?'

'If you do not leave, it will amount to a declaration of war,' Adrian said. 'I do not know *when* he will attack, in those circumstances, but he will. It would be an incredibly foolhardy thing to invite.'

'Then we may take it that you will not stay and fight with us against these savages?' asked one of the scientists.

'No, sir, I will not,' Adrian said. 'I did not come here to the high country to start a war. I have given you the chieftain's decision, and I have given you my advice. Now, I propose to leave the valley tomorrow morning. If you wish to accompany me, I will happily guide you out. If you are determined to stay . . . then your blood must be on your own heads.'

'There speaks a true Englishman,' someone in the group remarked contemptuously.

Adrian ignored him and looked at Fischer.

'I respect your motives, Herr Barclay,' the doctor said. 'You must therefore respect mine. You do not wish trouble with the Masai, because you have made your home here. However, there can be no doubt that one day, and it will be one day soon, this valley will be occupied and exploited by Europeans. I intend that those Europeans will be my own countrymen, sir. And I intend to make that plain to the Masai, now.' He gave Adrian a hard look. 'And *when* this country is a German colony, your failure to support us may well be remembered.'

Adrian nodded. 'When, Herr Doctor,' he said. 'I will say goodbye. I'm afraid I cannot bid you good fortune. Nor would it be of any avail.'

He summoned Safah, and the two of them left the encampment that evening, pitching their tent some miles distant and already on the climb out of the valley. The next morning they looked down on the Germans and saw them

184

breaking camp. For a moment Adrian felt an almost painful sensation of relief that Fischer was, after all, showing some common sense. Then the sensation became an equally painful one of distress, because the Germans, far from leaving the valley, were pressing on towards the lake. Fischer was actually challenging Uthuli.

'We will wait here,' he told Safah.

The Somali nodded. He too wanted to see what would happen.

They did not have long to wait. Looking down on the scene from some distance they were unable to make out much detail, but they watched the German advance guard pass beneath some high and apparently empty bluffs just short of the lake, followed by the main body a couple of hundred yards behind; and then suddenly the bluffs and the grass to either side were alive with Masai, who must have taken up their positions during the night and lain concealed until the right moment. Adrian and Safah could see the puffs of smoke and almost thought they heard the shouts of men and the reports of the rifles. Then they saw black men running through the grass – the Germans' porters. Behind them ran the Masai with deadly intensity, hurling their spears or waiting to catch up with the terrified men and thrusting at them. The Europeans were out of sight behind the bluffs, but it was obvious that they were surrounded and pinned down.

'We must get down there,' Adrian said. 'Or there will be a massacre.'

'There already has been a massacre, bwana,' Safah pointed out, but he was not disposed to argue with his master and they hurried towards the scene. It took them several hours, during which they listened to more rifle fire as they approached. It was late afternoon before they encountered the Masai and were taken before Uthuli, who sat on a large stone on a slope overlooking the bluff which was occupied by his warriors.

Uthuli was delighted to see them. 'Bar-clay,' he said, resting his hand on Adrian's shoulder. 'Truly am I pleased. We had supposed you had turned your back on us and fought with the white men.'

'I gave them your message,' Adrian said. 'And when they would not heed it, I left them. Are they all dead?'

'No,' Uthuli said. 'Not yet. Their long spears are difficult weapons to overcome. Several of my Morani have been killed.' He did not look disturbed about that; death in battle was an honour for a Masai. 'But several of them have been killed too,' he added. 'And their black men have run away. We killed all of them. We will finish the matter when the darkness comes.'

'Can you not let the white men go?' Adrian asked. 'Those who have survived?'

Uthuli gazed at him. 'To come again, with more men?'

'I do not think they will do that,' Adrian said. 'I am sure it will be a long time before they can do so. They will take with them tales of the strength of the Masai Morani, and think deeply before they return. But if they disappear altogether, others will certainly come looking for them.'

He was not telling the absolute truth, of course. Fischer would certainly also take with him tales of the magnificence of the country he had seen, and that would encourage another expedition – but he could think of no other way to save their lives, and he certainly could not just stand by and watch them being cut to pieces.

Uthuli was considering the points he had raised. Now he nodded. 'If they will now leave our lands, never to return, my Morani will not kill them. Tell them this.'

Adrian pointed at the setting sun. 'They will be afraid to leave in the darkness, my father. You will hold your men for this night?'

Uthuli inclined his head. 'They will leave at dawn,' he said.

Adrian and Safah went down beneath the bluff. They

186

were curious to see just how the battle between rifles and spears and arrow had worked out, and Adrian quickly realised that the rifles had by no means had the best of it; there were several white men lying with the deadly throwing spears of the Masai, the weapon they used to hunt the lion with, thrusting through their chests. Two or three had also had their throats cut, indicating they had been so unlucky as only to be wounded. Scattered around in the grass were also the bodies of dead Morani, but the Germans could hardly know the execution their rifles had done, while their own dead and wounded were too painfully obvious.

He had never crossed a battlefield before, and the dried blood, the stench, the flies and the croaking vultures were all nauseating.

'Stop right there, Herr Barclay,' Fischer called as he approached the tumbled rocks behind which the Europeans had taken shelter. 'Or I will cut you down.'

'Then you would be a fool,' Adrian told him. 'I have come to save your lives.'

There was a brief silence, while Fischer no doubt consulted with his men, then he said, 'Come in.'

Adrian climbed through the rocks and took in the situation. Some thirty Europeans and half a dozen bearers were all that were left of the original party, and several of them had wounds; one or two looked quite serious. Nor did the rocks provide adequate shelter from any of the Morani who could get close enough to hurl their spears – as they certainly would after dark.

Fischer understood his expression. 'They came at us very suddenly and very quickly,' he said. 'I will admit I had no understanding of how well they can conceal themselves and how far they can throw those spears. They are formidable fighters.'

'And terrible creatures,' said the scientist who had called Adrian's courage into account. 'Those of us who were wounded and could not keep up . . . they screamed for mercy before they died.'

'The Masai have you pinned down here,' Adrian told them. 'They intend to attack you again tonight. And even if you repel them, you will never reach the lake. How much water have you?'

'Enough for perhaps two days.'

'And then? You have some badly injured men here.'

Fischer gazed at him. 'You said you could save our lives.'

'I can. The Masai have agreed to let you live, if you leave at dawn. Their chief has given me his word he will not, in fact, attack tonight. But don't suppose you can take advantage of that fact; if you start something he will kill you all. He regards war as a sport, and will happily stretch this business into next month. But if you defy him, you will all die.'

Fischer looked at his men, who had gathered round.

'We are being invited to abandon even this scant shelter,' he objected. 'Once in the open we will be easy prey.'

'He has given his word you will not be molested,' Adrian said.

'Do you seriously suppose we will trust the word of a savage?' asked another.

'A savage word is too often of more importance, to the savage, than that of a white man,' Adrian said. 'Besides, I will add my word to his. I will take you back out of the valley. But we must leave at dawn.'

He actually had more reason for wanting to hurry than merely to get the Germans out of danger; he had seen no sign of Kainairju and his band of Morani anywhere around the scene of the battle, and that troubled him, even if he could not decide why. Nor did he have the time now to return to Uthuli and attempt to find out just what Kainairju was doing, if he was going to save the lives of these people. But the sense of urgency was growing on him, and he could hardly wait for the dawn.

188

Lacking his bearers, and with three men too badly wounded to walk, Fischer had to abandon almost all of his supplies and, to the distress of his scientists, most of their specimens as well. Then, carrying their wounded in improvised litters, the sorry band made their way back up to the highlands, casting anxious glances at the Masai warriors who stood on mounds and crags, looking down on them. Four days later they reached the edge of the forest, and here Adrian and Safah bade them farewell.

'Your best course is to make for Mombasa,' Adrian told Fischer. 'Keep the mountain they call Kilimanjaro always on your right hand. When you encounter the Kikuyu, treat them as friends and they will respond to you. Ask only a passage through their land. They may even supply you with bearers. Fight them, and they will destroy you.'

Fischer shook hands. 'You have behaved properly, Herr Barclay,' he said. 'We did not heed your warnings, and we paid the penalty. Next time . . .'

'If you are wise, Herr Doctor, there will not be a next time,' Adrian advised.

Fischer gave his crooked smile. 'There is always a next time, Herr Barclay. The white man is on the march. He will not be restrained until he has sown his seed over the entire earth.'

'Then God help us all,' Adrian said, and turned to the north.

He and Safah walked for the rest of the day and only camped when it was already dark. He slept restlessly, and Safah watched him with sombre eyes. But the Somali said nothing.

Next day they hurried on their way, and before long they encountered a Morani, standing still, spear in hand, watching them as they approached. 'I seek Kainairju,' Adrian said.

'He has been, and is gone.' The man's eyes smouldered at him.

189

'He has been to the white man's kraal?'

'He has been,' the warrior said.

'Did they fight?'

'He has been, and he is gone,' the warrior repeated. 'He seeks his father, that a wrong may be set right.'

Obviously they were going to get nothing more out of him. Adrian pressed on, and that evening, such good time had they made, they topped the last rise and looked down on the valley and the stream, the little wood and the smoking fire, the flock of sheep and goats, and the houses. Both houses. Adrian's heart did a leap of joy, and tired as he was, he ran down the slope, followed by Safah.

His coming was obviously observed, for Kurt appeared on the verandah, a rifle in his hand. Pitzer was at his side, Omar behind him. Adrian pounded up to the steps, Safah at his heels, but as he reached the house, he stopped. There were several spears sticking out of the wood. 'Kainairju has been here?' he shouted.

Kurt nodded briefly. His face was just as sombre as that of the Masai. 'What news of Fischer?'

'He would fight with the Masai,' Adrian said. 'And as I predicted, got cut up. I managed to intercede with Uthuli for the lives of the survivors, and they have left the high country; they are going down to Mombasa.'

'Damnation,' Kurt said. 'I had hoped you would bring them here, to give us some support.'

Pitzer had brought Adrian a drink, and he gulped it. 'Support?' he demanded. 'Do we need support?'

Kurt pointed at the spears. 'Do you not see that we need support?' He glanced at Pitzer. 'The best thing we can do is pack up and get out of here, and see if we can catch Fischer up before those devils come again.'

'Get out of here?' Adrian shouted. 'Attacked? What the hell has happened?' He pushed open the door and went inside. Amanda and Joanna and the two babies seemed unharmed, but their eyes spoke stark tragedy. Bar was by

190

himself in the corner, staring at his father with wide eyes but not moving. 'What happened?' he asked again, more in control of himself now he saw that his family appeared safe.

'We were attacked by that devil Kainairju,' Kurt said, following him into the room.

'But why, for God's sake? Amanda . . .' He looked at his sister.

She looked at her husband. 'Kainairju came here,' she said. 'I do not know what was said, but . . .'

'He had twenty Morani at his back,' Kurt said. 'He told me that you had been seen marching with the white men to make war on the Masai, and that I was no longer welcome here. He said you were no longer his brother, and that you would be killed with the other white men.'

'Jesus,' Adrian muttered. 'Uthuli told me they were out scouting. That was all a pack of lies.'

'Lies or not, he sounded plausible,' Kurt said. 'He told us his father had commanded him not to kill us unless we resisted, but that he was to expel us from this land. All of us, excepting Amanda. She was to go with him to his kraal.'

Adrian looked at his sister. That she was terrified was obvious. 'What did you do?'

'What did you expect me to do?' Kurt demanded. 'I sent a couple of shots over his head, got everyone into the house and barricaded the door. There was a great lot of shouting, and they threw spears at us, as you have seen. We fired back, and I think hit one or two of them. But they weren't going anywhere, and we had little water in here; they had us cut off from the stream. So . . .' he hesitated.

'He shouted at them through the window,' Joanna said in a low voice, 'that if they did not give us all safe passage out of their land, he would execute Lulu.'

Adrian looked at her, then at Kurt, and then left and right round the room. Lulu was not to be seen, and Bar had not come to him when he had first entered. His heart lurched.

'And?' he asked.

'They ignored the threat and launched another attack, so . . .' Now even Joanna could not continue.

'I did what I thought best,' Kurt declared. 'I went outside, holding the woman. I told them to leave or I would carry out my threat. When they attacked me, I shot her.'

7

There was a silence, broken suddenly by a wail from Catherine Barclay. Joanna hastily hugged her quiet again.

'I had no choice,' Kurt said. 'If I had hesitated, they would have cut all our throats.'

Adrian forced himself to concentrate on the situation as it was; grief and anger would have to wait. 'Kainairju saw you do it?' he asked.

'Of course he did. And it worked,' Kurt insisted. 'He withdrew his people the moment he understood I was determined to fight.'

'He will be back,' Adrian said. 'To avenge his sister's murder.'

'It was a necessary act of self-defence,' Kurt said stubbornly. 'Would you have had them take your sister? And if they had, they would have taken Joanna as well.'

Adrian looked at the women. Their eyes were wide with shock, and like Joanna, Amanda hugged her baby to her breast.

'That is why I say we must leave now,' Kurt went on. 'Before the Masai get themselves organised. If we can catch up with Fischer's party . . .'

Adrian looked at Bar, who had seen his mother shot. Then he looked at Kurt. 'Where is she?' he asked in a low voice.

'We . . . we buried her,' Kurt said. 'It happened three days ago.'

'Where?'

Kurt looked at Pitzer. He understood he was trembling on the brink of physical destruction.

'Here.' Pitzer led Adrian away from the houses, to where a simple grave had been dug in the earth.

'Erect a cairn,' Adrian said.

Pitzer nodded. 'Omar . . .'

'You,' Adrian said, pointing at the little man. 'You do it, or by God, I will break your neck here and now.'

Pitzer licked his lips, then nodded and hurried towards the wood in search of stones.

Adrian remained looking down at the fresh-turned earth. He almost wanted to dig it up to look at her. But three days was too long in this climate; he would see only horror. And he could remember her, her stately grace, her very real beauty . . . her sensuality. The disastrous course his life had taken had been no fault of hers, but her association with him had caused her death in the end.

He went back to the house, where Kurt and the women watched him.

'We really must hurry,' Kurt said. 'Every minute is precious if we are going to make it.'

'You are not going to make it,' Adrian told him. 'The Masai are already on their way, and they would catch up with you long before you could even reach the forest.'

'We cannot stay here to be murdered.'

'You can do what you like,' Adrian said. 'I have done with you. You tricked me, you tricked us all, into coming here. For your own profit. Your trickery has cost me the love of the woman I hold dearest in all the world, and now it has also cost the life of the woman who seems to have held me dearest in all the world. Because I believe you *were* saving the lives of Jo and Mandy, or thought you were, I will not kill you now. But I wish nothing more

193

to do with you. Try to stop me, and I *will* kill you.'

'So you will abandon us to the mercy of the Masai, and make off yourself,' Kurt sneered.

'I am abandoning *you*,' Adrian said. 'I am not running away.' He went to his house to collect his gear. Without a word, Safah followed him.

A foot sounded on the verandah. 'Where will you go?' Amanda asked.

'Away from here,' Adrian replied. 'Pack your things.'

She hesitated and licked her lips. 'Kurt is my husband.'

'He will not stop you leaving. I will see to that.'

'I did not mean that. He is my husband, and the father of my child. I cannot desert him.'

'He is a scoundrel and a murderer, Mandy.'

'He is my husband,' she said stubbornly. 'And he was saving my life.'

'And his own.' He gazed into her eyes. 'I cannot force you to come with me. But if you do not, I can no longer help you. Or protect you from that man.' He finished collecting his few belongings and hefted his pack. Safah was also ready. He went on to the verandah and faced Joanna; Catherine was in her arms.

'If you will wait for five minutes,' she said. 'I will accompany you.'

For a moment Adrian was too surprised to speak.

'I cannot stay here, either,' Joanna said quietly.

'Then I will wait for you.' He went outside, heart pounding. He could not believe it was happening.

Amanda followed him from the house.

'I must stay with my husband,' she repeated. Her face was more set and determined than he had ever known it. She did love Kurt, whatever his faults. And now, it seemed, whatever his crimes.

He sighed. 'I will speak on your behalf to the chief and ask him to allow you safe conduct out of his land. But you cannot stay here.'

Kurt gazed at him for several seconds. Then he nodded. 'I have no intention of staying here. Just get us that safe conduct.'

Adrian found Bar still sitting in his corner, staring into space. 'Your mother is dead,' he said in Masai. 'You saw this happen?'

Bar gazed at him.

'So now we must leave this place,' Adrian said.

'You must kill Bwana Von,' Bar said.

Adrian shook his head. 'I believe he acted as he thought necessary, no matter how horrible the deed. But we cannot stay here any more. Come.'

The boy hesitated, then got to his feet and went outside, where Safah waited with the packs, the rifles and ammunition, and some food. They could carry no tents or heavy gear.

'Where will you go?' Amanda asked. She had made her decision and she would not now change it, but she was mortally afraid. Her lips trembled and her eyes were filled with tears.

'In the first instance, to the Masai,' Adrian told her. 'To save your lives, if I can. But you must understand that there is no way you can remain here.'

Amanda nodded. 'Will I ever see you again?'

'Of course. I hope.' He kissed her on the cheek. 'Take care.' He looked at Kurt. 'She is your responsibility, Kurt. Or I swear, I will see *you* again.'

'She is my wife,' Kurt said with dignity.

Joanna was now ready as well, wearing her safari outfit of blouse and skirt, thick boots, knapsack, sun topee, and rifle slung on her shoulder, with Catherine in her arms.

'I will carry the baby,' Adrian said, and she gave her to him. Then she embraced Amanda. They did not speak.

'Let's go,' Adrian said. 'There is not much time.'

They walked away from the houses and the stream, and Adrian paused to look back. Kurt, Amanda, Pitzer and

195

Omar stood on the verandah, watching them; Amanda held Heinrich in her arms, but she raised one hand in farewell. He turned away from them and walked on; the inevitable had happened.

The sun was already low, so they pitched camp only some four miles from the copse. As they had no tents they lit a small fire, cooked a quick meal and settled themselves for the night. It was no time for reflections or plans. Joanna fed Catherine, took a morsel of food for herself and a sip of water, then glanced at Adrian; they had not spoken since leaving the ranch. Now she said, 'I want you to know that I am sorry about Lulu.'

'Thank you.'

'I hated her,' Joanna said, speaking quietly. 'But to see her shot like that, in cold blood . . . He was holding her arm and was only a foot away from her. He blew her head right off.' She shuddered. 'It was horrible.'

He made no reply, and she wrapped herself in her blanket, Catherine in her arms, and turned her back on the men.

Adrian dared not think about what she had said. Instead he followed her example, with Bar; he had spent sufficient time in this country now to know that wild animals will not willingly approach humans, unless attracted by the scent of freshly killed game; the fire would be sufficient to discourage even an inquisitive leopard.

Safah said goodnight, and then asked, 'You go to the Masai, bwana?'

Adrian nodded. 'But I think they will come to us first.'

The Masai were there at dawn, some hundred of them – all the Morani of the clan, led by Uthuli and Kainairju – standing gazing at them. Adrian went to speak with the chief.

'These are sad times, my son,' Uthuli said.

'Sad times,' Adrian agreed.

'Where are you going?'

'I was on my way to visit your kraal.'

'You have left Von?'

Adrian nodded.

'That is as it should be,' Uthuli said. 'He has murdered your woman, and my daughter. You have killed him?'

'No,' Adrian said.

Uthuli gazed at him, trying to understand. Then he nodded. 'You have left him to my vengeance. I am pleased.'

'No,' Adrian said again.

Uthuli gazed at him, and Kainairju snorted. Several of the Morani drummed their spear hafts on the ground. 'He has murdered your woman,' Uthuli repeated. 'And my daughter.'

'Lulu was killed because Kainairju in defiance of your promise of goodwill, sought to take Von's woman by force,' Adrian said.

Uthuli looked into his eyes, then turned to his son. 'You have not spoken of this.'

'Would you not have two lion-haired creatures in your kraal?' Kainairju demanded.

'She belongs to another,' Adrian said. 'And she is my sister. You have broken your father's word. You cannot condemn Von for defending her and himself.'

Uthuli considered. 'Then you do not condemn him for murdering your woman? And my daughter?'

'I cannot condemn him,' Adrian said. 'However much I may hate him for the deed. Thus we are no longer friends, and thus I have left his kraal with my servant, and . . .' He glanced back at Joanna. 'My other woman.'

'Where will you go?' Uthuli asked mildly.

Adrian took a long breath. But there was no help for it; he would only save Amanda by sacrificing himself. 'I will come to the kraal of the Masai.'

Uthuli nodded. 'I am pleased.'

'But only if Von is left unharmed, to leave this land with his woman and his servants and his child.' He looked at

Kainairju. 'I must have your word, and the word of your son, on this.'

Kainairju's lip curled. 'You seek to instruct us, Bar-clay? You have seen how we deal with white men.'

Adrian looked at him. 'I see only a coward who was sent by his father to scout the white people and instead took his men and attacked a man for whom he had sworn friendship.'

Again Uthuli turned to his son. 'You have not spoken of this. You spoke of tracking the white men into the forest, of returning by way of Von's kraal, of his hurling his long spears at you and your people. Can this be true?'

Kainairju snorted.

'His spears are still sticking from the wood of Von's kraal,' Adrian said. 'You may see for yourself.'

Uthuli continued to gaze at his son.

'He is a white man,' Kainairju growled. 'They are our enemies. Have we not seen this? They should be destroyed. All white men should be destroyed.' He stared at Adrian, afraid to utter the obvious.

'You have lied to me,' Uthuli said. 'And you have broken the word of your father and your people. I shall not look upon your face again.'

He spoke quietly, but there could be no doubting the finality of his decision, or the dreadful sentence he had just pronounced. Kainairju glanced at his father, then at Adrian. Then he looked at the Morani, but they stood silent, watching him.

Kainairju stamped his spear haft in the dust, then turned and walked away, towards the north. Adrian let him go. He did not doubt that if the Masai did intend to return to the ranch alone, Kurt and Pitzer and Omar would be capable of dealing with him.

'My son has broken my word,' Uthuli said. 'He is no longer my son. You are my only son. But Von killed my daughter. He must die. It is our law. It need be no concern of

198

yours. We will not harm your sister. Rather will we do as my son suggested and bring her into my kraal, to live with us and belong to one of my young men.'

'No,' Adrian said.

'You cannot interfere, my son. It is the law.'

'If you go to kill Von,' Adrian said, 'then you must kill me. Kill us all. First.'

Uthuli stared at him, and he stared back. Behind him he heard the click of the bolt being drawn on Safah's rifle. And then another click. Joanna might not understand what was being said, but she understood they had reached the critical point.

Uthuli was puzzled. 'You would die, for the man who murdered your wife, my daughter?'

'I gave him my word,' Adrian said. 'He must go unmolested. He will leave the high country and never return. But he must be free to go.'

Uthuli considered, and made a decision; he valued possession of Adrian even more than he wished vengeance on his daughter's murderer. 'Von will be allowed to leave the high country in peace,' he said.

'I must ask for your word.'

'You have my word,' Uthuli said. 'Von will be allowed to leave in peace.'

'And with him, his wife and child and servants,' Adrian insisted.

Uthuli inclined his head. 'None of his people will be harmed.' He turned to face the Morani. 'This is my word.'

'Then I am pleased,' Adrian said. 'Now, let us go to your kraal.'

'Are we free to leave now?' Joanna asked, walking at his side as they accompanied the Masai; he carried Catherine.

'We are going to their kraal,' Adrian told her.

'Oh.' She considered this for a few seconds. 'For how long?'

'For the rest of our lives, maybe.'

She stopped walking. 'You have to be kidding me.'

'They wish me to live with them,' Adrian explained. 'That is the price I have accepted, to save the lives of Kurt and Mandy. And Heinrich.'

'Oh, Jesus,' she muttered. Again she walked in silence for some minutes. Then she said, 'They have no use for me. I don't have yellow hair.'

'I suppose they don't.'

'Then . . .'

'I have use for you,' he said.

Her head turned sharply. 'You mean I am your prisoner?'

'I mean you are my wife.'

She looked away from him. 'No,' she said vehemently. 'I cannot be your wife. You were married already when you . . . took me to Gretna Green.'

'I was never married to Lulu,' he said. 'Not in any Christian ceremony.'

'That is specious,' she argued. 'She was your woman. She certainly thought she was married to you.'

He sighed. 'I suppose you're right. I did not take it so seriously. She was presented to me by Uthuli, and I accepted the gift. Then when Kurt and I escaped, I thought the episode was finished. Kurt reminded me that it might not be, when he asked me to come back up here with him, and I laughed at him. I feel very guilty about the whole thing, believe me. That does not alter the fact that I did not believe she was my wife when I married you – or that I love you.'

'Ha,' she commented.

'Or that you are now the mother of my child. And I have a son, as well, who needs a mother.'

Joanna glanced at Bar, walking on the other side of his father, and shuddered. 'I am sure you can find a willing mother for him from amongst his own people.'

'And for Catherine?'

Her chin came up. 'You would take away my child?'

200

'No. I am making sure that you stay to care for her.'

She stopped walking again and turned to face him. 'What are you going to do, rape me every night?'

'I'd rather appeal to your good sense.'

'Ha,' she said again. 'I'll kill myself before I ever submit to you again.'

When they camped that night, the Masai watched them with interest. As she was the only woman in the party, it seemed natural for her to take her meal by herself, but afterwards they certainly expected her to get beneath Adrian's blanket. 'I think you must,' he told her.

'I will not.'

'Listen, you can keep your drawers on, and I promise not to touch you. Bring Catherine with you. But if the Masai get the idea that you are *not* my woman, one of the Morani will take you for himself. Do you want that?'

She gave him a bitter look, but obeyed, retaining both blouse and drawers, and hugging Catherine in her arms as she turned her back on him. Lying there, with his thighs against her buttocks, he was very tempted to force the issue there and then. But he had given his word, and he did not believe she would hold out much longer. He rolled over himself, wedged them backside to backside, and slept. He had not had the time or the inclination to analyse what had happened, but he did know that he had reached a great watershed in his life. Their lives. For all his sadness over the death of Lulu, his anger with Kurt, his feeling of loss that it might be years before he saw Amanda again, if he ever did, he was happy.

Next day they reached the Valley, and even Joanna found it difficult to maintain her mood of anger and outrage. The Masai chose to descend by one of the more gentle escarpments, where the greatest drop was hardly more than a hundred feet, but for that very reason the game was even more plentiful here than on the high ground, and she

201

immediately wanted to shoot one of the impala that came inquisitively close. But Adrian restrained her. The Masai would not eat game, so the flesh would be wasted, and he had not yet made up his mind whether or not to reveal her artistry with a rifle to the Morani — theirs was a male-oriented world in which no female could possibly stand comparison, and clearly none of them understood the use of the revolver that hung from her belt, and with which she was as accurate as with her rifle.

But in any event, the walk northward towards Lake Naivasha and Uthuli's kraal soon drove thoughts of mere hunting from her mind. In the several years he had been away, Adrian had himself forgotten both the wonder and the beauty of this blessed land. Like Joanna he found himself staring at the volcanic cones which marked the valley floor, a constant reminder of the cataclysmic forces which must have led to the creation of this gigantic fault in the earth's surface. Like her he wanted to clap his hands at the sight of the first of the lakes, even if it was little more than a gigantic mud bath, surrounded by the gleaming white salt crystals which lay heaped on the bank.

'Salt water, so far from the sea?' she asked.

'It's caused by the high rate of evaporation,' he explained. 'But Lake Naivasha is fresh.'

That evening they came to Uthuli's kraal, and here again Adrian realised that his memory had often played him false. He recalled the clan as being far larger than it actually was, and in fact there were no more than forty huts surrounded by the thorn fence. The pasturage beyond contained however a good two hundred head of cattle.

'Are those all Uthuli's?' Joanna asked.

'Technically they belong to the clan,' Adrian said. 'But as Uthuli is head of the clan, I suppose you could say they are his.'

She was looking at the relatively small area under cultivation, the straight but shallow furrows filled with brown,

drooping barley stalks. 'I guess they're not great vegeta-
rians,' she remarked.

'Their crops are really emergency rations,' he agreed.
'Believe it or not, they live off milk.'

She shot him a glance, suspecting that he was making fun
of her, and he grinned. 'Diluted with bull's blood, of
course.'

'Ugh,' she commented, and then grew pensive as she
gazed at the women who had come out to greet them,
particularly the young girls, with their high, conical breasts
and slender, swaying hips. 'Do we spend the night here?' she
asked, uneasily.

'We'll camp on the banks of Naivasha,' he decided. 'It's
only a couple of miles away.' Because he knew that would set
a seal on her fascination with her new surroundings, and as
he had hoped, she exclaimed in wonder when she first saw
the flamingoes, even if she seemed more taken by the great
pelicans resting sleepily on the stumps of long-dead trees in
the shallow water.

'Here we shall make our home,' he told her.

She glanced at him, flushed and looked away again.

'Here will be a fine place, bwana,' Safah agreed.

'And for you.' Adrian clapped him on the shoulder. 'We
shall have to find you a woman.'

Safah gave one of his rare smiles. 'If a Masai will come to
a Somali, bwana.'

Adrian felt guilty that his grief over Lulu's death should be
tempered by the knowledge that she had been the great
stumbling block between Joanna and himself; if he would
never have considered sending Lulu away, both because of
Bar and because she was Uthuli's daughter, he could not
now escape a sense of relief that the episode was closed. He
knew this was an entirely dishonourable emotion, but he
was used to looking at situations honestly and realistically –
it was the only road to survival at sea and, he was beginning

to understand, in the primitive world as well.

If he was also concerned about Amanda, he reflected that she could hardly come to any great harm as long as she was so much in love with Kurt, a love which he, for all his coarseness and arrogance, seemed to reciprocate. If Adrian still believed that Kurt had married his sister simply as an additional possible negotiating factor with the Masai, it was equally tempting to believe that during their adventures together a true relationship had sprung up between them, cemented by the birth of Heinrich, and if they were returning to civilisation, it was possible that Kurt might introduce her to that society she would grace so elegantly.

His only real worry was that his brother-in-law, once he realised that the Masai were not going to attack him, might choose to stay. In which case he would have to be evicted, with all that would entail. But he would have to go; Adrian had given Uthuli his word on that.

And now he was living where he had always wanted to live, and amongst friends. As before, Uthuli had recognised that the white men did not live as the Masai did, and the chieftain was determined not to offend his 'son' – now his only son – in any way; by the happiest chance, not only had the previous year's harvest been the best within living memory, but the tribe's cattle had never been healthier. Adrian was well aware that these things went in cycles which had absolutely nothing to do with his presence, but he was not going to tell the chief that; if the next five years were as good as the previous had apparently been bad, then he could only benefit – and five years was a long time. Thus, to his enormous relief, when he refused to allow Joanna also to be inducted into the clan, Uthuli did not argue. Adrian did not tell Joanna from what he had saved her – the Masai also practised female circumcision.

Meanwhile, there was a great deal to do. He began with a house, helped as before by the Masai women as carriers, and the Morani, when they were in the mood, as builders, but now with himself as the driving spirit instead of Kurt. With Uthuli's agreement he chose a site about a mile from the Masai kraal, beside a bubbling stream which fed the lake some hundred yards away. Here he constructed, over the next six months, a solid, two-storeyed building, which comprised drawing room, dining room, kitchen and parlour downstairs, and three bedrooms upstairs, each floor fronted by a deep verandah. He even installed a bathroom, something his mother and father had not possessed in their Southampton cottage. Of course there was no piped water, and Safah had to empty the slops three times a day – but one day, he dreamed, there would be piped water. It was slow work, but so satisfactory; to see his own design rising solidly under his own hands; Uthuli came down every day from the kraal to inspect it in wonder. 'You build a kraal to last forever,' he commented.

'It is the white man's way,' Adrian told him.

To his pleasure, even Joanna could not resist the attraction of creation, and gave him her opinions and ideas. After the roof was on, one day she saw to it that there was a gourd of fresh-cut flowers in every room.

Then it was a matter of starting on the furniture. 'When I am finished,' he told her, 'we will have a palace. A palace fit for a queen.'

She gave a little twisted smile. She had allowed herself no surrender; she continued to sleep in a room to herself and Catherine, although during the day, with his warning about the Morani in mind, she played the attentive wife and willingly shared the cooking duties with Safah. She was marking time, Adrian knew. For what, he did not know. But escape was impossible, with Catherine to think of. And her imprisonment, if she did so consider it in her heart, was at least in the most beautiful surroundings on earth.

He did not revisit the ranch until Uthuli's Morani brought word that it had indeed been abandoned; they returned with the flock of sheep, which had been attacked

205

by a leopard. Typically Kurt, Adrian thought, just to abandon the helpless animals, but he was enormously relieved that his brother-in-law had indeed done the sensible thing in leaving, and that the danger of any further confrontation was past. Yet he could not help reflecting on the whims of fate, that he should be the one making their dream come true, while Kurt had had to admit defeat. Fate, or the faults in Kurt's character? But how would *he* have reacted, faced with a similar situation? Perhaps Fate had indeed intervened, and arranged his absence when Kainairju decided to abduct Amanda?

After the Long Rains, the Masai prepared for their annual migration. Uthuli came to the house to see Adrian. 'You will be here when we return?' he asked.

'I will be here,' Adrian said.

Uthuli gazed into his eyes. 'Once I had a son and a daughter,' he said. 'Now they are dead. I am an old man. My wives do not bear my fruit any longer. Now I have only you, my son.'

'I will be here,' Adrian promised again. 'But is not your real son still alive somewhere? He will come home, one day, and you will be reconciled.'

'My son is dead,' Uthuli declared. 'Even if he has escaped the lion and the leopard, the desert and the hatred of other men, to me he is dead. I have only you, Bar-clay.' He looked at little Bar, who was in fact no longer so very little and was clearly going to be a stalwart lad. 'And the boy.'

'I will be here,' Adrian said.

They stood on the verandah to watch the clan move out, Safah and himself and Bar. As before, they had been left with a stock of grain and some sheep to see them through until the end of the year. The Masai moved in a great cloud of dust, the cattle lowing and the sheep bleating, the children running to and fro, the women chasing them, the men walking with stately strides. The scene was almost biblical.

It was several hours before the sounds of their progress died away and quiet settled over Lake Naivasha.

'Four months of heaven,' Adrian said. 'Or can it be a heaven for you, Safah, without a woman?'

Safah smiled. 'There will be a woman, bwana, when they return in the autumn. It is arranged.'

'You sly old devil,' Adrian cried, and shook his hand.

'And for you?' Safah asked, his smile fading.

Adrian looked down the sloping grass to the edge of the lake, where Joanna was sitting in the sunshine with her daughter. A little way away Bar stood up to his knees in the water, fishing, but Joanna paid no attention to him.

'A man should have a woman,' Safah said. 'And when that woman is the mother of his child . . .' It was the nearest Safah had ever come to giving him personal advice.

Adrian walked down the slope. How beautiful she looked. She had allowed herself to relax in her dress; she had discarded stockings and shoes, as well as red flannel underwear; her blouse was open at the throat to allow that magnificent flesh to brown. Yet, incongruously, she still wore her topee with its veil, sadly torn, to keep the complexion of her face as pale as possible. Her hair was gathered in a bow on the nape of her neck. She was irresistible, a nymph playing with her child. He knew she must be aware of how much she titillated him.

He stood above her and she looked up. 'I would like to swim in the lake,' she said. 'It is so calm and peaceful. I have seen no sign of any crocodile, or even a large fish. Do you suppose you could take the boy and keep him at the house for half an hour?'

'You cannot swim in the lake,' he said.

Her chin came up. 'Because you say so?'

'Because the Masai say it is dangerous. There is some kind of disease in the lake which attacks the stomach and can be very dangerous. It is especially dangerous to small children.'

She hugged Christine to her breast, almost as if fearing he

207

was about to dip the child into the water. 'We drink from the stream.'

'Apparently the disease, whatever it is, only exists in still water. The stream is quite safe, but in those shallows, even, the disease can enter the body through any natural orifice. So the Masai say, and I believe them.'

She made no comment, but gazed at the lake as if it had suddenly become an enemy instead of a thing of beauty.

'The Masai have gone,' he said.

'I heard them.'

'We shall be alone for four months,' he said.

'Alone.' She shivered, every muscle quivering.

He wanted her. God, how he wanted her. He had to have her, or go mad with desire. 'Bar,' he called.

'Yes, Father,' the boy answered in English, coming out of the water. 'I have caught nothing.'

'Be sure you wash your legs with water from the stream,' Adrian said. 'Now, I want you to take your sister up to the house.'

'Yes, Father.' He came towards them.

'No,' Joanna snapped, starting to her feet.

Adrian caught her by the hair before she could run away.

'Oh,' she gasped, twisting her head so violently her hat fell off. 'You cannot let him touch her. He is a . . .'

'Say it, and I'll hit you,' he warned. 'He has Masai blood. But he is my son, and Catherine is his sister. Give her to him, or he will watch me beat you.'

She snorted in fury and bit her lip because the grip on her hair was hurting her scalp. After a moment's hesitation, she held out the baby girl, who was looking at her parents with enormous eyes. Bar took his sister with great care, hugging her to himself as he had seen Joanna do.

'Take her to the house,' Adrian said again, 'and amuse her until her mother can come to her.'

'Yes, Father.' Bar walked up the grass towards the house.

'And take good care of her,' Adrian called after him.

'Yes, Father.'

'Will you let me go now, please?' Joanna asked.

He released her hair, and she sank to her knees.

'I suppose it pleases you to humiliate me in front of the servants.'

'Bar is not a servant. Neither is Safah. Nor was Safah looking. Don't you think it's time you stopped acting the fool?'

She turned, her eyes blazing. 'The fool? I want out! I want to go home and forget that I ever saw you. I want to bare my bottom to Papa and tell him to beat me until I'm raw, for being such a fool. I deserve every punishment he can think of. See, I'm not denying the fault is all mine. You swam into my life and you were everything I had ever dreamed of. Tall, blond and handsome. And I was stupid enough to fall, hook, line and sinker. I guess the fact that you had lived in Africa clinched it. That's another area in which I need my head examined; I actually wanted to come to this Godforsaken place. So I made a set at you. Sure, I was escaping Papa and his absurd notions and that sickly sweet New York existence and Jerry Bailey and shipbuilding and petty hypocrisies and everything in life that I hate. Sure, I knew if I didn't run I'd wind up being crushed by those things for the rest of my life. Sure, the fault was mine. But I've suffered for it. Jesus, I have suffered for it. Now I want out. Out, out, out! You are breaking the law, keeping me here. You have kidnapped me. And now you have assaulted me. You are a louse and a rat and a bastard and . . . and a white nigger!' she shouted.

Adrian reached for her. She tried to duck under his arm, but he caught her easily enough and with no effort stretched her on the grass with a thump which left her winded. He knelt beside her and released the waistband of her skirt, then rolled her on to her face to unfasten the buttons, and gently slid the skirt past her thighs, looking down at her, desire swelling until he thought he would burst.

'It'll be rape,' she gasped.

'Not with my wife.'

'I'm *not* your wife,' she screamed. 'You married me bigamously.'

'That's not true.' He stood up and stripped himself. 'Anyway, there is no law up here, save my will. You'd better get used to that.'

She stared at him. 'Oh, God,' she whispered. 'Oh God . . . Adrian . . . please.'

'I love you,' he said.

'And I hate you,' she snapped and sat up.

He put his hand on her shoulder, gently laid her flat again and waited for her to fight him, uncertain how far he would really carry this. For a moment he thought she was going to, then she suddenly relaxed, like a punctured balloon. She lay absolutely still, staring at him, while he unbuttoned her blouse and sat her up to ease it from her shoulders, then took down her drawers – she wore nothing else. Still she did not move, even when he touched her as he wanted. When he was ready, he rolled her on to her face, then changed his mind, because he wanted to look at her face. Her eyes were wide when he turned her on her back again, but still she would not fight him, even when he parted her legs while he made his entry as gently as he could. It was all but eighteen months since he had touched her. Now she lay still as he climaxed.

Then she wept, softly and quietly. He got off her and looked down at her, and wanted to die. 'I am sorry,' he said.

She sat up, reached for her blouse and pulled it on, then stood up and stepped into her skirt.

'I do love you, so very much,' he said.

Still she would not speak. She stooped, placed her topee on her head, picked up her drawers, holding them crumpled in her hand, and began to walk up the slope to the house.

'All right,' Adrian said. 'You win. I will not touch you again.'

For a moment she stopped, waiting.

He went up to her. 'I have got nothing, save you and the child. But if it is what you truly wish, as soon as the Masai return, I will seek permission from the chief to take you and Catherine to the coast.'

'Is it really necessary to ask permission of an African chief?' she asked. 'There is nothing to stop us leaving now.'

'I gave Uthuli my word,' he reminded her, 'that I would be here when he returned. I shall not break my word, either to him or to you.'

She resumed walking again.

Suddenly they were almost friends. She had his word that she could leave, and in a sense it was a relief to him as well. Much as he loved her, wanted her, dreamed of her even when she was sleeping in the same house as himself, he was not mentally equipped to play the gaoler, or to be totally selfish. He knew that there was no physical force to prevent him keeping her here for the rest of her life, to rape her whenever his urge for her became overwhelming, to watch his daughter grow. But that would be to abandon the last civilised ethic he possessed. Besides, he could not stand seeing her unhappy, while her happiness was a joy to behold. Now she smiled, and even played with Bar from time to time. She could act the mother he wanted her to be, with an end in sight.

He and Safah worked at creating furniture for the house, and at adding various refinements. Safah was puzzled at this, as he was well aware of the arrangement for the following year, and while he knew that Adrian would honour his pact with Uthuli and come back, he could not understand the necessity for creating a somewhat European-style house, on a lavish scale, when the only woman Bwana Barclay was ever going to share it with would be a Masai. But as usual, he never argued.

Adrian was more than ever determined to create a proper

211

home in the valley. Of course he recognised that his motive was at least partly to make Joanna regret what she was leaving behind. But it was equally because, for the first time since the shock of arriving at Kurt's 'ranch' and discovering how he had been tricked, he was finding it possible to think of the future. He was here, living in paradise. It was undoubtedly a paradise which would attract other white men in the future. But he was here first, and had achieved a special relationship with the Masai. It would be criminal to waste the opportunity, however vague the future.

'What crops do you suppose would grow here, Safah?' he asked.

The Somali considered the matter. 'Almost everything, because you could irrigate your soil even in the dry season, from the lake. But the grain the Masai grow is the easiest to cultivate.'

'And they grow enough for their needs. I was thinking of a cash crop.'

Safah considered some more. 'Perhaps coffee would do well, if there was sufficient shade.'

'What do they use on the coast?'

'Banana trees, bwana. These have big leaves, which will shade the coffee plants until they are fully developed.'

'Well then, we must get some coffee seedlings.' He grinned. 'And bananas.'

'The Masai do not know of coffee,' Safah pointed out.

'I was not thinking of the Masai.'

'How would you get your crop to the coast?' Safah asked.

'I think the coast is going to come to us, soon enough,' Adrian told him. 'I am surprised it has not already done so. If we had a coffee crop ready and waiting . . .'

'It will be necessary to have the cash first, to purchase the plants,' Safah pointed out.

Adrian nodded. 'I am going to need cash in any event, to buy Bibi Joanna's passage and provide her with money for the journey. When we go down to the coast, we will hunt on the way. For elephant.'

'Oh, that would be superb.' Joanna had been listening to their discussion, obviously only stopping herself from joining in by sheer willpower. But now she could no longer restrain her enthusiasm. 'I've always wanted to hunt elephant.'

'Then we can market the tusks in Mombasa and be rich.' Adrian smiled. 'Kurt's idea. But it'll give us a cash base.'

That night she oiled and polished her rifle, imagining they were leaving the next day. But a week later, her enthusiasm vanished in a cloud of despair; she missed her period.

8

After another month there could be no doubt. 'I hate you,' Joanna screamed. 'God, how I hate you. Sometimes I feel like killing you.'

'I'm sorry,' he said. 'But it's additional proof that you and I were made for each other – every time I enter you, you become pregnant. However . . . you need not have the child.'

She stared at him.

'I am sure Safah and I could induce a miscarriage,' he said. 'Or, certainly, when the Masai women come back in January . . .'

'No,' she snapped. 'Never.'

He had not expected her to agree. She was, above everything else, instinctively a mother. 'Then we shall have to delay your departure,' he said.

'Until you make me pregnant again,' she said bitterly. 'I shall lay my bones in this horrid place.'

'That is up to you,' he reminded her. 'I have promised not to touch you again, unless invited to do so.'

'That'll be the day.'

'Well then, as soon as you and the child are strong enough to travel, we will leave for the coast.'

'Two God-damned years,' she moaned.

He grinned. 'I'll have the furniture finished by then.'

He was, of course, delighted. He could not believe that she hated him as much as she pretended, and if she were going to be here for another two years at the very least – one could hardly take a four-hundred mile safari with a baby at the breast – he firmly believed that two people living together, and sharing two children, had also to love. But he fully intended to keep his word this time, and set to work to build a dower house some hundred yards from the main building, in which she could install herself if she chose. As she did choose. He refused to take offence, and to make sure he kept his word – and also, he hoped, perhaps to inspire a little jealousy in her – he took a Masai woman when the clan returned in the new year.

Uthuli was delighted, as was Safah, who now also had a bride. The pair were sisters, called Sita and Saba – that these happened to be the Swaheli words for six and seven indicated the many years of contact between the Masai and the coast, however much the men of the high country regarded all others as their natural enemies.

Adrian had no idea whether or not the two girls were actually the sixth and seventh children, or daughters, of their mother. They were a charming couple, as beautiful as most Masai girls, whose sole aim in life appeared to be to please their husbands and masters, and they filled the house with laughter and sensuality, keenly aware that they were living in a situation achievable by none of their compatriots.

Joanna accepted the situation coldly, but by then her belly was swollen and she was in a fairly bitter state anyway. Yet Adrian noted that she did not turn him away when he went up to her cottage every afternoon to pass the time

214

of day and play with Catherine, nor did she send Bar away when the boy visited her, which was also almost every day.

Her incapacity, while frustrating for her, was also, he reminded himself, frustrating for him, and not in any sexual sense. In the spring of 1883 he was twenty-six years old and becoming aware that he could hardly count himself a success if he merely lotus-ate on the banks of Lake Naivasha for the rest of his life. The future, which now had to encompass three children to be educated and established, was becoming increasingly urgent. In addition, and even more frustrating, he had no idea what was happening in the rest of the world, and how Amanda was faring, or his mother. Whether, indeed, Molly Barclay was alive or dead. In the emotional upset of Lulu's murder, he only remembered long after the crisis that he had quite forgotten to ask Amanda to explain the situation to Molly, and had not even sent a greeting. Undoubtedly Amanda would have done so on his behalf, but that did not make up for the fact that he had not seen his mother for over two years, and there seemed little prospect of seeing her for longer than that.

He attempted to discuss the matter of a visit to the coast with Uthuli, to explain his aims and intentions, and found the chief both bewildered and suspicious. 'This money you say you need,' Uthuli observed. 'Is it food?'

'It can be used to buy food,' Adrian explained.

'Buy?'

'It is a form of barter,' Adrian said. 'But on a much wider scale. If I shoot an elephant and bring the tusks to you and ask you for cattle in exchange, you may agree, supposing you have cattle to get rid of, and you had a use for the ivory. But I could not exchange the tusks for anything you did not have to trade, and I could only do so if you wanted the ivory. But if I take the tusks to Mombasa, there are always people there who are willing to buy ivory for money, and with the money, I can buy everything I wish, from many different

215

people, each of whom may have only one of the things I need. But they will all barter for money, because they can then use the money to barter for themselves.'

Uthuli clearly did not understand, and fastened on one word. 'Mombasa?'

'It is a city, a vast kraal, far away from here, on the shores of the great ocean.'

'I have heard of this "ocean",' Uthuli said doubtfully, 'from the Arabs . . .' He glanced at Safah, still not wholly unsuspicious of the Somali's motives in being in his country. 'And I have never believed them. Can there be any water greater than Lake Naivasha?'

'Many times greater,' Adrian told him. 'Many, many times greater.'

Uthuli looked more doubtful yet, but he certainly was not going to call Bar-clay a liar. As usual, he preferred to concentrate on essentials. 'An elephant's tusk is very heavy,' he pointed out. 'Even you could not carry one very far. As for more than one . . .'

'I would go to the Kikuyu and obtain bearers,' Adrian explained.

'The Kikuyu are our enemies,' Uthuli announced, in a voice which firmly ended the discussion.

'Actually, I'm sure he can be persuaded,' Adrian told Joanna when he visited her that afternoon. 'All I have to do is work on him.'

'But you cannot go until I have had the child, and can travel,' she said. 'You promised to take me with you.'

'I will keep my promise. But we're talking about two years. If then. Taking small children into the jungle . . . it doesn't make any sense. And by then, just for instance, will you have anything which is not in rags?' He looked pointedly at her many times mended skirt and blouse.

'Sure I do. I have a complete outfit virtually untouched.' Now she looked at his equally tattered shirt and trousers. 'If you had been more careful with your clothes you'd have no problem either.'

'Maybe, if I had a wife to look after me, I'd have even less of a problem.' She made no reply to that, so he went on, 'I still think I should make one hunting safari now – pave the way, so to speak – and then we can make another when you can travel.'

'No,' she said. 'When you leave, I leave. You promised. And you cannot possibly leave me here by myself.'

She was absolutely right, of course, as she had made no attempt to learn Masai and relied upon Safah or himself to interpret for her. Nor could she possibly fend for herself while pregnant. And what was a year or two longer, in these surroundings?

The following month they received another invasion. This was a very odd one; the Masai appeared one day escorting a straggling band of terrified African bearers and a lone white man, who introduced himself as Mr Joseph Thompson, from Dumfriesshire, in Scotland. Adrian was amazed to see him, and still more amazed when Thompson told his tale.

Although only twenty-nine years of age, he had been in Africa for some eight years, arriving first in Zanzibar – just about the time he and his father had been putting their own expedition together in Mombasa, Adrian realised – to serve as geologist with an expedition commanded by another Scot, Alexander Johnston, to explore the lakes to the south. Adrian had heard of Johnston, the son of a partner in a prominent map-making firm in Scotland, who had died upon an African safari four years before. Thompson, following Johnston's death, had taken command of the expedition, young as he was, and led it safely back to the coast.

His ambitions whetted by this experience, he had returned to England for financial backing, and received it, at last, from the Royal Geographical Society. Returning to Africa to put together an expedition of his own, he had

217

encountered Dr Fischer, and from what the doctor told him, resolved that the high country was where he must head. On Fischer's advice, he had fitted out a very large safari – some hundred and forty men, apart from bearers, all armed to the teeth and quite capable, he had supposed, of taking on the Masai. Then he had retraced Fischer's route, up from the coast opposite Zanzibar.

All had gone well until he and his band had actually reached the high country, when they had come face to face with a band of the very Morani they had determined to defeat. Thompson's 'army' had promptly insisted on ending their safari there and then, and returning to the coast. He had refused, and been abandoned, with just this handful of loyal servants. The Masai had promptly surrounded them, and would certainly have cut them to pieces, Thompson felt, had he not saved their lives by using another piece of information Dr Fischer had given him: that if he was ever in dire straits in the Masai land, to say he was a friend of Bar-clay. So here he was, and if somewhat shattered by his recent nerve-racking experience – apparently he had encountered no people like the Masai on his earlier journeys – he was totally dumbfounded by the gracious house and beautiful surroundings in which he now found himself.

'Of course, your name is well known on the coast, Mr Barclay,' he said. 'But it is presumed you are a white African, living in the most degenerate squalor. This . . .' He threw his arms wide in admiration.

Adrian scratched his head and introduced him to the very pregnant Joanna.

'My word, but this is a marvellous thing,' Thompson declared. 'Man, woman and child living here with the savages, as if in an English village. The world will never believe it.' He smiled at Joanna. 'But I will tell them of it, Mrs Barclay. You may be sure of that.'

Joanna didn't look altogether pleased at the prospect.

Adrian wanted to seize the opportunity to learn what was happening in the outside world. But little appeared to have changed since he had left it. Europe was at peace. Gladstone was still prime minister. The Queen still reigned. The Liberal Government had, the previous year, reluctantly been forced to intervene in the affairs of Egypt, and there had been a full-scale war, with Alexandria bombarded by the Royal Navy, and in which the British Army, commanded by the country's premier soldier, Sir Garnet Wolseley, had been totally victorious. And everyone, Thompson said, was reading, and talking about, a remarkable book called *Also Sprach Zarathustra*, by some obscure German philosopher with an unpronounceable name – Nietzsche. Finally, New York now actually had an electricity-generating plant, invented by Edison.

Thompson wanted to talk about the Masai. In spite of their arrogance and their treatment of him – he had apparently been roughly handled while they were bringing him to Adrian – he thought them splendid people.

'Misunderstood,' he said 'On the coast, they are legendary, especially since Fischer's failure. I spoke to Stanley about my project, you know, and when he learned where I was meaning to go, he said, "Take a thousand men or write your will." And here I am with a handful, thanks only to yourself.'

'Did you ever speak with a man called Kurt von Schlieben?' Adrian asked, heart pounding.

'Oh, Indeed I did. Your brother-in-law.'

'Where is he now?'

'Sometimes in Germany, sometimes in Zanzibar, sometimes in Mombasa. He dreams of returning here. But with never less than a thousand men. He is contributing even more than Dr Fischer to the legend of the Masai.'

'Did you ever meet his wife?'

'Oh, indeed, a most beautiful lady. Your sister, of course, Mr Barclay. The resemblance is plain. And a wonderful

219

mother. She accompanies her husband everywhere, with her two children.'

'Two children?' Joanna cried in delight; they were keeping pace with each other.

'A girl and a boy,' Thompson told her. 'And bless my soul, she gave me a message to deliver, should I ever encounter you. Both of you,' he added hastily.

'Oh, do tell,' Joanna said.

'Well, to you, Mr Barclay, she sends her love, and that of your mother.'

'Thank God for that,' Adrian said. It was the first intimation he had had that his mother was still alive.

'And to you, Mrs Barclay, one I confess I did not understand. It was simply, all is forgiven.'

Joanna looked at Adrian, eyebrows arched.

'I imagine she means your papa,' he said. 'The prodigal daughter and all that.'

'I guess you're right,' Joanna said thoughtfully.

She would now more than ever determine to go home, he thought sadly. But there was more than just Joanna on his mind. 'Is Herr von Schlieben meeting with any success in his attempts to raise an army with which to invade the highlands?' he asked Thompson.

'Not when last I heard, sir, no. But there are straws in the wind. Oh, indeed, straws in the wind. These highlands and the Masai have, as I have said, become quite legendary. As well as the enormous quantities and varieties of game and wild life to be had here. Oh, indeed. And they will be even more famous when I return, sir. And yourself, and your beautiful wife, to be sure. I intend to write a book about my travels.'

'Oh, good lord,' Joanna remarked.

'Why, Mrs Barclay, do you not wish to be famous? Why, sir, Mr Barclay, do you realise that if *you* had written an account of your adventures up here eight years ago, of your sojourn with the Masai, you would by now be immortal?

You could still do so, in fact.'

Joanna looked at Adrian.

'My wife agrees with me,' Adrian said, 'that our fame is irrelevant beside the risk of having this beautiful country spoiled by a horde of European land-grabbers.'

'Land-grabbers? Well, as to that . . .' Thompson looked offended for a moment, then recovered. 'I am sure it will all be properly organised,' he said. 'And besides, surely there is room for all?'

'Dr Fischer had the same opinion,' Adrian reminded him. 'Unfortunately, the Masai are nomadic and, admittedly, wasteful in their agricultural habits. But it is their land, and there is not room for them and anybody else.'

'Hm,' Thompson said. 'Hm. Yes, I take your point. We could have a situation such as is currently destroying the American Indian. Yes. Be sure I shall make these points in my book, Mr Barclay. And I am grateful to you for raising them.'

'Will you now return to the coast?' Joanna asked. 'You'll have to hurry; it is all but time for the Long Rains.'

'The coast, dear lady? Good heavens, no. I am not to be deterred by a little rain. I am here to explore this country. To map it. I mean to travel to the north, as far as I can. At least as far as the great striped mountain. Now that the Masai are my friends, thanks to you, of course . . .'

'Ah,' Adrian said. '*These* Masai are your friends. There are many clans living in the north who know nothing of me and will certainly be your enemies.'

'That is a chance I must take,' Thompson said. 'I do not mean to leave this country until I have completed the task given me by the society.'

Joanna and Adrian exchanged another glance but made no comment.

Thompson's determination was commendable, while his interest in everything was absorbing. He wanted to explore the lake, and was dumbfounded when he discovered the

221

Masai had no boats and had never ventured upon the water. He went crawling through the mud-flats – the water level being low – to investigate the curious flamingo nests, which looked like upside-down coal scuttles made of mud, a procedure which did not amuse the flamingoes themselves in the least. He went out on to the plain to prod the huge, red-earth termite nests, which almost resembled miniature castles and were as well defended. If the Masai had been scandalised at his intrusion on the privacy of the flamingoes, they were horrified at his intentional stirring up of insects they tended to avoid wherever possible. Nor was Adrian very pleased about this, as keeping his wooden house free of termites was his biggest headache.

But after two days of frenetic activity, Thompson and his small band were gone, following his compass to the north.

'There is one ball of fire,' Joanna commented, as they waved him out of sight. 'Now all I have to do is get home before he starts writing scurrilous tales about me.'

'I don't think you have to worry about that,' Adrian told her. 'He's never going to write any book, much less have it published.'

'Why not? If everyone is so interested in the high country and the Masai, as he says?'

'He won't ever write it, simply because he won't be alive to do so. Not if he seriously intends to travel the length and breadth of the Masai country. That would be asking too much of fortune.'

But what Thompson had told him left him worried. He had underestimated Kurt, as usual, in supposing that his experiences would lead him to abandon his dream. Kurt was not that sort of man. And with his money and connections, if he were to return to the high country with an army . . . not even the Masai would be able to stand against him, and this paradise would be utterly ruined.

There was nothing he could do about it until Joanna was

222

fit to travel, and that was still many months away.

Towards the end of the wet season she was delivered of a baby boy, whom she named John, after both of his grandfathers. That she had taken her part in choosing the name pleased Adrian enormously, and he looked for better times. And encountered a rebuff. 'You promised me I could leave, as soon as is possible,' she said. 'With Catherine. I regard Johnnie as also mine to take with me, in view of the circumstances surrounding his conception.'

He could not understand her. He was sure she did not hate him; when she was in a good mood she would laugh and talk with him as if they were the oldest of friends. But was that merely perfect dissembling on her part – and wishful thinking on his? She had claimed to hate him when Lulu appeared. He simply did not know enough about women, or about life itself, to come to a decision as to how to treat her. He could now only be patient until he could fulfil his promise.

Meanwhile, he worked to make the houses ever bigger and more comfortable, and to create a garden; he planted a lawn sloping down to the water, and if it was largely weed and there were great brown patches, the next Long Rains turned it into a green delight. He dug flower beds and installed such of the flowers from the plain as he thought might prosper, and saw them wither in the sun where they were not eaten by Thompson's termites. But he persevered.

He and Safah both took their part in the life of the Masai, tended their cattle, hunted with the Morani and enjoyed their domesticity with Sita and Saba; before the next Long Rains arrived Safah was the father of a bouncing baby boy. Somewhat to Adrian's relief, Sita did not manage to conceive, however willing a sexual partner she always proved. This both embarrassed and frightened her, but he did his best to reassure her that he had already too large a family – even if he was shortly to lose three quarters of it. He had no doubt that the real reason he could not impregnate her was that all his thoughts were centred upon the cottage across the lawn. Once or twice he even attempted advances, but these were coldly, if politely, quashed before he could even frame the words. Joanna was determined to remain wrapped up in her mood of injured dignity, pride . . . and determined chastity.

His personal misery at the thought of losing her and the children was, however, tempered by the steady rise in her spirits as the days and weeks drifted by, and Johnnie turned out to be a happy and healthy child. Adrian was sure her feelings were actually equivocal. Whatever her emotions regarding him – and he liked to suppose these were equivocal as well – or her frustration at the absence of books or other white company or indeed anything to occupy her time, save the children and the household chores, she did love Africa. She would wander off by herself to make friends with the various antelope which would come right up to the house, and she soon had them eating out of her hand. But she was clearly still determined to leave at the first opportunity.

He himself was aware of becoming excited at the prospect of revisiting even the meagre civilisation of Mombasa. But first, he had again to try to obtain the permission of Uthuli to make the long journey; quite apart from his promise to the chieftain to live out his days with the Masai, there was no possibility of their escaping with two small children; taking Catherine and Johnnie through the forest would itself be a most hazardous undertaking.

He explained all his reasons, including his fears for the future if the white men came in great numbers, and his hope of being able perhaps to postpone that day – how, he had no idea – and Uthuli thought about them. Then he said, 'What you have told me, Bar-clay, saddens me greatly. Do you know that, many years ago, there was a great man amongst our people, a mighty warrior who was also a man of much brain and foresight, a prophet. This man spoke of our future as a people, and said we were doomed. He prophesied three great calamities falling upon the Masai, all in a short space of time. The first would be an illness which would destroy our cattle. The second would be a sickness which would destroy ourselves. But the third and greatest of the evils, the evil which would bring the other two and many more besides, would be the coming of the white man. When you and your friend Von first came to us, my thought was to destroy you. But your great strength and your colour, like that of the sun, made me wish to propitiate you, in defiance of the prophet's warning. I thought I was proved right when the rains came early and our cattle, which had been sick, became strong again. But now you say that you fear the greatest of these three evils may be about to invade us. This troubles me.'

'As it troubles me, my father,' Adrian agreed. 'That is why I would like to go to the coast and discover what is truly happening.'

'But you will return,' Uthuli said. 'You are the source of our prosperity, and besides, should the white men come again in great numbers, too great even for my Morani to defeat, I need you here to speak on our behalf.'

'I will return,' Adrian said. 'This is my home. Am I not leaving my principal son and my servant and the other woman here with you? Do you think I would ever abandon them? I must return. I ask only of your Morani to accompany me as far as the border of the Kikuyu country. There I will secure bearers for the remainder of the journey.'

'Go then, and come back,' Uthuli said. 'Before the white men reach here.'

It was October 1884, and John Barclay was fifteen months old. He would not again be less vulnerable until he was an adult; perhaps not even then, Adrian thought.

'You mean I . . . we, can actually leave?' Joanna asked in disbelief.

'If you really are determined to,' Adrian said. 'I don't like the idea of taking the children through the forest and the desert, I'll tell you straight. But . . .'

'That's nonsense,' Joanna declared. 'They're just as much at risk up here as they would be on safari. We're on permanent safari here. What about those leopards we saw prowling the other night? If we took our eyes off the children for one moment we could lose them. Well, I'm not going to take my eyes off them until we step ashore in New York.'

'I was thinking more of disease,' he ventured.

'What disease? They were both born in Africa. They're not going to get disease, any more than a Masai baby does.'

'They do,' he said. 'The infant mortality is very high.'

'But these are no longer infants,' she told him triumphantly. 'Because they've been cared for, and because they're strong. Don't tell me you're going to renege now, Adrian Barclay. That would be worse than breaking your word. It'd be a crime against the children, comdemning them to a life of savagery up here, no education, no civilised behaviour, no . . .'

'I am not going to renege, as you put it,' he said. 'I just feel you are putting the children, and yourself, at unnecessary risk.'

'You have got hold of the wrong end of the stick,' she snapped. 'You put me at risk, and my unborn baby, by bringing us here. You forced Johnnie on me, regardless of the risk. Now you won't let us leave.'

'Do you really hate me that much?' he asked.

She looked down at the baby, and then to where Catherine, now a vigorous three-year-old, played with Bar in the dust outside her cottage. 'I do not think any woman can hate a man who has fathered two children for her, Adrian. But I do not think I can ever forgive you for the wrong you have done me.'

'You mean my crime in having kidnapped you and taken

226

you to paradise,' he said. 'And kept you there against your will.'

She gazed at him. 'Your crime is having made that paradise into a hell for me,' she told him.

'I do not think she means what she says, bwana,' Safah said. 'I think . . .'

'Safah, old friend,' Adrian interrupted. 'I value your council above any other's, as regards Africa. As regards women of my own race, I followed your council once before, and I have regretted it ever since.'

Safah bowed his head.

'But what is done, is done,' Adrian said. 'And now at least I have three children, even if two of them are on loan, so to speak. I will return with news. And of your family.'

'I will be grateful, bwana. But . . .' His face was anxious. 'You will return?'

'I will return,' Adrian promised him.

He was under no misapprehensions as to the difficulties which lay ahead, for all Joanna's sanguine confidence – which he supposed was a compliment to him.

In the beginning there were few problems. They travelled with a dozen of the Morani, as well as both Bar and Safah, to the plain, and then down to the forest. Here, as it was two months since the end of the Long Rains and still a month before the coming of the Short Rains – which lasted only a few weeks – the glutinous black swamp which clung to the edge of the prairie was as dry as it could ever be, and presented no obstacle.

Adrian had made very careful preparations, and constructed from buffalo hides two harnesses, one for each child, so that they could be carried papoose-style on the back. Nor were they a burden at this stage of the march, as the Morani were willing to carry Bar-clay's offspring, however anxiously Joanna might watch them every step of

227

the way. On the edge of the thick forest, however, Adrian commanded the warriors to return. Any Masai found in the country of the Kikuyu was certain to be regarded as an enemy, and quite apart from his determination not to make his journey a cause for war between the two peoples, he could not risk involving the children in any hostilities. So here Safah and Bar bid them a final farewell, the boy manfully holding back his tears, while Adrian assured them he would be back before the Long Rains, no matter what; then they loped through the trees and back on to the plain.

Suddenly the forest seemed a very lonely place. Joanna obviously also felt so too. She gave a little shiver as she adjusted her haversack over her hip, and Johnnie on her back. Adrian had Catherine on his back, and the heavier pack; each also carried a rifle and bandolier, even if they were now down to fifty cartridges between them.

'All right?' he asked.

'Sure,' she said. 'Let's go.'

But these were early days, and a relatively easy forest. Although, as he suspected, she soon found the weight a considerable burden. He had to call a halt within four hours of their first march, to allow her to sink to the ground in exhaustion. He gave her some water to drink, and she gulped it, then put a little in Johnnie's mouth; he had slept peacefully most of the way, in contrast to his sister, who had pummelled her knees into Adrian's back and kept up a steady chatter.

'I think we'd better stay put for a couple of hours, to let you rest,' he decided.

'I am perfectly capable of walking through the jungle,' she insisted. 'I did it before.'

'Not with a pack and a baby on your back. I'm sure you're perfectly capable of walking until you drop, but what do I do with you then?'

She glared at him, but was asleep within five minutes. He played little games with Catherine, who was wildly excited

228

by the trees and the butterflies, the whole adventure of going for such a long walk with her father and mother. 'I want Bar,' she said. 'Bar coming soon?'

Adrian nodded; he had not the heart to tell her she would never see Bar again. 'Soon,' he promised.

From then on they walked only four hours in the morning, and four in the afternoon. But even with this slow progress it was distressing to see Joanna wilting, and sometimes staggering. For most of the time now, he took Johnnie and Catherine together, leaving her only her pack, but she still found the going terribly hard.

He reminded himself that with every step they were nearing the land of the Kikuyu. Indeed, after four days he was sure they were in it. But they saw no sign of any Africans, until he was awakened on the fifth morning by the hiss of arrows and a stifled scream from Joanna. 'My God,' she gasped. 'We're under attack.'

'Keep down,' he snapped, and wriggled over to lie beside her, pushing Catherine in front of him; the little girl was more excited than afraid. And surely, he told himself, there was no reason to be afraid of the Kikuyu. He had visited them three times before and never received less than perfect hospitality. But there was an arrow sticking out of the tree trunk above Joanna's head, and he could not doubt that it was poisoned.

'Where are they?' she whispered, huddling Johnnie against her stomach while she levelled the rifle with her arms.

'All around us. But they can't have identified us. Do you not remember me?' he shouted out to them in Swaheli. 'I am Bar-clay, the friend of the Kikuyu. My bibi is with me. She too is your friend. Why do you attack us?'

The forest remained silent, save for the distant wail of a bush-baby.

'Maybe we should try a couple of shots,' Joanna said.

He shook his head, and a few minutes later saw one, and

then several Africans leaving their concealment to approach him. 'Stand up,' he told Joanna, and did so himself, holding Catherine by the hand.

The Kikuyu did indeed remember their friend Bar-clay, as they also remembered their other friend, Von, who had passed this way the previous year and distributed presents. But Von had told them that Bar-clay was now their enemy, who marched with the Masai, and when he returned to them would be accompanied by a Masai army. This the chief told Adrian almost apologetically, although he kept looking into the trees as if expecting the dreaded Morani to appear at any moment, even if his warriors had assured him there was no sign of them.

'The wretch,' Joanna growled.

'Yes,' Adrian agreed. 'Something to remember. Von is a liar, my friend,' he told the Kikuyu chieftain.

'But he had many presents for my people,' the chief pointed out. 'You do not have any presents.' He glanced at the children, as if wondering if they could be of any use.

'I am on my way to the coast to purchase presents for you and your people,' Adrian said. 'But first, I must shoot elephant. If your warriors will help me with this, and with transporting the tusks to the coast, you will have all the presents you can use.'

The chieftain was doubtful about this, as his people had a mortal fear of elephants. But at last he recruited a few of the bolder spirits, and they descended to the plains above Tsavo, where the herds of giant beasts roamed at will. Joanna was desperate to have a shot at one, but equally she would not leave her children in the care of the Africans, so Adrian had to do the shooting himself. It was the first time he had set out deliberately to kill any wild beast, save for food; even on his first stay with the Masai, Kurt had done most of the shooting, and he had been little more than a gunbearer. But he had practised hard, for all his dwindling store of cartridges, and he managed to bring down two victims, although he knew real fear for the first time in his life when his opening shot merely wounded a bull, who charged him with a high-pitched shriek, its giant trunk flailing from side to side. It took him two more bullets to finish the job, when the beast was far too close for comfort.

Then he knew real remorse as he gazed at the mighty creature, so much more noble and powerful than any man could ever be, slain by a few lead pellets. He tried to remind himself that this was the law of the jungle, but the memory of the execution stayed with him a long time, and it took a great act of will-power to shoot the second of his victims.

Joanna was greatly relieved when he returned in triumph. Having heard several shots, she had been anticipating some disaster. But as she hastily pointed out, her fear had been that she might have to continue the journey alone.

The Kikuyu were delighted. Never had they seen such a display of power, and they anxiously asked him to bring them back rifles of their own. Indeed, they suggested he leave his with them, but he pointed out that was impossible, and they accepted his decision, although with somewhat ill grace. However, they were happy to supply bearers down to the coast, in anticipation of his return with the firearms, having, like most primitive peoples, a sublime trust in the value of a promise.

He also had to persuade the ferry operators to take his word that he would pay them once he had sold the ivory, and this took some time, but at last they were across the water and on the island. 'We must not attract attention,' he told Joanna, 'until we've unloaded this stuff.' And he left her sitting under a mango tree, like any native woman, with her two children, while he conducted the business.

The dealers, whom he knew from the past, were astonished to see him, but very happy to purchase the tusks, which were of the highest-quality ivory, and he found himself in possession of more money than at any previous period in his life. But obviously, after that, his arrival in

231

Mombasa could hardly be kept a secret. When he returned to the mango tree, he found quite a crowd had gathered. The natural curiosity of the Arabs had been heightened when one of them asked Catherine, 'Where do you come from, child?' in Swaheli, a language she spoke as well as English, and she replied, 'From the land of the Masai.'

'I thought we might be stoned,' Joanna confessed.

'I think they're all afraid of you,' Adrian said, and escorted them to the hotel, where the proprietor, Abdullah, was delighted to see them again after all these years. He sent his various wives and older sons scurrying about to draw hot baths and provide water for shaving – Adrian having let his beard grow on the safari down from the high country – and himself went out to procure his tailor, who measured Adrian and promised to have a suit of new clothes ready for him the following morning.

Then it was his turn to soak in a boiling tub before borrowing a kaftan from his host and joining Joanna and Catherine for a delicious couscous; Johnnie had already been fed and put to bed.

'My God,' she said, 'I can just feel civilisation beginning to fill my bones again, even in this God-forsaken spot.'

'In every possible way,' Adrian agreed, watching William Moore coming up the front steps of the hotel. 'You will act the part of my wife until you actually leave, I hope.'

She half-turned her head and nodded. 'Agreed.'

'Mr Barclay,' Moore said. 'Mrs Barclay. What a great pleasure it is to see you in Mombasa.'

Which was hardly what Adrian had expected to hear, but he shook hands.

'All but four years,' Moore said enthusiastically. 'But I must say, you are looking well. And this is your daughter?' He patted Catherine on the head. 'Are you going to be in town long?'

'Only a few days,' Adrian said, gesturing him to a chair. 'My wife is on her way back to America to visit her family.'

232

'You're not going too, I hope?' Moore asked anxiously.

'No,' Adrian said. 'But would it be important?'

'Oh, indeed, sir. Indeed. I can't tell you how happy I am to see you. As a matter of fact, I was even contemplating making a safari up to the Masai country to speak to you, and I will confess I was not looking forward to it.'

'Now, you have me all interested,' Adrian admitted. 'Why should you want to do that?' He decided against asking if the vice-consul might have a warrant to serve.

'Well, sir,' Moore said. 'How shall I put it?' He glanced apologetically at Joanna. 'You have managed to make quite a name for yourself, and your Masai. Not all of it good, mind. At least in certain quarters. I hope you do not mind my speaking frankly, Mr Barclay?'

'I appreciate it,' Adrian said, sipping his water and wishing it could have been wine; the presence of civilised surroundings was beginning to get to him, too.

'Well, our German friends seem to regard you as something of an eccentric. Neither did your German brother-in-law, Schlieben, have much good to say of you. He claims you have gone entirely native.'

'So I have been gathering,' Adrian said. 'But should that be considered a crime, as I live with them?'

'Good heavens, no,' Moore said hastily. 'It is the fact of your living with them that attracts me. And in such style. The things Thompson had to say . . .'

'Thompson?' Joanna and Adrian cried together.

'You mean that gink got out?' Joanna asked.

'Oh, indeed, Mrs Barclay. He returned to Mombasa, let me see, it would have been just after last Christmas. Why, that's very nearly a year ago.'

'Well, well, well,' Adrian said. 'We really never thought he'd survive.'

'I can tell you, sir, that he very nearly didn't. He was gored by a buffalo which he thought was dead . . .'

'It can happen,' Joanna agreed.

233

'And then he was captured by some very hostile fellows, Masai, who wanted to kill him. He had to pretend he was mad. Do you know what he did? He hastily took a mouthful of some Enos Fruit Salts which he had with him, then salivated like the devil, and of course frothed at the mouth. The Masai wouldn't harm him after that.'

'Sounds like our Joseph,' Joanna commented.

'And he told you of us,' Adrian said thoughtfully. 'So what is so very interesting about our situation?'

'Ah, well . . . may I speak in absolute confidence?' He glanced from face to face.

'I have no one to talk to,' Adrian pointed out. 'Except the Masai.'

Moore gave a nervous grin. 'Well, sir, I can tell you, in the strictest confidence . . .' Once again he glanced anxiously at Joanna. 'There are moves afoot. Here and in Europe. The fact is, Mr Barclay, Europe is waking up to the fact of Africa. The opportunities that lie here. Men like Stanley, and Fischer, have put Africa on the map, and if Thompson gets his book published, it is going to be even more on the map. The important thing, I can tell you, is that there is much interest in political circles. Now, obviously, if the attraction became too widespread, there would be the risk of a clash of interests, with heaven knows what international consequences to follow. For example, while we British claim to have, shall I say, a special relationship with the Sultan of Zanzibar, the Germans are thick on the coast opposite the island, and openly talk of it being under *their* protection. They have not made a claim on Mombasa as yet, but it could happen. We of the foreign service are of course making every effort to persuade our government that now is the time to declare a protectorate of our own, here in Mombasa. Unfortunately, Mr Gladstone is not really enthusiastic about colonies . . . ah, I meant to say, colonial expansion, as it were.'

'I think he's absolutely right,' Adrian remarked.

'Do you? Hm. You see, in these matters, possession is nine-tenths of the law. The Germans will not try to take over Zanzibar, because we were there first. But by the same token, we cannot do anything about their people on the mainland, because they were there first, in real terms. Now, there can be no doubt that the Germans are very interested in the Masai land, especially since Fischer's account of it. Is it really as beautiful and as healthy as he claims?'

'More so,' Adrian said.

'Hm. Well, you know, it would be a tragedy if the Germans were able to claim it for their own, merely by occupation. I mean, before we knew it, they'd have claimed all of East Africa. That wouldn't do. I mean to say, dash it all, we explored the country first. Livingstone, Burton, Speke, Stanley . . .'

'Stanley is an American,' Joanna pointed out.

'Oh, quite, Mrs Barclay. But your countrymen are surely not interested in Africa? No, sir, Mr Barclay, it really does come down to Germany and us, in this part of Africa, and who have the Germans really got to set against all our heroes? Gustav von Nachtigal, I suppose. One could hardly count Fischer, who was sent packing and only survived thanks to your intervention, as I understand it. But this is the point I am making. You are in possession, up there, now Schlieben has also been sent packing.'

'You are not being quite accurate, Mr Moore. The Masai are in possession of the high country.'

'Ah, well, I am speaking of Europeans, don't you see.'

'Meaning it doesn't matter to us Europeans what Africans may have title to the land?'

'One cannot stop the march of progress, Mr Barclay.' He was beginning to sound like Fischer himself. 'As I was saying, not only are you the man in possession, but you have recently seen off a German expedition. Now it would be idle to pretend the Germans are happy about this . . .'

'As you also just said, Mr Moore, I saved their lives. I did not see them off.'

'Well, the point is that if you were now to hoist the Union Jack outside your kraal, or bungalow, or whatever it is you have . . .'

'It is a house,' Joanna interjected, surprisingly.

'Indeed it is. How splendid. Well, by doing that you would proclaim that you held all of the land for the Masai in trust for the English Crown and the Queen, God bless her, and, well . . . it would put a spoke in their wheels, what?'

'And what would be the result for the Masai?' Adrian asked. 'Invasion by Sir Garnet Wolseley and a British army?'

'Oh, good heavens, no. Nothing could be further from our minds. It would merely be to forestall the Germans. But I imagine if *they* were to attempt to seize the country by force, you would not object to the sight of a thousand British bayonets, would you?'

'I prefer not to consider that point,' Adrian said.

'Well, I'm sure you would agree that your African "friends" would be much better off ruled from Whitehall than from the Wilhelmstrasse.'

'I can appreciate that *your* friends wish to forestall the Germans, Mr Moore,' Adrian said. 'But I would also appreciate a little less double-talk. Great Britain would not be interested in forestalling a German occupation of Masai land unless she intended to utilise that country for some purpose. I will have to know what that purpose is.'

'Ah, well . . . as a matter of fact . . . well, in the first instance, we have it in mind that free passage across the Masai land would greatly shorten the distance to the Kingdom of Uganda. You know of Uganda?'

'I have heard of it, but I have never been there. It lies in the centre of the continent, beyond Lake Victoria Nyanza.'

'Yes, indeed. Not very far west, as the crow flies, from your high country.'

236

'The trouble is that your crow is probably flying across a map,' Adrian suggested. 'It's a good bit further when you have to walk it.'

'Oh, quite. But if that is a long distance, consider how far it is from Cairo or the Cape. If we could go straight in from here . . .'

'What's so big about Uganda?' Joanna asked.

'Well, most importantly, the king there, a chap named Mtesi . . .' He looked at Adrian inquiringly.

'I have heard of Mtesi,' Adrian agreed.

'Well, he is very friendly to England. He was impressed by Stanley, and, ah' – he gave Joanna an apologetic glance – 'gained the impression that he was English, because he spoke the same language as the missionaries who had penetrated there. With a different accent, of course, but these things do not mean a lot to an African. Well, the long and the short of it is that he has invited our people in, missionaries and traders, and there is every prospect of, well, a lasting relationship.'

'You mean, a protectorate?'

'Well, King Mtesi seems to think it might be a good thing. So as I say, in the first instance, if we could cross the Masai land without having to fight every inch of the way . . .'

'And in the second instance?'

'Well, we would of course trade with the Masai. That would surely be for their good.'

'They are totally self-sufficient,' Joanna told him.

Moore gazed at her from beneath arched eyebrows. 'How can savages be self-sufficient, Mrs Barclay?'

'So maybe they don't have water closets, Mr Moore, but they don't have any tuberculosis or smallpox, either.'

'Well, of course, we would see that there were doctors available . . . or we could inoculate them. Yes, that would be best, I think.'

'What a brilliant suggestion,' Adrian said sarcastically, trying to imagine a regiment of Morani being told they must

237

all bend over to have their backsides scratched with a needle. 'Would there by any chance be a third instance?'

Moore turned the arched eyebrows on him.

'Can you, for example, give me a categorical assurance that the Masai will be left in sole possession of their country, that there will be no attempt made to alienate their lands or alter their way of life?'

'I can assure you that I have heard nothing to indicate that Her Majesty's Government is contemplating any such thing.'

'Then I would like that in writing, from Her Majesty's Government.'

'And if I obtained that, you would act as our agent in the Masai land? I may say that there is of course an emolument involved,' he added.

Adrian raised his eyebrows.

'A considerable emolument,' Moore said. 'One hundred pounds per annum. I am empowered to make you an advance of the first year's salary, here and now, should you accept my offer.'

'Sounds a bit like bribery to me,' Joanna said. 'A hundred pounds . . . wheee . . .' She almost winked at Adrian.

'My dear lady,' Moore protested.

'There is one small problem of which you are probably unaware,' Adrian said. 'I am wanted by the Southampton police.'

'Ah.' Moore gave a deprecatory smile. 'That incident with your father-in-law. Yes, indeed. There was a warrant issued for your arrest on a variety of charges; abduction of a minor, behaviour likely to cause a disturbance of the peace, illegal possession of a firearm and, of course, assaulting three police officers in the execution of their duty. But Her Majesty's Government is prepared to persuade the Southampton magistrates to drop all charges against you, if you are prepared to co-operate with them.'

'I reckon they want to fly their flag up in the high country real bad,' Joanna commented.

238

'Would it be possible to have that undertaking also in writing?' Adrian asked.

'Oh, certainly. Well, sir, supposing I can satisfy you as to all of those points you have raised, would you be prepared to act as our agent in the Masai land?'

'Yes,' Adrian said.

'My dear fellow, I am so delighted. Yes, indeed. Now, Mr Barclay, Mrs Barclay, my wife is having a small soirée tomorrow in honour of your visit to Mombasa. And your new appointment, to be sure. We so look forward to entertaining you.'

'Soirée?' Joanna asked faintly.

'We accept with pleasure,' Adrian said.

'You must be out of your mind,' she told him that evening. He had rented two rooms, explaining that one was for the children; that Joanna intended to sleep with them and not with him was nobody's concern but their own. But for the sake of appearances she undressed in his bedroom. 'A soirée? How can I possibly go to a soirée? What shall I wear?'

'That evening gown you still have tucked away.'

'That? It's five years old. Moore has seen it before. Anyway, I'll never get into it.'

'Oh, come now, you aren't that fat.'

She glared at him.

'And I will bet you whatever you like that Moore has forgotten it.'

She turned her glare on the mirror. 'My hair . . .' She had allowed it to grow throughout her stay in the high country, and although it retained its splendid sheen, it was certainly very long and slightly untidy.

'You have all tomorrow to do your hair. I'll help you, if you like.'

Another glare. 'And my complexion? It's ruined, thanks to that ghastly sun.'

'After what Thompson appears to have been telling everyone, your hostess will be disappointed if you turn up looking like a debutante, my darling.'

'I am not your darling,' she snapped. 'And you, accepting bribes to represent your government . . . You must see it's the thin edge of the wedge.'

'I do,' he agreed. 'But as I am afraid that wedge is going to be driven in anyway – and if the British aren't encouraged it might just be driven in by people like Kurt and his friends – I don't think I had any choice. This way I can at least look after the interests of Uthuli and his people.'

She made no further comment, and went off to bed. The next day she was highly nervous and seemed even more so when Adrian appeared with her steamship tickets.

'Here we are,' he said. 'One first-class cabin, for your exclusive use, Mombasa-Aden-Port Said-Naples. Then here is another ticket, again for first-class accommodation, from Naples to New York. The clerk at the British India Steam Navigation Company office assured me that, while his company does not sail the Atlantic route, this ticket will be honoured by any of the companies that do so, and he says to tell you his office in Naples will be happy to arrange your transfer to the ship of your choice. I assume you can manage all of that?'

'Of course I can,' she said.

'They were damned expensive,' he told her. 'I have just enough left to buy fresh cartridges and some calico for the Kikuyu. Of course, I suppose, without you hanging around my neck, and the children, I could always shoot a couple more elephants and return here to cash in before heading back to the hills.'

She knew he was teasing her, and was furious, even if she must have suspected the raging despair in his heart. 'My father will refund every penny of that passage,' she said. 'The money will be in Mombasa in six months. That is a promise.'

'I'll look forward to receiving it. As I probably won't be in Mombasa again for six years.'

She snorted, and began to prepare herself for the soirée, pinning up her hair with great determination and enormous effort, and then clucking her tongue sadly over her gown, which certainly revealed the passage of time. But she was prepared to fulfil her promise, and acted the perfect wife at the party itself, where they were the centre of attention, not only as guests of honour, but as two very unusual people.

It was a much larger party than they had expected, and a multi-national gathering, although all the skins were white. Joanna's gown displayed her sun-burned throat and shoulders and neck, which, combined with her mature beauty, had the men clustering around her while the ladies exclaimed in horror over such a ravaged complexion. They wanted to get her away in a corner and ask her questions about the Masai, about childbearing in the 'bush' – which was apparently any place in Africa not on Mombasa Island – and about a host of other intimacies, predominantly female circumcision, of which they had only heard rumours.

The men, once they had taken a good look at Joanna, were more interested in politics, and here again Adrian, an incongruous figure amidst the gathering of black jackets, as he wore only bush clothes – albeit new ones – and because he towered over everyone else in the room, found himself the objective of a barrage of questions. These he answered guardedly, as Moore had told him their conversation was strictly confidential. He was therefore both astonished and dismayed when the vice-consul declared expansively, 'Now, gentlemen, you must understand that Mr Barclay is obliged to maintain a proper reticence in answering your questions; he has just been appointed Her Majesty's vice-consul in the land of the Masai, a people with whom Her

241

Majesty's Government have reached a very proper under-standing.'

That took them all aback, and the party broke up shortly afterwards. 'My God, what an experience,' Joanna said as they walked back to the hotel beneath the huge tropical moon. 'To live here, on the edge of all that, and know nothing about it. To have such distorted concepts of it. To . . . Ouch! Got you, you beast.' She slapped, and the mosquito which had just bitten her dissolved on her arm in a splodge of blood. 'Ugh!'

'It's your own blood,' Adrian pointed out.

'They're still horrid things. I hate to see them on the children.'

'I thought Catherine has been coping rather well. Any mosquito who bites her is on a suicide mission.'

'I was thinking more of Johnnie. The poor little mite is a mass of bites and bumps. The sooner I get him out of this benighted place, the better. Oh, Mr Abdullah, good evening to you.' She frowned. 'Whatever can be the matter?'

The Arab was wringing his hands, and behind him all four of his wives were clustered together, yashmaks forgotten in their agitation. 'The boy, madam,' Abdullah said. 'He is so ill.'

'Oh, my God!' Joanna gathered her skirts and ran up the steps, Adrian at her heels. Johnnie was only half awake, but crying, and his flesh was terribly hot to the touch, while his complexion was blotched and he kept giving little muscular convulsions. In addition, it was easy to see that he had recently vomited. 'Oh, God!' Joanna screamed. 'He's been poisoned. God, he's been poisoned.'

'Now, I don't think that's really likely,' Adrian said. 'He has a fever. A doctor,' he told Abdullah. 'We must have a doctor.'

'I will wake one immediately,' Abdullah promised, and hurried from the room, driving his wives before him.

'Why in the name of God didn't he send for one earlier?'

Joanna moaned, sitting on the bed with the little boy in her arms, rocking him back and forth. 'Or send for us? He knew where we were. God, my darling, oh, my darling . . .'

Catherine was by now awake and sitting up. 'Jo-jo sick,' she commented.

'Oh, my darling, thank God you're all right. Adrian, we must do something. Get the temperature down . . .'

Her grief was terrifying to watch. Adrian ran downstairs to the kitchen, used the pump to wet several towels and took them back up. Joanna wrapped Johnnie in them, but the water was too tepid to have much effect. Adrian was just preparing some more when the doctor arrived. He was an Italian, and had actually been at the Moores' soirée with them. He needed only one look at Johnnie to know what the matter was. 'He has malaria,' he said. 'My dear lady, what a misfortune.'

'Malaria?' Joanna screamed.

'It is endemic here on the coast, and in the low-lying forests, as well,' Dr Giglioli explained. 'You have just passed through those forests, have you not?'

'Yes,' she said. 'But we all did. Oh, God . . .' She stared at Catherine in horror, as if expecting her to go into convulsions at any moment.

'Now, Mrs Barclay,' Dr Giglioli said reassuringly, 'there is no reason for your daughter also to catch the disease. No one knows what causes malaria. We do know that it arises from swampy land, and that it is probably some kind of noxious miasma. But equally, while it seems to be contagious in that where there is one case there are usually many more, human beings do not pass it from one to the other by bodily contact. Nor are all human beings susceptible to the disease.'

'But my son? What can we do?'

The doctor sighed. 'I will give him a quinine injection. This often helps to bring down the fever. And we must keep him cool, as you are doing, without of course allowing him

243

to catch a chill. It is **at any rate a** fast-acting disease, especially with one so young. The crisis will be here within forty-eight hours. All we can do is watch, and pray.'

Thirty-six hours later, John Barclay died.

They were within a few degrees of the equator, and it was the hot season. John Barclay died at dawn and was buried that same morning; Dr Giglioli had thoughtfully ordered a coffin to be made for the little child the moment he had diagnosed the illness – he had encountered too many cases of malaria during his sojourn on the East African coast to have the slightest optimism about the child's chances.

The Moores attended the funeral, and the doctor and his wife, and one or two of the other people they had met at the soirée. 'I don't know what to say,' Moore said. 'It is a terrible tragedy. But, well . . .' He looked at Adrian with anxious eyes, wondering if his carefully constructed plan for the Masai country had suddenly come crashing down in pieces.

'I shall be returning to the high country,' Adrian promised him. 'My wife was meaning to travel by herself, in any event.'

'Of course,' the vice-consul said. 'Well, if there is any thing either Margaret or myself can do . . .'

'You've been very kind,' Joanna said. When she realised that Johnnie had actually stopped breathing, she had collapsed in screaming tears. But now she was quite in control of herself. Yet it was obvious that she wanted to be alone, as the small hole was slowly filled in by the Arab gravediggers.

Adrian walked with the Moores back to the gate of the Christian cemetery. 'I shall of course send your emolument round to the hotel this afternoon,' Moore said, anxious to make quite sure that his new colleague had not changed his mind. 'I would have done so yesterday, but hearing of the child's illness, why . . .'

'That was thoughtful of you,' Adrian agreed.

244

'Well, old man, I am most terribly shocked. But life must go on, eh?'

'Indeed,' Adrian said, and shook hands. He felt no resentment; grief over the death of a small child is an intensely personal matter – it can never be shared. He only worried for Joanna's state of mind, and waited by the gate until she had knelt at the graveside for some time, then walked with her back to the hotel. They had left Catherine in the care of Abdullah's wives and children. She was totally confused, poor little thing, but had responded to the lively young Arab girls.

'There's not a lot I can say,' Adrian admitted. 'Except . . .'

'Forget it,' Joanna told him. Her eyes were dry, as if she had wept all the moisture in her body. Certainly she was exhausted, and there were black shadows under her eyes. Neither of them had slept for forty eight hours. 'I killed him.'

'Now, Jo . . .'

'For God's sake, it was my idea, wasn't it, to take him through the bush and bring him to this pesthole? You said so at the time. Crazy to take children into the jungle, you said. But it was what I wanted.'

'Well, it was a risk you had to take,' he argued. 'If you were to get him out of Africa.'

'I thought, being born here, he'd be immune to things like malaria,' she muttered, and went up to their bedroom.

'You'll feel better at sea,' Adrian comforted her. 'I suggest you go to bed right away, and stay there until tomorrow morning. You don't have to be on board until noon. Giglioli gave me a sedative powder for you. He says it'll make you sleep for twenty hours. That's what you need. Then when you wake up you can board, and by dusk tomorrow you'll be on your way.'

She sat on the bed, gazing at her suitcase. It was brand new, but still had to be packed.

'I'll mix it up now,' Adrian said, going to the door.

'Don't you hate me?' she asked. 'I have just murdered your son.'

'Oh, Jo,' he protested.

'I guess I've done a lot of stupid things,' she said, half to herself. 'Crazy things. Criminal things. Maybe I should now start doing some sensible ones.'

She got up and went to the dressing table, where the steamship tickets still lay. She picked them up, held them in her hand as if about to tear them across, then changed her mind. 'I'm going to be sensible, remember,' she said, still speaking to herself. 'Let's go cash these in.'

'You're not serious?'

She shrugged, but her eyes were again full of tears. 'I have no place to go, Adrian. Not now. Not until I've made up for Johnnie.'

PART III

The High Country

9

Adrian was not sure how much she meant what she had said, how much he dared give way to a sudden, surging happiness which seemed grotesquely out of place when he had just buried his son. But for the time being, at least, his life, and therefore hers, took an entirely new direction.

They decided to waste as little time on the coast as was possible; it had become hateful to them, and they were both anxious to get Catherine back up to the healthy air of the highlands as quickly as possible. The tickets were cashed, and the refunds, added to Thompson's 'emolument', made Adrian again quite wealthy, in Mombasa terms. They each wrote letters, she to her parents, and he to his mother, relating their adventures and their present situation, telling them of Catherine and Johnnie, and of Johnnie's death, of the house and the Masai and their determination to make their lives in the high country. Adrian also told Molly about the 'pardon' he had received, and of his appointment as an officer of the Crown. He knew she would be delighted that he had become a man of what she would regard as substance and respectability, and also that she would relay the news to Amanda, and thus Kurt.

Then it was simply a matter of preparing to leave. They bought everything they supposed they might need during the next few years. The list included books – both for their pleasure and to school Catherine and Bar, additional clothing, a huge supply of cartridges, some cloth and beads for the Kikuyu, as well as several rifles. The boring on each rifle had been mutilated with a file so that there was little chance of the bullets flying true; Adrian knew he had to fulfil his promise to bring them firearms, the ones Kurt had given them so long ago having dwindled into rust, but he certainly did not want to think of the Kikuyu armed with accurate modern rifles as well as poisoned arrows.

He also bought a large store of seeds, which he hoped would survive the journey. But he was determined to plant a cash crop, especially if there were going to be regular caravans passing through the highlands on their way to Uganda.

Finally, it was necessary to arrange for porterage up to the forest. It took them several days to prepare the expedition, days in which they spent almost every moment on their feet, happy to be so preoccupied there was little time for thought, and at night collapsed into their beds exhausted. But with such a cloud of grief hanging over them, he could not have taken advantage of Joanna's offer, even had he been as fresh as a daisy; and he had no doubt she was grateful.

But on their last night in Mombasa, when everything was ready and most of their gear had already been transported to the mainland, she donned her evening gown for dinner, and they sat facing each other across the table as they ate. 'I promised to wear a good gown every night on the ranch,' she said. 'I never did.' She gave a twisted little smile. 'I guess because there was no ranch. But we do have a house. A fine house.'

It was the first time she had ever admitted that.

'Still,' he said, 'I absolve you of the necessity to wear anything you don't feel like, ever again. I'd be happy to look at you in sack cloth.'

There were a million things on his mind. Top amongst them was whether or not they *could* pick up the ruins of their lives after nearly four years. But surrounding and supporting that overriding problem were so many others. She would wish to know what he intended to do about Sita, and learn he could do nothing about her; one simply did not send a Masai bride back to her family – it was the deepest disgrace that could befall a girl. In Sita's case, too, the disgrace would be all hers, as she had failed in her primary duty of motherhood; she would become the outcast of the clan, a total pariah. He could not contemplate that. But neither could he contemplate reducing her to the level of a mere servant in his own house; he might as well take her out and shoot her, because she would surely die of shame.

But this evening, Joanna obviously only wanted to forget the past, and will him again to love her. 'I have always loved you,' he said, in answer to her expression.

She gave another little smile, but this one was more genuine. 'I know. That's what makes me feel so bad. I guess I have always loved you, too. But . . . maybe if you'd hated me for the way I was treating you, or at least got angry; if you'd thrown me across a bed and beaten me, or raped me more often . . . I might have realised that sooner.'

'Safah's advice.'

She made a moue. 'But then again . . . I might not.' She pushed her plate away. 'I guess we should make an early start in the morning.'

He nodded.

'Then I think we should have an early night as well.'

He followed her upstairs and into the second bedroom, to kiss Catherine good night. The little girl was fast asleep. She had spent the past week being entertained by Abdullah's wives and daughters, and the fact of her brother's death had clearly not penetrated her consciousness. He hoped she would be much older before it did. For the moment, she was just aware that a large and enjoyable toy had been taken away from her, by accident rather than design, and she did not resent that when there was so many other things to enjoy. So she snuffled happily into her pillow, her cheeks a bloom of health.

'Adrian,' Joanna said. 'If anything were to happen to her, I'd kill myself.'

'So would I.' He put his arm round her shoulders. It was the first time he had touched her intimately for nearly eighteen months. 'Nothing is going to happen to her,' he promised.

She turned, into his arms, and he lifted her from the floor to kiss her, as he had done when she first appeared at the cottage in Southampton. The kiss was like that first one too: long, and slow, and exploratory; he had not actually kissed her for four years.

He carried her into the adjoining bedroom and laid her on the bed. She undressed lying there, wriggling the gown down to her thighs while she stared at him. 'Is there something very terrible,' she said, 'about life, about us . . . that a child . . . that dear little boy' – a tear rolled out of her eye – 'had to die to bring us back together?'

'I think we'd have got back together, somehow, sometime, even if I'd had to come to the States to fetch you,' he said, lying beside her.

'But you wouldn't stop me going. Oh, Adrian . . .' Now she was weeping freely. 'Oh, Adrian . . . Johnnie . . . oh, God, Adrian, if one could only put back the clock.'

He held her close, her head on his shoulder. 'As long as there is tomorrow, my dearest girl. As long as there is tomorrow, yesterday doesn't really matter, save as a memory, which perhaps we can use to guide our tomorrows. We'll never forget Johnnie, or how he died. Maybe it was out fault. *Our*,' he repeated as she would have stopped him. 'If we knew what causes malaria . . . I can't believe it is just a matter of walking through the forest, or why didn't we all get it? One day people *will* know these things, and then maybe they'll be able to avoid our mistakes. But right now, all we can do is live, and love . . . and remember.' He looked

252

down at her. 'I think we'd better leave it for tonight.'

She gave a huge sniff. 'No,' she said. 'No. Make me pregnant, Adrian. For God's sake, make me pregnant.'

Suddenly life had indeed taken on an entirely new direction. It was as if a vast cloud had cleared from over the earth to let in the sun. They returned from the coast with a well-equipped bearer party, and Joanna was able to do some shooting herself when passing through Tsavo, while Adrian took care of Catherine. Included in her bag was a full-grown lion, shot in the act of attacking the camp; it was her proudest trophy. The Kikuyu welcomed them as friends, especially when Adrian presented the chief with the new rifles, but that was nothing compared with their welcome when they regained the high country.

Safah was ecstatic to have both the bwana and the bibi back again, even if he showed a suitable sorrow at the news of Johnnie's death. Bar was equally delighted with the return of both of them, and Adrian's eyes were moist when Joanna embraced and kissed the boy.

Uthuli had always been somewhat confused as to just what Joanna intended, or indeed even what function she fulfilled in Adrian's life, and did not display great interest in her return, but he was very pleased to have Adrian back again, and listened gravely as his adopted son explained his new appointment.

He was not entirely happy about the situation. 'Why do the white men roam so?' he asked. 'Why cannot they be content with what they possess?'

'Well, you roam every year,' Adrian pointed out.

'We do not leave our own land,' Uthuli replied. 'We follow well-known paths, and we return to this kraal every year. But the white man . . . why does he want to go to the land of the Uganda?'

'Heaven knows,' Adrian said. 'Why did I want to come here? As you say, my father, we are wanderers. And there is

253

also trade. These caravans, as they pass through, will bring many things of use to the Masai.'

'What things?' Uthuli asked.

Adrian couldn't immediately think of an adequate reply.

'And they will want our cattle in exchange,' Uthuli said sadly.

'No,' Adrian said. 'They will be paying for passage through your land. You need trade with them nothing you do not wish to.'

'They will want our women, too,' Uthuli said, as if Adrian had not spoken.

'No,' Adrian said again. 'That will not happen, my father. You have my word.'

This seemed to reassure him, at least partially, and the entire clan gathered round the house as Adrian and Safah, having cut down a tall and straight sapling, erected it on the lawn and hoisted the Union Jack to its top. The Masai clapped enthusiastically, and Safah gazed at their handiwork with a quizzical expression. 'That is a very pretty flag,' he commented. 'I have seen flags like that on the British men-of-war in Mombasa harbour.'

'That's right,' Adrian said.

'Is this land now a British man-of-war, bwana?'

'The flag will keep away the Germans,' Adrian assured him.

Thus far his consular duties were simple enough. Life went on as before, but with an added impetus. Joanna opted not to return to the main house, but to maintain her own establishment – in view of the continued presence of Sita. She never sought to discover what Adrian's relations were with the Masai girl, but she welcomed him to her cottage whenever he chose to come, and if he stayed to share dinner with her, after Catherine had been put to bed, she was eager to be his wife.

In part he recognised this was because she had known so

little sex since her self-imposed chastity of four years earlier. Equally, in part he knew it was because she desperately wanted to conceive, to replace the child she had lost. He could not bring himself to tell her that was impossible, save in the physical sense; one human being can never replace another. But it also proved to be physically impossible. 'God is punishing me,' she would groan, and he would sigh and hold her close.

But he was certain he could not impregnate her because, despite their mutual resolve, they did not love, at least not as they had done at first. They had fallen into love desperately, youthfully, romantically and irresponsibly. Then she had fallen out of love, again with all the ardour of youth, angrily and in despair. Now she could not fall into love with him again, simply for the asking. Nor, he was discovering to his consternation, could he love her with the desperate desire of a few years before. Her very coolness, allied to such beauty – and her body daily seemed to increase his urge to touch her, stroke her, possess her – heightened her desirability; and so did their peculiar living arrangements, in which she shared his bed only for sex. But there remained an invisible barrier between them. They had shared too much, and too much of it had been unshareable. They needed a catalyst to tear aside the emotional reserve that had been erected. And he did not know what the catalyst could, or should, be.

Yet they played at happiness, reading aloud to Catherine, taking her for walks along the banks of the lake, teaching her to shoot, even teaching her to ride on the back of a zebra they caught and Joanna tamed, with the assistance of Bar. Here at least was one perfect result of that tragedy which had brought her back to the high country: she was prepared to treat Bar as the son she had lost.

And they worked, for she took an equal interest in his plans for a plantation. He had read books and taken advice, and the coffee seedlings were carefully planted at the pre-scribed intervals and the bananas planted behind them, while the Masai watched with interest. Planting, just before the Long Rains, was something they could understand, but they had no idea what the coffee seeds were going to produce. The following year they were pleased with the banana crop, and gazed in wonderment at the huge leaves and the clustering fruit, but were sadly disappointed that the coffee plants, which had grown to a good size, had as yet yielded nothing. When Adrian explained that they would not do so for at least another year, they shook their heads at such careless confidence. Two years was too long to expect the termites not to become interested.

But the following year there was a crop, most of which Adrian had to throw away; Uthuli solemnly tasted the black drink and pronounced it poisonous, and his people would not touch it. Adrian and Joanna made the discovery that, having planned a coffee crop, they had forgotten to bring any sugar from the coast. But they were both excited by the proof that they could perhaps contribute something to this land.

Thus passed a few years of contentment, rather than true happiness, contentment which was the sweeter because Adrian neither heard nor saw anyone from the coast. However anxiously he spent his time, at first, waiting and watching, the caravans prophesied by Moore did not appear, and indeed his visit to Mombasa might never have been, except for its personal repercussions. He was relieved that this should be so, even if he had received no more salary. But Moore had no doubt been replaced, and his harebrained schemes disavowed and abandoned.

Then Kurt von Schlieben returned.

The Masai were in a state of high excitement. Their scouts came to the house to report the presence of a white army encamped by the swamp and approaching the highlands. The Masai had few numbers, and regarded ten, multiplied several times by the opening and shutting of the hand, as indicating a vast array. Now they despaired of being able to open and shut their hands sufficiently. Adrian frowned at them. 'White men, you say? With bearers?'

'Oh, yes, Bar-clay. Many bearers.'

His frown deepened. 'Were they flying any flags?' He pointed at the now somewhat faded Union Jack flying above his lawn.

The Morani considered, then shook their heads.

'What does this mean, my son?' Uthuli asked. 'Is this the fulfilment of the prophecy?'

'I sincerely hope not,' Adrian said. 'And it is my business to make sure that it *is* not.'

'What are you going to do?' Joanna asked him.

'Go out and have a look at these people, and discover what they want. And what they intend.'

'Do be careful. If they were to turn out to be enemies . . .'

'I'll be careful,' Adrian promised. 'Expect me back in a week.'

He was more worried than he would admit. If it really was an army . . . A British army would be bad enough. But supposing it was a German force? What would he do? What *could* he do? Moore had talked airily of sending a thousand British bayonets. But even if it had been possible to summon such a force, and possible for them to get here within five years, would he really want to turn this magnificent country into a battlefield? Or to be responsible for perhaps a full-scale war between Britain and Germany?

He stood, with Uthuli and several other elders of the clan, on a bluff to look out over the plains and the approaching multitude. And held his breath, because there were certainly several hundred men down there.

'It is the whole world, come to our land,' Uthuli said dolefully, and looked over his shoulder to where his Morani, themselves less than two hundred strong, were gathered to await his orders. He could, of course, send messengers to all the other clans, as he had done when Fischer invaded his

257

land, and summon up an army of several thousand, but he clearly did not relish the prospect. He added, even more gloomily, 'They will have the long spears which kill our people.'

'Let me talk with them,' Adrian said. 'Stay here, and only advance if I fire my rifle into the air.'

He walked down from the bluff, his heart pounding, feeling even more exposed than when facing the charging elephants three years before. But he was so obviously a white man, and he had Moore's word for it that people like Fischer and Thompson had made him famous. That was a reassuring thought.

His approach certainly caused some commotion. Men ran to and fro, presumably summoning superiors, and then three men left the encampment and came towards him. He observed that they were unarmed, and slung his rifle – then caught his breath as he recognised the leading figure.

'Adrian!' Kurt von Schlieben shouted. 'My dear fellow, how very good to see you.'

Adrian took the outstretched hand without thinking what he was doing – he was looking past Kurt at the other two men, very well dressed, with feathers in their slouch hats, neat moustaches and precise countenances, trousers thrust into stout gaiters over their boots.

'This is the man himself, Your Excellency,' Kurt said. 'Mr Adrian Barclay. Adrian, may I present Count Teleki von Szen, and Lieutenant von Hohnel.'

'Gentlemen.' Adrian shook hands with them in turn.

'I cannot tell you how pleased we are to make your acquaintance, Mr Barclay,' the count said, in perfect English. 'We have heard such tales of this country, of the fierceness of the Masai, who can only be overcome with your assistance. Fortunately, we have as yet seen none of the savages.'

Von Hohnel, the younger man, stared at Adrian as if wondering if he might not in fact be one of them; for all his

258

European clothes, Adrian wore his yellow hair quite long and, both for coolness and convenience, in a pigtail exactly as any Morani.

'They have seen you, Your Excellency,' Adrian told the count. 'They are watching you at this moment.'

'The devil.' Now von Hohnel looked from left to right anxiously, and then back at the encampment some hundred yards distant. 'Shall I sound the alarm?'

'They will not molest you without reason,' Adrian assured him.

'Or unless you give them the order, eh?' Kurt shouted with a bellow of laughter.

'They are prepared to take my advice, yes,' Adrian said evenly.

'As they should, seeing that you represent the Great Queen, their foreign mother, eh?'

Adrian frowned. 'You know about that?'

'Who doesn't?'

'Will you not join us for a schnapps, Mr Barclay?' the count asked.

'I might, Your Excellency. Once I have ascertained your purpose in coming here with such force.'

'Why, I am on safari.'

'With five hundred men?'

'Seven hundred, to be precise,' the count told him. 'Why, yes, sir, I believe in travelling in both comfort and security.'

'We are but passing through Masai land, Adrian,' Kurt explained. 'It is all in order. We have passports, signed by the consul general in Mombasa, to cross British territory. Our intention is to head north, doing a little exploring, a little shooting, a little mapping – enjoying ourselves.'

'We also intend to climb some of these spectacular mountains that we see in the distance,' the count said. 'Especially the famous striped peak.'

'I would like to see these passports,' Adrian said, totally

259

mystified by what he had just been told. Consul general in Mombasa? British territory? But why else should these Austrians – as he assumed the count and his people to be – go to the trouble of obtaining permission to come up here, almost as if Great Britain *had* established a protectorate over the land of the Masai?

As it turned out, they had, although the word was not mentioned. The passports were documents drawn up by a man called Williamson, who certainly signed as consul general in Mombasa, graciously giving permission to the Count Teleki von Szen and a party not to exceed seven hundred and fifty men to proceed through the territories 'generally acknowledged to be within the sphere of influence of Her Majesty the Queen'. There was even a note attached requiring the count to have the documents countersigned by Her Majesty's vice-consul in Masai land, Mr Adrian Barclay.

Kurt laughed at his obvious bewilderment. 'There have been momentous happenings, Adrian. They have held a great conference in Berlin, attended by your Lord Salisbury, as well as our Prince von Bismarck . . .'

'Lord Salisbury?'

'He is your prime minister, now,' the count explained. 'The Conservatives are again in power, and they are the party of empire, eh?'

'Well, the long and the short of it is,' Kurt said, 'that the great powers, which means in effect England, France and Germany, although there have been some concessions made to Spain, Italy and Portugal, have agreed that, to avoid perhaps dangerous clashes of ambition, all Africa shall be divided into spheres of interest, within which each power may pursue the policies it regards as being in the best interests of itself and its peoples. Here in East Africa, England and Germany have divided the country. We have all the territory south of Mount Kilimanjaro, down to the borders of your claims in the lands of the Matebele, and you have all the territory north of the mountain, up to the borders of Ethiopia.'

'Good God,' Adrian commented, aghast that half a continent could be so divided. But according to Kurt, the *whole* continent had been chopped up, like a large cake being offered to greedy children. 'What did the Africans have to say about this?'

Kurt gave another bellow of laughter. 'Why, do you know, I don't think they were consulted? Or have even been told yet. Except perhaps the Sultan of Zanzibar, and he is perfectly happy about it; he is getting a salary from your government.'

An emolument, Adrian thought, feeling sick.

'But they will all find out in the course of time,' Kurt assured him. 'They will have to accept the inevitable.'

'I would have to say that as far as I can gather, not all the natives seem very happy about this arrangement,' the count put in. 'Are you not having some trouble in the south, Schlieben?'

Kurt shrugged. 'A few minor disturbances, Your Excellency. Nothing that we have not been able to quash with a Maxim gun. The British are also having trouble. Far from extending their influence, they have been expelled from Uganda.'

'Have they?' Adrian asked. 'I had supposed King Mtesi was a friend of ours.'

'Oh, he was. But he died, about three years ago, and his son, King Mwanga, holds a different point of view. He promptly murdered the Anglican bishop, Hannington, and as I say, virtually expelled your people from the country. There is much resentment of this in London, I understand. I am sure that Mwanga will also discover the power of the Maxim gun before too long.'

Adrian said nothing. Mtesi must have died, and Mwanga taken power, at about the very moment Moore was outlining his vast plans – which after all had apparently been endorsed by the British Government – to Joanna and himself in Mombasa. So much for dreams of empire. And that explained the absence of any of the promised caravans. But according to Kurt, it was still going to happen, and on a larger scale than even Moore had envisaged.

'However,' the count was saying, 'let me hasten to assure you again, Mr Barclay, that we are on nothing more than a long holiday. We intend to offend no one, harm no one . . .'

Adrian looked past him at the huge collection of trophies, ranging from elephants' tusks and lions' manes to the great curved buffalo horns and zebra tails which adorned the camp. 'Except all the game you can shoot.'

The count gazed at him, then glanced at Kurt.

'Why, do you not shoot game, Adrian?' Kurt asked. 'I have heard that you took some of the best tusks ever seen to Mombasa, a few years ago.'

Adrian flushed. 'It is sometimes necessary. Oh, do not worry, Your Excellency. I will countersign your passports, when you are on the point of leaving this land and I am sure the Masai have nothing to complain of.'

'Do you not trust the word of the count?' demanded von Hohnel hotly. 'Why, sir, if you require proof of our intentions, look in our bales. We left Zanzibar with twenty-four thousand yards of calico for distribution as presents to the natives along our route, as well as many other things. Your Masai are welcome to a reasonable share.'

'I am sure I can accept the word of Count Teleki von Szen, Herr Lieutenant,' Adrian said. 'But can he pledge his word for every man in his safari?'

The count smiled, easily. 'You are right to be cautious, Mr Barclay. But I have given you my word that we are on a peaceful expedition and are just passing through. Any man of mine who steps out of line will answer to me, personally. Is that satisfactory to you?'

'Indeed it is, Your Excellency. But I still think it would be safest for everyone if your people remained up here on the high ground and did not descend in force to the Masai kraal. However, my wife and I would be pleased to entertain *you* and your friends, if you would care to visit us when you are close enough?'

'Your wife?' Kurt demanded. 'Not Joanna?'

'Joanna has determined to make her life up here with me, yes,' Adrian told him.

Kurt gave one of his tremendous shouts of laughter. 'I knew you'd bring her round. Oh, what a shame I was not here to see it. To help you, perhaps. And you have not asked after your mother and sister?'

'I was hoping you would tell me about them.'

'I can tell you they are well, and send you their love. I have letters. Many letters. Amanda indeed would have accompanied me on this safari, but she is nursing our third child; we now have two boys and a girl. She longs to see you again. Who knows . . . it may be possible to return here to live, one day.' He gazed at the expression on Adrian's face, and added, 'Perhaps.'

Neither Uthuli nor Joanna were particularly happy to have Von once more in their midst.

'He killed my daughter,' Uthuli said. 'I shall go unhappy to my grave that I have not avenged her. And how he comes back . . . You told me he would not do that.'

'He has not returned to live, my father,' Adrian said. 'He is but passing through, and has been given permission to do so by the Great Queen, who rules over all men. He will be gone like a spurt of dust, and you need not even look upon his face.'

Joanna was easier to placate, principally because in the satchel of letters Kurt had given him there was one from her father, expressing his pleasure at the way her life had turned out so successfully, and his deep regret at the news of Johnnie's death, as well as sending the love of all the family, with the hopes that she would be able to visit them before too long.

The letters for Adrian included, in addition to those from his mother and Amanda, a long epistle from Moore, apparently written the previous year, just before his departure for England and reassignment. The letter brought him up to date on the Ugandan situation, and enclosed, as Moore had promised, not only Adrian's official appointment as British Vice-Consul in Masai Land and a note that there was a steadily accumulating balance to his credit in Mombasa, but also the official discharge from his crime in Southampton.

'It appears I can now return to England whenever I wish,' he remarked.

Joanna put down her letter and gazed at him. 'Will you go?'

'No,' he said. 'Not right now, anyway.'

She looked disappointed, but did not press the matter, and in any event it was swept aside by what Kurt and Teleki had to tell them when they came to dinner several days later, an occasion for which she dressed her hair and wore the new evening gown she had made up from material purchased in Mombasa three years before.

Both the count and Kurt were clearly impressed by her beauty, as well as their surroundings, especially as they had had to undergo the ordeal of walking past a line of staring Morani to get there.

'Amazing,' the count remarked, fingering the silver cutlery, also purchased in Mombasa on that last visit. 'But I suppose only to be expected. Everything they say of you is absolutely true.'

'And what exactly do they say of us, Your Excellency?' Joanna asked.

'Why, did you not know that you and your husband are famous, Mrs Barclay? Have you not read Mr Thompson's book?'

'We have not even seen it.'

'We have copies here,' Kurt said, producing another satchel. 'As well as some others you may find interesting. Thompson has apparently inspired an English novelist, a man named Haggard, who also, it seems, has an acquaintance with Africa, although not this part of it. He has recently published two books – each a great success – set in East Africa and obviously based in part on Thompson's tale. One, called *King Solomon's Mines*, is set here in this high country. It is a far-fetched tale about a huge depository of emeralds which seem to have belonged to King Solomon, David's son, but somehow got hidden away in some gigantic caves Thompson discovered in the mountains to the north. These emeralds are found by a white party searching for a long-lost relative.' He grinned. '*You've* never heard of any emeralds in those mountains, have you, old friend?'

'That'd be the day,' Joanna remarked.

'The second book,' Teleki said, 'is to my mind even more interesting, although it is even more far-fetched. It is called *She*, and tells of a lost tribe of Africans, again hidden away in those mountains, ruled by a fabulously beautiful blonde white woman who has found the secret of eternal life. Well, I have had the pleasure of meeting Frau von Schlieben, and I would say she was certainly his model. And, listen to this, Mrs Barclay, this tribe is eventually found by an expedition headed by a tall, handsome young man who is also very blond. A perfect picture of your husband. The names are different, of course.'

'You flatter me, Your Excellency,' Adrian said. 'But your theory collapses on one point; my sister was not up here when Thompson was. Have they ever met?' He looked at Kurt.

Kurt grinned. 'Always the stern realist, eh? Who cares? I can tell you this: all the world will soon be on your doorstep. You should employ Messrs Barnum and Bailey to handle your affairs and make you into a millionaire.'

'Gee, I'd *give* a million to get Papa out here,' Joanna said. 'I hope he's read these books.'

Adrian was more interested in getting Kurt to himself after the meal. He found it as difficult as ever to resent or dislike his brother-in-law, partly because he did seem to be making Amanda so very happy, and partly because, apart from the killing of Lulu, which was now a long time in the past, his efforts to denigrate him had been so very puny. But to have him back here, and transparently envious . . .

'You have indeed made your dream come true, Adrian,' Kurt remarked, sitting beside him on the verandah after dinner and offering him a cigar; the count had remained inside to flirt with Joanna. 'A splendid home, a magnificent location, not one, but two beautiful wives . . .' Sita had been presented before the meal although she had not joined them for it. 'Tell me,' Kurt went on, 'does Joanna no longer object to receiving you straight from black arms? Or have you beaten sense into her?'

'It would not go amiss if someone were to beat the vulgarity out of you,' Adrian remarked.

Kurt merely smiled. 'And on top of all that, a British official, with the Masai eating out of your hand. And now a planter into the bargain. That was a very good cup of coffee. Tell me, who do you sell it to?'

Adrian could smile just as easily. As Kurt had just reminded him, he was the one who had made their dream come true. 'I throw most of it away,' he admitted. 'But it passes the time. Now, you tell me the truth about this little expedition of yours.'

'Have I not done so?'

'I'm trying to decide. What is the count's real purpose?'

'My dear Adrian, the count is a totally honourable man. He would not know how to begin to lie.'

'I'll accept that. Then, what is *your* purpose in coming back? You must have known it would be dangerous; the Masai have long memories. I have heard how you tried to

266

raise an army to return on your own terms. Forgive me, but that looks very much like an army camped up there on the ridge.'

Kurt grinned. 'But it is not mine. Oh, when I first left here I was filled with ideas of returning in vengeful triumph. I hate being beaten, Adrian, and you know that. But I decided to return to Germany first, and see to my estate, and introduce Mandy to my family. They adored her . . . but then she became pregnant and, frankly, the high country faded into a sort of fantasy world. I even managed to forget about it from time to time. But when Teleki approached me and asked me to act as guide, I couldn't resist it.'

'And you felt that with seven hundred men at your back you didn't really have to fear the vengeance of the Masai.'

'Why,' Kurt said, 'that is exactly right.'

'Three days ago you said you would like to return here to live.'

'Having seen it again, I know that I would.' Kurt gazed at him. 'Would you forbid it?'

Adrian shrugged. 'I am a paid servant of the Crown, now. If you secured a passport I would of course have to honour it. But I would strongly advise against it. Uthuli has certainly not forgotten you. In any event, I would have thought that you would be more at home in your German-controlled territory to the south.'

'Tanganyika,' Kurt said. 'That is what it is called now: Tanganyika. Oh, it is splendid country, Adrian, but not as splendid as this. Tell me, has there been any news of that scoundrel Kainairju?'

'Nobody has heard of him since the day he was banished. He's almost certainly dead.'

'But you still do not recommend that I return. Not even with Mandy and the children?'

'Especially not with Mandy and the children.'

Kurt grinned. 'Unless I can bring with me a thousand bayonets, eh?'

'Well,' Adrian said, 'thank God, no British Government would ever allow that.'

Kurt guffawed. 'Unless they were British bayonets, eh? Unless they were British bayonets.'

10

'Do you think he meant it?' Joanna asked, after their guests had left, and Adrian had related his conversation.

Adrian shrugged. 'One always feels that Kurt means everything he says. But he may be the least of our worries if all he has told us is true. And with this Uganda business on the boil . . . I really would like to know what's happening. And that means a visit to Mombasa.'

'Yes,' she said thoughtfully.

'And you would really like to go home,' he said.

She glanced at him. 'Only for a visit.'

'Then you shall,' he promised.

'Couldn't you come with me?'

He shook his head. 'I think it's more than ever necessary for me to remain here, right now. You'll have to be my ears and eyes, my love. But you'll take the children.'

By the end of the next Long Rains he was approaching his thirty-third birthday, and Joanna was nearly thirty. Into the past eight years they had crammed a great deal, but now once again he was beginning to wonder about the future, which had so suddenly become uncertain. On the one hand, he solemnly grew a coffee crop every year and then threw most of it away; on the other, he remained intensely grateful that Moore's ambitions were taking so long to be realised, and that there was no one to sell his crop to. On the one hand he recognised that he was living in paradise, and that he did not have any financial worries – quite apart from the money on deposit in Mombasa there was always ivory to be obtained whenever he needed cash; on the other, he felt he was stagnating, accomplishing nothing that would not disappear with his death. On the one hand, he felt keenly the fact that it was now eight years since he had seen his mother; on the other, even with his 'pardon' for that Southampton affair, he had absolutely no desire to return to England. And on the one hand he dreaded the coming of anything to harm the Masai, whom he had truly grown to love and respect, but on the other, if change and challenge were inevitable, he wanted it to happen soon, while he still had the determination, and the power over Uthuli, to cope with it. Nor was it any advantage to reflect on the fame which everyone said he had achieved; as far as he could see, he was famous as a freak rather than as a man of accomplishment.

He wondered if Joanna considered those points. It was a measure of their odd relationship, so very intimate and yet so very separate, that they never discussed them.

Uthuli, who was far older than Adrian – it was impossible even to attempt to guess at the age of any Masai one had not known from birth, but Adrian was pretty sure the chieftain was nearly sixty, a tremendous age for a Masai – was as usual unhappy at the thought of his favourite human being leaving for the coast, even if only for a few months. But, as usual, he accepted the situation. Safah was this time able to accompany them; he had four sons by now, and three wives, and his domestic establishment was thriving. Bar, who at thirteen was as tall as any warrior, also went on this occasion, as Adrian had long determined not to have the boy inducted into the tribe, which would sway him permanently towards Africa, whereas he wanted his son to be entirely international in outlook. So he arranged with Joanna to put him to school in England on her way to the States; they both decided his opportunities would be better there than even in North America, where people of black or mixed blood were far more numerous, and for that reason far less socially acceptable, whatever the rights they had won for themselves as a result of the Civil War. Bar, like all of them, had decidedly ambivalent feelings about his departure – excitement at launching out into the world, tempered with sadness at leaving the only home he had ever known.

Catherine, who was now eight, would also remain away for a while with her grandparents. She was definitely unhappy at the prospect, but Joanna had no doubt she would change her mind when she actually got to New York.

Joanna's feelings remained a mystery. Excitement certainly. But also regret? 'I am coming back,' she promised. 'I am coming back.'

He kissed her. 'I believe you,' he said. But he didn't really.

So what did *he* truly feel about it all? He knew going home was something she should have done long ago, and he was still optimistic enough to believe that such a trip *could* bring them back together again. He was prepared to be utterly lonely, as Sita was in no sense a companion, and on their safari down to the coast indulged in almost a second honeymoon, hoping desperately she might become pregnant. They shot elephant together, to finance her trip, and laughed and joked as they had not done since that first unforgettable safari, and he felt she was genuinely happy for the first time since then as well.

In Mombasa, however, any grief he might have felt over her imminent departure was shadowed by the evidence of increasing British presence all about him. There was now a warship; it seemed permanently based on the coast, a steam sloop whose business was keeping an eye open for slavers. There were British soldiers everywhere, wearing their new tropical uniforms of drab brown, which they called 'khaki' from the Indian word. And there were officials, merchants and missionaries by the dozen, all perfectly at home and regarding themselves as permanent fixtures. The word 'protectorate' was still carefully avoided, but what was happening had to be fairly obvious to the Africans. Equally disturbing, as he had observed on his way down to the coast, the Kikuyu were becoming distinctly restless under the constant probing of the white man; even their old friend Bar-clay had been made to feel less than welcome, and there had been no *ngoma* to entertain them on this occasion.

'I am sure there is going to be some trouble with them, fairly soon,' he told Mr Williamson, who actually was the consul general.

Williamson shrugged. 'One accepts that possibility, Barclay. Indeed, one regards it as a probability. It is a pattern which is being repeated all over the world. Empires are not won without some bloodshed from time to time. But we will soon be ready for any aggression on the part of the Kikuyu.'

Aggression on the part of the Kikuyu! Adrian thought.

Moore had always treated Adrian as a figure of awe whose opinions had to be respected, and who had to be cajoled into accepting the necessary decisions from Whitehall. But Williamson, a much older man and a senior civil servant, who had been consul in a variety of out-of-the way places during his career, regarded Adrian as one of his junior assistants – and with some suspicion, as a man who might very well put the interests of the African over the European, a truly unforgivable point of view.

Adrian now discovered that the first of the caravans Moore had spoken of several years before was being prepared. A military force was accompanying it, as it was intended to reach a decision with the arrogant King Mwanga of Uganda. No one appeared to be considering the points of view of the people, the Kikuyu and the Masai and the other tribes whose lands had to be crossed before the lake was reached.

Adrian and Safah left as soon as Joanna and the children had steamed out of Mombasa harbour, hurrying to return to warn their people of the impending crisis. The Kikuyu took the news grimly. Uthuli as usual sat and pondered for some time. Then he asked, 'What must we do, my son? My Morani will regard this as an invasion of their lands, by men seeking to take their cattle and their women.'

'You must restrain them and tell them to be patient, my father,' Adrian told him. 'These people are but passing through. They will not trouble either your cattle or your women.'

It was an immense caravan, more than a thousand men, no doubt as recommended by Stanley, Adrian thought. They had both horses and dogs with them, animals entirely strange and frightening to the Masai, as well as a large detachment of khaki-clad British soldiers bound for the garrison in Uganda. They had had a brief clash with the Kikuyu and lost a couple of men to the poisoned arrows.

'But we gave them a bloody nose,' declared Major Spencer, their commander, as he dined with Adrian by the lake. 'Not that I do not realise those black scoundrels will have to be dealth with, once and for all, in the near future. I intend to recommend that in my report.'

'Can men be scoundrels for wishing to preserve their land from invaders?' Adrian asked quietly.

Spencer stared at him, uncertain whether or not his leg was being pulled, then decided to change the subject. 'What really worries me is the incidence of malaria. But there it is. One must accept the misfortunes of nature if one sets out to earn the Queen's penny, eh? At least we have not had to do battle with the Masai. Thanks to you.' But he glanced nervously at the kraal, where Uthuli had assembled several clans to make a total fighting force of more than a thousand men, just in case; Spencer's own command had been encamped some distance away, with strict instructions not to enter the Masai township.

'Nor will you, unless you provoke them,' Adrian promised.

'Not our business to provoke people, old man. Just to

272

keep the Queen's peace, eh. Besides . . .' He smiled. 'We would hate to have you evicted from this delightful spot. My word, but I envy you.'

After that, the caravans became a fairly regular feature of life in the high country, passing through at least twice a year. Adrian hated to see them, not only because each one represented a potential crisis, but because of the insidious effect they had on the Masai. At first, the Morani stood in clusters on high ground, each man with a spear, hungrily watching the straggling humanity beneath them – who watched *them* with a proportionate anxiety. But as time passed, and the men from the coast realised that the Masai were not going to attack them, their fear dwindled. Then they wanted to trade with the proud warriors and the beautiful women, and they came well equipped to do so, with all the irrelevant bric à brac which had for so long appeased the Kikuyu. The Masai were utterly childlike in their passion for bright colours and gaudy trinkets, and it saddened Adrian to see the stalwart young Morani exchanging their knives and their hard-won lions' manes for a necklace of coloured glass beads. The beads indeed soon became an important article of attire. Not only did the warriors wear them, but they took to making presents of them to their wives and girl friends, and before long the esteem in which a woman was held by her man was indicated by the number of necklaces she wore. Even Sita succumbed, and after a stream of complaints Adrian was forced to follow fashion and drape half a dozen of the valueless glass chains round her neck.

Even more disturbingly, the contact with the people from the coast also had an immediately deleterious effect on the health of the Masai. The common cold, previously unknown in the high country, quickly became endemic, and ugly streaming mucous stained every face. It occurred to Adrian, but fortunately not to Uthuli, that here might be the beginning of the fulfilment of the dreaded prophecy.

Of course the caravans had their useful sides too. They did buy Adrian's coffee crop, both for themselves and for resale, either in Uganda or when they regained the coast. They also brought news, although most of that was invariably bad. The forest tribes were in arms almost everywhere; British troops had fought a pitched battle with the Kikuyu, as Spencer had prophesied, and there was a continuous guerilla war going on with the Kamba people, while hunting parties from Mombasa were apparently descending on Tsavo in droves, massacring untold quantities of game. No one seemed excessively concerned by all this – it was accepted as part of the process of 'civilising' the country.

Adrian could only be grateful that the high country lay too far from the coast to be the object of anything less than a most expensive safari, and equally that with the forest tribes in an uproar, it had become a most hazardous journey to and from Mombasa. But he felt obliged to protest when the soldiers began to construct a fort on the river which formed the traditional border between the lands of the Masai and the Kikuyu. The Masai called the river *enairobe*, because its water, flowing down from the mountains, was always cool – the British immediately corrupted this to nairobi. When Adrian pointed out that this was actually Masai grazing land, he was informed that the fort was intended to prevent the Kikuyu, who were now apparently regarded as far more dangerous than the Masai – they were certainly far more numerous – from expanding into the Masai country and causing additional trouble. Adrian was prepared to accept this, but felt he had to point out to the commanding officer that the fort was constructed in about as unhealthy a spot as could be imagined, to be told, stiffly, that British soldiers were expected to face the perils of malaria with the same spirit in which they faced any human enemies.

The caravans also brought letters, which was always a pleasure. His mother wrote, as did Amanda, and Jo. She explained that she was having to delay her return because of her father's illness, but hoped to be back in another year or so. *Year or so*, he thought; then she would have been gone four years. She wrote to him regularly, and he understood that it had taken her nearly a year even to get back to America, with her lengthy stopoff in England. Her letters were always filled with terms of endearment and considerations of their joint future; and he had always replied in kind, but he still wondered if they were both not fooling themselves, much less each other. Four years was too long to be apart. They had shared a splendid dream, but the dream had soured too early in their marriage to have any hope of being realised now. Johnnie's death had thrown them back together, but it had not been able to restore their love. He did not really expect to see her again.

And Bar? The boy wrote regularly as well, letters obviously composed with great care and concentration as he slowly mastered the art of using words to express his ideas. He spoke with wonder at the sights he had seen, the hugeness of the world into which he had been launched. He did not mention the loneliness of his position or the hostility which he would undoubtedly have encountered from some of his schoolmates, but Adrian could sense that there was an underlying unhappiness marring his son's life. So, Bar would undoubtedly come home – but what kind of Bar would it be? This was another cause for consideration of his own position.

Thus he was in a sombre mood when Uthuli came to see him, just after the Rains, and thus several months since the last caravan had passed through. Uthuli was in an even more sombre mood. The cattle were dying.

Adrian was horrified at the news, and even more when he hurried off to inspect the herd. He was no vet, but he could see that the animals had some sort of disease. And they were dying at the rate of several every day; the plain was littered with dead animals, the vultures were having a field day, and the stench reminded him of the afternoon of the battle with Fischer's men, multiplied a hundred fold.

'It is good that we leave this place,' Uthuli said, for the clan was preparing for its annual migration. 'But you . . . it is not good that you stay, this year, my son.'

'I must stay, my father,' Adrian pointed out. 'It is my duty to be here. But . . . it would be best if you did not take your cattle.'

Uthuli frowned. 'How may we leave our cattle, to be slaughtered by the lion and the leopard? Who will milk our cows? And what is a man, without his cattle?'

Adrian scratched his head, because there was really no answer to any of those questions; he and Safah alone could not cope with the entire herd. Obviously the only sensible course was for the Masai to forego their wandering for this year – but he knew neither Uthuli nor his people would accept such a break with tradition . . . and it would mean great hardship. Yet he tried to explain. 'The trouble is, my father, if these cattle are diseased, and the disease is contagious, you could be carrying it with you, to infect the cattle of the other clans.'

'Contagious?'

'That means they can pass their illness from one to the other very easily.'

'I know nothing of that,' Uthuli declared. 'The cattle are dying because the great powers which control the skies and the earth are punishing us for allowing our country to be invaded without resisting.' Adrian had never known him in such a dark mood. 'I will take my cattle with me,' he insisted, 'and pray that by the time I return these caravans will have ceased to trespass upon the lands of the Masai.'

Adrian sighed. 'They will not do so, my father.'

'Then you must stop them, Bar-clay. My Morani ask me why we should suffer the loss of our cattle, so that these people may pass.'

276

Adrian had no reply to that either. But he knew there was a crisis hovering about him. As soon as the Masai had left, he and Safah went down to Fort Smith, which was only a short safari away. There they found, as he had predicted, that most of the garrison were down with malaria; indeed, several had died. But there was a veterinary surgeon there, with nothing to do because all the horses had also died. 'Some kind of fly,' he complained. His name was Alderton, and he immediately agreed to return to the high country with them, to look at the situation. 'That place is a pest-hole,' he remarked of the fort as they left it. 'I must say the Government seems to have an instinct for sending its people to die in faraway places.'

He was a cheerful soul, for all his awareness of death and disease all around him, but even he grew serious when he inspected the scattered entrails of the dead cows and bulls, took specimens – such as had been left by the vultures and had not rotted away – and made little experiments. 'Rinder-pest,' he said briefly.

'Is that serious?' Adrian remembered Kurt saying there had been an outbreak of rinderpest shortly after their departure in 1875 – but the herds had recovered.

'It can be, very serious. The herd must be quarantined at once.'

Adrian gave a mirthless grin. 'That herd is several score miles away by now, Mr Alderton. Mixing with a lot of other herds.'

'Then we may be on the verge of an unimaginable catas-trophe, Mr Barclay. Am I right in supposing the herds represent the main food supply of the Masai?'

'Well, not entirely. They use the milk more than the meat. And they use grain more than meat, too. The loss of their cattle will have more of a moral effect. They regard it as their wealth, you see. But I agree with you that it could be serious. They feel it is a judgement on them from heaven for allowing their territory to be invaded. If the cattle do not quickly recover . . .'

'They can hardly do that,' Alderton pointed out, 'while they are busy reinfecting each other. You say there is no hope of this particular herd being recalled?'

'Not without an army.'

Alderton wiped his brow. 'I must get down to Mombasa and report this. It is most terribly serious. Will you accompany me?'

'I think I had better go north and see if there is anything I can do to bring them back. But I doubt anything will come of it. Is this disease dangerous to man?'

'Not in itself. It will destroy all the cattle, though, if it is not checked. And possibly the sheep as well. Whether they are great meat-eaters or not, I would say your friends are well on the way to having a food problem over the next few years.'

Adrian and Safah packed up the house, took their wives and Safah's children, and trekked north, following the trail of Uthuli's clan. This was not difficult to do, as everywhere they found the evidences of the disease in the decimated herds of cattle, and everywhere, although Adrian was by now as well known throughout the Masai land as he apparently was on the coast, he encountered increasing hostility. He might have brought the Masai ten years of good fortune, but now their herds were dying.

And not only their herds. He was aghast when they finally caught up with the clan in its winter grazing area. Here the cattle were not only dwindling, but the people themselves were sick. Adrian and Safah saw the blisters on the skin of one dying woman, and knew immediately that it was smallpox. 'How the hell . . .' Adrian asked.

Safah gave a doleful shrug. 'Someone in one of the caravans, perhaps, bwana.'

'It is the fulfilment of the prophecy,' Uthuli said. 'You are my son, Bar-clay, and I love you like a son. No man of my

278

people will ever go against you, as long as I live. But not even you are powerful enough to change the prophecy. The white man has come to our land, and our cattle and our people are dying. Soon the white people themselves will come in sufficient numbers to destroy the rest of us. These are sad times, my son.'

At least he was uttering no threats. Yet. 'I will go to Mombasa,' Adrian said. 'And arrange for doctors.' Moore had promised those, as well as the caravans.

But getting to Mombasa was no longer simply a matter of making a safari, as he had done with Jo back in 1884. He had to return to Fort Smith and convince the commanding officer, Major Winter, of the urgency of his mission in order to obtain an escort of soldiers – no other way could he dare to pass through the land of the Kikuyu. But Winter had, two months previously, sent an escort with Alderton, and now he simply could not spare the men – in view of the enormous sick parade every day – without weakening his garrison to a dangerous level. 'I'm afraid you will have to wait for either the next east-bound caravan, Mr Barclay, or for reinforcements to reach me from the coast.'

Adrian returned home, his despair growing. He seemed totally unable to do anything about what was fast developing, as Alderton had prophesied, into an unimaginable catastrophe.

In the new year the clan was back, and was now definitely in the grip of a smallpox epidemic; some score of them had already died. He could not help being concerned with the health of Safah and the women, and tried to keep them at home as much as possible, but of course it was impossible to stop them visiting their relatives in the kraal, and it was equally impossible to explain to them how easily they could catch the disease. The herd, too, had been decimated, although the death rate had declined.

The Morani were, naturally, in an ugly mood. They could not understand how their great friend Barclay had permitted this to happen. 'But you will put a stop to the caravans, and these evils will go away,' Uthuli said confidently.

'I am certainly going to try,' Adrian said, and in March an eastbound caravan finally arrived from Lake Victoria. They were in a hurry, having heard about the smallpox, and were reluctant to let Adrian join them – especially when he proposed to bring along Safah and their joint families – in case they were contagious. But Adrian insisted, and for once Uthuli was happy to see him go, confident that he could put an end to their troubles.

Adrian knew just what he was up against, for as usual Williamson was not disposed to take the matter seriously. 'Rinderpest,' he remarked. 'I have had that fellow Alderton bleating about rinderpest for weeks. Now you are talking about smallpox. I have British soldiers dying every day of malaria when they are not dying of something else – do you realise that one of our officers actually went and got himself killed by a lioness the other day? Now you want me to start worrying about a smallpox epidemic amongst the Masai. Have you been inoculated?'

'A long time ago, when I first sailed this coast.'

'Well, there is a good doctor here in Mombasa. Have it done again before you return. And see that your domestics are also vaccinated. As for the Masai, I'm afraid they will have to take their chances; we certainly do not have sufficient serum to vaccinate an entire nation, even were they likely to allow us to do so.'

Adrian kept his temper with an effort. 'A lot of them will die,' he agreed. 'I think they can stand that. But they feel, correctly, that the disease, and the illness of their cattle, comes from the caravans. They want them stopped. I want them stopped, at least until this thing has cleared up.'

'My dear fellow, you know that is quite impossible. You simply must get it through your head that opening a continent is bound to involve a considerable amount of dislocation, and even hardship, for the indigenous inhabitants.

280

Indeed, for everybody. But it is the duty of British officials to face these problems with courage, and above all, equanimity. It never does to let the natives know there is a crisis. They can't take it. Next thing you know you have panic and God knows what else. Surely you understand that by now?'

Adrian felt like throttling the man in sheer despair; everything he had spent the last ten years in doing seemed to be falling apart, and no one was prepared even to worry about it. Still, he made himself keep calm, had himself and Safah vaccinated, as well as Sita and Saba and Safah's other two wives and his children, and dashed off a letter to Joanna, after several hours of unhappy thought, recommending that she stay away a while longer – and that she have herself and Catherine vaccinated as well before thinking of returning to Africa.

In fact, as she had now been gone nearly four years, and here he was suggesting she prolong her stay, he was more than ever convinced he would never see her again. His feelings about this alternated between despair that another aspect of his life should have turned out to be such a blind alley of wasted hopes and dreams and opportunities . . . and a certain relief. They had lived a sham for too long, and if she could find some real happiness back in the States, or in England, then he was content that she should do so; in the present state of affairs in the high country there was no hope of finding any happiness there.

But the thought that he would never again hold that pulsing beauty in his arms induced total misery, a frame of mind which Sita seemed to understand, as she watched him with her huge black eyes filled with anxiety – but which she was quite unable to alleviate.

His misery was compounded by having to wait for a caravan going west, when his whole being was wrapped up in the high country and the tragedy that might be taking place there – or might already have taken place. As the Long Rains had now started, and as he had passed a westbound

281

caravan on his way down to the coast in the spring, it was obviously going to be several months before there was another. He felt the delay was driving him mad, so he attempted to secure purely military support. But there were no troops available, as sporadic little revolts kept occurring among the Africans. Nor were these confined to the British territory; the situation seemed to be even worse in Tanganyika. The whole of East Africa, that dreamland which his father had discovered for him, was collapsing into chaos. 'Except,' Williamson told him as they dined one night at Abdullah's hotel, 'for the Masai land. They may have some sickness up there, and be losing some of their cattle, but they alone have never attempted to resist our advance. Thanks to you, of course, Barclay,' he added in one of his rare moments of condescension. 'I do wish we'd had the foresight to plant someone like you in the heartland of each of the tribes.'

The man's complacency was insufferable. Adrian was very tempted to resign as vice-consul, if only to allow himself the pleasure of telling Williamson just what he thought of him, but he reflected that that way he would be even less able to help the Masai. He was more tempted to risk passing through the land of the Kikuyus with just Safah and the women, but he knew that in the present state of anger and hatred which existed in the forest it would be suicide. So he smiled politely and controlled his impatience, and was at last approached by a burly Scotsman named Andrew Dick, who it appeared was going to lead the next caravan through the high country, as he was on his way to Uganda to set up a steamship service on Lake Victoria. 'I'm carrying every God damned thing I can possibly need, save for the timber out of which I'll make the hulls; I'll cut that on the spot. But I'm going to have to build up my own engines right there. I'll do it. It'll be a goldmine. And I'm pleased to have you along, Mr Barclay. I've heard a lot about you, and read more, eh? You're my passport through

282

the Masai land. That's a good thing. You'll keep those thieving black hands off my machinery.'

Another totally dislikeable would-be frontiersman, Adrian thought in disgust. But there was nothing for it save again to smile politely. 'When do we leave?' he asked.

'Won't be for a couple of weeks yet. I've some more gear coming in on another ship and she's not due till then. I'll be in touch.' He winked. 'I won't leave you behind, man.'

Another couple of weeks! Even Sita and Saba, who initially had been entranced by Mombasa – the sights and the sounds, the minarets and the prayers, the clothes of the people and the exotic foods, the immensity of the ocean and the heat of the air – were beginning to fret as they felt themselves entirely cut off from their own people. Adrian could only counsel them also to be patient. But he counted the hours until a fortnight later the missing ship did actually drop anchor in Mombasa harbour. He was there to see it, and watch the precious machinery being unloaded, as the passengers were brought ashore – and he found himself looking at his wife. Behind her was her father, and a young woman who was clearly one of her sisters.

'Jo?' he muttered. 'Jo Oh, my God!'

Her smile faded. 'Aren't I welcome?'

'Oh, my darling . . .' She was in his arms, despite the crowd of onlookers, her new topee slipping down her head, her magnificent hair uncoiling down her back, her eyes moist. But also anxious. As was he, suddenly. He held her away from him. 'Didn't you get my letter? I wrote you, telling you not to come.'

'I must have been already on my way.' She frowned at him. 'Telling me not to come?'

'We are having all kinds of trouble . . .' He remembered his manners, and smiled at John Meachem. 'Well, sir, it has been a long time. Welcome to Africa.'

'Glad to be here, boy,' Meachem said, shaking hands and

283

looking into Adrian's eyes. He had aged a great deal since that unforgettable evening in Southampton, and his hair was quite white – but his grip was as firm as ever. 'No hard feelings, eh?'

'None, sir.' Adrian looked at the girl, who was simply a young edition of Joanna.

'I'm Hetty,' she said. 'I guess you don't remember me.'

'Oh, I do,' he lied.

'Say, boy, what does a guy have to do to get a drink around here?' Meachem demanded. 'My throat's dry as this dust that's getting everywhere.'

'You have to bring your own, I'm afraid, sir.'

'That's what Jo's been telling me. Well, I sure have done that. Where the hell are those boys?'

Several Arabs were at that moment staggering ashore carrying an enormous assortment of trunks and boxes, sporting rifles and tropical gear, two cases of Scotch whisky and one of brandy . . . Meachem was clearly planning a long stay.

'It's all so *exciting*,' Hetty said, looking around her with wide eyes. 'We're going on safari. Have I said it right?'

Adrian looked at Joanna, who looked back at him. Her eyes were at once anxious and brittle; she clearly did not feel his welcome had been what she had hoped for. 'You spoke of trouble,' she said, as they walked to the hotel, followed by John Meachem's equipment.

'You name it, we've got it,' he said, and told them over lunch. 'So you see it's not really the place to be, at the minute.'

'Well, boy, we sure didn't come all this way to go home again without seeing this paradise Jo's been telling us about.'

'Have you all been vaccinated?'

'Sure thing. No smallpox is going to trouble us. Shame about the cattle though. That sure does upset a man. Say, now, who's this pretty little thing?'

'Ah,' Adrian said, his heart sinking as Safah and the women entered the building and came across to greet him. Joanna's face was freezing. 'This is Sita. My . . . my housekeeper. She understands some English. And this is Safah, my right-hand man, and Saba, his number one wife. Our establishment, you might say.'

Thank God, he thought, that the girls, being in civilisation, had been persuaded to wear clothes.

'I see a great deal has changed,' Joanna remarked, as he followed her into his bedroom, where Abdullah had already had her boxes placed. 'Nowadays you take Sita with you when you travel.'

'I could hardly leave her up there for several months, alone, when her people were moving north,' Adrian pointed out. 'And frankly, I wanted her, and Safah's family, to be vaccinated. Things really are bad up there. I don't honestly know what I'm going back to.'

'Well, then, the sooner we are back, the better.'

'Are you sure? I mean, if anything were to happen to your father or Hetty . . .?'

She stared at him. 'Are you sure you want me back, Adrian.' Then she flushed. 'Thanks, anyway, for telling them Sita is your "housekeeper". Does she sleep in here? I'd better have my things moved out.'

'Jo!' He caught her arm. 'I really am quite overwhelmed to have you back. I'm sorry I was so surprised . . .'

'So am I.'

'I've just had so much on my mind,' he said. 'I can see it all falling apart. Ten years, just being crumpled up and thrown away like waste paper. Oh, Jo . . .' He drew her close. 'I have missed you so.'

She tilted back her head to look up at him. 'Have you honestly? Oh, how I have missed you. I had no idea everything took so *long*. Four years . . . And to come back to a cold shoulder . . . You haven't even asked me about the children.'

'I haven't had the time. I'm asking now.'

'Well . . .' She sat on the bed, and he sat beside her, holding her hands. 'I don't know how many of my letters got to you. But you remember I told you Bar had to go to what you people call a crammer, before any school in the UK would look at him?'

'I remember.'

'Well, he did very well. He really is a very bright boy, and he is so anxious to learn. So, with Mr Edmonds' help, I finally got him a place at one of your public schools. That's what they call them, right?'

'Right. But that's tremendous. Which one?'

'A place called Winchester. It's convenient for South-ampton and his grandmother.'

'Winchester? Good God! That's a *very* good school.'

'I can tell you that it's darned expensive. Bar will only be there for two years, of course, as he's going to be seventeen this year. The headmaster agreed to take him because of the exceptional circumstances, but he did tell me there's no chance of him qualifying or anything. They're just going to try to turn him into an English gentleman.'

'Which is more than I ever was,' Adrian said.

She made a moue. 'I like them rough. Anyway, I bor-rowed the necessary off Papa. He says we can repay him by letting him shoot a couple of elephants.'

'Um,' Adrian agreed, not altogether happy to be indebted to John Meachem.

'And Cathy is at school in New York, living with Mama and Pru. She settled in very well, once she realised she couldn't grab a gun and shoot anything she felt like. She's going to be a proper lady when next you see her.'

'I wonder if they'll want to see me,' he murmured.

'You don't approve?' she asked, in a mixture of anxiety and annoyance.

'Of course I approve, my darling girl. Do you know, you haven't actually kissed me?'

'I feel I'm in a bedroom with a strange man,' she confessed.

'Well, after four years, maybe that's the best way to start off,' he agreed.

They *were* strangers again, and yet, perhaps because they had both dreamed of this moment for so long, and wanted to give so much to each other, they were more hesitant than strangers could ever have been. She had put on a little weight, but that only made her always petite body more exciting. It had never crossed his mind that she might not have spent an entirely celibate four years until now, but he would not have blamed her had she had an affair – just to hold her naked in his arms was totally reassuring. And she had come back! That fact was only slowly dawning on him. She was back, and she was never going away again, at least, he resolved, not for a very long time.

'Did you see Mandy?' he asked, as she lay with her head on his shoulder.

'Oh, yes, they came across to England to visit with me. She's looking great. Well . . .' She hesitated.

'What?'

'I think she has a hard time with Kurt.'

'Yes,' Adrian said, remembering their first safari, and also how Kurt had made her strip for the Masai.

'He told me he'd been up here to see you with some Austrian count.'

'Did he tell you he still dreams of coming back?'

'I sort of got that idea. Would you stop him?'

'I don't know that I can. It's still a free country. I'm just hoping he has more sense. It's Mandy I'd worry about.'

'And their children,' Jo said. 'They are the most adorable kids. She has three,' she added wistfully. But she had something else on her mind. 'Adrian,' she said very softly. 'Is there nothing we can do about Sita?'

He looked down at her. 'I'm afraid not.'

287

'For God's sake!' She sat up violently, her always ready temper flaring. 'Am I being so unreasonable? All I want to do is be your wife. To have you, and be yours. I don't want to share you. I won't share you! Adrian . . .'

He sighed. 'My darling girl, if we are going to live with the Masai . . .'

'Oh, God damn the Masai!' she snapped, and lay down again with her back to him.

The Masai, he thought. The burden he had taken on, first to save the lives of Kurt and Amanda, and then because he wanted to, because they were such splendid people. Now they were dying, and his membership of their nation was hanging around his neck like a millstone. Of course Jo was right; no civilised woman should be expected to share her husband with another, certainly not on a permanent basis. But there was nothing he could do, save pack up and leave. And she knew that, he was sure, just as she must know he loved her, and no one else. He kissed her shoulder, but she merely gathered the bedclothes about her.

Next day he was grateful for the presence of John Meachem and Hetty, who had to be shown the sights of Mombasa, taken up to inspect the massive ruins of the old Portuguese fortress overlooking the town, guided through a mosque and the souk, the open air market, and taught how to eat mangoes without immediately needing a bath. Then they had to be introduced to Dick, and Adrian had to make the necessary arrangements to have them included in the caravan. The idea didn't please Meachem. 'Say,' he remarked, 'I thought we were going into the real bush, just so. This is a God damned army.'

'I'm afraid it has to be, the way things are now,' Adrian told him. 'But you'll find you're in the real bush, just the same.'

He and Joanna were not alone again until that night, and then she complained of a headache brought on by the heat.

288

He couldn't argue with that; he had one himself. He could only reflect with relief that the caravan was due to leave in three days' time. Things would be better when they reached the high country, and Jo had got back in the feel, and the ethics, of Africa.

Meachem's fears that he might be cheated of adventure disappeared within a couple of days of leaving Mombasa, when a blacknecked cobra – called the spitting snake because of its habit of ejaculating its venom into the face of an adversary rather than actually biting it – got into his tent. He got out before actually being blinded, landing panting on the ground, and Jo despatched the reptile with a single shot from her revolver, proving that she had not forgotten how to shoot.

The incident put her back in the best of humours, but before Adrian could capitalise on that, Hetty was less fortunate than her father in that she picked up a scorpion, thinking it was a pretty insect. Adrian was sure her screams would be heard back in Mombasa, and certainly her hand swelled up to a horrendous size, but all caravans nowadays travelled with a doctor, and he had the necessary medicines and salves both to soothe the pain and to bring down the swelling and the fever, and after four days of being carried in a litter she had recovered sufficiently to be able to walk; but throughout the four days Jo remained at her side, sleeping in her tent at night, caring for her baby sister.

There was the usual confrontation with the lions as they crossed Tsavo, and John Meachem was delighted to bring down one of the huge creatures, while he found enough tragedy for reflection when three of the bearers were swept away as they forded the Tsavo river; as this was the wrong time of the year to be making this journey, just after the rains instead of just before they commenced, the waterways were still deep and fast running; even the huge seasonal lake at Amboseli, which Adrian had only ever seen as a vast mud swamp, was now an even vaster expanse of still water.

In the savannah land above Tsavo they halted for a week to let everyone really enjoy themselves, and from dawn until dusk the sound of rifles echoed over the plain, while the pile of trophies within the camp grew and grew. Adrian never hunted save for a very good reason, and he let the others get on with it, but Joanna was especially delighted when she encountered one of the rare bongo species of antelope, normally a nocturnal creature, whose reddish-brown skin was marked with exquisite narrow white stripes. 'Do you think there is any chance of preserving this hide?' she asked Adrian. 'Safah could skin it for me.'

'Why not?' he agreed. 'If that's what you want to do.'

Her temper flared. 'What the hell is the matter with you?' she demanded. 'Everyone else is having one whale of a time, and you just sit around the camp looking miserable.'

'Maybe I think there are more important things to do, like seeing if any of the Masai are still alive, than shooting everything in sight,' he replied. 'And maybe I don't get all that much amusement out of taking life just to be able to say I shot something. Or from watching other people do it.'

'Oh . . .' She realised that Sita was, as usual, nearby and both watching and listening, which merely made her more angry. 'You know what you are? You're a prig,' she stormed, and marched off to be with Hetty and her father. He began to wonder if things *would* be any better up in the valley, but he observed that she abandoned the idea of keeping the bongo skin.

They were in sufficient strength to prevent any trouble from the Kikuyu, who had in any event been thoroughly cowed by Kurt's old remedy for black independence: the Maxim gun. Adrian doubted relations with the tribe would ever be the same again; not only was there no *ngoma*, but several of the villages they passed were burnt-out shells. Even more disturbing, those Kikuyu they did encounter were in a state of great agitation, and not with the British invaders. They spoke of some great calamity having taken

290

place up in the high country, but would not say more than that.

Joanna's mood towards Adrian softened, but he was concerned only with getting on into the upper forests – he would allow Dick no more long stops, to the disappointment of John Meachem and Hetty, who were entranced by the scenery. And at last they reached the Nairobi river and Fort Smith, where to Adrian's consternation they were told by Major Winter that they could go no further.

'What do you mean, we can't go on?' Dick demanded. 'I have a contract to fulfil, man.'

'There has been an outbreak of the most serious trouble with the Masai, Mr Dick,' Winter explained. 'I was only waiting for you to arrive to send a message down to the coast calling for reinforcements.'

'Trouble with the Masai?' Adrian asked, uncertain whether to be pleased or aghast. If the Masai were capable of making trouble, then the smallpox epidemic could not have been as severe as he had feared. But if the Masai *were* making trouble . . . something very remarkable must have happened.

'Why, Mr Barclay, good to see you back. I wish to God you'd been here last spring. Yes, the last caravan going through, well, it came a cropper. I always knew it would happen, one day.'

'*What* happened?' Adrian shouted.

'Well, I imagine there were faults on both sides. For one thing, the caravan leaders had recruited a large number of Kikuyus as bearers for the whole trip.'

'Into the Masai land?' Jo asked. 'I thought the Kikuyus were afraid of the Masai?'

'Not any more,' Adrian told her. 'The Kikuyu think the Masai are soft, because they are the only people in this part of Africa not to have opposed the British penetration.'

'I'm afraid that too is a thing of the past,' Winter said. 'The caravan was attacked and cut up. I mean, really

291

massacred. Of some six hundred people, only a couple of hundred got back here.' That explained the Kikuyu attitude, Adrian thought. 'All the white men were killed,' Winter went on. 'It is the most serious incident to have taken place, anywhere. The Kikuyu went fleeing back to their forest as if the devil himself was after them.'

'We met them,' Adrian agreed. 'But there had to be provocation for the Masai to go to war.'

'Well, Mr Barclay, as to that, I am not in a position to judge, in the absence of reliable witnesses. The surviving Kikuyu swore there was not, other than the mere fact of their presence in Masai land in the first place. But that is hardly relevant. The point at issue is that the Masai simply cannot be allowed to massacre any member of any caravan they do not like. And when we consider the European lives that were lost as well . . .'

'We'll make the bastards pay,' Dick growled. 'Oh, yes. You don't have to wait for reinforcements, Major. I have a hundred fighting men with me. Add them to your soldiers, and I reckon we can sort out any God-damned Masai.'

'If you attack the Masai,' Adrian said, looking down on the smaller man, 'before I discover the truth of what has happened, I am personally going to break your neck.'

'Now look here, big fellow . . .' Dick was taken aback by the sudden vehemence in Adrian's normally mild and polite voice.

'Gentlemen,' Winter protested. 'Let us maintain a sense of proportion. You say you wish to find out the truth, Mr Barclay? What exactly do you have in mind?'

'That the caravan rests here, as you have indicated, and that I proceed with my man, Safah, and discover just what the Masai feel their grievance is.'

'Grievance?' Winter demanded. 'I'm afraid this business has gone too far to be described as a grievance. We are at war.'

'We'll slaughter the bastards,' Dick growled.

This time Adrian ignored him. 'I am the vice-consul for Masai land, Major Winter, and as such am responsible for their actions. I have known these people for twenty years. In that time, as you well know, Chief Uthuli has not undertaken hostilities against any white men since the attack on Dr Fischer's expedition, which was immediately before I achieved a position of influence with the chieftain. I am telling you that for him to have broken his pledge to me and attacked a caravan, whether I was there or not, there must have been a most enormous ill done to his people. Now, sir, common justice demands that I go to his kraal and find out what that ill was. I will then report back to you, and to Mr Williamson in Mombasa. But any decision as to future action must wait on that report, and must be decided by the proper authorities, not by you. Or . . .' He glanced at Dick, 'by any itinerant trader.'

'Why, you big gorilla,' Dick shouted, becoming red in the face.

'Mr Dick,' Winter said sharply. 'You realise you may be going to your death, Mr Barclay? If the Masai really have declared war . . .'

'There is no chance of that. Just understand me, Major; no one moves from this fortress into the Masai land until I return.'

The major nodded. 'Very good.'

Adrian looked at Dick.

'I do what I think best,' Dick declared.

'I suggest you lock this fellow up,' Adrian said. 'Or at least put him under restraint. He's a menace to us all.'

'But the major is right,' Joanna said that evening at dinner. 'If they really are on the warpath, you could be killed out of hand, long before you got near Uthuli.'

'I agree with Jo,' Meachem said. 'I think your idea is crazy. They're a bunch of God-damned savages, boy, not to be trusted. We've had the same trouble in the States. Let the

293

Army pacify them, that's my motto. We sure pacified the hell out of the Sioux, like we're doing to the Apaches right now.'

Adrian decided to ignore him as well, before he lost his temper. As soon as he could, he took Jo aside. 'There has been some great injustice done,' he said. 'And I have to prevent an even greater one, which could happen if the Government gets the idea they have to despatch a punitive expedition up here. We're talking about our home, my darling girl. Do you want that to become the centre of a bloody war? I have to go. These are my people.'

She sighed. 'Yep. I sometimes reckon they're more your people than anyone with a white skin. Well . . . I guess I never did have the time to get to know you again.'

He grinned. 'I had sort of got the idea you didn't too much care to do that.'

'Oh . . . you drive me up the wall. Too often. But I guess I love you, despite all. I always have. I fell in love with you at first sight, remember? I guess I'm a one-man woman.'

'If you mean that,' he said, 'then I can conquer the world.'

Her eyes were moist. 'Just conquer me, my love. One more time. And then . . . please come back.'

Sita and Saba and Safah's other wives were also alarmed at the thought of their men going off alone together, even to confront their brothers and uncles; they suggested that their presence might be a peace-keeping factor. But Adrian, for all his pretended confidence, had no idea what had really happened, and just in case Uthuli had been replaced as chief by some hothead, he couldn't risk the women. But in fact, for all his euphoria at Joanna's word, he felt sick with despair; it seemed that all his dreams had crashed to the ground in a single bloody afternoon – six months before.

Safah understood his feelings, and indeed, shared them; the Somali regarded himself as almost a Masai, nowadays, as his sons were of course half-Masai. They had no need to speak, as they travelled west as fast as they could, pitching camp as dusk fell and resuming again at dawn, loping across the high plain, and encountering their first Morani, clearly a look-out, as they were about to descend the escarpment into the valley.

'Bar-clay,' he said, leaning on his spear. 'These are busy times.'

He looked fit and healthy and strong – and unmarked. And as arrogantly confident as any Morani who had recently been to war.

'Troubled times, you mean,' Adrian said.

'Where are the white soldiers?' the Masai asked.

'In their fort, where they belong. Safah and I have come to find out what has happened.'

The Morani peered across the plain. 'We have expected them for many days. They do not follow you?'

'They do not follow me,' Adrian said. 'I give you my word.'

'Uthuli would speak with you,' the warrior said, and joined them for the climb down the escarpment.

That was good news. Equally was it reassuring to find that the smallpox epidemic seemed to have spent itself, at least temporarily. Even the cattle, although the herd appeared to have been approximately halved in size, seemed far healthier than when he had left. Not so good was the number of people, and especially Morani, gathered around the kraal; clearly there were several clans assembled here – in anticipation of a war? Or to start one?

But his house still stood, undamaged, by the lake. And Uthili himself was waiting in the kraal. 'Bar-clay,' he said. 'It is good to have you back. You have been away for so long I had feared you would not return. Have you put an end to the caravans?'

Adrian looked at the assembled Morani; there were a good five hundred of them, leaning on their spears, staring at him. 'They will not stop,' he said. 'They will never stop

295

now, because you have broken your promise, my father. You have summoned your people to war, and you have killed.'

'How could I restrain my young men?' Uthuli asked. 'And it is the white men who have broken their words, not I.'

'Tell me what happened.'

'Before the Long Rains, a caravan entered our land. We bid them welcome, before we realised the bearers were Kikuyu. Many, many Kikuyu. These people have always been our enemies. You know this thing, Bar-clay.'

'I know it, my father. But there have been Kikuyu bearers with caravans before.'

'Never so many.'

'They were just passing through. They could have done you no harm.'

'When has a Kikuyu not harmed the Masai? Since time began there has been warfare between the Masai and the Kikuyu. We have raided their lands for cattle and women, and they, when they have found the courage, have raided our lands. In recent years, you said to keep the peace, and we have done this. So the Kikuyu have come to regard us as a nation of women. We did not oppose their passage through our land, because they were with the caravan. But while we watched them and let them pass, they entered our kraals and carried off our maidens. My young men would not be restrained.'

'They carried off some of your women?'

'Many women.'

Adrian looked into his eyes. 'You will swear to this, my father?'

'It is the truth, my son.'

Adrian nodded, totally relieved. 'Then all will be well. The Kikuyu are at fault. I will return to the fort and tell the soldiers. I may even have to go down to the coast to explain what really happened to the white men there. But your action was justified, and I will make them understand that.

No harm will come of this, provided you return to the ways of peace, and there is no more killing.'

'We desire only to be left alone, Bar-clay,' Uthuli said.

That night they sat together to eat and drink, and Adrian slept soundly in the kraal, relieved at what he had found, and that he had a case to present. But he was awakened before dawn by the firing of guns; the Masai village was under attack.

11

Adrian and Safah both grabbed their rifles and their clothes and ran outside; it was near dawn, and the kraal was in an uproar, women screaming, babies wailing, men shouting. But after the initial shots, the rifle fire had ceased.

The Morani were gathered outside the village, on the pasture where the herd had been grazing the previous evening. Adrian pushed his way through the crowd and found Uthuli, surrounded by his elders, gazing at the bodies of three young men – they had all been shot. Of the cattle there was no sign save for their hoof prints and pats.

'This is the value of Bar-clay's word,' one of the men remarked. 'He speaks peace, while his friends steal our cattle.'

'Who did this?' Adrian asked Uthuli.

'The white men.'

Adrian could not believe his ears. 'The soldiers from the fort?'

'I do not know if they were soldiers, my son. They were led by white men, armed with long spears. You see, they have shot and killed my people who were guarding our herd. Now they have made off for the escarpment with our cattle. My son, I promised you there would be no more

297

bloodshed. But my warriors must go after these men. They have robbed us of everything we possess.'

Adrian did not have to think very long about what he was going to do. He simply could not believe Major Winter would have permitted any of his men to carry out such a raid, which, apart from being illegal, could do nothing less than inflame the situation. It must have been some other party, who deserved the most drastic punishment. 'I'll come with you,' he said, and Safah nodded his agreement.

They left the kraal within half an hour, five hundred warriors loping into the dawn. The trail was easy to follow, even had they not been able to hear the lowing of the cattle and the cracking of whips in the distance. The Masai made no sound, and they could travel far faster than men driving cattle; when dawn broke they could see the cloud of dust, already halfway up the escarpment, marking their enemies, and as they drew closer, they could make out some hundred men in front of them.

Equally, their enemies could now see them. Someone fired a shot into the air, and while some dozen of the invaders – who seemed divided equally into white men and black – continued to drive the cattle upwards, the remainder turned back to choose defensive positions amongst the rocks. Then one of them fired, and a Morani fell without a sound. Immediately the rest of the Morani also took shelter behind rocks and trees and in the grass, Adrian and Safah with them.

Adrian's brain seemed to have gone numb. He knew he was about to witness a massacre. Those men had attempted to steal the most valuable of all the Masai possessions, killing three men in the process. And now they had killed another of the warriors. No power on earth would now check the anger of the Masai. He could only watch and wait, as Uthuli, with the skill of a born general, directed his men to left and right, by brief words of command to aides who crawled off through the grass. A detachment of the

Morani moved up the escarpment itself, by a steeper, more difficult route than that taken by the cattle, aiming at regaining contact with them as quickly as possible. The remainder dispersed through the rocks and the tall grass and the trees in front of the main body of the invaders, slowly advancing. Occasionally one would show himself to draw fire – often sacrificing himself in doing so – in order that his compatriots might make a further advance.

Meanwhile the white men expended their ammunition in senseless volleys which were mostly wasted on empty grass.

It was a slow process, as the sun climbed into the sky and the day grew hot, but there was no cessation in the Masai movement. By noon the Morani were close enough for their first charge, and suddenly the hillside was alive with darting black figures, thrusting and carving. The cattle thieves grouped together and withdrew up the escarpment, while they poured volley after volley into the Morani, and after a furious five minutes the battle died down, as the Africans again went to ground.

Adrian estimated they must have lost a good twenty men, but the white men and their allies had suffered even more, and the cries of their wounded, lying in the grass and suffering from thirst, made the day hideous. And now, to complete their discomfort, the Masai who had climbed the escarpment appeared above them, brandishing their spears in triumph: they had regained their cattle and undoubtedly despatched the rustlers.

Adrian had been unwilling to fire upon his own kind, however much he condemned their action. Now that they were so clearly lost, he made his way forward, Safah at his heels, until he had regained Uthuli's latest command position, close to the white men's circle. From here he could recognise the burly man who was organising the last-ditch defence. 'Andrew Dick, by God,' he muttered.

'You know this man, my son?' Uthuli asked. As usual

when there was fighting to be done, the chieftain looked utterly contented.

Adrian nodded. 'He commanded the caravan with which I came up from the coast. The man must be mad.'

'Bring him down,' Uthuli suggested. 'Use your long spear, my son, to punish him for this crime.'

Adrian considered. He was so angry he was certainly tempted. But it was necessary to show Winter that the Masai had acted here with judgement and humanity. He shook his head. 'Let me speak with him, my father.'

'You would save his life?'

'I would attempt to stop further bloodshed. He will have to surrender and stand trial. He will be sent to prison for many years. But he must know he has no choice.'

Uthuli considered in turn. Then he nodded. 'The ways of the white man are strange. But if you assure me that he will be punished by his own people for the harm he has done to mine, then speak with him.'

Adrian crawled to the shelter of a thorn tree, and there stood up, cupping his hands. His rifle was slung on his back. 'Dick!' he shouted.

'I see you, Barclay,' the Scotsman shouted back. 'Nigger-loving scoundrel. You have had my men murdered.'

'As you have murdered the Masai,' Adrian replied. 'And committed a most senseless crime. Throw down your arms.'

'And be cut to pieces? Not on your life. Winter will be along soon enough. He'll sort your savages out. We'll hold until then.'

'Listen to me,' Adrian shouted, stepping from behind the tree and walking forward, his hat in his hand so that they could see he was carrying no weapon. 'You won't last another hour. To surrender is the only way you can save your lives. Listen to me.'

Dick levelled his rifle and fired. The bullet struck the

ground only feet from where Adrian stood, and he dived for shelter. Before he had regained his breath, and without a command from their chieftain, the Morani rose again from amidst the boulders and long grass through which they had been steadily crawling throughout the parley, taking the cattle thieves entirely by surprise. The spears were flung from a range of not more than a few feet. One took Dick in the chest, and he fell backwards, his rifle exploding a last time, harmlessly, into the air. His followers threw down their arms, but it was too late. By the time Adrian had regained his feet and got to the scene, there was not one left alive.

'I trust you will believe that Mr Dick left the fortress without my permission – indeed, against my express orders,' Winter said, when Adrian summoned him to inspect the site of the battle. 'But I have no jurisdiction over white civilians. My orders are very precise about that.'

'Then I think your orders will have to be changed,' Adrian told him.

'He said he wished to reconnoitre, and be at hand in case you needed help. As I say, I told him that was against your wishes . . . but he seemed to want to help. I had no idea he was after stealing cattle.' He wiped his brow. 'I cannot understand his reasoning.'

'It's very simple to me,' Adrian pointed out. 'He meant to lead the cattle back to the fort, knowing the Masai would follow, and reckoning that you would have to take his side if it came to a fight within sight or sound of the fort, simply because of the colour of his skin. He did not realise how fast the Masai can move, or how organised they are. Or, perhaps, how highly they value their cattle. For God's sake, they value their herds more highly than they value their women, and they killed close on four hundred Kikuyu for attempting to steal some of *them*. They may be the most generous of hosts,' he said, remembering the way Kurt had

301

been allowed to enjoy himself on their first visit here, so many years ago. 'But they don't like thieving.' He could have added, except when they are doing it. But he was determined to allow himself no weaknesses of conscience here, especially over the way Dick and his friends had met their ends. If they had underestimated the Masai, they had also made the mistake of supposing, with civilised hypocrisy, they could save their lives, when they chose, by surrendering. And if the Christian in him had been revolted by the sight of them being cut to pieces while begging for mercy, he had also to remember that they had shot the three herdsmen in cold blood, and would have killed every African they could see, had they been able to.

For the Masai, it was now a simple matter of survival, and he was their spokesman.

'It has been a most dreadful business.' Winter stood on the escarpment, half a dozen soldiers – all he could spare from the fort – at his back. He looked down. The scene was peaceful enough now, but the bodies and discarded weapons still lay amongst the rocks, and if the hyenas had sullenly withdrawn from their feast on the appearance of the white men, the vultures still circled hungrily overhead, the bees and insects still hummed busily, and the stench of death lay over the hillside. 'This has to be considered an act of war.'

'There need be no war, if you, and everyone else, are sensible,' Adrian insisted. 'These people have been provoked beyond endurance, their women attacked, and finally they were assaulted without warning by Dick and his thugs. They defended themselves, and they regained their cattle, as they were surely entitled to do. The number of dead is horrifying, I know; but Dick refused a very fair offer of surrender.'

Winter pulled his ear. 'I'm not at all sure what the Government is going to say to this.'

'They will have to listen to me, and then, I hope, adminis-

302

ter nothing less than justice. Isn't that their claim? That they carry British justice throughout the world?'

Winter pulled his other ear. 'Well, I would say your best prospect is to return to the coast as rapidly as possible. I will put an embargo on any more caravans coming through here until I get sufficient reinforcements to protect them, and I will put the fort into the best state of defence I can, for when the Masai decide to attack us.' He continued to stare down into the valley. There was not a Morani in sight, on Adrian's instructions, but clearly he was expecting the worst.

'Now wait just one moment,' Joanna said, when the men returned to the fort. 'Are you saying we can't go home?'

'If you mean you wish to return to your house in the valley . . .'

'My home,' Joanna pointed out.

'Yes, well, I'm afraid that would be foolhardy in the extreme, Mrs Barclay,' Winter said. 'Your house is within a mile of the Masai kraal. You'd not survive a moment.'

Joanna looked at Adrian. They had not had a chance to be alone since he came back. 'Do you believe they'll trouble us?'

'Frankly, no,' he said. 'But the major is probably right to suggest it might be unwise for you to go there. You've been away a long time, and I won't be there.'

'Why not?'

'I have to return to the coast to inform Williamson what has happened, and try to stop any punitive expeditions being launched.'

'Well,' John Meachem said. 'That's it. We've had our safari, I guess. Like you said, Jo, things have changed a bit since you were last up here. We'll come back with you, Adrian. There sure would be a fuss if I was cut to pieces by marauding Africans.'

'I am going home,' Joanna declared. 'I have been away from my home for four years. That's too long. And I invited

303

you, Papa, and Hetty, to come and visit with me here in the high country. You haven't even seen it yet. I agree with Adrian. The Masai were provoked beyond belief. But I have lived amongst them, and am known to them. They won't have forgotten me. And they won't trouble my father and sister, either.'

'My dear Mrs Barclay,' Winter protested.

'Now, see here, Jo,' her father said. 'There comes a time when it's sensible to pull up stakes and sidle off.'

'Gee, I wonder what it *feels* like to be cut to pieces by a marauding African,' Hetty murmured, not altogether in terror.

'I am going *home*,' Joanna said again, and looked at Adrian. 'Can you spare the time to take us there?'

Adrian felt as if she had just offered him the moon. 'Oh, yes,' he said. 'I'll take you there.'

'Are you sure?' he asked her, three nights later, as they stood at the windows of the main bedroom in the house and gazed out at the lake. 'I'll leave you Safah, of course. But there's really no saying what might happen. Uthuli entirely trusts me, of course, and knows I will do my best for him and his people. But if word has already reached the coast about Dick's death, and an expedition has already been launched, and I can't stop it . . . you could find yourself on the wrong side of a shooting war before I can get back to you.'

'I'll take my chances on that,' she said. 'I was never more sure of where I want to be in my life. No matter what happens, I'm certain Uthuli won't turn against me, simply because I'm your wife. He seemed to like Papa too, although I thought Papa was going to have another heart attack when he was offered that blood and milk to drink. But he's really tickled pink by everything he's seen on this trip.' She pointed down the lawn to the bank of the lake, where John Meachem was standing staring at the immense expanse of still water. 'He's absolutely spellbound, and I'll bet that's never happened before. This is the Africa he always wanted to see. The Africa I told him about.' She giggled. 'Hetty's the one I'm going to have to watch. Did you see her eyes roll at the sight of all those naked willies?'

He was still not entirely reassured. 'You do realise the Masai will be migrating in another couple of weeks? Then you really will be all alone up here . . .'

'With Safah, and Safah's sons, and Papa. Hetty and I can look after ourselves too, you know.'

'I do know.' He held her shoulders, drawing her back against him. 'I am so proud of you, my darling. So very proud.'

'Are you?' She tilted her head back to look at him. 'Do you know, that's the very first time you've ever said that to me?'

'Maybe that's where I've been going wrong. I've always been proud of you.'

'But you were too British to say so.' She turned in his arms. 'Are you going to be away long?'

'God knows. I hope not. But with things the way they are . . .'

'I'm so proud of you, too,' she said. 'Going off alone to speak with Uthuli, when he might have been deposed or something . . . Papa was impressed too. He told me so. And now, going down to the coast to defend your people . . .'

'Our people.'

'Our people,' she agreed. 'Oh, Adrian, we have made *so* many mistakes. Or maybe I'm the one who has made them all. You know what my father once said to you, that I was a spoiled brat. I guess I haven't changed all that much.'

'Wouldn't you say you've changed now?'

'I'm going to try. Oh, I'm going to try. Adrian, I'm going to become friends with Sita. I promise. Only . . . can she stay being your housekeeper, at least until Papa and Hetty go home?'

'Of course.' He hesitated. 'You know I have to . . .'

305

'I know. Or she'll go off into the bush and commit suicide or something. I know. Only . . . do it quietly, please.'

'Haven't I always?'

She kissed him. 'Sure you have. As far as I know you might have serviced the whole God-damned Masai nation without me being aware of it. Just so long as you save some for me, some time.'

'Some time like now?'

'Like now,' she said. 'I feel I'm home, really and truly, for the first time. Some time like now.'

Here was happiness again, a total loving of each other, a total sharing, made the more bitter-sweet by the fact that they were about to be separated again. Almost he changed his mind about going; he could wait here for the men from the coast to arrive and sit in judgement. But he knew if he did that, they would arrive with their judgements already made, and with Maxim guns in their baggage. As Winter had said, the Masai could not be allowed to go killing indiscriminately whenever someone annoyed them. His job was to convince the authorities, which basically meant Williamson, that they would not do so again, providing they were left in peace. He never doubted he could do that. But only in person.

The Masai themselves recognised the gravity of the situation, and turned out to see him leave. Uthuli embraced him. 'You have long proved our strong right arm, my son,' he said. 'Now more than ever are your powers needed by our people. We do not seek to fight with the white man. I at least understand that he is not to be defeated, not even by my Morani, because of his numbers and his long spears. We desire only to be left in peace.'

Adrian nodded. 'That I intend to see happens, my father.'

Then there was Joanna. They had spent a last tumultuous night together. Now she gazed into his eyes. 'Now I must say to you . . . come back.'

He smiled at her. 'No doubt about that. I have nowhere else to go.' He looked at Sita, standing anxiously a few feet away, and Joanna understood his meaning. She left him, put her arm round the black girl's shoulders. 'We'll be waiting for you.'

'Gee,' Hetty said. 'I thought all one did up here was live, and shoot game.'

'Wouldn't that be boring,' Adrian pointed out. He shook hands with John Meachem. 'I'm glad you're going to be around till I get back, sir.'

'Glad to do my bit,' Meachem said. 'But you, boy . . . you've taken on quite a responsibility here, and you're handling it well. I figure Joanna married the right guy, after all. Don't you worry about a thing. I'll take care of the girls till you're back again.'

Adrian picked up a military escort at Fort Smith, travelled hard for a month, and reached Mombasa in November. The news of what had happened had indeed already filtered through to the coast, and Adrian was just in time to prevent a punitive expedition, comprising every soldier who could be spared, together with a detachment of sailors from the warship, from leaving. The soldiers went anyway, but Adrian succeeded in having their orders changed, so that they simply went as reinforcements for the garrison at Fort Smith, pending the outcome of the investigation of what had happened.

Williamson was more full of himself than ever, even if he was apparently shortly to be relieved. The reason was that the British Government had at last ceased sitting on the fence and had formally announced the formation of the East African Protectorate. This was partly because the East Africa Company, the consortium of merchants and ship-ping lines which had conducted trade with Mombasa and financed the caravans to Uganda and paid for the soldiers, had fallen into financial difficulties and was in the course of being dissolved. It was also to prevent the risk of encroachment by the other ambitious European powers, the Germans in Tanganyika to the south, and even more, the Belgians, who, having established themselves in the Congo basin, were casting covetous eyes upon Uganda, where King Mwamba, despite several defeats by British forces, was still always liable to start trouble.

All of this was news to Adrian, and he was not sure whether it was good news. Williamson assured him that it was. As he said, in the circumstances, there would now have to be a commissioner in Mombasa instead of a consul-general, and thus he was in the process of being replaced by a more senior official – but for the moment he was acting commissioner, and both enjoying his new authority as well as being determined to make the most of it as regards establishing his reputation. 'This is a most serious business, Barclay,' he declared. 'And an urgent one. We must display to the world, but most of all to the Africans, that British justice is not only expeditious but impartial.'

In fact, he was more energetic than Adrian had ever known him. After expressing the opinion that Adrian must be mad to have left two white women virtually in the hands of the Masai – he seemed to regard them as some kind of hostages and another reason for haste – he determined to use the circumstances to deal with the problem on the spot. Engaging in a lengthy discourse with distant Whitehall might take months and might well leave the matter unsettled until after his recall.

He therefore convened a tribunal, consisting of himself, the captain of the Navy ship, and the commander of the garrison in Zanzibar, together with a representative of the Sultan. Even getting this small body together took time, however, and it was after Christmas before the tribunal actually sat. It was an odd court, because virtually the only witness was Adrian, who had to present both sides of the coin, as it were. None of Dick's men had survived, and although Williamson endeavoured to round up some of the

Kikuyu survivors of the first massacre, none could be found. The Kikuyu despatched a chieftain to act as a character witness for his people, but, as their long enmity with the Masai was well known, his evidence was of little value.

Adrian was openly biased. He pointed out that the Masai were the only tribe in East Africa who had willingly accepted British suzerainty, and that all they had ever asked was that their lands not be alienated, and their cattle and women left in peace. He stressed that taking a large body of armed Kikuyu into their land had been an act of the most wanton provocation; the two nations had been at war since time immemorial, and the Kikuyu had carried out the first act of aggression in attempting to steal the Masai girls. To this, which of course could not be proved, he added the indisputable fact, supported by a written statement from Major Winter, that Andrew Dick had engaged in an equally irresponsible act – that of attempting to steal the Masai cattle, apparently in an effort to lead the tribesmen back to the fortress and there embroil them with the soldiers. Dick had miscalculated both the speed and the anger with which the Masai would pursue him, but that did not alter the fact that he had sought to stir up a real war.

The risks of this were his final argument. 'These are a proud and most warlike people,' he said, 'who have, with reluctance but in good faith, agreed to change their ways in order to cooperate with the requirements of Great Britain. We must beware of pushing them too far, or they will resist, out of despair as much as anger, and then you may well find yourself engaged in another Zulu war, or Matabele war, or a war such as the Germans in Tanganyika have only just completed against the Wahehe people, with enormous expense and loss of life. That grim spectre has never hung over British East Africa more heavily than now. But it can be averted by simple common sense, and British justice.'

The tribunal listened to him gravely, retired briefly and then returned to issue their judgement: that the Masai had been unreasonably provoked, and that while their action in taking so many lives could not be condoned, they were understood to have acted in defence of themselves and their property.

'I thank you,' Adrian said, his heart bursting with happiness.

'They will, of course, have to be made aware of the horror of what they have done,' Williamson said. 'I do not suppose any Christian reflections as to guilt will have much meaning to them. As I understand it, there have been few missionaries operating in Masai land.'

'None at all,' Adrian told him.

'Because of the reputations of these fierce warriors. We shall have to do something to rectify that shameful situation. Then the penalty will have to be something the Masai will be capable of understanding. I will impose a fine equal to the value of the cattle Mr Dick was carrying off.'

Adrian could not believe his ears. 'But that is monstrous. You have just conceded that they have committed no crime.'

'No, Mr Barclay, we have just conceded that their crime, for it was certainly that, was justified in all the circumstances. Just. But a crime must be atoned for.'

'You are asking them to hand over the cattle they regained from Dick at the cost of so many lives? You may as well declare war. In fact, you have just done so.'

'I am not asking for their cattle, Barclay. I am asking for a payment in equal value. Should they, for instance, undertake to supply Fort Smith with grain for a period of five years, that I am sure would cover the fine.'

'It is still not justice,' Adrian growled.

Williamson sighed. 'My dear Barclay, justice is always part expediency. The findings of this tribunal will have to be confirmed by the Colonial Office, where there may be some very self-righteous gentlemen in positions of authority, without experience of African affairs, who will be horrified at the knowledge that we have condoned what will appear to them as cold-blooded murder on a great scale. However, in my experience, such gentlemen find it easier to reconcile their consciences if they can feel there has been solid, and if possible financial, gain to the English taxpayer. We should all hate to think that the decision of this tribunal might be overturned, would we not?'

'Now that sounds sensible,' Adrian agreed, calming down, and for the first time in their acquaintance actually beginning to like Williamson. 'Then I will undertake to supply the garrison with coffee, free of charge, as part of the arrangement, and I know the Masai will provide sufficient grain. All right, Mr Williamson, you have made your point. Now I should like to make one or two, without which your decision is worthless. First, in all future caravans, the leaders have to be men of character, and either familiar with the African and his point of view and his history, or accompanied by someone who is. Otherwise I may wind up shooting a few of these gentlemen myself.'

'Point taken.'

'Second, it is essential that in future caravans the numbers of bearers drawn from tribes which are hereditary enemies of the Masai, such as the Kikuyu, should be severely limited.'

'We shall certainly see what we can do about that,' Williamson agreed. 'Believe me, Barclay, I have no intention of upsetting your applecart, or of driving the Masai into open antagonism to our rule. I appreciate your efforts to prevent this, and I am sure that with good will on both sides we can reach a permanent condition of peace and mutual respect. In fact, I think I can promise that.'

'I'll say amen to that,' Adrian said. 'And I can't tell you how relieved I am, or how relieved Chief Uthuli will be, when I return with this news. He is a soldier to the backbone, but he is also a sensible man, and he knows that to go to war with Great Britain would mean the destruction of his people. His big problem is convincing them of that. This will go a long way to accomplish that.'

'When do you plan to leave?' Williamson asked.

'I have an escort standing by. I shall leave tomorrow.'

'Can you postpone it for a couple of days? There is someone I want you to meet. He's actually on the mainland at the moment, doing some surveying. But I think you may be seeing a lot of him over the next couple of years. And he may be the answer to all of your, all of our, problems.'

It sounded interesting, and Adrian reflected that a couple of days wasn't going to make all that much difference. He agreed, and three days later met George Whitehouse.

Adrian was immensely impressed by the man – tall, saturnine, determined – but equally aghast at what Whitehouse was planning to do. 'A railway?' he asked in consternation. 'From here to Lake Victoria?'

'And beyond, if necessary. Railways are the key to opening up a country, Mr Barclay. Frankly, with King Mwanga constantly threatening to go to war, it is felt essential that a fast and certain means of communication with Uganda – a means by which troops can be rushed to the lake at short notice and without losing half their ration strength to malaria – is essential.'

'From your point of view, Barclay,' Williamson put in, 'it'll mean no more caravans to cause trouble with the Masai. The train will carry everything and everyone right through Masai land in a couple of days. That's why I said Whitehouse's project could mean the end of all your problems.'

'That would be too good to be true,' Adrian agreed. 'But have you any idea of what is involved, Mr Whitehouse?'

'I'm hoping you're going to show me,' Whitehouse said. 'But first of all, tell me.'

Adrian obliged. He told him about the Taru desert, and

Tsavo, and the forests, and the rivers, and the steady climb up to six thousand feet and more.

Whitehouse nodded. 'I think we can cope with all of that,' he said seriously. 'Now tell me about the escarpment. How deep a drop is it?'

'About two thousand feet.'

'Very sheer?'

'From the point of view of a railway line, precipitous.'

'Hm. I've been thinking about that, studying maps . . . it certainly looks as if that will be our biggest problem. What about after we pass it?'

'If you can negotiate that, the floor of the valley shouldn't prove very difficult. And the western escarpment is by no means as steep as the eastern.'

'What comes after that?'

'It's not country I have explored personally,' Adrian admitted. 'But from what I have gathered, it's then a pretty steady slope down to Lake Victoria. If you can pass the Rift Valley, you should have no more difficulties. *If* you can pass the Rift Valley.'

'We'll pass it,' Whitehouse said confidently. 'It may be necessary to use some kind of a funicular, at least to start with. But we'll find a way.'

'You're going to need one hell of a lot of labour.'

'I've thought of that. I've government permission to import Indian coolies, where we cannot hire sufficient Africans.'

'You're going to bring Indians to Africa?'

'Why not? They've been employing them in South Africa, and in the West Indies, for some time. With success. They're a hard-working people, and the climate doesn't destroy them the way it can a European.'

'Have you any idea how much all of this is going to cost?'

'The accountants are talking of perhaps a million pounds. But that's not your concern, old man. The British taxpayer is footing the bill; the Government is determined to have its railroad.'

Adrian scratched his head. 'And the Masai?'

'Well, as I've told you, it will be necessary to cut across their land, to be sure. Nothing more than that. I'll even offer them employment.'

'Masai, doing manual labour? You might get a few women.'

'I can manage without either. What I want from you, Mr Barclay, apart from your technical advice regarding terrain, is an assurance that they won't attack my crews. I've been hearing some pretty grim tales about the way they've massacred various caravans.'

'I will give you an assurance that the Masai will not attack your crews if you will give me an assurance that your railway crews won't interfere with the Masai. If you'll forgive me, *I've* heard some pretty grim tales about railheads and what happens there.'

'I can give you a personal assurance on that,' Whitehouse said. 'No man steps out of line on my crew and remains there another day.'

Adrian believed him, just as he had taken Count Teleki von Szen's word on the same subject – and not been disappointed. The two men could not have been more unlike . . . but they both had a chill in their eyes.

He turned to Williamson. 'I will also require an assurance from you, sir, that the laying of a railway track through the Masai land will involve no massive influx of population, save for the transient work gangs, of course.'

'Why should it?'

'I'm thinking of what happened in the American West, is happening there now, as a matter of fact, as the railway spreads.'

'This is hardly the American West, Barclay. It's a good deal hotter, for one thing, therefore there is no growing white population bursting at the seams and desperate for land. I can certainly give you a categorical assurance that Her Majesty's Government has no plans for allowing the expansion of any African tribe outside its traditional homeland – which is one of the reasons for Fort Smith, you may recall, erected over your objections.'

'Then you will have the entire cooperation both of the Masai and myself,' Adrian promised him.

'I'll safari with you up to the Rift Valley, if I may,' Whitehouse said. 'Of course, you do realise the railway won't even reach the Masai land for a little while yet; the first track hasn't been laid. You'll have time to prepare your friends for the iron horse.'

'How long is a little while?'

Whitehouse shrugged. 'A year or two, certainly. Everything depends on what we find when we start building. And what you show me over the next couple of weeks.'

Whitehouse was a most pleasant and stimulating companion. He had built railways in practically every country of the world where there was a British presence, from Canada to Ceylon, from the Argentine to Australia, and was disappointed because the British Government had been outbid by a Belgian consortium to build the first railway in China, from Peking to Tientsin. 'Now there's a country which needs railways,' he said. 'So does Australia, of course, with such vast distances to cover. But so much of it is over desert, it really is the unpleasantest terrain in the world in which to work.'

'You haven't seen anything yet,' Adrian told him. He was in the very best of spirits. He had obtained for the Masai an honourable acquittal for the attack on the Kikuyu and on Dick's rustlers, he seemed to have got Jo back again, and now he could even tell Uthuli that he had solved the caravan problem. That last was somewhat specious, of course, but Uthuli was concerned mainly with the disruptive presence of the vast numbers of men and animals crossing his territory; if they were to do so on one continuous line and hidden away in sealed boxes, Adrian was sure the chieftain would feel his troubles were over — if it really was possible to construct a railway over such a country.

Whitehouse, with his vast experience, was neither depressed nor impressed by the desert or the Tsavo plain. At every stop he and his assistants got to work with their theodolites, tested the consistency of the ground, studied gradients. 'Excellent railway country,' he pronounced. There was the usual confrontation with lions, but this did nothing more than excite him. The forest was actually a great relief to him. 'It's not the hot, tropical rain forest one finds in West Africa or in northern South America,' he explained. 'There the undergrowth is so thick, and grows so fast, you can hardly tell tomorrow what area you have cleared today. This is going to be relatively easy, and these trees we're going to fell will make perfect sleepers.'

He was equally pleased when they reached Fort Smith and he was able to look at the level ground through which the river flowed. 'How far to the Rift Valley?' he asked.

'Two, maybe three days, for men moving steadily.'

'And that plain out there is flat?'

'No, it's quite up and down, really. But there are no deep valleys or high hills before you reach the Rift.'

'Then right here is the place for our central marshalling yards; we shall have to have a headquarters closer than Mombasa. It's close to the fort too, which may be useful just in case there ever is trouble, and close to water. Ideal.'

'I think you might want to reconsider that decision,' Adrian suggested. 'This area floods and becomes a vast swamp in the wet season. In fact, it never really dries out. This soil' — he stooped and dug out a piece with his fingers — 'has a most unusual consistency. We're quite well into the dry season now, and yet you see it's quite moist. I don't know what the connection is, but it means malaria is a real hazard here.' As he spoke he slapped a mosquito.

316

'This high up?' Whitehouse queried. 'I thought malaria was a coastal disease. Anyway, there's no doubt that disease, of some sort of other, is going to be a problem. I never built a railway, certainly in a tropical country, where it wasn't. The important thing about this place is that it's flat. That's essential for a marshalling yard.'

Clearly it was pointless to argue further, and undoubtedly Whitehouse knew a great deal more about building railways than he knew about malaria, Adrian reflected.

They went on across the high plain and looked down on the Rift Valley. Whitehouse whistled. 'Some country,' he said. '*Some* country.' He was thinking less of the beauty than of the difficulties of carrying a line down the escarpment. But he was again pleased when they had descended the slope and reached the floor of the valley. 'This is going to be a treat,' he declared.

Adrian took him first to the kraal, but the Masai were away on their migration. Then he took him to the house. Now he himself was quite excited, as they approached Lake Naivasha. He had been away only three months, but three months could be a very long time, and his first sight of the house made him pause – he could see no sign of life. Then Safah gave an excited shout, and a moment later people appeared from everywhere, Safah from the garden, Sita and Saba from the kitchen, John Meachem from the verandah on which he had been taking a nap, and Hetty from the bank of the lake, where she had been sketching.

Adrian introduced Whitehouse, who was struck dumb by the splendour of his surroundings, while he looked from right to left, seeking Joanna.

'A railroad, eh?' John Meachem said. 'Now, that's progress. I'd like to see how you're going to manage that, young fellow.'

'Oh, it's been so heavenly here,' Hetty cried, embracing Adrian. 'I never knew there was a place like this on earth.'

'No problems with the Masai?' Adrian looked at Safah.

317

'None, bwana. They left about a month ago. They had faith in your mission, bwana.'

'Well, I've nothing but good news for them,' Adrian said, and at last saw Joanna, also coming up from the lakeside.

He ran towards her, and stopped, as she continued to move slowly. Could she possibly have undergone another of her devastating changes of mood?

But she smiled at him, and there were tears in her eyes. 'Welcome home,' she said. 'Was it a success?'

'Oh, yes,' he said. 'Oh, yes. A great success.' He took her into his arms.

'I'm so happy about that,' she said, and kissed him. 'And I'm happy about something else, too.'

He held her away from him to look at her, her radiant face, the slight bulge to her dress. 'You're not serious,' he said.

'Never more,' she said. 'I'm so glad you came back, my dearest man.'

12

She was thirty-six years old, which Adrian felt was a considerable age to be having a baby – when she was so out of practice, as it were. Fortunately, there was now a doctor resident at Fort Smith, and he came over to stay for a week when the delivery was due, which was in the middle of the Long Rains; the child was another boy, to the great joy of both Adrian and Joanna.

'We'll call him John,' Joanna decided.

'Are you sure?' Adrian asked.

'So sure. Nothing is going to happen to this John.'

Hetty and John Meachem were also delighted, and relieved; they had stayed over for the birth, but now it was

318

time to plan their departure. Joanna was perfectly happy for Adrian to escort them down to the coast, although she had no intention of leaving Naivasha herself again for a long time. This was her home, and she was staying put.

In the autumn the Masai returned from their migration, and Adrian had been able to tell Uthuli the great news that in a very few years' time, the caravans would cease to trouble him. Instead there would be a road of iron, and one of those impossible-to-understand white man's magic boxes, to hurry people through the land of the Masai. He saw no point in explaining about the change in status, that in the eyes of the British Government, at least, the Masai were no longer an independent people; that could hardly be apparent to them for a long time to come.

Uthuli, as usual, considered the matter in silence and at great length. Then he asked, 'This metal road, will it not harm the soil?'

'Where it is laid, of course,' Adrian agreed. 'But it will be a single track, not more than as wide as two men are tall, including the embankment. That is a very little amount of soil to give away to stop the caravans.'

Uthuli considered that also, but did not make the obvious comment, that there was no valid reason, save that of naked power, why the Masai should have to give up even a twelve-foot-wide strip of land. Instead he asked, 'But this moving box, will it not kill our cattle? And even ourselves?'

'Only if you get in the way of it, and that will be easy to avoid, my father,' Adrian promised. 'I give you my word that it will be for the better, not the worse.'

'And I must accept your word, my son,' Uthuli said. 'As you have been proved right so often in the past. Now you must listen to what I have to say. Do you remember my first son, Kainairju?'

Adrian frowned. 'I'm not likely to forget him.'

'I had supposed him dead,' Uthuli said. 'But now it seems he is alive. When I banished him from my lands and my

319

kraal and my love, I expected him to go away and die. Instead I have learned that he went north, right out of the land of the Masai, and made a new home for himself with the Gusii. Now he has heard of our battles with the Kikuyu and the white man, and he has sent word demanding, as we are again a nation of warriors, to be allowed to return, to lead our Morani into battle. Should I permit this, my son?'

Adrian's heart gave a peculiar thump. The fear of a hothead like Kainairju eventually succeeding Uthuli as one of the senior Masai chieftains had long haunted him. 'Do you wish him to return, my father?'

'How can a father not wish his son to return?' Uthuli replied, very reasonably. 'Whatever his crimes. But Kainairju will wish to lead my warriors into battle.'

'And that would be a grave mistake. Send word to Kainairju that the day of battles is now over. That while you would welcome his return, it must be to pledge peace with the white man.'

Uthuli considered. 'It would be better if he did not come,' he said sadly, and returned to the kraal.

Reluctant as he was to leave Joanna and the baby, Adrian had a more urgent reason for descending to the coast than just to see his father and sister-in-law safely on board a ship; he was anxious to learn what was happening with the railway project, as the caravans were still passing through the Masai country and Uthuli was beginning to look unhappy again, having told his Morani that Bar-clay had promised they would cease.

In Mombasa, he bid his in-laws a fond farewell. 'I'm coming back,' Hetty promised. 'Oh, I'm coming back.' Then he found that the work on the track had actually started, Whitehouse being a bustling ball of energy, as usual. Now Adrian met the new commissioner, Sir Charles Eliot, for the first time. Sir Charles, a career diplomat who obviously did not regard assignment to British East Africa as an upward step on the ladder of promotion, was some-what sceptical about the state of affairs he had inherited, particularly the present status of the Masai; the Kikuyu were now peaceful, because they had been cowed – the Masai had never actually experienced the mighty power of Great Britain.

'I may say, Mr Barclay,' he remarked, 'that there has been considerable adverse comment in England given to the decision of Mr Williamson's tribunal not to punish the Masai, severely, for their unchristian behaviour and aggression, their predeliction for murder and mayhem on a horrifying scale.'

'They are not Christians, Your Excellency,' Adrian reminded him.

'That is not the point. They are living in a Christian empire. Mr Gladstone may no longer be a potent force in political matters, but his principles are still, thank God, a potent force in the beliefs and in the conduct of our affairs.'

'With respect, sir,' Adrian argued, 'the Masai did not ask to be included within our so Christian empire.'

Eliot stared at him for several seconds, then continued as if he had not spoken. 'What is more serious even than that, however, is the apprehension that, having been allowed to get away with such an atrocity by the mere imposition of a fine, the Masai will undoubtedly be encouraged to suppose they can repeat the deed with impunity, as and when they feel like it.'

'They will keep the peace, Your Excellency,' Adrian promised him, concealing his irritation, and indeed his alarm, at the mettle of the man who was now the supreme arbiter of British East Africa. 'They understand their vulnerability. That smallpox epidemic of a few years ago, coupled with the disease of their cattle, has had a disastrous effect, especially in the north. It is impossible to say how many people must have died, but I doubt the nation is more than half what it was ten years ago. *That* is a horrible thought to have to consider. They won't cause trouble unless they are provoked beyond endurance, as they were by both the Kikuyu and by Mr Dick, and I have Whitehouse's assurance that he will keep his people under firm control.'

'Well,' Eliot said. 'I sincerely hope he can. Have you seen them? Do you know how many Bengali thugs he is importing? Thirty-two thousand. My God! It is like transporting an entire nation, all for the sake of a railway. Oh, I concede it's important. A quick and direct link with Uganda is very necessary. But the cost . . . questions are being asked in Parliament. They are calling it the lunatic line to nowhere. If there should be another massacre . . . well, heads will certainly roll.'

'There will be no more massacres,' Adrian promised him. 'At least, not by the Masai.'

Within a year he was heartily glad he had added that last proviso. Whitehouse was very anxious to utilise his knowledge of the country, which was so much more complete than that of the swarm of 'white hunters' who were earning their livings escorting shooting parties out of Mombasa for a short distance inland. And he was happy to oblige, although it kept him away from his home a good deal over the five years it took to complete the railway. But it was an amazing and epic-making five years. He often wished that a Joseph Thompson, or his friend, Henry Rider Haggard, could have been there to record it for posterity; he could not believe any more difficult task had been carried out anywhere in the world before, since the building of the pyramids.

It was nearly all hand labour. The myriad of coolies, with a substantial contingent of black labourers, supervised by white overseers who in many cases had their families with them, found the going easy enough in the beginning, as Whitehouse had predicted, even if the incidence of malaria was high – as Adrian had predicted. They carried the tracks

322

across the Taru desert, and then bridged the Tsavo river, which in itself was a tremendous feat. Adrian left them for a season, hurrying home to plant his next coffee crop, thus he was not with them as they made their way across the Tsavo grassland, and so he only heard about the massacre when he returned two months later.

It was a massacre of a totally unexpected kind. The lions of Tsavo had always had a fearsome reputation, and he had always regarded the grassland as the most dangerous part of the journey from the coast. But he had never supposed the mighty beasts would assemble to fight a pitched battle with human beings, or that if they did so, they would not be defeated. Instead, they routed the entire work crew. Figures of casualties varied according to the continuing terror of the reporter, but Whitehouse, if unable to estimate the number of Africans killed, himself counted the mangled remains of twenty-eight of his coolie work force, together with that of a white foreman, into whose tent a lion had broken to drag him away before the horrified eyes of his wife and child.

That halted proceedings for some time, and there was even talk of abandoning the entire project, but it was to the credit of Whitehouse that he refused to be defeated by man, beast or bug. Adrian, aghast at learning that, in such a place, there had been no more than the usual couple of sentries posted on the night of the attack, recruited a capable body of marksmen to see them through on their next attempt. He stayed with them, and had to cut down several lion.

After that the forest was simple, again as Whitehouse had predicted, and the line crept on, mile after mile, until it reached the river and the swamp, where it halted, two years after leaving the coast. In accordance with Whitehouse's previous decision, a marshalling yard was constructed. Naturally, there rapidly grew up around the yard a shanty town, especially as it was now possible to make the journey from the coast in no more than two days, providing one could obtain a place on the always crowded train; but where the railway gangs were, with their relatively high wages and their mainly easy come easy go attitude, there was money to be made keeping them in food and drink and clothing. Adrian did not much care for the idea of a regular town being built so close to the Masai land, and in fact actually on one of their pastures, but it was still a good distance from the Rift Valley and he was prepared to accept that it was necessary. However, he felt obliged again to warn Whitehouse that the place he had chosen was possibly the worst in the entire high country, from every point of view.

'It's flat,' Whitehouse responded, as usual. 'That's the important thing.'

Then he proceeded to take the line across the high country itself.

The building of the railway as far as the marshalling yard of Nairobi, as it was called after the corrupted name of the river, took place during two years of growing African unrest, as there had been ten years before, when the white man had first decided to exploit East Africa. The principal trouble originated in Uganda, where King Mwanga once again decided to oppose the British, being aided by a mutiny of part of the garrison, which was comprised mainly of Sudanese troops.

The reason the British Government had always valued Uganda more highly than the eastern part of the region – and had indeed only taken on the coast and its immediate hinterland as a means of gaining access to the inland country – was that the Nile, which was essential to the prosperity of both Egypt and the Sudan, rose in Lake Victoria. Whoever controlled the source of the river obviously controlled, and could entirely stop, the flow of water. It had thus seemed reasonable, and more economic, both in men and money, to employ Sudanese soldiers to protect the river course – their own families would be the only losers should that course be diverted or dammed. This costly mistake was rectified by Major James Macdonald, after a bloody campaign; and Mwanga, together with his ally, King Kabarega of Unyoro, was sent into exile in the Seychelle Islands in the Indian Ocean.

The Germans in Tanganyika also continued to have their troubles, and the Portuguese in Mozambique were also faced with a native insurgent movement. But in British East Africa, for all the frantic activity of Whitehouse and his moving nation of labourers, all was quiet. While the Masai waited for the coming of the iron road, with patience if with mixed feelings, the Kikuyu suddenly realised that here was at last a golden opportunity for them to make money out of the white man, rather than make war upon him, especially when they were bound to lose. Forty thousand odd men, multiplied by an almost equal horde of camp followers, needed a lot of feeding, and not all the white hunters in the world could bring down sufficient game. Nor could men live off meat alone, especially the coolies, who comprised the greater part of the work force, many of whom would not touch meat in any form. The Kikuyu turned themselves into a nation of vegetable farmers almost overnight, and prospered greatly, hawking their wares the length of the line.

For Adrian it was a period of intense activity, but also of intense happiness as well. If he had to spend several months in each year with Whitehouse at the railhead, and if he regretted the enormous influx of people and the consequent decimation of the animal herds that roamed Tsavo, he was also able to spend much of each year at his home on the banks of Lake Naivasha, and savour the beauty, and now the real prosperity, of his surroundings. He was being paid a retainer by Whitehouse which more than made up for the loss of his 'emolument' as vice-consul, which had naturally ceased with the announcement of the protectorate, although the British Government had also graciously granted him a pension to continue as adviser in native affairs. In addition, his coffee crop – and he was now planting several hundred acres – as well as the yield he was obtaining from his banana plantation, was earning a good income.

But the house on the banks of Lake Naivasha had never needed money to be a gracious and happy place; it had required only the presence of a happy Joanna. Baby John was the best and healthiest of children – although remembering that his brother had also appeared perfectly healthy until his sudden and fatal illness, Joanna kept him under constant surveillance. As Adrian passed his fortieth year he could once again reflect on the joys of fatherhood, which were increased when Bar came home, having completed school and now able to read and write, and even to speak with a marble in his mouth. Over six feet tall, his skin the colour of rich mahogany, entrancingly set off by his yellow hair, his high-cheekbones, thrusting-jawed Masai features strangely muted by the small Barclay nose, and amber-eyed, he was a splendid figure of a man. Now he wanted nothing more, despite his experiences in England – or perhaps because of them – than to live out his days with his father and stepmother. Adrian could not possibly refuse him, even if he felt in his bones that not all of the future could conceivably be as good as the present; while Joanna was delighted to have, as she put it, both her sons in residence.

Uthuli too was pleased to have his grandson back, and immediately approached Adrian on the subject of Bar's initiation into the clan, with the suggestion that the boy would be his natural successor as chieftain; Uthuli would be approaching seventy by now, and was far older than any of his relatives.

The idea was an attractive one. If Kainairju had refused to return to live in peace with the white man, he was still there, somewhere in the northern forests, and the thought of his appearing on Uthuli's deathbed to claim his rights was a

326

frightening one; there could be no doubt that he retained his popularity with the Morani, and had indeed grown into something of a legend. If Bar could step naturally into Uthuli's shoes . . . but he could not possibly condemn his son to a lifetime in the high country, and as an African rather than a white man, unless it was a personal choice.

He and Joanna and Bar discussed the matter at some length. 'This is my home,' Bar said. 'I have seen the world, or at least England, which regards itself as the centre of the world. It has many good things in it, but many bad things as well.'

'That is true of anywhere,' Joanna pointed out.

'I agree, Mother. But these are my people in a way the English can never be. If you are agreeable, Father, I will accept initiation into the tribe.'

Adrian shook his hand. 'I think it's probably the wisest decision.'

Joanna shuddered as she thought what he would have to undergo, Adrian having explained to her the ritual – and equally that the Masai men were physically quite different to the average white man, something that she had slowly been working out for herself, if only from observing her own sons. But Bar was confident, and Uthuli was delighted with his decision. As seemed his warriors. There was no more talk of Kainairju.

His initiation complete, it was immediately necessary for Bar to be married, and this was arranged to a maiden named Lili. Adrian was a little apprehensive as to Joanna's reaction to acquiring a black daughter-in-law, but she seemed perfectly happy. For his own part, however, he was determined that Bar would always retain his English characteristics, and at his invitation the newly-weds moved into the dower house he had once built for Joanna, and which had been empty for several years. Within a year he was presented with his first grandchild, named Ade.

This same year there was a further cause for pleasure in

the return of Cathy. She had completed her schooling, and wished to revisit her parents, and her birthplace, before going off to a Swiss finishing school. She had no idea what she wanted to do with her life, but she was enjoying it to the full, and had grown, at seventeen, into a beautiful girl, with something of her father's height and with all of her mother's looks, while her hair was a splendid dark gold. 'Her marriage will be next on the agenda,' Joanna prophesied.

Cathy stayed in the high country for a year, during which they had the pleasure of entertaining the mountaineer Halford Mackinder, on his way to make the first successful ascent of Mount Kenya, as the great striped peak of the Masai was now called. There was also a very odd character, who appeared one day out of the north and riding on a camel, accompanied by only a few Somalis – he had apparently come all the way from Somalia to find the high country, nor was he concerned that he had chosen the most difficult of all the possible routes.

Small, red-haired and aggressive, he introduced himself as Hugh Cholmondeley, the third Baron Delamere. Joanna was impressed; she had never before entertained a member of the British nobility. Delamere was also impressed, but less with what Adrian had achieved on the banks of Lake Naivasha than with what he had seen of the country. 'Damned fine land,' he remarked. 'A man could well make a home here. As you have done, eh, Barclay?'

'By courtesy of the Masai, my lord,' Adrian reminded him.

'Oh, quite. Fine-looking chaps, aren't they? But really, all this land going to waste . . . You're growing coffee.' It was not a question, but rather a statement, almost a condemnation.

Adrian nodded.

'Waste of time,' Delamere declared. 'Too much coffee in the world today already. One can't compete with Brazil, old boy.'

'We're not trying to compete with anyone,' Joanna told him. 'Our coffee earns sufficient for our needs.'

'Oh, quite, Mrs Barclay. But needs . . . some people need more than others. Now, this magnificent prairie . . . cattle is the answer. Think what they've managed to do in Texas. That's where the real money will lie.'

'Texas has slightly easier access to markets,' Adrian suggested.

'What about this railway they're building? Damned fine idea, in my opinion. Mombasa in three days, that fellow Whitehouse says.'

'I'm sure he's right, when he gets it finished. But it'll have to be one hell of a big train to carry enough cattle to be economically worthwhile. Even in the States they have to drive their cattle to market – across grassland, not through forest. They don't have the lions of Tsavo in Texas. And still they lose a fair proportion of every herd.'

Delamere held up one finger. 'Refrigerated cars, old boy. Refrigerated cars. How far is it from here to this settlement they call Nairobi?'

'Two, three days, driving cattle.'

'Well, that wouldn't be a problem, would it? Slaughter them there, pile the good meat into refrigerated cars, and there's your profit. I'd like to meet these Masai of yours.'

Adrian looked at Joanna, who shrugged and agreed. His lordship was obviously impressed by the stalwart Morani, who towered over him, if not by their cattle, which still showed the effects of the rinderpest outbreak of a few years before. But the Masai were totally captivated by this newcomer – they had never seen red hair before, and obviously wondered whether he might not also possess exceptional powers, perhaps to replace those of their ageing demigod.

Adrian was quite relieved when Delamere and his camels went on their way towards Nairobi and the coast. He never expected to see him again.

As Johnnie was now four years old, when the time came for Catherine to leave, Joanna accompanied her daughter to Mombasa and thence Europe, before returning to the States for another visit. This was now a perfectly simple thing to do, as on the railway it was a matter of only a couple of days to Mombasa, all in the most perfect comfort in a Pullman sleeping carriage, while with modern steamships operating one could reach England from Port Said in a week, and the Atlantic took no longer than that to cross.

In her absence, the railway forged steadily ahead. White-house did put in a funicular system for the descent and ascent of the escarpment, and a hairy business it was, the carriages having to be pulled up or lowered by a combination of man and horsepower. But it worked; Joanna was just home in time to join in the celebrations when, on 26 December 1901, the line finally reached Lake Victoria Nyanza.

The Masai had from the first viewed the railway with the gravest suspicions. Unlike the Kikuyu, they wanted nothing to do with either the iron road or the horde of labourers who camped over their country for months on end. They steadily refused, again unlike the Kikuyu, to offer any of their grain or cattle to the invaders, which was a source of some concern to Whitehouse, who had to bring in all of his food supplies during the crossing of the Rift Valley, as well as to exert all of his authority to stop his people from stealing the odd cow now and then.

But, as with the first caravans, time went by and only a couple of careless bulls wandered on to the track to be killed, and there was no more trouble with Kikuyu marauders or with anyone else – because Whitehouse was as good as his word, and did indeed keep his coolies under the strictest discipline – they somewhat relaxed their attitude. Bar, now generally acknowledged as their next chieftain, worked hard to convince them that the line could only bring prosperity, in time. For the moment it did nothing but pass

330

through, although a regular stop was always made beside Lake Naivasha, both for the convenience of the Barclays and to take on water.

Adrian was entirely reassured by the way things had worked out, and he had no idea that anything could possibly be amiss, when he received a message urgently requesting him to visit Mombasa for a conference with Sir Charles Eliot, early in the year following the completion of the track.

It was actually the first time Adrian had ridden by the train for any distance, and equally the first time for a year he had visited Nairobi. He was amazed at the way the place had grown, with even some substantial buildings sprouting amidst the shacks. It wore something of a Wild West atmosphere, as the white men and the merchants from the coast were beginning to come in and set up shop, all carrying weapons, as if expecting an imminent native revolt. There were missionaries in large numbers to be seen — one or two had actually visited the valley, but had found it difficult to communicate with the Masai, either linguistically or in terms of the Christian philosophy. Even more interesting was the way in which several of the so-called coolies had hived off from the railway gangs, set up shops for themselves, and were prospering with all the industrious ambition inherent in the Indian. It occurred to Adrian that in the course of time Nairobi could well become as prosperous a township as Mombasa, although of course it would still have to use the seaport as its only outlet to the world.

Then the train took him on the exhilarating journey down through Tsavo and the desert. It was an overnight passage, and it was a peculiar sensation to be sleeping in a comfortable bed while the train rumbled through the night, oblivious of lion and leopard, snake and scorpion, burning sun or choking desert.

'I have to congratulate you, George,' he said to Whitehouse

331

when they met in Eliot's study. 'It was an immense undertaking, but a most successful one.'

'Oh, *Sir* George, please,' Eliot said. 'He has been rewarded by our new king for his efforts.'

'Well, then, doubly congratulations.'

Whitehouse did not look terribly pleased. 'I've an idea you may change your mind about that very shortly,' he remarked.

Adrian raised his eyebrows. 'I've just travelled by your Pullman service for the first time, and it seems perfection to me.'

'Oh, there's nothing wrong with the line,' Whitehouse said, and looked at Eliot. 'You'd better explain the situation, Charles.'

Eliot played with his pen for a moment, as if uncertain how to begin, while Adrian suddenly felt a cold grey cloud seem to settle on his shoulders. 'I'm afraid,' Eliot said at last, 'that where George went a little wrong was in his costing. We recognised some time ago, of course, that the original estimate of perhaps a million pounds was far too low, and might even have to be doubled. Unfortunately, the cost has exceeded even that.'

Adrian looked at Whitehouse, who sighed. 'Five million.'

'*Pounds?*' Adrian could not believe his ears. Five million pounds would have built, just for example, five modern battleships for the Royal Navy.

'There was no use stopping halfway,' Whitehouse said defensively. 'Or skimping where the safety and comfort of the line might have been put at risk.'

'Oh, entirely,' Eliot agreed. 'But nevertheless, the House of Commons is up in arms. It had been our hope, and our intention, that the line would be run as a government service, with only the most nominal charges made to nongovernmental persons using its facilities, but now it's going to have to pay for itself.'

'I don't see how that's possible,' Adrian said. 'There

332

'simply isn't sufficient traffic up and down.'

'Exactly.' Once again Eliot played with his pencil. 'At the moment.'

Slowly Arian raised his head.

Eliot cleared his throat. 'It is the opinion of His Majesty's Government that the railway could become a self-supporting, and even a profitable undertaking, were, for instance, the high country to be turned into a cattle and sheep and cash-crop area on a large scale. I would give you the example of the Kikuyu, who have quite literally turned their spears into ploughshares, and are doing very well at it.'

'No chance,' Adrian told him. 'You'll never be able to educate the Masai into growing, or developing, sufficient surplus to make it worth your while. They are nomads. They waste an awful lot of ground, but it's their way of life, has been since time began.'

'Yes,' Eliot said, looking acutely unhappy. 'I'm afraid they are going to have to stop being nomads and learn to do with less land, as they are going to have to share it with others.'

Adrian's brows drew together. 'I was given the most solemn assurance by your predecessor, Sir Charles, that there would be no mass movement of African tribes as a result of the railway. Indeed, there cannot be. You'd have the bloodiest war of the last hundred years on your hands if you attempted to move the Kikuyu into Masai land.'

'Good heavens, no one would dream of doing that, Barclay,' Eliot protested. 'Williamson's assurance holds good there. No, no, it . . . well, it is the intention of His Majesty's Government to encourage *white* settlement in the highlands.'

Adrian stared at him. 'You must be mad.'

'Don't you wish some company? I'm sure it must get pretty lonely up there for you and your good wife. My dear fellow, the scheme has everything to recommend it,' Eliot went on as if he hadn't spoken. 'We have the evidence of your own successful venture – and indeed, your own health and that of your family – that the climate up there in the high land is ideal for Europeans, far more suitable than it is down here. We have the evidence of your own success in growing coffee that there is an ideal soil for the production of cash crops. We now have the railway to provide easy access to and from the coast. We have . . .'

'The Masai to think about,' Adrian said quietly.

'As you yourself have said, theirs is a wasteful way of life,' Eliot pointed out. 'We live in a shrinking world, Barclay. The Masai will have to conform to its changing patterns. My own opinion is that it would be best for everyone if a system of reserved lands were set up, to prevent any possibility of a clash where the Masai might seek to graze their herds over one of the settler's land. Unfortunately, the Colonial Office does not quite see it this way . . .'

'You'd herd the Masai on to reservations?' Adrian shouted. 'That would be the crime of the century. Taking away part of their grazing land is bad enough.'

'I may say that the reservation I have in mind would cover a very large area,' Eliot protested. 'And I should remind you that His Majesty's Government has never, to my knowledge, given any undertaking that any part of this country would not, at some future date, be used for white colonisation.'

'Because the point never arose. I asked Williamson whether or not the Masai lands would ever be alienated, and he assured me not.'

'Mr Williamson was never in a position to make any such assurance. But in any event, as I understand it, his assurances extended only to the movement of African peoples. I stand by *that* assurance. No Kikuyu will be permitted to settle in the Masai land without permission.'

'Without permission,' Adrian said bitterly. 'You mean, no more than the white men may require to hew their wood and draw their water.'

'The situation will be most carefully monitored,' Eliot said, speaking very carefully himself. 'By a Crown Office which will be set up in Nairobi, whose ultimate reference will be myself and my successors. In any event, I should point out that these white settlers we are hoping to attract are hardly likely to be the scum of the earth. Only those applicants with the most impeccable backgrounds, retired army officers and that sort of thing – it is even hoped that a fair smattering of the nobility may come here – will be considered. In fact, one of the moving spirits behind the whole concept is Lord Delamere, who has a personal acquaintance with the highlands. I believe you met him when he was up there a few years ago.'

'Delamere!' Adrian said. 'My God! So he was serious. He wants to ranch cattle.'

'Well, the Masai ranch cattle, do they not?'

'That's exactly it. If the herds were to get mixed up, even to the extent of one cow . . .'

'I am sure the matter will be settled peacefully. The point is that Lord Delamere is a man of infinite wealth, and an equal determination. He has already applied for, and been granted, a hundred thousand acres in the valley.'

Adrian could only stare at him in horror.

'And with such an example,' Eliot went on, 'we expect many more men of his standing and financial background will come in. I can hardly tell you what a boon that would be to the protectorate. Now before you go off the deep end again, Barclay, I should say that we have no intention of allowing anyone to possess land he does not intend to work. This is being made perfectly clear to all applicants. Any land left idle after a suitable period of time will be returned to the Crown and reapportioned.'

'And it simply does not occur to you, or to the Government, or to Lord Delamere, that this land actually belongs to somebody else?' Adrian asked.

'With the proclamation of the protectorate, all the land in

335

East Africa within the borders of that protectorate became the property of Great Britain, that is, the British Government, except where it has been purchased from the Government, or has been granted.' He was starting to sound like a lawyer. 'And such transactions have been, and will be, recorded for posterity.'

'For God's sake, Sir Charles, the Masai have never heard of a record office or a land deed. That land is *theirs*. It has been since time began.'

'Hardly, my dear fellow. Most anthropologists, following Thompson, have deduced that the Masai must have come from the north, therefore it is pretty certain they dispossessed someone when they arrived in the high land.'

'Ah,' Adrian said. 'Now at last we're dropping the cant. So you are telling me that the British Government has conquered that land, without firing a shot, and is telling the Masai to accept it or face the consequences.'

Eliot gazed at him. 'If we are all sensible, Barclay, we will never state any situation in such cold terms. That way lies chaos, when a more moderate consideration of the problem should bring satisfactory results. I may say, at this moment, that His Majesty's Government, in recognition of your invaluable services on their behalf over the past ten years, and in anticipation of your continued efforts in the future, have authorised me to tell you that the land around your house and coffee plantation, which has been extended and rounded out at ten thousand acres on the shores of Lake Naivasha, has been granted to you and your heirs in perpetuity.'

'Your generosity astounds me,' Adrian remarked. Although he supposed giving him ten thousand acres of somebody else's land was hardly an insult where a lord who was also apparently a millionaire had only been given ten times that. 'Unfortunately, Sir Charles, I cannot accept the gift, because ten thousand acres around my house will certainly include the Masai kraal of Chief Uthuli's clan.'

'Indeed it does.' Eliot glanced at a map on his desk, which Adrian noticed for the first time. 'The clan of which you are actually a member, is that not so?' He gave a wintry smile. 'I have read Mr Thompson's book, you know. Well, the land is yours, already registered in your name. If you do not work it, it will, as I have indicated, revert to the Crown after a period of years. As it is in a prime position, by all accounts, it will certainly then be released to someone else, who may not be quite so friendly to your, ah, relatives. It is entirely up to you, of course, whether you evict these people or allow them to remain. But I would suggest the latter. From them you will be able to draw all the labour you need. It is, indeed, anticipated by the Colonial Office that the Masai nation will form an inexhaustible labour force for the European settlers.'

Adrian drove his hands into his hair. 'God, the ignorance of those people. And you believe that, Sir Charles? You must know the Masai do not work for other people.'

Eliot's gaze was as frosty as his smile. 'I am sure they will soon learn.'

No doubt he did know better, but was carrying out his instructions from Whitehall as phlegmatically as he would perhaps have faced a convicted murderer with whom he sympathised, to inform him that his appeal for clemency had been refused. Adrian felt rather like that. He was, not for the first time in his life, being faced with a *fait accompli*; he had been outfoxed, outwitted and out-thought, not by an ambitious German scoundrel, but by a government, drawn from his own people, which he had supposed above all others he could trust. He got up. 'I will let you have my resignation as a government agent this afternoon, Sir Charles,' he said. And looked at Whitehouse. 'And as adviser to the railway. I won't bid you good day. It isn't one.' He went outside, and Whitehouse, who had remained a silent spectator of the argument, hurried behind him.

'I want you to know how desperately sorry I am about

337

this, Adrian,' he said. 'I had no idea, until one hour before you arrived, what the Government intended.' He gazed at Adrian's stony expression. 'What are you going to do?'

'What can I do? Save go to the Masai and tell them that I have betrayed them.'

'It needn't be as bad as that. The scheme might work.'

'When you can pour sulphuric acid into a barrel of gunpowder, and come back and tell me you have made milk, then I'll believe it'll work, *Sir* George,' Adrian said.

'Steady on, old man. I didn't ask for the damned knighthood.'

'And I apologise.' Adrian shook his hand. 'I'm just so angry I could tear this damned building apart.'

'But . . . you won't incite the Masai to violence?'

'Of course I'll not incite them.'

'And you'll stay there?'

Adrian gave a mirthless grin. 'Why, do you mean if I packed up and left, the scheme would fall to the ground? If I thought that, George, I would do it on the instant. No, I'll stay. I'm nearest to Uthuli's kraal. I'll be the first to go when they realise what's happening.'

'You can't be serious,' Whitehouse protested. 'If they start a war they'll be wiped from the face of the earth.'

'That,' Adrian agreed, 'is the best of all reasons for not starting a war. Unfortunately, George, it is the worst of all formulae for making men. And a man who isn't a man and prepared to act like one, is an animal who is indeed fit only to be slaughtered at the whim of his betters. But the Masai are *men*. Now do excuse me. I have to catch your train back up to Naivasha.'

For the first time in his life he simply had no idea what to do next. Giving way to a wild, despairing anger, he knew, was no answer at all. He had never done that, whatever the provocation, not even when Kurt had treated him like a

338

naïve child, which he had been – and still was, he thought bitterly – or when Kurt had murdered Lulu. He had always reasoned, always trusted, that the motive behind another's activities had been based on at least survival, and therefore to a certain extent been justifiable. He had always persuaded Uthuli that what was going to happen was for the best. In that spirit and that belief, he had told the chieftain that the railway could bring only good. Now, his only thought was that he had been used from the very beginning, it seemed, for the benefit of others – and that he had innocently used the Masai for that same purpose. It was a sombre reflection for a man of forty-five.

His mood deepened all the way home, which was now reached far too quickly. There was insufficient time for reflection, and seated, or sleeping, in a comfortable railway carriage did not require the utter concentration of mind that had been necessary to make this journey on foot. Three days after leaving Mombasa he was stepping off the train at the Naivasha halt. Here there were the usual half-dozen Morani waiting to see the iron horse through. They no doubt considered themselves as sentries, to make sure no unwelcome visitors got off the train, but they were undoubtedly utterly fascinated by the hissing, clanking monster, which always stopped at Naivasha, whether there were passengers or not, to take on water from the tower Whitehouse had constructed, which drew its reserves from the lake.

But the return of Bar-clay was always an occasion for pleasure. 'Bar-clay,' they said. 'These are good times.'

'Good times,' Adrian agreed savagely, and humped his pack to walk over to the house.

Joanna immediately realised something was wrong. She put Johnnie to bed, and sat with him on the verandah, while he told her what had happened. And what was now going to happen.

'What are you going to do?' she asked.

'I don't know,' he said. 'Save cut my throat.'

339

'Sweetheart.' She laid her hand on his. 'It may not be quite the catastrophe you envisage.'

'What can possibly prevent that?'

'Any number of things,' she said. 'In the first place, do you really suppose the British Government is going to attract a million settlers here tomorrow? Or a thousand? Or ten?'

'They've attracted Delamere, haven't they?'

'From what you've just told me, I have a suspicion Delamere has attracted them. So he's one hare-brained aristocrat with more money than sense. I'll bet there aren't too many others like him around. And why should he cause trouble?'

'Taking over a hundred thousand acres of Masai land?'

'Well, even he can't do that all at once. And the Masai seemed to like him, didn't they? Besides, if he *were* to put in some capital up here, and maybe introduce a newer, stronger strain of cattle . . . would *that* be so terrible a thing?'

'If I could believe he would be the *only* one,' Adrian growled.

'Of course he won't be the *only* one. We have to accept that. But the others won't just descend on us all at once in a cloud. They'll come one by one, and they'll look at the country, and some will decide to invest here and others won't. Twenty years ago you were expecting the white man to invade the high country, and it's only just beginning to happen. We're talking about a period of years before they'll be any significant change, you'll see.'

'It'll still happen.'

'Slowly. During that time, you, we, can perhaps persuade the Masai that it is all for the good. Maybe it *will* be all for the good. The idea has some merits. It'll bring prosperity . . .'

'Money prosperity. The Masai don't understand about money. They're lucky. Up to now.'

'Well, maybe they'll have to learn. It *is* a changing world.

It'll certainly bring prosperity to us. Ten thousand acres. Wheee! That's a lot of land.'

'If I accept their offer. You once damned me for accepting a bribe from Bill Moore.'

'So, then I didn't have quite the family I have now. But with all that land, and a regular, and quick, communication with the coast, why, we can sell all the coffee we can grow, and then some. We can diversify. We can become rich. We . . .'

'Now you're interested only in our prosperity, and hang everybody else.'

'Adrian, don't fight me. I'm on your side, one hundred per cent. Sure, I'm interested in our prosperity. I'd be crazy not to be. And so would you; you've worked hard enough to make it come about. And even if you turned your back on it all and walked away, it would still happen. You're the one who can make it happen, without bloodshed. You and Bar.'

'Bar,' he said thoughtfully. He squeezed her hands. 'You always did have a lot more sense than I. I think the key to this whole thing is Bar.'

Bar listened as thoughtfully as his grandfather had ever done, and then said, 'I agree with Mother that there is no use turning our faces away from what has always been bound to happen. I remember you, Father, years ago, saying that other white people were certain to discover this land, some day.'

'And *your* people?'

'Well, I agree with Mother there too, that any white settlement up here is bound to be a slow process. It is up to us, up to me, to make it as painless as possible to my people. They are changing all the time. It is how long, seven years, since the battle with Dick's rustlers? They have kept the peace all that time. If there is no white invasion for another seven years, why, the Morani will have followed the

341

example of the Kikuyu and turned their spears into plough-shares.'

'Does that thought make you happy?' Adrian asked.

Bar gazed at him. 'No, my father,' he said, speaking Masai. 'That thought does not make me happy. But while I was at school in England, I learned about a great king named Canute, who understood, where his courtiers did not, that no one, however powerful, can stop the tide from rising. If we cannot change the world, then we must accept it, and learn to prosper in it as best we can.'

Words of necessary wisdom, Adrian thought, from his own son. He still hated duping Uthuli, and would have preferred to tell the chief exactly what was going to happen and face the consequences of his own second-hand duplicity; but he did as Joanna and Bar had recommended, and merely told his old friend that the little red-haired Englishman, who was well remembered, would also like to settle in the land of the Masai.

'Will he become one of us, as you have done, Bar-clay?' Uthuli asked.

Imagination could not cope with that. 'You'll have to ask him. But this man is a great man in my country. He is close to the Great Queen, the mother of all men. He will farm on a much greater scale than I have ever done.'

'And he will stay in one place all the year, like you,' Uthuli said thoughtfully.

'Yes, he will. It is our way.'

'Is he then a greater man than you, my son?' Uthuli asked, clearly not prepared to accept that.

'He is closer to the Great Queen than I,' Adrian said carefully. 'It would be a bad thing for you to quarrel with him. Or any of your people.'

'He comes to us because you have told us so,' Uthuli said. 'He will be our friend.'

Adrian wanted to weep.

In fact, the arrival of Lord Delamere in the high country was the most important thing that had happened to the Masai since the battle with Andrew Dick, and not a whit less enjoyable. Here was a type of white man they had not encountered before, except in passing. Delamere was accompanied by a retinue of servants, very much as if he were on an extended safari, like Count Teleki von Szen ... but he had come to stay.

He constructed a mansion rather than a house, on the shores of the next lake along the valley from Naivasha, called Elmenteita. He played music from a gramophone every morning at dawn, even if he only possessed a single record, 'All Aboard for Margate' – the Masai had never heard such a sound before. He not only possessed silver cutlery, but silver crockery as well. He imported wine by the case, and a string of polo ponies, although he had no one to play against. He rode to shoot lion with a string of gunbearers and porters. He bred huge Irish wolfhounds, which the Masai regarded as far more dangerous than any lion. He sat on his verandah and smoked huge cigars, and he always wore a revolver, with which he was fond of shooting, with consummate accuracy, at anything which caught his eye and represented a target. The Masai were entranced by such omnipotence. Adrian realised sadly that they had at last truly found a worthwhile god.

For all his eccentricities, at least against an African background, he was a very good neighbour. He rode across to Naivasha at least once a week, and encouraged Adrian and Joanna to return his visits with similar regularity. In part this was certainly due to the fact that Joanna, although several years his elder, was a most handsome woman. But also in part it was due to a very obvious respect not only for Adrian's age and status with the Masai, but to a regard for his experience, which his lordship certainly meant to put to good use. Joanna enjoyed this hob-nobbing with the aristocracy enormously, even if Adrian suspected she was

343

getting a somewhat distorted view of the British upper classes. But he was pleased to see her pleased, and so relieved that Delamere, far from being resented, was actually being worshipped by the Masai, that he would have forgiven him anything.

But Delamere, although he listened to everything that was told him about the problems of farming or ranching in the high country, was so self-confidently an individualist that not even he could immediately turn the great prairie into gold. He had early decided against cattle, having gone into the question of the prevalence of rinderpest. But the land was equally obviously good for sheep. The Masai kept sheep, albeit on a small scale, and here was a vast pasture waiting to be populated. He had, however, chosen his acreage at random, except with an eye both to beauty and to the proximity to water, and Uthuli came over to speak with Adrian, as the sheep began to arrive in large numbers. 'You must tell Lord,' he said, 'that they will all die.'

'Oh, come now,' Adrian protested. 'I would have said there was enough grass for all the sheep in the world.'

'Enough grass,' Uthuli agreed. 'But enough good grass, no. Where he has put his sheep to graze, no. Our forefathers taught us this.'

And it was a fact, Adrian realised, that he had never seen sheep grazing by Elmenteita. He suggested this to his lordship, who was not impressed. 'Grass is grass, old boy,' he declared.

But Uthuli was right. The sheep began to die, certainly due to a lack of something in their food. Delamere was not to be put off by that. He imported an expert to tell him what was wrong, and was informed that there was a mineral deficiency in the grass, and the sheep could not survive. Having taken further advice, he ploughed up the pasture, while the Masai watched in amazement, and sowed English clover, which had everything a sheep could desire. Then he re-stocked his herd. But before they could benefit from their change of diet, the clover in turn started to die: the African bees were unable to pollinate it.

His lordship, with whom money was obᵛiously no consideration, followed a logical path. If his sheep needed clover to thrive, then clover they would have. He replanted, and imported English bees to deal with the problem. With enormous success. As he said when next he visited Naivasha, 'Wait until you see my pasture of clover. I am going to have the finest sheep in the world.'

Adrian went to visit, and realised he was right. The clover was growing like the weed it basically was, running wild. Unfortunately, it kept right on doing that. In its native habitat, northern Europe, it would normally have had a dormant period during the winter; in the high country, beneath an African sun and soaked by African rain, it just grew and grew, far more quickly and luxuriantly than it could ever be eaten by the sheep, or than it could be cut by Delamere's gardeners. Often the sheep were entirely lost to sight behind the great deep green thickets. Then they started dying again, from foot rot.

His lordship then decided that perhaps sheep were not the ideal source of wealth in the high country, and returned to his first idea, cattle. To negate the risk of rinderpest, he imported British bulls to cross breed with the best strain of African cows. This time, the Masai, who had watched the sheep experiment with polite pessimism, were really interested, and Uthuli formally invited Lord Delamere to be initiated into the clan. This his lordship, having discussed the pros and cons with Adrian, declined, but his prestige still grew as his cattle appeared to be impervious to all the local diseases – until a new strain of some unknown variety of fever swept up from German East and wiped out his herd. The Masai could understand this sort of tragedy, having experienced it often enough, and were very angry on his lordship's behalf. Uthuli himself went to Elmenteita to offer condolences. His Morani themselves took over the restocking and herding of the surviving cattle. With or without initiation, Lord was now one of them.

His experiences naturally did not encourage vast numbers of others to join him, which pleased Adrian. There *were* new arrivals over the next few years, most of them scions of the nobility as well, such as the brothers Berkeley and Galbraith Cole, younger sons of the Earl of Enniskillen, who also tried various methods of farming, without notable success. But the Masai welcomed them all, regarding them as protégés of their red-haired idol, who was in turn a protégé of their blond giant.

They were less popular in the now thriving township of Nairobi, which was trying hard to become an English provincial town in the high country, noxious odours and mosquitoes notwithstanding, where whist parties and tea parties and rustling gowns and parasols were the order of the day, and where an enterprising entrepreneur had actually built an hotel, which he called, for no very obvious reason, the Norfolk. This hotel became the rendezvous for the 'farmers' when they decided to make a night of it in town. They would descend upon the unfortunate establishment in a drove of perhaps a dozen, invariably led by Delamere himself – which should have been good for business. But they saw themselves very much as frontiersmen, went nowhere without loaded revolvers on their hips and invariably got very drunk. Then their normally excellent breeding would dissolve into an extreme form of sixth form humour, a vice which the cowboys of the Wild West had lacked. Shooting out windows and knocking down bottles was bad; shocking the good ladies of Nairobi with their language and their noise was worse; impromptu rugby matches when anything or anyone might discover itself, himself – or even herself – being used as the ball was worst of all.

Adrian and Joanna, who thoroughly liked Delamere and most of his friends when they were sober, and who could outshoot any one of them, drunk or sober, decided they were a little old for this kind of entertainment, and besides, as neither of them had ever been to a public school, they could not always appreciate the joke. They soon made a point of staying away from Nairobi as much as possible, and certainly when the crowd were in town.

This caused no offence. Indeed, it heightened the already exaggerated respect with which the newcomers, at Delamere's instigation, treated the 'veteran' as Adrian was called. Adrian was so relieved that the long-feared invasion had passed off without a major clash of interests that he was inclined to think of the boisterous youngsters as *his* protégés. For life went on much as it had done since he could remember. The Masai still went on their annual migration, if nowadays by circuitous routes to avoid crossing the various crops being sown by the white men. There continued to be problems of the occasional poor harvests or outbreaks of rinderpest, with a distressingly high incidence of mortality from influenza and measles and various poxes, all unknown in the high country before it had been 'opened up'. The railway train chugged relentlessly once a week, each way, across the high land and down the escarpment – the funicular having been replaced by a series of hair-raising gradients – and thence across the Rift Valley to Kampala in Uganda, on the western shore of the Great Lake.

For the Barclays it was a period of great domestic bliss. Because of the stormy beginning to their marriage, the lengthy period when they had lived together not as man and wife, the equally lengthy separations, they were still discovering, in their forties, facets of the other to admire and to love. No doubt, Adrian reflected, every criticism levelled against their determination to marry in such rushed circumstances had been absolutely justified. He had known nothing of women. She had been, as her father said, a spoiled rich girl, capable of withstanding any hardship, climbing any height, enduring any discomfort – so long as it

347

was chosen by her, and did not go against anything she conceived was proper. But what a waste there would have been had they taken all that advice and separated, because now they loved, and more, they trusted each other, morally and physically. Out of the molten heat of their earlier disagreements they had become welded into a single entity, a relationship stronger than that shared by any two people of their acquaintance.

They were equally blessed in their family, with Bar's progeny increasing by one every year and Johnnie growing into a strong little boy. Cathy was savouring the delights of Europe under the protection of her aunt Hetty, who had certainly got the wanderlust and was pleased to act as chaperon to her niece, which also enabled her to keep in close touch with the sister she most envied.

There was sadness too, as both John Meachem and Molly Barclay died. But as each had reached a ripe old age, their deaths seemed in the natural order of things. Adrian felt bitterly guilty that he had not seen his mother during the last twenty-five years of her life, but he had the evidence of Amanda's letters as well as Molly's that she had never ceased to love him and to admire him for what he was doing with his life – and he also knew that she had lived in total luxury, thanks to Kurt's generosity, until the day she died.

John Meachem's death meant a considerable difference to their wealth, for when the shipyard and the ships had been sold and everything totted up, each of the four daughters received a million dollars.

'What shall we do with it?' Joanna asked.

'Oh, God knows. Invest it, I suppose,' Adrian said. 'I'm not going to ask you to waste it on futile experiments like Hugh.'

'There are a couple of things I would like,' she said, and proceeded to install her own stable and import two magnificent Alsatians – to the alarm of the Masai. Her final extravagance was also a copy of his lordship's; he had recently had an automobile sent up from the coast on the train, in which he would drive across country, horn blaring and natives rushing out of his way. Soon Joanna was doing the same.

'Happy?' he asked, as they sat on the verandah and sipped their whisky sundowners on a January afternoon in 1906.

'Oh, happy,' she said. 'I never thought life could be so blissful. Here we are, rushing at fifty' – which was an exaggeration in her case, as she was only just forty-six – 'all of our troubles behind us.' She sat up. 'The train's in. Now what is all that hubbub?'

'Some other lordling arriving,' Adrian grunted, not bothering to look up.

But Joanna was on her feet, and running down the steps. 'Mandy!' she shouted. 'Oh, Mandy! How marvellous to see you.'

Adrian also got up, following more slowly, and walked across the lawn to gaze at his sister. She was well over forty now, but as tall, and elegant, and blondely beautiful as ever. Then he looked at the two children, young teenagers who both took after their mother, and then at Kurt. 'Good God!' he remarked. 'Without even a word?'

Kurt grinned, and shook his hands. 'We wanted to surprise you.'

'Well, you have done that. But welcome, welcome. If you'd told us you were coming, we'd have made some preparations. It's going to be a bit of a squash.'

'Oh, we are not coming to impose on you,' Kurt told him. 'Save perhaps for a night. We are bound for our property.'

Adrian's brows began to draw together in a frown. 'Your property?'

'But of course. We always intended to return here to live. Now that circumstances have changed so much for the better, I have taken land. I am to make my dream come true, at last.'

349

13

'You'll have to explain it to me,' Adrian said that night after dinner. Kurt had, as usual, travelled with a case of champagne and another of claret, and they had dined very well. It was a splendid celebration, in which Joanna's transparent joy at seeing Amanda again had quite dissipated any initial apprehensions Adrian might have had over the reappearance of his brother-in-law. Although both he and Joanna were saddened by Bar's point-blank refusal to attend the meal – he would not sit down with his mother's murderer – Adrian entirely symphathised with him. But he could not help but be delighted to see his sister again, and to see her looking so well. Additionally, he now knew that Kurt had cared for his mother throughout the last years of her life, in a way he had never been able to do: Joanna's inheritance had arrived too late for that. He really had every reason to welcome them back . . . but he could not prevent the worry tension that immediately began to accumulate in his brain.

'Explain what?' Kurt asked. 'I always intended to come back. But after my differences with the Masai, I felt I should wait until things were more settled up here. Besides, Mandy did not want to leave dear Molly, or to bring the children up here until they were old enough to travel well, so I had to practise patience. I think it has worked out very well. Next year I shall be sixty. I have done everything I wanted to with my life, save settle here. And now is the time to do it, to

350

make my dream come true and enjoy this beautiful country. It is Mandy's dream too. She has always wanted to return. Heinrich will soon be joining us; he is in the army. But Willi and Inge have heard so much about this place that they are quite wildly excited.' He offered Adrian one of his cigars, and Adrian bit the end with satisfaction.

'The Masai have long memories,' he remarked.

'Indeed they do, and I observed one or two of the Morani giving me a close look when I got off the train. I was rather relieved old Uthuli was not there, I can tell you. But as I understand it, there are no teeth left in the Masai.'

'I wouldn't altogether count on that,' Adrian said. 'Now tell me the truth about why you did not let us know you were coming.'

'Don't you like being surprised?' Kurt asked.

'Was it because you knew I would try to put you off? Or have you stopped?'

Kurt raised his eyebrows. 'Could you have done that?'

'Possibly. Things have changed since the last time you were up here. The high country has been opened to British officers and gentlemen. Nobody else.'

Kurt grinned. 'And I qualify on neither count? But I am married to a British lady. Would you argue with that?'

'No,' Adrian agreed. 'And I am glad to see her. Where is your land?'

'Oh, where it always was. I have reclaimed my land. It seems nobody else has taken it. The fact is, all these newcomers have opted for land here in the valley. Give me the high plain, any time.'

'And what do you propose to farm?'

'Sheep and cattle. I always did.'

'You've heard of Lord Delamere's experiences?'

'Indeed I have. And I shall profit from his mistakes. But I should like to benefit from your experience, too.' He leaned across, held out his hand. 'Bygones, Adrian. Bygones. We have known each other too long to be enemies.'

351

Adrian hesitated, sighed, and took the offered fingers.

Kurt was, as ever, a bundle of energy. He might have been nearly sixty years old, but he worked like a young man, and his ranch – the remains of the buildings still stood, the timbers sadly gnawed by termites – grew up again at great pace. None of the Masai would work for him, so he obtained permission to bring in Somalis and some Swaheli from the coast, and treated the Masai cold shoulder with apparent indifference.

'He is a murdering swine,' Bar declared. 'He should not be allowed to live here.'

'Would you like me to make a formal protest?' Adrian asked. 'I very much doubt if he mentioned in his application that he had once killed a Masai woman. The government might very well revoke his grant.'

'It would mean the expulsion of Aunt Mandy as well,' Joanna pointed out.

Bar scowled – sometimes he could look very much the Masai Morani, although he usually wore European dress except on ceremonial occasions or for hunting. Then he shrugged, and gave one of those delightful smiles which so illuminated his essentially sunny personality. 'He will join my mother in the shades, soon enough. It is not necessary for us to send him there.'

'He doesn't mean what I think he means, I hope,' Joanna asked Adrian that night.

'He means what he says,' Adrian said. 'I'm quite sure he'll never do anything to harm Mandy.'

'I sure hope so,' Joanna commented. She was in a seventh heaven. Much as she had always loved the high country, she had always acutely felt the absence of any compatible female companionship, a lack which had been pointed up during the gloriously happy couple of years she had had her sister Hetty staying with her. She had, by sheer exposure to the language, picked up enough Masai and Swaheli to carry on a conversation with the Masai women – she and Sita would often chatter away at each other – but there was no intimacy; their talk was confined to recipes and ways of cooking the native food, and the health of the various children and grandchildren, and the weather. Nor had she been able to make friends with any of the new breed of English bibis daily arriving in Mombasa with their husbands and spreading up to Nairobi, and even on to the plain and down into the valley. They were generally of the upper classes, and were terribly aware of it; she might be an American millionairess, but she was still an American.

They also regarded her as a considerable freak, a white woman who had lived for a quarter of a century amongst the most fearsome tribe left in Africa, and clearly assumed she had been raped and circumcised and even dunked in the cooking pot from time to time, and had survived only by a variety of fortunate accidents. Certainly her sunbrowned complexion was, to their eyes, utterly ruined, and her habit of going shooting whenever she felt a change of diet utterly unladylike. She lacked other social graces, too, in that she didn't play whist, didn't beat her servants – which had apparently been instilled in the bibis as an essential part of coping with the African native – because, worst of all, she didn't *have* any servants, only friends who helped about the house, and her husband's peculiar housekeeper . . . all the bibis knew what *that* meant, even if they found it difficult to denounce Adrian as a roué when both his women were older than most of them.

From Joanna's point of view, these new arrivals were a joke; they persisted in indulging in all the old absurdities she had suffered when she first came to Africa – they wrapped themselves in red flannel underwear, wore spine pads and sweated in horrible discomfort.

But Amanda was her oldest friend, and one whose experience of the high country went back as far as her own; she regularly rode up to visit her sister-in-law – not even her automobile could cope with the escarpment – invariably accompanied by Johnnie, at ten years old already an excellent horseman and the darling of his German cousins. As Kurt had promised, they were soon joined by Heinrich, a tall, grave young man with a professionally Prussian bearing, who clicked his heels and bowed over his aunt-by-marriage's knuckles every time they met, to Joanna's delight.

Adrian only occasionally accompanied them, as Kurt only occasionally accompanied Amanda when she returned the visits. Both men were fully occupied with their farms, but they also knew they could never be friends, especially after Kurt was joined by his old friend Pitzer as foreman – a man Adrian could never see without wanting to throttle on the instant. And Kurt, for all his bravado, had no intention of making his presence too obvious to the Masai, or of finding himself near Uthuli's kraal after dark. But Adrian was pleased for Jo's sake that she had at last a companion of her own sex whom she could enjoy.

On their own domestic front, there was suddenly a problem. Cathy at last found the man she apparently wanted to marry, an Englishman who was distantly connected with the nobility, and Adrian therefore expected he would settle in very well to the new society which was taking root in the high country. His name was Ralph Price, and he was tall enough to match his fiancée, and handsome in a somewhat drawing-room fashion. She brought him out for a visit, chaperoned as ever by her aunt. Hetty was clearly never going to marry; she was interested only in finding a husband who would lease land in the high country and, as she was now past forty herself, this was growing increasingly difficult. But she had the wealth, inherited from her father, to do what she pleased with her life, and Cathy was the apple of her eye.

Cathy's great ambition was to be married at Naivasha, and Joanna naturally encouraged her in this. Ralph was less sure. Adrian had enthusiastically set to work to show him every aspect of the life in the valley, in the hopes that he might indeed be interested in settling there. Delamere was pleased to welcome him, and entertained the young couple to dinner. But although he sat a horse well and could shoot accurately, and was not unduly affected by the heat, he was too obviously bored. 'I mean to say, sir, there's no life up here, is there?'

Adrian didn't know what to reply to that. If there was no life in the high country, then he did not see that there was life anywhere else in the world. But Ralph apparently meant night life. He also missed sculling, which had been his previous favourite occupation. Joanna suggested they try Nairobi for the former, at least, and he and Hetty and Cathy went in for a short visit, but returned soon enough; someone had shot the hat off Ralph's head, for no reason save that it had been a brand new topee. Cathy was furious and had wanted to shoot back, but Hetty and Ralph managed to dissuade her. Ralph's only desire, after that, was to leave the high country as rapidly as possible. However, before doing so, he formally asked Adrian for Cathy's hand in marriage, and Adrian, with Joanna's approval, gave his permission.

But the concept of an East African wedding had necessarily gone by the board. 'I'm afraid the mater would never go for it,' Ralph explained to a thunderstruck Joanna.

The wedding was fixed for the following spring, in England. 'You are going to attend,' Joanna said, not prepared to risk making it a question.

Adrian sighed. 'I don't want to.'

'You mean you have no desire ever to set foot in your native country again?'

'Frankly, none.'

'Well, then, have you no desire to see your only daughter married?'

'I suppose I do. But not to that chinless wonder.'

355

'But you will come,' she said, sticking to essentials. 'Cathy would be crushed if you didn't.'

There was not a lot of argument he could put against her. Keeping the peace was no longer his province; Uthuli, quite without realising it, had become his tenant, and the rest of the Masai nation seemed to have accepted the white influx in good heart. Because it had not been quite the influx Adrian had feared, and because as Eliot – now long retired – had prophesied, most of the settlers were from the upper crust, and if their eccentricities could never match Delamere's, they were yet regarded as being superior beings by the Morani; their Nairobi antics when drunk did not interest the Masai. It would have to be a very remarkable mishap to upset them now – and there would be nothing he could do about that either, he supposed.

Nor could he really pretend he was still needed for every harvesting or sowing of his crops. Bar and Safah between them were quite capable of taking care of that, and as Bar had early got the message that Ralph Price did not consider him 'quite right' because of his African blood, there was no question of him attending the wedding; the suggestion that her new daughter-in-law might have a 'coloured' half-brother would most definitely upset the mater.

Yet he still would have preferred to stay. He had, as usual, studied Delamere at work. Now that he had some money of his own to play with, courtesy of Joanna, he had diversified into sisal and flax – crops which his lordship was also growing, in addition to some coffee, in an attempt to set off some of the losses he had suffered through his experiments in livestock; even the Delamere millions were not apparently inexhaustible. In fact both the new crops were doing well, but it was too early as yet to be sure if they would prove a success, and the thought of being away during the critical first couple of years – even for a few months, which were all he was prepared to spare – was disturbing.

He had, fortunately, resisted the temptation to follow his

lordship into wheat. Delamere was convinced that the climate of the high country must be as conducive to wheat growing as the American Midwest, some thirty degrees farther north. He thus sowed a vast area with wheat, over Adrian's scepticism, and chuckled happily when it had indeed grown as luxuriantly as ever his clover had done. Unfortunately, the game – which was far more abundant in the high country than in North America – rapidly discovered it to be the best food they had ever tasted. Every cereal-eating animal in East Africa, it seemed, from buffalo to kongoni, accumulated on Delamere's property for this unexpected feast. His lordship was furious. He assembled all his friends, cursing angrily when Adrian merely laughed and refused to join in, and shot every living creature, short of man, he found on his acreage. The slaughter was immense, but it didn't save the wheat, which was by then dying of disease. It merely got his lordship into further bad odour in Nairobi. The government officials were beginning to think in terms of shooting licences to alleviate the indiscriminate slaughter of the wild game in the valley. And Delamere's latest drunken exploit – sliding the full length of the main bar in the Norfolk Hotel and exiting through a plate-glass window – also caused a stir. Relations between the farmers and the government promptly deteriorated further, especially when the deputy commissioner called his lordship a 'damned scallawag', an epithet Delamere had never before suffered.

But as usual, Delamere's antics had little effect on the farm at Lake Naivasha, where, if there were diseases and other minor problems from time to time, the crops on the whole prospered.

With the coming of the new year, Joanna became quite excited at the thought of the wedding, and their own imminent departure. She began planning outfits from vast catalogues of the latest fashions, noting with relief that bustles were out, as were wasp waists and Gibson Girl figures – King Edward VII liked his ladies to be full bodied, and that was sufficient for English society. Joanna had become quite full bodied with the passing of time.

Amanda was also excited. Kurt had agreed that she too could attend the wedding, although he did not intend to do so himself; Inge and Willi had already gone off, to their various colleges, and Heinrich was going to accompany his mother. Departure was in the air, and some of the excitement even communicated itself to Adrian.

Then, the morning after the return of the clan from its migration, Uthuli appeared on his front verandah. Adrian had expected him and was waiting to greet him, but frowned as he saw his foster father's expression, which was that of a man labouring under a most severe burden.

'There are grasshoppers, in the north,' he announced.

Adrian wasn't sure what to make of that. 'Grasshoppers?' he queried. There were always one or two grasshoppers around, and they were a nuisance in that they ate the young leaves, but it was simply a matter of keeping a look out for them, as a rule, and flicking them away. They had never in any way suggested a critical situation. But Uthuli obviously expected to be taken seriously.

'Word has come,' Uthuli said. He looked at Bar, who had hurried across from his house to greet his grandfather. 'There are grasshoppers in the north,' Uthuli repeated sombrely.

Bar stared at him, then at his father.

'You'll have to explain what's so terrible about that,' Adrian said, in English.

'If there are enough of them, they will eat everything,' Bar said, aghast.

Adrian frowned. 'There would have to be one hell of a lot of them to do that. Has this ever happened before? Have you ever seen it happen?'

Bar shook his head. 'There has not been one within living

memory. Except . . .' He switched back to Masai. 'You have known a plague of grasshoppers, my grandfather,' he said. 'You have told me of them.'

'When I was a boy,' Uthuli said, 'the grasshoppers came. They ate everything. There was no grain, no fodder for the cattle. Many died, and many cattle, too. Everything was dead, when the grasshoppers had left us.'

'Jesus Christ,' Adrian remarked. He looked at the sky to the north. It was a simply superb day. He could see only birds. 'When?' he asked.

'No man knows,' Uthuli said, positively enjoying his Cassandric role.

'But they are definitely coming?'

'The grasshoppers are coming,' Uthuli said solemnly.

Adrian told Bar not to mention the matter to his stepmother at this moment. He didn't know what Joanna's reaction might be if, at this late stage – they were due to depart in less than a fortnight – he announced he wasn't going after all. But the thought of leaving the farm, the entire high country, just as it was about to be struck by the greatest catastrophe of the past sixty years, was impossible. But he could hardly believe it was really going to happen.

He mounted his horse and rode across to Elmenteita, where his lordship was supervising the laying down of a croquet lawn. 'These chappies don't seem able to understand that it has to be as smooth as a billiard table,' he grumbled. 'Because that's what croquet is: billiards on grass.'

'The grasshoppers are coming,' Adrian said.

Delamere gave him an old-fashioned look. 'Bit early for me, really, old man, but I think you could do with a hair of the dog.' He led the way into the house.

'I am perfectly sober,' Adrian protested. 'I think what they mean is, a plague of locusts could be on the way.'

Delamere decided to pour two whiskies instead of one.

359

'You'd better tell me about that,' he said. Then he listened, pulling his nose from time to time. 'So far it's just hearsay,' he pointed out when Adrian had finished.

'Uthuli seems to take it seriously.'

'Uthuli has always struck me as a bit of a pessimist. Tell you what I'll do: I'll send some men up north to find out what's happening, if there's any truth in this rumour. No use starting a panic, eh?'

'Do you reckon we *should* panic?' Adrian asked. 'If they are coming?'

'Don't you know?'

'I've never experienced it. It's a once in a lifetime event, fortunately.'

'Hm. And the little buggers really eat everything?'

'Apparently. Everything green, anyway.'

'There'll have to be one hell of a lot of grasshoppers to eat everything green on this plain.' Delamere echoed Adrian's own first reaction. 'I'll find out what's really happening, and we'll talk about it then.'

He was as good as his word, and sent some of his Somalis to the north. They were back in a week, to say that the land up there was like a desert. Even Delamere took that seriously, and more so when they spoke of a cloud of grasshoppers so thick it obscured the sky. He drove over to Naivasha to consult Uthuli and Adrian.

'Fire,' Uthuli recommended. His Morani were already cutting down trees and stacking great piles of timber and maize stalks to set alight.

'Where?'

'Everywhere. In the fields.'

'But if you set fire to the fields, my father,' Adrian said, 'at this time of year, when there has been no rain for some months, you will burn all the grass just as if the grasshoppers had eaten it.'

'It will burn the grasshoppers as well,' Uthuli said, with an unusually vicious intonation. 'There is also noise.'

'Noise?' Delamere asked.

'It may send them away.'

'Where?'

'Anywhere but here,' Uthuli said.

His lordship came up to the house for tea with Joanna, one of his very favourite pastimes. 'When are you leaving?' he asked.

'The day after tomorrow,' she said, and gave Adrian one of her steely looks. 'I hope.'

'Ah,' Adrian said. 'Well . . . that depends.'

'Tell me.'

He had finally mentioned the risk of a grasshopper invasion to her, but playing down the seriousness of the situation. Now he said, 'Well, Uthuli seems to feel it could be a fairly destructive happening, and . . .'

'I don't believe a word of it,' Joanna declared. 'Do you, Hugh?'

Delamere pulled his nose. 'Those Arab chappies I sent up north are bright lads. They say there has been a drought in Ethiopia, and in their own Somaliland, these couple of years past, and this is what has started the grasshoppers moving. They say they really are a menace. In fact, they say the old chief is right, and the only possible remedy is to discourage them from attacking your land and drive them on to the next fellow.'

'Sounds rather unneighbourly,' Joanna commented.

'Well . . . if we could drive them right across the high country and into Tanganyika . . .' he grinned. 'That'd put a spoke in the Germans' wheel, eh? I really think I must warn the other fellows.' He drove off in his motor car, leaving a plume of dust behind him as he crossed the valley.

Joanna was thoroughly annoyed. 'You're going to use this as an excuse for staying, aren't you?' she asked bitterly.

'I think I'd better have a word with Kurt,' Adrian decided. He didn't really care whether Kurt's pasturage got eaten up by locusts or not, but it was just possible, with his experi-

361

ence of other parts of Africa, Kurt might have encountered this problem before.

Kurt had never seen a plague of locusts before, but he had heard the rumour that one was imminent. And was as usual disposed to regard it as so much nonsense. 'Grasshoppers,' he said contemptuously. 'It is a native fantasy.'

'I'll see you and Jo tomorrow, when I ride over to catch the train,' Amanda said. 'With Heinrich.'

'Um,' Adrian said, and returned to Naivasha.

'Aren't you going to pack?' Joanna asked that evening.

'Tomorrow will do. I haven't all that much to take.'

He lay awake half the night, listening and thinking. Grasshoppers. He found it difficult to visualise just how much damage they could do. He thought of a myriad grasshoppers settling on his coffee plants, his flax and his sisal, his bananas. But there were surely sufficient Masai, added to himself and Safah and Bar and Safah's sons, to drive them away, or indeed to slaughter them. He fell asleep in a more relaxed frame of mind.

Joanna was up early, and dressed for the train journey, as was Johnnie. 'I'm so excited,' she said, as they breakfasted on the verandah. 'Cathy, marrying, well . . . I know he's going to turn out all right.' Then she became agitated. 'I wonder where Mandy and Heinrich are? I expected them for breakfast. I do hope they won't keep the train waiting. Oh, Adrian, I'm so . . . oh, Lord,' she muttered, as she saw Uthuli crossing the lawn. 'Good morning, our father,' she said, using the somewhat disrespectful form of address she had cultivated for him, but which always pleased him. 'We must say goodbye.' She got up to take his hands as he came up the steps. 'And not a grasshopper to see us off.'

Uthuli gazed at her, and then turned and pointed at the northern sky.

Joanna frowned. 'What an odd-looking cloud,' she remarked. 'Are the Long Rains going to be early, this year?'

'That is not rain,' Uthuli said. 'Grasshoppers.'

362

'Oh, my God,' Joanna said. 'Oh, my *God*!'

Both Adrian and Johnnie got up and ran to her side, looking in the direction of Uthuli's pointing finger. The northern horizon was obliterated by what appeared to be a heavy bank of cloud drifting slowly in the air, but with a peculiar shape to it, two distinct points, like a tornado suspended in mid air. There was blue sky above the cloud, and there was blue-green landscape beneath. But between the two there was that heavy dark mass, moving slowly nearer.

'What do we do?' Joanna asked.

'You and Johnnie get into the house, for a start,' Adrian snapped. 'Summon all the women, and make the children come in as well. Shut all the windows. Safah!' he bawled. 'Bar! Let's get those fires lit.'

He had arranged a series of bonfires at various places throughout his acreage, having carefully cleared the crop from around it; he was hoping that the flames and smoke might discourage the grasshoppers from alighting, without at the same time doing too much damage to the crops themselves. Uthuli was already hurrying back for his kraal as Adrian, Safah, Bar and two of Safah's sons mounted up and rode off. Safah pointed as they entered the fields, and Adrian saw a grasshopper on the track in front of him. And then another, already alighted on a banana stalk and eating the leaf. He rode off the track and swung at it with his crop. The creature fell dead with a somewhat surprised air. When Adrian looked back at the stalk, there were at least a dozen where the dead insect had been before.

As they lit the fires, they became aware that the air was slowly thickening. Grasshoppers lodged in their hats, their hair, got down the front of their shirts and into the tops of their boots, each one about the size of a man's little finger, with enormous, long, bent legs, flapping wings and hungry proboscis. The volume of insects was unbelievable; when Adrian looked up he could not see the sky, when he looked back at the lake he could not see the house. With every breath grasshoppers seemed to be sucked against his nose and mouth, and he had a sudden claustrophobic feeling of being about to be smothered to death.

It was impossible to communicate with any of the others because of the noise; the flapping of the billions of tiny wings and the scissoring of the legs against each other was like being in the middle of a gale at sea, only it reached a much higher timbre than any wind could, and as they fought their way back towards the house they could hear the dogs barking inside. They stabled the horses and closed the doors, but there were already grasshoppers inside the barn. When they climbed the steps to the verandah of the house they trod on them; grasshoppers formed a ghastly seething carpet on the floor. Adrian paused to look back at the lawn, which after twenty years of constant effort was at last a green sward . . . or had been a green sward. Now it was a dull brown, a seething mass of hungry insects.

The morning, then the day, took on a surrealistic tint. Everything had turned a dull brown colour – the air, the fields, the lawns, the house, any human being who went outside – while across the landscape there drifted a pall of brown smoke from the various bonfires. From the Masai kraal there came a tremendous shouting, and the sounds of spears and cooking pots being beaten together, while Bar even tried firing a few shots into the air. Nothing made any difference to the grasshoppers. For twenty-four hours they hung above Lake Naivasha, whirring, hissing, whining – and eating.

During the night the noise ceased, and when at dawn Adrian went outside, they were gone from the air. He trod on a bed of dead grasshoppers as he went down the front steps. He looked at thousands, perhaps millions, of dead insects as he crossed the lawn and went down the track to the fields. But there were still some living. Safah, following him, turned over a desiccated branch to show Adrian the eggs that had been laid during the night. 'These will be grasshoppers next year,' he said.

Adrian felt consumed with a total hatred for the ghastly creatures. 'Stamp on them,' he said. 'Stamp on every one you can find.' But, of course, they would not find more than a fraction. And in the meantime . . . he continued on his way, to look at the destruction. Remarkably, the coffee trees, with their unusually hard fibre, were relatively undamaged; the grasshoppers had discovered easier food to masticate. The other crops were just a withered accumulation of empty stalks. But crops could be replanted. The real damage was beyond the fields; there was not a blade of grass to be seen on the pasturage.

They listened to the train whistle, mounted their horses and rode down to the station to meet the eastbound locomotive. 'It is bad,' the conductor said. 'All the valley is eaten out.'

This was the train they had been supposed to catch the previous morning, delayed twenty-four hours by the catastrophe. Adrian waved it on.

The Masai had been fortunate, to a certain extent, in that they had not yet planted their yearly crop of maize, but the grasshoppers had been sufficiently disastrous. 'Now all our cattle will die,' Uthuli said. 'This is a terrible misfortune, my son. It is a punishment by the great gods of heaven and earth for our misdeeds. For putting away our spears and ceasing to live as the lion hunters should always live. For permitting the murderer of my daughter to live amongst us, unpunished. These are sad times.'

The Masai, Morani and women, stood outside the kraal and gazed at Adrian. Once he had brought them prosperity. Now he had brought them disaster.

'No one will die, my father,' Adrian said, and rode back to the house.

Joanna waited on the verandah. She wore her bush clothes. 'I heard the train whistle,' she said.

'I'm sorry. But these people will starve if they are not helped; they will lose all their cattle for a start.'

'Don't you think I understand that?' she asked. 'But there's money in the bank, isn't there?'

He took her in his arms. 'I thought you might be angry at missing the wedding.'

'There are some things more important than weddings,' she said, and kissed him. 'Cathy will understand. Now we'd better get cracking.'

They rode into Nairobi and bought all the fodder available, then sent down to the coast to procure more; a special train was laid on. Delamere and his friends – who had all lost the major portion of their crops, and would also have a fodder problem – joined them in the desperate rush to avoid a cattle famine, but there was insufficient time, and too many cattle.

'We will save some,' Adrian promised Uthuli, gazing at the dying animals. 'And we will rebuild your herds, my father.'

'But they say, why has this thing come upon us?' Uthuli asked. 'They say Bar-clay is a false god, and so is Lord. They say more . . .' He looked up at the escarpment.

Kurt had ridden over the day after the locusts had passed through, trying to suppress his smile. His ranch had been assailed by the plague the night before the insects had reached Naivasha, which was why Amanda and Heinrich had not appeared for breakfast, but it was virtually undamaged. 'Brains, boy,' he told Adrian. 'Brains, and determination. That is what is needed to survive up here. I fought the damned things face to face. I lit a line of fires so thick nothing could get through. I must have burned up near a thousand acres north of the ranch. And I kept the fires going. So I saved the rest of my pasturage. When the creatures saw that pall of smoke, they swerved off.'

'And came down to Naivasha,' Adrian said.

Now Kurt did grin. 'Wouldn't you have done the same?

366

But I'm here to help, boy. Anything I can spare is yours.'

He meant what he said, but it *was* anything he could spare, and the fact remained that his pasturage was all but intact and his cattle were not dying. Amanda and Heinrich also cancelled their departure and helped wherever possible, but nothing could alleviate the glaring difference between Kurt's situation and that of the Masai.

'They say he is an evil spirit,' Uthuli growled, 'who has always brought misfortune upon my people. You came to us with your father, and Von took you away again.'

'Well,' Adrian said, preparing to explain it had been his idea as well to leave.

'Then he returned, to murder my daughter. Now he has come back, to bring destruction upon our land.'

'He saved himself by his own efforts,' Adrian insisted. 'And your cattle and your land will recover. And your people.'

'These are sad times, my son,' Uthuli said, and returned home.

'Will there be trouble?' Joanna asked.

Adrian shook his head. 'Not as long as he lives.'

'And when he dies?'

Adrian looked at Bar.

'There will be no trouble, Mother,' Bar said. 'My people will never go to war against the house of Barclay. But that German swine . . . I think now it would be correct for us to ask for his grant to be revoked.'

'But Mandy . . .'

'I am sorry, Mother. Mandy will have to go as well. Besides, knowing that Schlieben is so disliked, and more than ever now, I cannot believe she can be happy here.'

Joanna looked at Adrian, who sighed. 'I'm sorry too, my love, but I think Bar is right. As long as Kurt lives here, every misfortune will be laid at his door, and the resentment against him will grow and eventually poison the whole happy atmosphere of the high country and the valley. I'm going to go into Nairobi and have a word with the deputy commissioner.'

Joanna said nothing. She knew they were right.

Adrian was up early next morning, his horse saddled for him. He walked it down the drive, and there drew rein, aware of a curiously breathless feeling. Before him was an assembly of Morani, at least twice the number who composed the warriors of Uthuli's clan. To his relief, Uthuli was with them, but then he looked at the black man beside him, tall and strong, although by no means young, wearing the lion's mane headdress and smeared in red mud.

Uthuli's face was a peculiar mixture of happiness and apprehension. 'Kainairju has come home,' he said.

14

Every muscle in Adrian's body seemed to tighten as he stared at that arrogant countenance. Kainairju must be older than himself, he reflected, and he was in his fiftieth year. But the Morani had worn well, and where Adrian would have confessed to a slight sag behind his belt, Kainairju's naked body was as powerful-looking as ever in the past. And his expression was every bit as hostile as the last time he had seen him, twenty-five years before.

Nor could he doubt *why* his foster brother had come back at this moment, especially supported by a contingent of Morani from the other clans. But he had to pretend otherwise, until he could decide what had best be done. He dismounted and held out his hand. 'It has been a long time, my brother.'

Uthuli looked relieved.

But Kainairju ignored the offered fingers. 'For my people, Bar-clay,' he said. 'Too long.'

Adrian listened to hoofbeats behind him. Others had observed what was going on. He continued to look at Kainairju. 'And you come upon us at a sad time,' he remarked.

'A sad time,' Kainairju agreed. 'Because my people have turned their faces away from the old ways, and submitted to the white man. They have become a nation of women,' he added loudly.

The Morani at his back stirred restlessly. Many from his own clan could never have seen him before today, however many tales they had been told of his deeds and the way he had been banished.

'Your people have accomplished great deeds in your absence, Kainairju,' Adrian said, also raising his voice. 'They have won great battles. Now they wish to live in peace.'

'How may a Masai, a Morani, live at peace?' Kainairju asked, and looked past Adrian.

Adrian knew who had to be there, and himself turned. 'Your nephew,' he said. 'Bar.'

Bar dismounted. Safah was also there. Joanna had had the sense to remain at the house, but Adrian was certain she would be watching, probably with a rifle at her shoulder.

'Bar is the agreed successor to your father and his grand-father,' Adrian said, just in case no one had thought to inform Kainairju of that important fact.

'That cannot be,' Kainairju declared. 'I have returned, to succeed my father and lead my Morani into battle.'

Adrian shook his head. 'You have been away too long.'

'Too long,' Kainairju said. 'Too long. While my people have dwindled. Now I have returned to save them from destruction. Can Bar do this?'

'Yes,' Adrian said. 'By the way of peace and friendship with the white man.'

'That is the way of destruction,' Kainairju insisted. 'I have come back to lead my people, to reclaim our pastures from

369

the white man. I have come back to rid my people of Von and his friends, who have brought calamity upon us.'

'Von has no friends,' Adrian told him.

Kainairju turned to face the warriors. 'Was there ever a plague of grasshoppers when I led the Morani?' he demanded.

Spear hafts thudded into the dust.

'Or before the white man came?'

Thud went the spears.

'Wherever I have been in my wandering,' Kainairju said, 'men say to me, this has not happened before.'

'It has happened before,' Adrian asked. 'And before the white man came to this land. Ask our father. Is that not so, my father?'

'Many, many years ago,' Uthuli said. 'Many, many years.' His tone implied there had been some reason then too. Adrian wished he could be more certain of exactly where the old man stood in this clash of beliefs, of principles.

'The gods of heaven and earth were angry then,' Kainairju declared. 'So they are angry now. They are angry because we have made peace with the men who have taken away our pastures. I will succeed my father, and I will lead the Morani.'

'No,' Bar said, speaking for the first time.

Kainairju turned back to face him, slowly. 'You are a white man yourself,' he said contemptuously. 'Have you ever killed a lion, save with a long spear?'

Bar bit his lip, because he had not; Adrian had never let him.

'You seek to lead my people,' Kainairju went on, even more contemptuously. 'Then you must prove you are a better man than I.' He turned his spear in his hand, and drove it into the earth at Bar's feet.

Adrian listened to the whistle of breath through Safah's teeth, audible even above the drumming spear hafts; the

Somali knew they were facing the biggest crisis they had ever encountered, since the day of John Barclay's death.

'Don't touch that spear,' Adrian muttered, in English.

'I must, or leave this land,' Bar replied. Unaware when he left the house of what he would have to face, he was wearing European clothes. Now he kicked off his boots, unbuttoned his shirt.

Adrian looked at Uthuli. 'This is not the way, my father,' he said.

Uthuli looked acutely unhappy, but made no reply.

While Kainairju sneered. 'It is the way of the Masai, Bar-clay,' he said. 'Let your son face me as a man, or crawl away to your kraal like the animal he is.'

Bar dropped his shirt on the ground, threw his hat behind it and plucked the spear from the earth; the Morani drummed their spears in anticipation of the coming duel.

More hooves sounded from behind them. Joanna had realised what was going on.

'Go back,' Adrian shouted at her, but she had already reached them. Both horse and rider were panting. As he had known she would, she carried her rifle, but that counted for nothing with the Morani. She was a woman, and none of them had seen her shoot or was aware that she could knock out his eye at a quarter-of-a-mile range.

'You must stop this,' she said in English.

'He cannot,' Bar said, standing still, the spear in his hands. 'If I do not fight him, then we must all leave this place.'

Adrian knew Bar was right. He watched Kainairju back away, waiting for another spear to be thrust into his hands. Perhaps Kainairju was afraid, he thought. Perhaps he had not expected Bar to respond to his challenge. He was fifty years old, Adrian reminded himself. Bar was thirty-one, in the very prime of life, very nearly as tall and as powerful as Adrian himself. Kainairju must realise he was out of his class.

371

But there was no fear in his face, only an increasing arrogance as he stared at Bar, never taking his eyes from the younger man's face, while he grasped the offered spear without ever looking at it, and stepped forward, as did Bar, into the space before the Morani.

Adrian backed to where Safah and Joanna waited.

'Adrian,' Joanna said urgently. 'You cannot let this happen.'

'I cannot stop it now,' he said. 'And perhaps it is the only way to end it without major bloodshed. Otherwise we could have a war on our hands.'

Her hand reached down to squeeze his shoulder as she watched the two men slowly circling each other, testing footholds with their toes. Then Kainairju grinned, and thrust. Bar leapt backwards with easy confidence and let his own spear swing; the two weapons thudded together, and Kainairju grinned again. Then he moved forward once more, spear darting to left and right, seeking an opening. Joanna held her breath, but Bar was equal to every thrust, parrying every movement of his more experienced adversary with consummate skill. Kainairju's advance brought the two men together, spears crossed, pressed into their chests. Kainairju strained to push his rival backward, but then Bar exerted his greater strength, and Kainairju suddenly disengaged and sprang away, panting.

Now Kainairju's grin wore a tinge of desperation. He stood still for a moment, reaching for breath, chest rising and falling, while Bar waited for his next move. Adrian stamped his foot in despair. Now was the time for Bar to go on to the attack, while his opponent was at once exhausted and dispirited. But Bar had not yet made up his mind that it was necessary to kill his uncle.

Kainairju feinted to left and right, moving closer as he regained his breath, and then, from a distance of about ten feet, hurled his spear. Adrian and Joanna gasped together, but Bar simply ducked, and the spear passed over his shoulder, to land point first in the earth, quivering.

Again Kainairju stood still, breathing deeply, muscles tensed as he realised he had lost. The Morani were also still, waiting for Bar to administer the *coup de grâce*.

'Now,' Joanna whispered. 'For God's sake, *now*.'

But Bar stepped aside, moving to his right, leaving Kainairju's spear exposed, watching and waiting; he could not bring himself to kill an unarmed man.

'Winchester,' Adrian muttered savagely.

Kainairju hesitated, then realised he was being given a second chance. He leapt across the intervening space, grasped his spear, turned and threw it again, from the side. It shot through the air like the javelin it had become, and entered Bar's chest, high on the left side; taken quite unawares, Bar had not the time to raise his own weapon to parry the missile.

Joanna gave a low whimper of distress, while Adrian stood as if turned to stone. Bar was killed instantly as the spear pierced his heart. His knees gave way and he slumped to the ground, his blood drifting away from his body to coagulate in the dust.

Kainairju raised his arms on high, his chest rising and falling. The Morani drummed their spear hafts on the ground, and Adrian listened to the click of the bolt being cocked on Joanna's rifle. 'No,' he muttered, and stepped away from her. He knew only white-hot anger that he had allowed this tragedy to happen, that he had taken away from Bar the instincts of the savage, which, left untarnished, would have given him so easy a victory – in the mistaken idea that he was making him into a better man. But he had never fallen into the habit of wearing a gun like Delamere and his friends. Neither was Safah armed, and for Joanna to gun down Kainairju would cost them all their lives to no purpose. There was only one way he could right this situation, and avenge Bar as well.

Joanna understood what he intended, and was instantly afraid. 'No,' she begged.

Adrian ignored her, as he went towards Kainairju. 'You have killed my son,' he said, his voice harsh.

Kainairju turned to face him, the arrogance for one moment fading from his face as he realised they were both unarmed; he had no desire to find himself within the grip of those immensely powerful hands. 'We fought as men should,' he said. 'I have no quarrel with you, Bar-clay.' He leapt away from Adrian and stood immediately in front of the Morani. 'We fought by the law of the Masai.'

'Now you will fight me,' Adrian said.

'No,' Joanna shouted. 'Oh, God, no!'

'I have no quarrel with you, Bar-clay,' Kainairju said again. 'Are you not my brother? How may brother fight with brother? I will not fight with you. If you oppose me, it will be to oppose my Morani.'

Once again six hundred spear hafts drummed on the earth.

Adrian looked at Uthuli, seeking support for his claim to vengeance.

'He is right, my son,' Uthuli said. 'They fought according to the law of our people. I grieve for the death of my grandson, but Kainairju has proved he is my rightful heir.'

'I am chieftain,' Kainairju declared.

Uthuli turned his head to look at him, and past him at the warriors; he could not doubt that he had just been deposed by unanimous decision of his young men. 'Your weakness has brought calamity upon our people,' Kainairju said. 'I will lead the Morani into battle now.'

'That is madness,' Adrian declared, his anger momentarily receding as he realised he could indeed be witnessing the start of a war. 'You cannot oppose the white soldiers.'

'The white soldiers,' Kainairju said in contempt. 'They will not stop us now. Go back to your kraal, Bar-clay, with your woman, and' – his gaze played over Safah – 'your servant. And remain there.' He looked down at Bar's body. 'Take that with you. Leave me and my people to our work.'

Adrian hesitated. He wanted to seize the man and throttle him, but Kainairju had threatened that would mean taking on some six hundred Morani, and he was supported only by an elderly servant and a woman, and with a single rifle between them.

He stooped, lifted Bar into his arms and turned away.

'Put him on his horse, bwana,' Safah said.

'I will carry him,' Adrian said, and walked back up the drive to the house, perhaps half a mile away. There he laid Bar on the verandah. Sita, Saba, Lili and the other women gathered round, and Safah's sons, and Bar's children as well, three sons and two daughters. The eldest, Ade, was only eight years old.

Lili gave a sob, and sank to her knees.

Joanna dismounted. 'What will you do?'

'We must send messengers,' he said. 'One to Delamere, to warn him what is happening, one to Nairobi, to alert the garrison, and one to Kurt. He is in the gravest danger. He and Amanda.'

She shivered. 'Shouldn't we all just light out of here?'

'I don't think they'll let us,' Adrian said.

She turned to look down the drive. Some fifty of the Morani had followed them home and now stood in a group, watching them. 'Then they won't let anyone go.'

'I think a couple of men might sneak out after dark,' Adrian said. 'And if they can mount up once they are out of earshot . . . I only wish I had sufficient horses for all of us.' But there were only eight in the stable.

'I will go,' Safah said.

'No,' Adrian said. 'We need you here.'

'Then I will go, bwana,' said one of his sons.

'And I,' said another.

'And I,' said the third.

Safah nodded. 'My sons will carry the messages and bring help.'

Adrian assented. 'For the time being, act as if nothing will happen. But prepare yourselves. Everyone inside the house, and let's get these windows closed and shuttered.'

'Will they attack us?' Joanna asked, calmly taking out and checking all the rifles, one after the other, then placing the boxes of cartridges on the table.

'Not at the moment. Kainairju could have killed us then, had he intended to do that. What will happen when he discovers we've sent for help . . .'

'When do you think he'll move against, well, whoever he's meaning to attack first?'

'Kurt, you mean? He's only just got back. My guess is that it'll take him at least twenty-four hours to establish a system of commands and signals; these people take their fighting very seriously. If we can get a message out, and stay alive long enough for the soldiers or Delamere's people to get here . . . it's our only chance.'

She touched his arm. 'I know how you feel.'

'Do you?' he asked savagely.

'Yes,' she said. 'I wanted to kill him too, there and then. Then I got to thinking about you, and Johnnie . . . I know you were thinking of us.'

'That doesn't stop me feeling a coward,' he said.

'I know.' She sighed. 'Bar . . .'

'I'll do it.'

He went outside, and took the body down by the lakeside. There he dug the grave. Safah came to help him. They dug together, while the women and children, having been forbidden to leave the house, watched from the verandah – and the Masai watched from the drive.

'I did not think he would lose, to Kainairju,' Safah said. 'Perhaps he was too confident of winning.'

'He did not understand that Kainairju meant to kill him,' Adrian said. 'He thought it was a game. That is the curse of

376

the English, until it is often too late.'

'Will you avenge his death, bwana?' Safah asked with his usual directness.

Adrian straightened from throwing earth on top of the still body, and looked him in the eye. 'Yes,' he said. 'When I can.'

Safah nodded, satisfied.

They returned to the house and had a meal, although no one felt like eating, and endeavoured to pass the day. Adrian told the women to fill all the utensils they could find with water from the stream; that way they could stand a siege of several days, he thought, supposing it came to that. They went outside at regular intervals to look at the Morani, who continued to look at them.

When darkness fell, Adrian did not light the lamps, but left the house in darkness. After another meal, Safah's three sons crept down to the stable and took out three of the horses, which had been saddled earlier. The animals were well used to the young Somalis, and made no sound; there was only the slightest jingle of a harness as they were led away along the north shore of the lake. Adrian and Joanna waited on the verandah, rifles in their hands, watching the Morani, who were now lost in the gloom but still definitely there. Nothing moved, and they never heard a hoofbeat. The Somalis had walked their horses out of earshot.

'They are good men,' Adrian told Safah. 'Now all we can do is wait.'

The three of them took turns at keeping watch. They listened to considerable noise from the Masai kraal, where a great fire had been lit, and from where there came much stamping of feet and chanting of songs, all of which contributed to the chances of the messengers being unobserved. Adrian wondered what Uthuli thought of it all, if indeed he was still alive. But for the chieftain, as for himself, the day had brought only heartrending calamity. Apart from the death of Bar – the second son he had had to watch die, unable to help – this would mean the end of the Masai as a free people. Yet the Morani believed they had to fight the white man, or die of recurring diseases and disasters. Adrian understood that, yet at this moment he felt no sympathy for them. His whole being was too consumed with anger and hatred, and if he had possessed a Maxim gun, he would have cut them down without a moment's hesitation. He could only dream of avenging Bar . . . but for all his bold words to Safah, he wondered if *he* would ever be in a position to do it. Kainairju might well hang for murder, but it would be a judicial process . . . and he would be left with nothing but a bitter memory.

He was awakened by Safah touching his arm. 'Kainairju,' the Somali said.

The dogs, carefully confined all night so as not to provoke an incident, were growling, and Joanna was already up, rifle in hand. 'Stay out of sight,' Adrian told her. 'And keep those dogs under control.' He went to the front door, unbolted it and stepped on to the verandah. His heart constricted at what he saw, and his throat was dry, even as he found himself unable to understand how this second tragedy had happened. Safah's sons had the horses . . . a horse could surely outrun even a Morani.

'Why do you not bury your dead, Bar-clay,' Kainairju said. At his back were his Morani, several hundred strong, filling the lawn, leaning on their spears . . . and at their feet were two dead bodies. 'It is better to do this than fight against your brother.'

Safah gave a howl of the purest agony and ran from the house, waving the huge, two-edged sword he had carried since Adrian had first known him. Adrian caught his arm just in time to stop him from charging down the steps and on to the spears of the Masai. 'Now we both have reasons for hate,' he said. 'But not for sacrificing our women.'

Safah sobbed, and sank to his knees, the sword blade

378

gouging into the wood of the verandah.

Kainairju smiled. 'You have not lost your wisdom, Bar-clay,' he said contemptuously. 'But you have forgotten how to fight. Did you suppose I would not post men to guard every side of Naivasha, every way from the valley? These Muslims rode straight on to the spears of my Morani. They are children at war. Now listen to me well, my brother. Because you are my brother, and my father's adopted son, I have no quarrel with you, unless you force me to it. Now I tell you, do not attempt to leave this kraal, or to send any other messengers. I will leave men to watch you and your people. If anyone attempts to leave, my men will kill him, or her, and then kill everyone else in your family.' He looked past Adrian at Joanna standing in the doorway, and at little Johnnie peering round her skirt. 'Everyone,' he said, and turned away.

Adrian remained on the verandah, watching the Morani leave, every pulse of his heart shrieking for him to seize Safah's sword and dash into their midst, and cut and slash until he fell himself . . . and as he died, listen to Joanna's screams? He went down the steps with Safah, to stand above the two young men. Behind him Saba wailed and pulled out her hair, and Sita tried to comfort her. Lili hugged her children protectively.

'You have another son,' Adrian said.

Safah said nothing. He picked up the spade they had used to bury Bar, and went down to the bank of the lake.

Joanna came down the steps. 'Isn't Ali also dead?' she asked. 'If they rode straight into a Masai patrol . . .'

'If Ali were dead, Kainairju would have brought his body here as well,' Adrian said. 'I don't know how he escaped, but I would say Kainairju isn't even aware that he did.'

'So where was he going?' Joanna asked.

'I don't know,' Adrian confessed. 'They were to decide that amongst themselves. But wherever he went, it'll be to bring help, either from the garrison in Nairobi, or from

Hugh . . . he has fifty men over at Elmenteita. And Kurt has a dozen . . .'

'Kurt,' she said. 'Will *he* come to our aid?'

'It's Kurt I'm worrying about. Or rather, Mandy.'

'And Heinrich.' She went back up the steps, waited until the grave was ready, then came down with the women, to stand and watch as Safah buried his sons. Afterwards, she asked Adrian, 'Is it the end of everything?'

'The end of a lot.'

'Will you leave here?'

He looked at her. 'I do not want to.'

She shivered. 'Neither do I. But to go on living amongst these people . . .' She looked along the drive. Twenty Morani stood there, motionless, leaning on their spears, gazing at them. 'To feel so helpless. To be ordered about . . . but they still haven't learned, Adrian. We could rush them, especially if we used the automobile. You, me and Safah, with our rifles . . .'

Adrian pointed. Another twenty Morani stood at the back of the house, on the driveway leading to the track to Elmenteita. He recognised none of their faces. Kainairju had left the men from the north to watch Barclay, just in case Uthuli's people might still be susceptible to his influence. 'While we were rushing one lot, they'd be in the house killing the women and children.'

'Well, maybe they're the ones to rush. If we loaded the automobile with all the women and children, and drove straight at them . . .'

'We'd not do it without casualties,' he told her. 'And the Morani can run faster than that car of yours can travel.'

'We'd at least take some of them with us. Just to *do* something . . .'

'We will do something. When we can without risking all of our lives.'

'Do our lives matter so much, now? I just want to kill

380

somebody.' She gave a twisted grin. 'Kainairju, mainly. But anybody will do.'

'And Johnnie?'

Her shoulders slumped. 'Oh, hell, sometimes I wish we had never had children, or that you were not quite so level-headed and patient.'

'Either way, we wouldn't have had each other.'

She came to him and put her arms round him. 'I can feel your tension,' she said. 'Just promise me one thing: that you'll get Kainairju.'

'I'll get Kainairju,' Adrian promised. 'When you, and Johnnie, and the others, are at no risk.'

'But suppose he gets away with it, with this war, secures Masai independence . . .'

'There's no chance of that, my darling. The Masai cannot take on the British Army.'

'But he sure can run riot until the soldiers arrive.' She gave another shudder.

There was nothing to do but wait, and wonder what was happening, where Ali was, and Kainairju. And stay aware of the Morani watching them. The temptation to attack their guards, as Jo wanted, was enormous. But Adrian had seen the Masai at work, when Dick's men were destroyed, and earlier, in the attack upon Fischer's expedition. He knew just how good they were; how ruthless, and how fearless, and how undeterred by losses. He and Jo could probably bring down half a dozen of them; Safah was no marksman. But the others would go to ground and work their way towards the house, using all the shrubs he had so carefully and lovingly replanted after the locust plague, taking all day over it if they had to, until by nightfall they would be within feet of the verandah, poised to come in. He could barricade the doors and windows, but the Masai would merely set fire to the house. And when they broke in, or the heat and smoke drove the defenders out, he and

381

Joanna could probably take yet another half-dozen with them. But a single spear thrust would account for him, and then Jo would be in the hands of the Morani, and Johnnie . . . and the massacre would begin.

Well, then, *could* they break out in the automobile, and on horseback? The car simply could not travel fast enough to escape the Masai. If they had enough horses . . . but there were only five left, and there were thirteen of them. To attempt to charge the Masai, two and three to a horse, would cost lives, their lives. While if they attempted to go north, there was Kainairju's patrol to be encountered.

Was he creating obstacles because of fear? Or being, as Joanna had said, a logical, thinking, patient leader? He had never doubted his own courage, when he had known what he had to do, when it was his life alone at stake. But to risk Jo and Johnnie, and Sita and his grandchildren, especially when all the time either Hugh Delamere or a rescue column from Nairobi might be coming to his aid . . .

Leaving Kainairju to attack Kurt – and Mandy? But Kurt had Heinrich and his old friend Pitzer with him, together with a dozen Somalis. He could withstand a siege even from five hundred Morani, for a couple of days, if need be.

But Christ, to know what to do, to be sure what *had* to be done.

'Listen,' Joanna snapped.

A rifle shot echoed through the still morning air. Then another. Then silence, while the echoes still ringed the lake.

Adrian went outside. The Masai had heard the shots too, and were muttering to each other, discussing what to do in a situation for which they had received no orders from Kainairju. But there had only been two shots; there was no army out there.

'I see him,' Safah said. It was the first time he had spoken since burying his sons.

There was a horseman on the northern bank of the lake, and thus on the far side from the kraal and the warriors,

382

perhaps two miles away. Adrian levelled his binoculars. 'Kurt, by God!'

'Kurt? But how?' Joanna snatched the glasses.

'He's broken through. God, you have to hand it to the man. He always seems to know the right thing to do, and know how to do it too.'

'But . . . he's alone.'

'Of course he's not alone,' Adrian snapped. 'He could never have broken through, alone. Mandy and the others will be behind him. But they mustn't come here.' He pointed his rifle at the sky and fired twice. Kurt certainly got the message; he drew rein.

Joanna lowered the glasses. 'What are we going to do?'

Adrian's hesitation had disappeared, now he knew all his remaining family was safe. 'We break out too,' he said. 'If we can link up with Kurt and his dozen men, we can fight our way to Elmenteita, if we have to. Listen, we'll use the car . . .'

'There's no road along the lake,' she objected.

'Well, drive it as far as you can. Load the children in, and just go like a bat out of hell. Kurt's people will cover you.'

'Yippee,' she shouted. She had already slung a bandolier over her shoulder.

'Safah,' Adrian said, 'saddle all the horses. We'll need them when the car can go no further. Let's go, Jo.'

'It'll be a squish,' she said, calling the women and the children.

'Then squish.' He looked again at Kurt who had remained sitting his horse, watching the house. But his people must be close behind. Then he looked at the Morani. Now they were definitely alarmed. But still their orders were only to prevent Bar-clay from leaving; they had not as yet seen Kurt, and had no idea where the shots had come from, or why Bar-clay had returned them.

Everything was ready. Jo was behind the wheel of the touring car, the seats beside her and behind her crammed

383

with people; Johnnie was virtually in her lap, and Safah was waiting with the five saddled horses.

'The dogs,' Jo said.

'They're coming too,' Adrian promised. 'But I'm afraid I'll have to use them.'

She sighed, and nodded. But she was too excited to feel grief at this moment. 'Geronimo!' she shouted, engaged gear, and bounced across the lawn and the first field.

The Morani realised what was happening, and began to move, those to the south running straight at the house, those to the west making for the car. Adrian took careful aim at the southern group, and fired. One of the warriors threw up his arms and tumbled backwards. Adrian emptied his magazine and the Morani disappeared as they went to ground.

Adrian whistled. 'Come on, lads.' The dogs bounded out as he vaulted into the saddle. Safah held the reins of the three spare mounts. 'Let's go.'

Joanna was already on the far side of the garden, bouncing over the uneven ground, everyone holding on for dear life. But the second band of Morani were, as Adrian had feared, travelling much faster than the car could, and were gaining on her. Meanwhile Kurt still watched. Adrian fired into the air to tell him to bring his people into action, but had no time to do anything more. He had both to hold off the men behind and distract those in front. He loosed the dogs. 'Sic 'em,' he said, pointing.

The faithful Alsatians charged at the Morani in front of them, uttering low growls. Adrian looked back once more. The men behind them were on their feet again, and running at full speed towards them. He levelled his rifle and fired, and another Morani tumbled over. The remainder went to ground.

'To the car,' he told Safah, and they urged their horses forward. But even as they left the garden, there was catastrophe in front of them. The Alsatians reached the Morani and checked them, but only for an instant; spears flashed and the gallant beasts were stretched dead on the ground. Whether Joanna had been distracted by the sacrifice of her pets or not Adrian didn't know, but in the same instant one of the car wheels entered an unforeseen rut; the vehicle slewed half round, and then fell over on its side. People spilled out to left and right; the Morani were only a hundred yards away.

Adrian and Safah were at full gallop now, but they were a quarter of a mile back; and shooting from the heaving horses it was impossible to be accurate. Still Kurt had not moved.

Joanna seized her rifle. She stood, leaning against the overturned car, levelled her weapon, and fired five times in as many seconds. The Morani were taken entirely by surprise; they had expected the women to be an easy prey. Five of them fell. The rest hesitated in uncertainty, and while they did so, Joanna fitted another clip to her rifle and fired again, five times. Ten Morani were stretched on the ground, and Adrian insensibly drew rein. 'Holy Jesus Christ,' he muttered. He had never seen such consummate shooting.

Neither had the Morani. For the first time in his experience, Adrian watched the proud warriors running backwards, while Joanna calmly fitted a third clip into her magazine.

'Hold your fire,' he shouted, riding up to her. 'They have something to think about.' He leapt from the saddle. 'But my darling . . .'

'I've been wanting to do *that* since this time yesterday,' she said with satisfaction. And then added wonderingly, 'I've never killed a man before.'

'Well, they'll come again. But we've got a breathing space. Let's get mounted.'

He dispersed the children so that the lightest were in threesomes; he himself took Ade; Joanna had Johnnie seated behind her, his arms tight round her waist. 'Where the devil are Kurt and his people?' she demanded.

They rode through the brush and saw him, where he had been throughout the fight. 'You stopped the devils,' he said. 'That was good shooting.'

'They'll come again,' Adrian said. 'Did you meet any coming down the escarpment? Or see any over towards Elmenteita?'

'No,' Kurt said. 'No. They are all up on the plain.'

'Right. Let's link up with your people and make for Elmenteita. We'll be safe there.' Then he frowned, taking in his brother-in-law fully for the first time. Kurt had lost his hat, his shirt was soaked with sweat and his thinning hair was windswept. His face was grey with fatigue and fear.

'I have no people,' he said. 'They are all dead.'

Adrian couldn't speak for a moment.

'Amanda?' Joanna gasped.

'All dead,' Kurt repeated.

'They overran you so quickly?' Adrian asked. 'But how did you . . .'

'They took us by surprise. They came on us while we were dispersed in the fields. We had no inkling of what was going on. I was farthest out when I saw the Morani on the skyline. There must have been six hundred of them.'

Adrian stared at him. 'What did you do?' he asked, his voice low, as a dreadful suspicion began to tear at his mind.

'They were already between me and the house,' Kurt said. 'I knew I could never get back. I had to get help, but they were between me and Nairobi as well. So I came down here. I heard shots behind me, one or two, and then nothing. No one was ready . . . I looked back and saw nothing. I . . .' He looked from face to face.

'You rode away and left Amanda?' Joanna asked in horror. 'And Heinrich? You abandoned your wife and son?'

'I could not get back,' Kurt explained. 'I could not. And I knew it was me those devils really wanted. I . . .' He looked at Adrian. But Adrian was past restraint. He rose in his stirrups, leaned forward and swung his fist. Kurt uttered no sound as he tumbled out of his saddle and struck the ground.

No one said anything for a moment. Then Joanna asked, 'What are we going to do?'

Adrian looked back at the house. The Morani had joined forces now, but were staying a good way back. They had no desire to come within range of that dreaded rifle again. 'He got here,' Adrian said, scarcely recognising his own voice. 'He said he saw no Masai between here and Elmenteita. So ride over there. You can travel faster than they, even doubled up.'

'I will take them to Elmenteita, bwana,' Safah said. 'And him?'

Adrian looked down; Kurt was just beginning to stir.

'Leave him for the Masai,' Joanna said.

'He'd deserve it. But you'd better take him with you.' He pulled his horse round.

'Were are you going?' Joanna asked, as if she did not know. 'You cannot,' she said. 'One man? You would be going to your death.'

'She is my sister.'

'You cannot,' Joanna said, and levelled her rifle. 'I will not let you.'

'Then shoot me,' Adrian said, and rode to the north.

Within five minutes he was out of range. Not that he had thought for a moment that she would carry out her threat. He had been more concerned that she might come after him. But she could not abandon Johnnie.

His horse was still fresh, and he urged it up the escarpment and on to the high plain. He had no idea what he was doing, what he was planning. He only knew that the years of patience and self-restraint had suddenly been rolled away. If it cost him his own life, he had to find Amanda . . . and Kainairju. Nothing else mattered.

Within an hour he knew he was on Kurt's property. Now he looked for the Masai, and saw a warrior standing like a statue on a bluff perhaps two miles away. Kainairju would know he was coming.

He kicked his now tired mount into a trot and moved swiftly over the ground. He saw some of Kurt's cattle, away to his left, gathered together as if sheltering from a storm. He came to a rise and looked down on the copse, and the stream, and the houses, and the vultures.

His heartbeat seemed to slow as he urged his reluctant horse down the slope. He saw a hyena moving close by the main house, unslung his rifle, aimed and fired, all in a single movement. The scavenger dropped to the earth as the sound of the shot echoed into the distance, and the vultures squawked into the sky.

He walked his horse past the stream and looked at the dead bodies floating half in and half out of the flowing water. Morani. Kurt's people had not died without a fight. But he could still hope they had not all died, yet. He drew rein before the house and looked at the dead bodies on the verandah. Three Morani, two Somalis and one white man. He dismounted, went up the steps. It was Pitzer. The little man had faithfully followed his employer to the end. Like him, he had not dared to go near the Masai village since his return to the high country. Now the Masai village had come to him.

Adrian kicked in the already half-open front door, nostrils closing against the growing stench. Here was horror. Again two Morani lay dead, but also half a dozen Somalis, and Heinrich, sprawled over upturned chairs and tables, their entrails torn by the savage spears. Heinrich still clutched his revolver; unlike his father, he had died facing his enemies.

Scarcely breathing now, Adrian opened the bedroom door. Amanda lay across the bed. Kainairju had taken her in there, Adrian estimated, to realise an ambition he had held for twenty-five years. And from the cuts and bruises on her naked body, the shameful mutilations, he had not spared her a moment of humiliation and pain and terror before he slit her throat.

The horse whinnied. Adrian turned and went back on to the verandah. The ranch was ringed with Morani, and Kainairju stood in front of them. 'You are a fool, Barclay,' Kainairju said. 'I offered you your life, as you are my brother. Now you will die. And your people with you.'

'No,' Adrian said. 'You are the one who will die.' His fingers were tight on the rifle, but for all his unspeakable anger, the sight of Amanda had made his brain into an ice-cold weapon. To cut Kainairju down with a single bullet, and then die himself, would be a waste of time, a waste of vengeance, a waste of hatred. He had suddenly realised how he could end this business, if only he had thought of it yesterday morning. But now was no time for regret, only for determined ruthlessness. 'I challenge you,' he said. 'For the right to be chieftain of the Masai.'

Kainairju snorted. 'You? You are a white man.'

'Is the colour of my skin important?' Adrian asked. 'I am a member of the clan, a Morani like yourself.' He spoke loudly and clearly, that every man present should hear what he was saying. 'You yourself officiated at my induction. I am Uthuli's adopted son. This is well known.' He looked from left to right, at the smooth-complexioned faces. 'I have the right to claim the succession for myself.'

If *only* he had thought of that yesterday morning.

Kainairju started to sneer, but there was the thud of a single spear haft on the ground behind him, immediately followed by several more.

'You, and me,' Adrian said, and walked down the steps.

Now Kainairju did sneer. 'You wish to fight me with the long spear?' he asked. 'I have no long spear.'

Adrian stood the rifle against the upright of the steps and

walked towards him. 'We will fight as the Morani fight,' he said.

Kainairju hesitated, staring at him, but one of the warriors had already run forward, a spear in each hand; these he now hurled, point first, into the earth between the two men. If Kainairju was a legend amongst the Masai, so was the yellow-haired white man. The Masai knew they would witness history here today. They knew too that the outcome of this quarrel would decide their fate, perhaps forever.

Kainairju moved forward, picked up his spear and kept on coming. Adrian side-stepped him and grasped his own weapon. Kainairju had already turned, and now attacked again, a quick flick of his wrists sending his weapon to and fro. Adrian had never fought with a spear before. He was taken unawares by the speed of his opponent, and before he knew what had happened, the spear had been knocked from his hands and sent rolling across the dust.

The Masai watched in silence; they were disappointed that the contest should have ended so quickly and abruptly.

Kainairju grinned, and came forward, more slowly now. Adrian glanced at the spear; he knew he would never have the time to pick it up again. But he felt no fear, only the anger and hatred surging through his body, seeming to make his heart swell as if it would burst. Kainairju was within ten feet, the spear poised. But this time he was not going to throw it; he meant to make very sure. He tensed his muscles and thrust at Adrian's chest. Adrian swayed to one side, but not far enough; the sharp point ripped through his shirt, and he felt an agonising pain down his right side.

The Morani began to drum their spear hafts, and Kainairju jerked the spear back for the *coup de grâce*. But Adrian's hand had already closed on the haft, just below the point. Kainairju jerked again, and then tried to thrust, but Adrian now gripped the spear with his other hand as well, and held it immovable. Then he exerted his giant strength and snapped the spear into two pieces, leaving the longer piece in

Kainairju's hand, retaining the shorter, pointed end.

Kainairju retreated, staring in horror at the thick wood which had just been treated like a twig. Adrian threw the point to the ground and walked towards him. For a moment Kainairju clearly contemplated flight, but he knew the Morani would not let him through. He stood his ground and tried to use the broken spear as a club, swinging it to crash on Adrian's head and shoulders. Adrian ignored the blows, the blood which dribbled into his eyes, and went right up to him, to grasp him round the throat. Then he lifted him from the ground.

The Morani stared in a mixture of amazement and wonder and consternation as Adrian held their chieftain at arm's length. Kainairju wriggled and kicked and tried to reach his tormentor with his hands, but Adrian held him away, just clear of the ground, while he slowly squeezed the life from Kainairju's body. While he did so, he gazed into Kainairju's eyes. And as the murderer of his son and his sister died, he smiled.

'These are sad times, my son,' Uthuli said. He stood with his people, his Morani and their women and children, and gazed at the white soldiers who had hurried from Nairobi to ring his kraal, at the horses and the long spears and the Maxim guns, the flags and the uniforms, all the panoply of the white man about to wage war, the power against which he was helpless.

'Which you have brought on yourself,' Adrian told him.

'But now that Kainairju is dead . . .'

'Your people still let him lead them to war,' Adrian pointed out. 'Who can say when another Kainairju may arise? Now you must pay the penalty for your foolishness. It is the will of the Great King that you be confined to certain lands, and that no Masai, no Morani, may leave that reservation without permission, or he will be adjudged an outlaw and locked up in prison.'

391

'You are sentencing my people to death, my son,' Uthuli said.

'It need not be so, my father. The Great King has been merciful, and has granted you many hundreds of acres for your reserved land. It will be sufficient for you.'

'And the men from the north? Will they too be sent from their lands?'

'To the reservation, yes. It is the will of the Great King that all the Masai shall be confined.'

Uthuli considered. Then he said, 'Perhaps I should have killed you and Von, the day I first saw you. That would have been best for my people. But I saw you, and loved you from that moment. And all the time you were planning the destruction of my people.'

'I did not plan that, my father, and it grieves me to hear you say such things. I have done my best for you, have fought to save you from the reservation. But you yielded to Kainairju at the end. That was your mistake. I will still do my best for you, but you must obey the Great King.'

Uthuli turned away. 'These are sad times,' he said again, and went towards his people.

'I have to congratulate you, sir,' Major Templeton said. 'Leading all those black devils back here . . .'

'It was quite simple, Major,' Adrian said. 'They accepted me as their chief.'

'Nonetheless, sir, when I heard what this young man had to say . . .' He glanced at Ali. 'I really assumed we had a major war on our hands. All Nairobi is in a state of defence, and I have sent to the coast for reinforcements.'

Adrian nodded. 'You acted very promptly and well, Major. Ali, tell me how you managed to get through Kainairju's cordon?'

'I separated from my brothers, bwana, before we got to the north end of the lake. Where it narrowed, I swam my horse across to reach the other side.'

'By God,' Adrian said. 'The Masai would never have

thought of that, because they never used the lake themselves. That was brilliant.'

'But my brothers . . .'

'Died like heroes,' Major Templeton said. 'Oh, we shall not forget them. Thanks to their sacrifice, and your courage, Ali, and your diplomatic skills, Mr Barclay, in seizing control of the Morani, why, we really have averted a major catastrophe. I mean, when you consider, only one family overrun and murdered, and them not exactly English, well . . .'

'Oh, quite,' Adrian said, mounting his horse. 'Just one family, Major. We have been very fortunate.'

He rode to Elmenteita, which was still in a state of defence, bristling with guns and eager men. Delamere was in his element, and somewhat disappointed that he had not had to repel hundreds, or preferably thousands, of raging Morani.

'You did a great job, Adrian,' he said. 'A great job.' He lowered his voice. 'I can't tell you how sorry I am about your sister and nephew. And your son, of course.' He jerked his head. 'God, what a pitiful thing that man is. Won't eat, won't drink . . . do you want to speak to him?'

Kurt sat alone on the verandah, staring down at the lake and the re-sown croquet lawn. Adrian went towards him, and he started to his feet in alarm. 'I had no choice,' he said. 'I was not one of them, like you. I could not challenge Kainairju. Had I returned, I would have been killed too. Where would have been the sense in that?'

'Sometimes,' Adrian agreed, 'it is difficult to see the sense in anything.'

Kurt licked his lips. 'What are you going to do? You are my oldest friend. What will you do?'

'To you? Nothing, oldest friend. Nothing. I am going to leave you to live with the memory of what you let happen to my sister, and your son, and your faithful servants, for the rest of your days. I hope you live to be a hundred. Now, get out of here on the next train through, Schlieben, and do not ever come back.'

Joanna stood on the verandah of the house at Naivasha, and watched Safah and Ali erecting headstones, helped by Johnnie and Ade, and surrounded by the women and younger children. The graves apart, the lawn and garden looked almost as they had done before the coming of the locusts. 'Why do these things happen?' she asked.

'God knows,' Adrian said. 'And I sincerely hope he does.'

Johnnie came back up to them. 'You fought with Kainairju, Dad. Man to man. And killed him. I wish I'd been there.'

'I'm glad you weren't,' Adrian said. 'I wasn't really a very nice person, at that moment.'

'But I'm so glad you got him,' Joanna said, and put her arms round his waist, hastily releasing him as he winced. 'Is it very painful?'

'Just sore. It's coming along very nicely.'

'But it was quite deep. I'm so very proud of you, my darling. But God, the risk you took . . .'

'No risk,' Adrian said. 'Kainairju killed Bar because Bar lacked the ruthlessness to kill him when he had the chance. I set out with only murder in my heart, and Kainairju didn't realise that.'

'You'll be a legend in the Masai kraals forever more.'

'I wonder,' he said thoughtfully.

'Does what Uthuli said hurt you?'

'Of course it does. But there was no alternative. And they got off lightly, really.'

'And now?'

'Now?' His shoulders sagged for a moment, then squared again. 'We pick up the threads and go on living. We try to make it all worth while. Right?'

'Oh, so right. We are going to make this place, this entire valley, the entire high country, the most magnificent place on earth. We have to do that, as you say, for the sake of

Mandy, and Bar, and Heinrich, and Safah's sons. We have to.'

'We will,' he agreed.

'For ever and ever.'

Adrian considered. 'I doubt that.'

She turned her head to look up at him.

'Not forever,' he said. 'This is the land of the Masai. We are the trespassers. We took this land by brute force, and we have held it by brute force. But I think, one day, the Masai will be back. Or some other Africans will seek to regain what is rightfully theirs. Then we may have a price to pay.' He kissed her forehead. 'But let's enjoy it while we can.'